Also by Colin Forbes
in Pan Books

Tramp in Armour
The Heights of Zervos
The Palermo Ambush
Target Five
Year of the Golden Ape
The Stone Leopard
Avalanche Express

First published 1981 by William Collins Sons & Co. Ltd
This edition published 1982 by Pan Books Ltd,
Cavaye Place, London SW10 9PG
in association with William Collins Sons & Co. Ltd
© Colin Forbes 1981
2nd printing 1982
ISBN 0 330 26769 8
Reproduced, printed and bound in Great Britain by
Hazell Watson & Viney Ltd, Aylesbury, Bucks

Colin Forbes

The Stockholm Syndicate

Pan Books
in association with Collins

For Jane

Author's note

I would like to record my appreciation for the help and time the following provided in my research, and to emphasise that they are in no way responsible for any errors of fact,

Henry Augustsson (goldsmith), Iwan Hedman (the Swedish Army), Otto Holm (the Swedish police), Marie-Louise Telegin, and two others who must remain nameless.

1

The deadly game had begun. It was close to midnight, and Jules Beaurain started across the *Grande Place*. His manner apparently relaxed, his eyes were everywhere as he scanned windows, rooftops, doorways for any sign of the slightest movement.

"I don't like the idea. You'll be a sitting duck for their best marksman," Sergeant Henderson had warned him.

"A *mobile* duck," Beaurain had replied. "And your men will be all along the route."

"I can't guarantee they see him before he sees you," the Scot had persisted. "It only takes one bullet ..."

"That's enough talk, Jock," Beaurain had said. "We're going to do it. Warn all the gunners I want him taken alive."

So now they were doing it, and Brussels was almost deserted on this warm June night. A few tourists stood on the edges of the square, reluctant to go to bed but unsure of what to do next. Beaurain continued towards the far, dark side. Forty years old, five feet ten, thick hair and eyebrows dark, the hair brushed back over a high forehead, he had a military touch in the way he held himself, an impression reinforced by a trim moustache and strong jaw.

Born in Liège of an English mother and a Belgian father he had by the age of thirty-seven risen to the rank of Chief Superintendent in the Belgian police in command of the anti-terrorist division. A year later he had resigned from the police when Julie, his English wife, was caught in terrorist crossfire during a hi-jack at Athens airport, and died. Since then he had built up Telescope.

A curtain moved in a high window. It was at third-floor level, an excellent firing-point. The curtain parted. A man in a vest leaned on the window ledge, peering down into the *place*. Beaurain ignored him. The window was well lit, silhouetting the watcher. A professional wouldn't make that mistake.

This was the third time he had followed this route at the same hour. Always before he had varied both route and timing. It was the only way to stay alive once you were the Syndicate's target. He paused at the entrance to the rue des Bouchers, a cobbled road which led uphill away from the great open space of the *place*. He wished to God he could smoke a cigarette.

"No cigarettes," Henderson said. "It would help pick you out from a distance. Make it difficult – make him come to you ..."

Beaurain took one last glance over his shoulder into the *place*. He shrugged, confident that the tourists were innocent enough, and started up the cobbles. Instinct told him the attack would come in this narrow street. Leading off it were half-a-dozen possible escape routes, alleys, side streets.

"Keep to the shadows," Henderson said. "It will upset his aim ..."

Maintaining an even pace, Beaurain climbed the street. Henderson had twenty armed men at strategic positions along his route. Some would be at street level; others at upper floor windows overlooking the route. Some would be on the rooftops, he felt sure. And somewhere Henderson would have his command post, linked with every man by walkie-talkie. That was the moment the drunk appeared, staggering down the street towards him. He was singing softly to himself. Then he stopped, leaned against a wall and upended a bottle with his left hand. It was Stig Palme, one of Henderson's gunners. He was keeping his right hand free for his pistol. He stood against the wall as the Belgian passed. A pattern was beginning to emerge. Palme was the back-up man, the gunner who would change direction and reel up behind Beaurain covering his rear. Now there was a fresh problem – more light.

Through windows open to the warm night he heard the babble of diners' voices, the laughter of women and the clink of glasses. He had no option but to walk through the shafts of light, a slow-moving silhouette.

Beaurain was dressed casually, in a dark polo-necked sweater, dark blue slacks and rubber-soled shoes. He carried a jacket over his right arm. And then he saw something which really worried him.

Ahead on his route he saw a van parked at an intersection with a side street. *Boucher* was inscribed in large white letters across the rear doors. Each door had a window high up, like portholes. Why had he assumed that the Syndicate would send only one man? Supposing they had surrounded his route with a team to guide the killer to his objective. Above all, who would be taking delivery of meat at this hour of the night? Something brushed against his leg.

He didn't jump. He didn't pause. He glanced swiftly down. A fat tabby brushed against him again and then padded ahead, tail waving like a pennant, stopping at intervals to make sure Beaurain was still with him. As he passed a side street on his right he saw two lovers entwined in an embrace. Good cover for a gunman, Beaurain realised. If only Palme, whose voice he could just hear, were nearer. But the couple hadn't moved before he lost sight of them. And it was too late now to do anything about it. Palme would have to cope with them if they were trouble. Beaurain's eyes were now glued on the two windows at the rear of the parked van. The enemy could be watching his approach, and he had to watch several ways at once – the van, the various branches of the intersection and the windows above the restaurants.

And then it happened in the one way they had felt sure it would not happen. The assassin chose the direct approach. He appeared out of nowhere at the corner close to the parked van, a short, heavily-built man wearing a light raincoat, lifting with both hands a large Luger pistol, the muzzle obscenely enlarged with the attached silencer.

Beaurain had a brief impression – a plump face, cold eyes – then he flung away his jacket as he dropped to the cobbles, rolling sideways with great agility. The gunman had two choices – swing the gun in an arc and lower it to the target, or lower the gun and then swing it in an arc. He chose the latter. The wrong one. It gave Beaurain two extra seconds.

Raising the gas-pistol he had been holding beneath his jacket Beaurain aimed and fired in one movement. The tear-gas missile hit the gunman in the chest, exploded, smothered his face. The van doors were thrown open and Henderson had leapt from his command post. Using both hands he grabbed the assassin's gun arm, wrenched it upwards and backwards in one violent movement. Something cracked. The man opened his mouth to scream.

Palme had covered an astonishing distance uphill. His clenched fist hit the open mouth, stifling the scream, then his knee drove into the gunman's stomach. The man would have jack-knifed forward under the impetus of the blow, but he was held in Henderson's fierce grip, Henderson was wearing a gas-mask, but the tear-gas was affecting Palme and he was forced to retreat.

Others, also in gas-masks, had appeared from inside the van and they crowded round Henderson and his prisoner, helping to haul and lift their captive into the vehicle. The rear doors closed. Henderson tore off his gas-mask, handed it to the driver and told him to get moving. Palme picked up the gunman's Luger, gave it to Henderson and climbed in beside the driver.

Beaurain had retrieved his jacket and hidden his pistol. "I have a car down this side street," Henderson said; but Beaurain was momentarily distracted. Framed in the nearest restaurant window he saw a woman's head appear as she allowed a waiter to light her cigarette. The woman had dark hair; she was dining alone.

"We'd better move, sir," Henderson urged.

Only when he was settled in the passenger seat, and Beaurain behind the wheel, was the Scot able to relax a little, to relay his information. Beaurain started up the Mercedes 280E and began to follow a circuitous route which would take them out of the city to the south.

"Chap we grabbed was Serge Litov. I tailed him once in Paris."

"They sent a Russian? It doesn't make sense," Beaurain said. "Although we did hear he'd defected. Do we know who to?"

"I'd expected they might send Baum. He's even more dangerous."

"Odd, isn't it?" Beaurain agreed. "And how did your command post happen to be just at the right place?"

"Partly luck, partly reconnaissance. The gunners scoured the area and came up with a concealed Suzuki near that intersection. A powerful job – and I guessed it might be the getaway machine. So I told Peters to shift the machine. Then we parked the van at the intersection. Seemed the obvious place. Are you all right, sir?"

"You know something, Henderson? For some reason I

10

seem to be sweating."

"That'll be the warm night, sir."

"We may have left a little early."

"I thought the plan was to get clear of the area and back to base as soon as we had the fish in the net."

"No, I don't mean the van – I mean you and I. Supposing Litov had succeeded, had killed me. And then you in turn killed him, which could easily have happened. The Syndicate must have foreseen that possibility. So, what would they do?"

"Leave someone in a position to observe what happened and report back. But was there anywhere they could safely have placed a watcher?"

"In that restaurant opposite the side street."

To let in more cool air Beaurain pressed the switch which slid back the sun-roof of his beloved 280E. "Probably I'm wrong," Beaurain concluded, and speeded up to overtake the van transporting Litov somewhere ahead of them. But he still couldn't forget the slim white arm of the girl extending her cigarette-holder towards a waiter. It bothered him that he hadn't seen her full face.

2

Sitting by herself at the window table in the Auberge des Roses, Sonia Karnell had witnessed the violent events in the rue des Bouchers with the aid of her compact mirror. Constructed of the finest glass and always kept highly polished, the mirror was one of the tools of her trade. While all the other diners were enjoying their meal and noticing nothing, Sonia was giving an imitation of a vain thirty-year-old who could not stop looking at herself.

She watched the swift and decisive assault on Serge Litov. The murderous efficiency of Telescope's operation impressed Sonia and she decided she must include this in her report. She waited ten minutes and called for her bill.

As she left the restaurant, she ignored the admiring glances of several males. She walked rapidly to the hired Peugeot she had parked a quarter of a mile away. With the roads almost clear of traffic once outside the city, she reached her destination in under two hours.

Entering Bruges was like travelling back through a time machine five hundred years. The old city was a labyrinth of waterways and medieval streets and squares. Her nerves started to play up as she approached the Hoogste van Brugge. It was the man she had come to see who worried her. He did not take kindly to the bearers of bad tidings.

It was two in the morning when she parked the car and walked a short distance down a side street and then turned into the confined and cobbled alley which was the Hoogste van Brugge. Dr Otto Berlin resided at No. 285 during his rare visits to Bruges.

As she used the key to open the heavy door of No. 285 Sonia Karnell never gave a thought to the building opposite.

The cine-camera equipped with an infra-red telephoto lens was operated by a patient Fleming. He started up the camera as soon as she approached the building although he then had no idea whether the dark-haired woman had any, connection with No. 285. He kept it running until she had closed the door behind her. The windows opposite were masked by heavy curtains.

"It didn't work – Litov failed. Worse still, Telescope captured him alive and took him away in a van they had ready waiting."

Sonia was anxious to get over the worst at once, not knowing how her chief would react. Dr Berlin sat behind a baize-covered table in a tiny room on the first floor. The only light came from a milky globe on the table, shaded with dark red cloth. She faced him across the table, her chair drawn up close to support her back. As he said nothing she went on talking, to appease him. Although a native of Stockholm, she was speaking in fluent French.

"Telescope had men everywhere. I saw it all from the restaurant Litov told me to go to. Beaurain came up the street on foot again ... it all seemed so innocent and natural .. the van I hadn't taken any notice of, but that was where some of them were hidden ... they poured out of it when Litov was about to shoot at point-blank range. Litov of all people! How could he walk into such a trap?"

"He didn't."

Berlin was a fat man, no longer forty certainly but probably not sixty. His greasy black hair hung across his forehead. He wore a dark moustache curved down to the sides of his mouth and his glasses had heavy rims and thick pebble lenses. He wore a pair of pigskin gloves. He had replied to Karnell in the language she had been speaking. She stared in amazement at the reply.

"He didn't?" she repeated. "But I'm sure it was Litov!"

"It was Litov," Berlin agreed.

"Then if it was Litov I don't understand," she burst out. "His job was to kill Beaurain and escape."

"No. His job was to infiltrate Telescope and locate its main base. Only then can we mount a plan to destroy Telescope and all its works."

"And Litov," Karnell protested, "having been taken to this base, simply has to observe its location, escape and come running back to us with the information? Litov, of course, will have no trouble escaping ... "

Berlin leaned across the table. By the glow of the lamp his huge shadow loomed across the ceiling. He hit the side of her face with the back of his hand. "Never speak to me in that tone again," he said.

"It was just the shock of what you said," she stammered. "The fact that you had not trusted me."

"You know how we work, my dear Sonia." His voice was a soothing purr now, but still with the guttural accent which could not disguise completely the harsh menace he conveyed. "Each knows only what is necessary to know to do his or her job at the time. I think we will leave now. You have parked the car in the T'Zand? Good. On the way we will warn the entire network to keep alert for Beaurain's next move."

The blow to the side of her face had not really hurt her; it had been little more than a rather bear-like caress. Had Berlin really struck out, she would have ended up sprawled on the floor against the wall, possibly with her neck broken. He stood up and she wrinkled her nose at his soiled and crumpled suit. Berlin took two hand grenades from a cupboard, each of which he examined with care before depositing one in either jacket pocket. They were primed ready for use.

He led the way down the staircase, squeezing between banister rail and the peeling wall-plaster. Sonia Karnell checked the time. 2.30 a.m. Berlin was a man who preferred to conduct his business and to travel by night. "Who lives during the dark hours?" was one of his favourite sayings.

She turned on the pocket torch always kept in her handbag and followed Berlin into the street. The houses in the Hoogste van Brugge, all joined together and all built centuries ago, were like up-ended match-boxes – the thin side facing the street. Berlin had taken a beret from somewhere and crammed it on his head.

"You're sure you mean the word is to go out at all levels?" she said. "Right up to the top?"

"Right up to the top," he assured her.

There was no change of expression behind the thick pebble glasses as her torch caught the lenses for a second, but Berlin knew the reason for her checking, for her surprise. The word would now go out which was rarely invoked, the word which would alert a whole army of watchers to observe and report on the activities, movements and conversations of Jules Beaurain, head of Telescope. The code-word was *Zenith*.

It would go out to hotel receptionists, airport personnel, railway staff, petrol station attendants, Customs and Immigration officials at ports. Theoretically it would be impossible for Jules Beaurain to move in western Europe without his movement immediately being reported to Berlin.

But the word would also go out to a much more exalted level. Most important of all – and this was what had so shaken Sonia Karnell when she had fully grasped this was a *Zenith* call – the word would go out to men controlling banks and industries who, with the same urgency and motivated by the same fear as the lowliest baggage handler, would report on all and any contact they might have from now on with Jules Beaurain. It would become known throughout western Europe that the Belgian was a marked man. The next code-word would be the one sent out to kill him.

From the first-floor window of the house opposite, Fritz Dewulf had busily operated his cine-camera. The pictures of the woman would be good. The results on the man should be even better – Dewulf was confident. He had him on film full-face as he had stared up and down the street. He hoped it was the man Dr Goldschmidt was most interested in because the doctor paid according to value – the market value.

And I wonder who Goldschmidt hopes to sell these pretty pictures to in due course, Dewulf mused as he settled down to wait out the rest of the night vigil. It was just possible the owner of No. 285 would return later, although Dewulf doubted it; there had been an air of finality about the way the fat man had shuffled off down the street. For the next few hours at any rate. A sudden thought crossed the photographer's mind and he grinned. Maybe Goldschmidt would sell the film to the fat man who starred on the reel! It had happened before. It was not a conclusion Dewulf would have drawn had he known anything about the personalities involved.

Berlin sat silent and motionless in the passenger seat of the Peugeot as Sonia Karnell headed towards Ghent and Brussels. Sonia, who could drive almost any car with the expertise and panache of a professional racing driver – just one of her many talents which Berlin appreciated – was careful not to break the silence. Experience had taught her to be sensitive to her chief's moods; the slightest misjudgement could provoke a vicious outburst. When taking a decision he might not speak for an hour.

"The darkness helps my concentration," he had once explained. "I am a natural creature of the night, I suppose. Most people fear it – I like it."

They were passing open fields on both sides with no sign of human habitation visible in the dark when she turned off the main road, slowing as she negotiated a sharp downward incline and proceeded cautiously along a cinder track with her headlights full on. Berlin stirred as though emerging from a coma.

"We are there already?" he demanded in some surprise.

"Yes, you have been thinking." She said it in the way someone might say, *You have been sleeping*.

"Turn the car round so if there is an emergency ... "

Only with a considerable effort of will was she able to stop herself bursting out in irritation. Unlike Berlin, who never seemed fatigued, she was tired and edgy and the prospect of bed seemed infinitely desirable. *Of course* she would have turned round. And what Berlin meant was that if she ran into trouble where she was going he must be in a position to drive away from the danger, leaving her to fend for herself. Sonia did not resent this; she understood the necessity for it. But the fact that he thought she needed reminding infuriated her.

She dipped the headlights, switched off the engine and left the key in the ignition. Next, without a word, she reached under her seat for the Luger. She placed the weapon in his lap and turned away, opening her door.

"Be careful to check that Frans and that bitch are alone before you go on board."

The warning astonished her. Something momentous was imminent, or he wouldn't treat her like this. They must be close to the climax of the operation against Telescope, she decided. Gripping a torch she made her way down the little-used track. The stench of the canal was in her nostrils. Now she had to climb again, to mount the embankment to where Frans Darras' barge was moored. As she reached the top of the track her thin torchbeam shone on the large bulk of the

16

barge. Then a searchlight – so it seemed to her – blazed on and glared into her eyes. She could see nothing at all, for Christ's sake. Was it the police? And inside her bag was a Walther automatic with a spare magazine. She raised one hand to fend off the fierce glare. From nearby she heard Frans' voice speak in French.

"It is her, Rosa. You can put out the light."

Sonia, blinded still, gave full vent to her feelings.

"You stupid bitch! You could have called out instead of lighting up the whole world with that bloody lamp."

It was Frans who came out of the darkness, holding a shotgun, and with her own torch pointed the way onto the barge.

"We've got a *Zenith*, Frans. That's why I'm here."

"*Zenith!*"

"Keep your voice down, man."

Frans took the lamp from Rosa and handed her the shotgun. "Keep a lookout on deck," he said. He continued in hushed tones to Sonia, gesturing to where the car was parked. "He is here?"

"He is here. He won't be pleased with that idiocy with the searchlight." They went below-deck.

"It was my fault – I told her to aim the lamp while I stayed in the dark with the shotgun. We heard the car – how could we be sure it was you and not the police or the other people?"

"What other people?"

Sonia forced herself to speak casually, but could not meet his eyes for fear of revealing her shock at what he had just suggested he knew.

"I mean Telescope, of course ... " He stopped in mid-sentence. "I will transmit the signal," he mumbled, opening a cupboard. "What is the complete message? I'll write it down."

"Yes, you had better do just that," she said coldly, watching his every movement now. "Transmit over the whole network, 'Jules Beaurain ex-Chief Superintendent Belgian police lives apartment off Boulevard Waterloo Brussels Zenith repeat Zenith'."

Removing a bundle of screwed-up clothing from the lower shelf of the cupboard, Darras fiddled with a corner of the roof and the apparently solid back slid aside, exposing a high-powered transceiver. He pressed another button and a

17

power-operated aerial emerged on deck and climbed into the night alongside the TV mast. Now he was ready to transmit and the signal he would send out was so strong it could reach any part of western Europe. He also set a clock-timer for three minutes, which must be the duration of the transmission. Police radio-detector vans normally needed five minutes to get a fix on any transmission their listening posts picked up.

"I will leave you," Sonia said in the same cold voice. "You will get the barge moving before you actually transmit?" she demanded of Darras.

"I was just waiting for you to leave."

"Then hurry."

Climbing the greasy steps to the deck, she felt the planks under her feet vibrate gently as Darras started up his ancient engine. Rosa was nowhere to be seen. Sonia scrambled back down the path and then up the nettle-bordered cinder track. Berlin had put out the side-lights. He was clasping the Luger which he handed to her without a word. His hand closed over hers as she reached for the ignition.

"You were longer than usual. And what was that with the light?"

Being careful to keep her story concise – he couldn't stand long-windedness – she told him what had happened. With shoulders hunched forward he listened with great concentration.

"What do you think?" he asked eventually.

"I'm worried. I don't like the Rosa woman, but that's not relevant – but I think she has influence over Frans."

"And Frans himself?"

"He worried me even more. I think he's losing his grip. I'm sure he was going to operate his transmitter while the barge was stationary."

"That was the point which struck me," Berlin said thoughtfully. "Turn on the engine now."

"You think we should cut the Darras' out of the network?" she asked as she started the car up the track towards the road.

"It is more serious than that," Berlin decided. "I think we shall have to send a visitor."

3

When Serge Litov was manhandled into the butcher's van and the doors slammed shut, he was already in pain from the arm Henderson had broken. But in his grim life one of the qualities he had been trained in was to endure pain and his mind was still clear as the van moved off.

He had been placed on a stretcher on a flat leather couch bolted to the floor on the left side of the van which was equipped rather like a crude ambulance inside. A man wearing a doctor's face-mask loomed over Litov and by the aid of an overhead light examined the arm and then spoke in English.

"I am going to inject you with morphine to relieve the pain. Do you understand me?"

Litov glanced at the two other men in the van, sitting against the other side. They wore Balaclava masks, dark blue open-necked shirts and blue denim trousers. One of them held a machine-pistol across his lap. Two pairs of eyes stared coldly at Litov, who spoke English fluently, as he considered whether to reply in the same language – a decision which might influence his future vitally. It would conceal his true nationality.

"How do I know there is morphine in that hypodermic?" he asked.

"You are worried it is sodium penthotal – to make you talk? As a professional man I would not do that – not to a man in your condition." The Englishman's voice was gentle and there was something in the steady eyes watching him above the mask which made Litov – against all his training – trust the man. "Also," the doctor continued, "you have a flight ahead of you. Why not travel in comfort?"

As soon as he had been flopped onto the stretcher Litov's undamaged left arm had been handcuffed at the wrist to one of the lifting poles. Both ankles were similarly manacled and a leather strap bound his chest. He was quite helpless and waves of pain were threatening to send him under.

"I'll take the needle," Litov agreed, exaggerating the hoarseness in his voice. The doctor waited until the van paused, presumably at traffic lights, then swiftly dabbed the broken arm with antiseptic and inserted the hypodermic. When the van moved on again he waited for a smooth stretch of road and then set Litov's arm and affixed splints.

Time went by, the van continued on its journey, speeding up now as though it had left the outskirts of the city behind. Litov was trying to estimate two factors as accurately as he could: the general direction the van was taking and its speed, which would allow him roughly to calculate the distance it covered.

Earlier there had been several stops, traffic light stops, but now they kept moving as along a major highway. He chose his moment carefully – when the van paused and the trio on the opposite couch looked towards the front of the van as though there might be trouble. He glanced quickly down at his wrist-watch; something they had overlooked. Two o'clock.

As the vehicle started up again and his three captors relaxed, Litov half-closed his eyes and calculated they had roughly travelled two hundred kilometres, allowing for the van's speed and twelve pauses. They had to be a long way outside Brussels. West towards the coast? They would have reached it long ago. South towards France? They would have crossed the border long before now – which would have meant passing through a frontier control post and there had been nothing like that. North towards Holland? The same objection. The frontier was too close for the distance travelled. Same applied to Germany – which left only one direction and one area to account for the distance covered. South-east: deep into the Ardennes.

Following the same route, Beaurain had long since over-taken the van. He had by now passed through Namur where vertical cliffs fell to the banks of the river Meuse. At this hour there was hardly any other traffic and they seemed to glide through the darkness. Beyond Namur he drove through Marche-en-Famenne and Bastogne where the Germans and Americans had fought an epic battle during World War

Two. The country they were travelling through now was remote, an area of high limestone ridges, gorges and dense forests.

"Jock," Beaurain said as he slowed down to negotiate the winding road, "on the surface I was lucky back there in Brussels. Had Litov been just a second or two faster it would have been me you'd have carried inside that van."

"We had it well-organised. You were quick yourself."

"That motor-cycle, was it difficult to locate?"

"Not really, although we were looking for something like that. It was propped against an alley wall very close to that intersection."

"I see." Beaurain glanced at Henderson's profile. His sandy hair was trimmed short, he was clean-shaven and his bone structure was strong. A firm mouth, a strong jaw and watchful eyes which took nothing for granted. Beaurain thought he had been lucky to recruit him when he had resigned from the SAS – although really it was the other way round since Henderson had left the Special Air Service to join Telescope. The bomb in Belfast which had killed the Scot's fiancée had decided him to change the course of his life. He was by background, by training, the perfect man to control the key section they called The Gunners.

The radio-telephone buzzed and Beaurain picked up the receiver, driving with one hand. The telephone crackled and cleared. "Alex Carder here," a soft deliberate voice reported in French. "Any news re delivery?"

"Benedict speaking," Beaurain replied. "Expect the cargo in thirty minutes. Have you the manifests ready?"

"Yes, sir," Carder replied. "We can despatch the cargo immediately on arrival. Especially now we have the time schedule. Goodbye."

Beaurain replaced the receiver. "The chopper's ready as soon as Litov arrives. To make it work we need a swift, continuous movement."

"I have been thinking about what you said in the rue des Bouchers. I think you're right – the Syndicate *would* leave someone close by."

"Which means that by now they know we have Litov, so we have to work out how they will react to that news."

"Something else worries me." The Scot stirred restlessly in his seat. "I didn't mention it to you at the time because everything was happening so fast."

"What is it?"

"The safety catch was still on when we took the Luger away from Litov."

They were now well inside the Ardennes forest. The full moon oscillated like a giant torch between the palisade of pines lining the road. They hadn't met another vehicle in twenty kilometres. Ahead, at a bend, the headlights shone on stone pillars, huge wrought-iron gates were thrown open. The scrolled lettering on a metal plaque attached to the left-hand pillar read *Château Wardin.*

The Château Wardin – this was where it had all started, Beaurain reflected, as he drove up the winding drive. The formation of Telescope. For three days after the burial of his wife he had remained inside his Brussels apartment, refusing to answer the doorbell or the phone, eating nothing, drinking only mineral water. At the end of the three days he had emerged, handed in his resignation as chief of the anti-terrorist squad and asked the owner of the Château Wardin for financial backing.

The Baron de Graer, president of the Banque du Nord and one of the richest men in Europe, had provided Beaurain with the equivalent of one million pounds. His late wife's father, a London merchant banker, supplied the second million. But it was de Graer's gift of the Château Wardin as well, which had provided the training ground for the gunners whom Henderson trained as Europe's deadliest fighters.

Recruitment had been carried out with far greater care than by most so-called professional secret services seeking personnel. The motive had to be there: men and women who had suffered loss in the same way as Beaurain. Wives who had lost husbands in the twentieth-century carnage laughingly known as peacetime. Henderson had brought with him several Special Air Service men – taking care the motive was never money. The Scot despised mercenaries.

Telescope had been involved in three major operations. At Rome airport it had shot four terrorists who had hi-jacked an Air France plane. No one had spotted Henderson's snipers who escaped dressed as hospital orderlies in an ambulance. And Düsseldorf: a bank siege involving hostages. No one ever worked out how unidentified men wearing Balaclava-type helmets reached the first floor and then descended one flight to destroy the heavily-armed robbers with stun-grenades and machine-pistols. Vienna: a hi-jack with Armenian terrorists – unidentified snipers operating at night had killed every Armenian and then disappeared like ghosts. But in each episode – and many others – the local police had found the same object left as a trademark. A telescope.

Most West European governments were hostile to this private organisation which achieved what they were unable to. But rather than risk the general public knowing of Telescope's existence, they compromised – allowing their own security forces to take responsibility for the events in Rome, Düsseldorf and Vienna.

"It would make the politicians look so stupid, Jules," René Latour, head of French counter-espionage, had explained when he was dining with his old friend Beaurain during a visit to Brussels. "Do you remember that remark I once made to you about three years ago," he continued. "That the President regards me as his telescope because I take the long view?"

"No, I don't remember," Beaurain had lied.

"It came back to me when all our security services were holding a meeting about Telescope – and wondering who could be the boss of such an outfit."

"Really," Beaurain had replied, ignoring Latour's searching glance and changing the subject.

Information. The Belgian had foreseen from the very beginning that the transmission of swift and secret information to his organisation was essential if it was to be able to act with the necessary speed and ruthlessness. And in this direction only, money was used; large fees were paid to an elaborate network of spies in all branches of the media, in many branches of government, in many countries. And always they operated through two watertight cut-outs, phoning a telephone number where someone else called another number.

But it was the Château Wardin with its seclusion, its variety of terrain, its hidden airstrip and helipad, which was the key to Telescope. This was Beaurain's main base.

As soon as the van drove in, the gates of Château Wardin were closed behind it. Litov was still awake. He was concentrating furiously, trying to make out what was happening, why there had been a slowing down in speed. Before the sudden almost right-angled swing at a sedate pace they had been travelling fairly fast along a road which had many bends. They had to be somewhere out in the country because he had not heard the sound of one other vehicle for a long time.

Also there were other indications that they might be nearing their destination – a restless stirring among the guards; one of them came over to check his handcuffs and the strap; the doctor was putting his equipment away in a bag. The van was moving very slowly, turning round curves all the time, first this way and then that. Litov began to worry about the English doctor's remark. "You have a flight ahead of you, a trip by air ... "

The directive given to Litov by Dr Berlin personally had been clear and straightforward. "You will be taken prisoner by the Telescope organisation who will then take you to their base for interrogation. It is the precise location of the base I need to know. Once you have discovered it, you use your many talents to escape. It does not matter how many of their people are killed. And when you are taken in Brussels they will definitely not kill you – or injure you more than necessary ... "

It was this last prediction which had not ceased to puzzle Litov, which had almost caused him to ask Berlin how he could possibly know that for sure; except that you did not ask Dr Berlin questions. How could Berlin have known they would take trouble to preserve his life?

The van negotiated the bends of the sweeping drive lined with trees and dense shrubberies. Half a mile from the gates it swung round another bend, the drive straightened and the moon illuminated a large Burgundian-style château with a grey slate roof. The windows were long and crescent-shaped at the top and a flight of stone steps led up to a vast terrace.

The driver swung onto a track round the side of the château and continued through dense woodland. Well out of sight of the château, he pulled up in a huge clearing.

Litov tensed. The rear doors were thrown open and a hellish sound beat against his ear-drums, the sound of the starting-up of a helicopter's rotors.

Litov had the powerful scent of pinewood in his nostrils.

The guards, taking one end of his stretcher each, lifted him out. Litov, out in the open, saw above him a half-circle of dense pine trees, the halo of a moon behind cloud.

He had guessed right: he was somewhere in the Ardennes. As they carried him away from the van he saw Beaurain standing by a ladder leading into a chopper. What type he couldn't identify.

Knowing this would be his last chance, Litov opened his eyes wide before they carried him up the ramp. The chopper, throbbing like some huge insect eager to fly away, stood in the centre of a pine-encircled clearing. No sign of a road or house anywhere. It would be impossible to pinpoint it later, even from the air. A long straight main road, a winding smaller one, presumably a house, probably a big one, and a clearing among pines nearby. There must be scores of such places in the Ardennes.

They carried him up a ramp into the rear of the machine and laid his stretcher on another leather couch with an iron rail running alongside it. Litov couldn't hear the purr of the ramp closing above the roar of the rotors, but he was aware of sudden total darkness. One of the guards produced hand-cuffs and linked the stretcher with the iron rail. They were very thorough, these bastards. As if on cue, the machine began its climb into the night.

In the front cabin, which was isolated from the flying crew and from the cargo hold where Litov and his guards were, Beaurain and Henderson sat drinking the coffee made for them by Louise Hamilton, Beaurain's personal assistant. A dark-haired English girl of twenty-seven, dressed in slacks and a blouse which did not entirely conceal her excellent figure. The strong bone structure of her face showed charac-ter. The tools of her trade were not those of what the business world knows as a personal assistant. She carried a 9 mm. pistol made at Herstal in her handbag and she faced Beaurain across the table. For the whole of the journey, while he was forced to be in one place, she would brief him on what had happened through the day and take his dictation. She began by reporting, "Alex says it's a straightforward fracture. It will hurt for several days, but it will mend as good as new if he doesn't mess about with it." Beaurain was momentarily too tired to answer her.

Henderson said nothing.

"I've read his file, Jules," Louise persisted. "He's got a record that makes me shudder. You think he'll break?"

Beaurain studied her across the table before replying. They had now climbed to two thousand feet and were flying smoothly. The pilot had his instructions and would carry them out to the letter. Through the window on his right the early streaks of dawn, the start of another glorious day. He sipped his coffee.

"Litov doesn't have to break," he said.

"He doesn't? Then what the hell is all this about?"

"Chief's right," Henderson said. "Litov doesn't have to get the thumbscrew treatment, although we may have to drop him down a few flights of stairs so he doesn't catch on. He just has to be tricked."

The helicopter spent three hours in the air as far as Litov could reckon it, though he could no longer see his watch. He had no way of telling the direction the chopper was taking. All the windows had been blacked out so he hadn't even the moon or the dawn light to go by. At one point Beaurain and the man he took to be his chief of staff came to look at him and to talk briefly with the doctor and the guards.

Fatigue was taking its toll of his powers of endurance and he was having trouble staying awake, when he felt the chopper lose altitude. Three hours. They could be in England, Italy, Spain, anywhere. The doctor left his chair and came over to Litov.

"I'm going to blindfold you," he said. "Don't feel too helpless – I'll take this off as soon as we have arrived."

Litov kept his eyes closed as he felt the band of cloth tied round his head. The chopper was descending at speed, dropping vertically. The doctor inserted ear-plugs so he heard nothing except the faint roar of the rotors. With a bump the machine landed. Within minutes he was being lifted and carried and he knew he was in the open.

They had not, however, deprived Litov of his sense of smell, and the first thing he noticed on leaving the helicopter was the acrid stench of a bonfire. An English bonfire. How could he forget it? He had once been attached to the Soviet Embassy in London. There were, of course, bonfires in other parts of Europe, but ... The men carrying the stretcher paused and the doctor removed the ear-plugs. He assumed it was the doctor. The men transporting him began walking again. Complete silence for several minutes. They had switched off the engines of the helicopter. No sound of traffic anywhere. Then the silence was broken by the roar in the sky of a large jet lumbering upwards. Litov made a mental note. Only a crumb of information, but Berlin gathered in every crumb available.

"Careful up the steps," a voice said, in German.

Germany? Yes, or even Austria. Telescope's base could be in either of these countries. Feet scrunched on gravel, the first time he had heard their feet since leaving the chopper. The smell of the bonfire had disappeared. Litov strained every faculty to gather clues.

The stretcher tilted; his head was lower than his feet. He thought there were six steps and then the stretcher levelled out. Footsteps on stone, another slight lift, the footsteps became a padding sound – presumably they were now inside a house moving over carpet. A door being unlocked, the stretcher set down on a hard surface, a heavy door closing, a key in a lock. His blindfold was removed.

The same precise routine had continued for a week. So precise, Litov was now almost convinced he was somewhere in Germany, that Telescope was mainly controlled by Germans – something no-one had even guessed at so far as he knew. There was the bus, for example. The room he was imprisoned inside measured sixteen feet by twelve, the walls were stone as was the floor, and the window facing his single bed was high in the wall and made of armoured glass, he suspected. But it was louvred and kept open.

It was through this high window that he heard the sound of the bus stopping each day, always precisely at 3.50 p.m. He could hear passengers alighting and getting aboard; at least he assumed that was what was happening, but he could never catch the language they spoke in. Then there was something else which he couldn't work out.

At 3.55 p.m. each day another vehicle stopped, smaller, it seemed from the engine sound. There would be a pause of about twenty-five seconds followed by the slam of a metal door. Then the vehicle would drive off.

The daily incident puzzled Litov. His frustration was all

the greater because he stood five feet six tall and the window was six feet above floor level. Without something to stand on he was never going to see through the window. And there was nothing to stand on. The only furniture in the cell-like room was his single bed against the opposite wall whose leg-irons were screwed into the stonework. And there was nothing he could use in the small, spotless toilet leading off the cell.

One thing Litov felt sure of: the building where he was imprisoned must be in the country and the window must overlook a country road. A bus only once a day suggested a remote spot. Nor was there any chance of his taking the risk and shouting while the bus was stopped – his interrogator infuriatingly always chose this time of day to visit him and he had with him an armed guard. Each day he arrived sharp on 3.30, bringing his own chair which he later took away.

Beaurain himself introduced the interrogator on the day he arrived at nowhere. "This is Dr Carder. We need the answers to certain questions he will ask. Until we get those answers your diet will be restricted."

This was a blow to Litov, predictable but still a blow. A non-smoker and a man who never touched alcohol, he did like his food and generally ate three cooked meals a day. Perched on the edge of his bed, he regarded the men Beaurain had left with him. One was a guard and, because he now always wore the Balaclava, Litov would not recognise Stig Palme, the man who had attacked him in the rue des Bouchers. The other, the doctor, puzzled him.

"I believe you smoke?"

The Englishman, who had used his own language, extended a packet of Silk Cut cigarettes. Litov shook his head, secretly a little triumphant. They had no idea who he was, no dossier on him – otherwise his non-smoking habits would have been recorded.

Dr Carder wore no mask. He sat on his wooden chair with his legs crossed and began to light an ancient pipe. Litov guessed he was in his early sixties. He wore a tweed jacket with leather patches on the elbows, grey trousers, a pale check shirt and a dark green tie. His thick hair and moustache were brown, his weatherbeaten face lined, his grey eyes mild and slow-moving.

"Shall we begin with your real name?" Carder enquired.

"James Lacey."

"That's what your passport says. We can come back to that and try again, if you'd rather. Where were you born?"

"I've forgotten ..."

The guard standing by and holding a machine-pistol made a menacing gesture but Carder restrained him. "Our guest has every right to make any reply he wishes – after all, we are in no hurry. All the time in the world, if need be."

Carder reminded him of a man who spins out his job to fill the day, not caring whether he completes a task or not. It was all so different from what he had expected. No threats, not a sign that they would resort to torture. Carder went on asking his questions, relighting his pipe every few minutes, showing no reaction to Litov's answers or when he gave no reply at all. At the end of half an hour Carder stood up, yawned and stared down at Litov.

"It's going to take time, I can see that. You know something, Mr Lacey? I once had a man in this room for two years before he came to his senses. I'll see you tomorrow. Same time."

Then the door had opened and closed, the key turned in the lock on the outside, and Litov was alone with his thoughts. *Two years!* To stop himself thinking about it he concentrated on working out how to get a sight of the bus which stopped outside.

Carder's wooden chair. After several days of the afternoon interrogation routine Litov decided he needed the chair to stand on if he was ever to see out of the louvred window. That posed two problems. Carder had to forget to take the chair away after one of his visits, and he had to leave the cell soon after he arrived. He came at 3.30; the bus stopped at 3.50 p.m.

There was also the spy-hole above his bed, a small glass brick in the stone work. Litov had stood on his bed and examined the small square, but he could see nothing. Presumably they stationed guards there on a roster basis and he would be seen if he ever did get the chance to see out of the louvred window. But after one week, when the opportunity presented itself, he grabbed it.

It was his seventh day in the cell. Suffering from the steady pain of his arm and a diet of orange juice and water Litov felt it was more like seven months since his capture in Brussels. Carder arrived precisely at 3.30 and began with the irritating ritual of lighting his pipe. When he had it going nicely he looked at Litov without speaking for a minute, which again was what he had done each day.

"Changed your mind?" he asked at last.

"About what?" Litov glanced at the guard, wondering whether he could knee him in the groin and snatch the machine-pistol. But they had it all worked out. The guard stood well back, his weapon held across him so he could point the muzzle in half a second. Carder, as always, had placed his chair six feet from the bed, so Litov could not snatch him as hostage and threaten to break his neck. The Telescope people seemed to know their business. Then they made their first mistake.

"About your name," Carder said.

"John Smith."

"Ah yes, of course. It's a good job we have all the time in the world," Carder mused and peered into the bowl of his pipe. "Can't make out what's wrong with this thing today. It's been playing up ever since I first ... "

The cell door swung open and another masked guard stood in the entrance. "Telephone for you, Doctor. Sorry for the interruption, but they said it can't wait."

Carder got slowly to his feet. "Well, if you'll excuse us just for a minute, Mr Smith," he said, and left the cell, followed by the guards. The door was slammed shut and locked from the outside. Litov sat very still, expecting someone to come back at any moment, but they didn't. The chair was still there. *They had forgotten the chair.*

He checked his watch. 3.47. The bus was due in three minutes. He waited for two everlasting minutes. He stared at the square of glass brick above his bed. If anyone was watching they would be back soon enough, but it was a risk he had to take. He wanted his first look at the outside world in seven long days. He needed to see the bus. He moved swiftly, marked in his mind where the chair stood and then lifted it to the window and climbed onto it.

As he had guessed, it was a country road, a narrow tarred road with a grass verge and trees. The bus came round the corner almost at once, a red single-decker. It stopped, the doors opened automatically and three people got off, two women carrying shopping baskets and a man with a labrador on a leash. The bus was there only a few seconds, and then was driving off out of sight. But Litov had seen its destination in the window at the front above the driver.

Fascinated, he watched the passengers walk away off down the road. Another vehicle came round the corner, and pulled up almost underneath the window. Leaving the engine running, the uniformed driver attended to the emptying of the pillar-box while Litov studied the legend embossed on the side of the van which was also painted bright red. *E II R*. Her Majesty's mail-van was collecting the post. He watched the van until it too had disappeared, got down off the chair and put it back in exactly the position Carder had left it. Then he lay down on the bed and closed his eyes.

Guildford. That had been the destination on the front of the bus. Telescope's base was in Surrey, England. And now he came to recall his earlier calculations of time spent aboard the chopper, everything fitted. He was being held at some house out in the country on a bus route to Guildford.

"He certainly took his first opportunity," Henderson observed, clearly pleased.

"Not a man to underestimate," Beaurain agreed.

"And the dossier says ... " Carder was reading from a folder. " ... Litov was attached to the Russian Embassy in London between July 1975 and December 1977 when he was returned to etc., etc."

"Which suggests he is reasonably familiar with southern England," Henderson pointed out. "He was followed by Special Branch to Woking, which is just north of Guildford, several times. They lost him every time, of course, the stupid buggers."

Beaurain, Henderson and the doctor were finishing their cold drinks. It was another ferociously hot day.

"We'll keep him here a few more days," Beaurain said. "Let him have a few more sessions with the doctor. Then he can go." He stared hard at Henderson. "You had better start making arrangements at once to organise the biggest underground dragnet you possibly can. Litov will head back for the Syndicate's base, but he will expect to be followed."

"He's an expert at losing tails," Henderson said.

31

"Exactly. So you'll need to use the leapfrog technique. Whatever happens he mustn't succeed in shaking loose from that dragnet."

"I'm on my way, sir."

"And I," suggested Carder, "had better get back to Litov. You'll be about, sir?"

"Not for the rest of the day – I have a meeting in the city and won't be back until late."

Beaurain made his way to the front of the house, nodded as a guard opened the door for him and ran down the steps from the terrace to his Mercedes. Louise was waiting in the passenger seat. From a track into the woods walked a man wearing an English bus driver's uniform.

Beaurain acknowledged his salute and drove away. At the bottom of the drive he turned right and speeded up as he passed a signpost. *Bruxelles 240 km.* "Well, Louise, we've won the second round. I think we may have shared round one, but round two is ours."

The imposing double doors of the Banque du Nord on the Boulevard Waterloo in Brussels were closed. Beaurain left Louise in the car and pressed the bell, giving the pre-arranged signal. The left-hand door was opened a few inches. The uniformed guard recognised Beaurain and then swiftly closed the door again when he was inside.

"Monsieur le Baron is expecting you," the guard said, and escorted him to a small, gilt-framed door. He unhooked a phone and spoke into it while the lift descended. Beaurain approved of all this security: the people upstairs were being informed he was on his way.

"You will be met at the top," the guard said, and stood aside to let him step into the lift. The lift stopped on the second floor and a second uniformed guard waited for him, a man Beaurain did not know. The guard checked a photograph after a searching glance at Beaurain's face, then led him along a marble-floored corridor to a heavy panelled wooden door at the end. The guard ushered Beaurain in; it was one of those locks you could open by turning the handle from the inside but not from the outside. The door was closed behind him.

"My dear Jules, it is good to see you. And again my apologies for phoning you at the château and asking you to travel all this way at this hour." The Baron shook his hand and gestured towards the telephone. "You know I do not trust that instrument for important conversations."

Something was amiss. Beaurain sensed the atmosphere as the Baron de Graer, president of the Banque du Nord, ushered him to a leather armchair and then mixed two double Scotches and soda without saying anything. The Baron was small and slim, his hair still dark, his eyes had the sparkle of a man of forty though he was a good deal older than that, his nose like the beak of an owl. Then his guest spotted what had alerted him to the tension. The Baron's usually smiling mouth was compressed tight, like that of a man struggling for self-control – or of one who was terrified. The latter was surely out of the question.

"Cheers! As the English say!"

The Baron managed the pleasantry with an effort and sat down next to Beaurain in another armchair. Beaurain studied him closely, remaining silent.

"I am so sorry for dragging you all this way at such short notice ... "

He was finding excuses to delay saying what he had called Beaurain to tell him. Extraordinary: de Graer was a man of immense character. "It made no difference," Beaurain replied, watching his host very carefully. "I had to come in anyway for a meeting with Voisin."

"The Police Commissioner?"

What the devil was going on? The Baron's tone was sharp and anxious. Beaurain had the strange sensation that his world was being shaken all round him, a feeling of instability and of menace such as he had never known. Was he growing too sensitive to people, to atmospheres? Perhaps Louise was right when she said he badly needed a holiday?

"Yes," Beaurain replied as evenly as he could. "The subject is how to co-ordinate efforts to eradicate terrorism and there should be top people there from the States and from all over Europe. Is something wrong, Baron?"

"You may well be refused admission to the conference." The Baron swallowed his drink in one gulp and stared at the far wall.

"I have a specific invitation to sit in on the meeting, I don't anticipate any difficulty when I arrive there. What on earth has caused you to make such a suggestion?"

This time the banker looked directly at Beaurain. His grey eyes had a haunted look and, yes, there *was* fear in his expression. He used a finger to ease the stiffness of his starched collar. "There are things you do not know, Jules. Power so enormous it is like a vast octopus which has spread its tentacles into every branch and level of western society. This morning the Syndicate sent out world-wide a signal naming ex-Chief Superintendent Jules Beaurain formerly of the Brussels police. It was a *Zenith* signal."

He stood up and walked quickly to the cocktail cabinet. He refilled his glass, adding only a nominal dash of soda. Then he did something else out of character. He went behind his huge desk and sat in his chair, as though conducting a formal interview. Beaurain stood up, put his glass carefully on the desk, and began strolling slowly round the room, very erect. The Baron recognised the stance as the one Beaurain used when on duty in charge of the police anti-terrorist squad.

"Do you mind telling me," he began, "how you know about a signal sent by the Syndicate which, so far as I know, has not yet been proved to exist? And," he ended with deliberate coarseness, "what is this crap about *Zenith*?"

"*Zenith* means that the person named is to be kept under constant surveillance, that every move they make, everything they say, everyone they meet – all their activities down to the smallest detail, so far as is possible – must be reported to the Syndicate."

Beaurain stopped in front of the desk and took his time lighting a cigarette, standing quite still, studying de Graer as though he were a suspect.

"I'm sorry, Jules, but I felt I must warn you ... "

"Shut up! Shut up and answer my questions."

"You cannot speak to me like that!" de Graer protested. He was standing up, his right hand close to the buzzer under his desk that would summon his secretary.

"If you press that buzzer I'll throw whoever comes in down your marble stairs. Then I'll probably break your wrist. For God's sake, are you telling me you're one of them – the Syndicate?"

"No! How could you believe ... "

"Then tell me how you know about this *Zenith* signal? Who transmitted it to you?"

"A woman phoned me. I have no idea who she is or where she is when she phones. No clue as to ... "

"And why, de Graer," Beaurain interrupted, "do the Syndicate phone you if you're not one of them?"

"You're not going to like this ... "

"I haven't liked any of it so far."

"The Banque is a very minor shareholder in the Syndicate. That is how I have been able to pass information about them and their possible future activities to you from time to time. You know, surely, that after what I have been through I would never help them in a major way."

After what I have been through. Beaurain had trouble not allowing his manner to soften at the banker's use of the phrase. Just over two years earlier his wife and daughter had been held hostage in the Château Wardin by Iraqi terrorists seeking to bargain for the release of two of their comrades held in a Belgian prison. It was just before Beaurain had given up command of the anti-terrorist squad. The negotiations had been botched, a clumsy attempt at rescuing the hostages from the château had led to the death of the Baron's wife and daughter.

Soon after the brutal killings the Baron had made over the Château Wardin and its ten thousand hectares of wild forest and hills and cliffs to Telescope's gunners and other staff. The Baron would no longer go near the place.

"It is because of what you went through," Beaurain told him in the same distant tone, "that I cannot understand your having anything to do with this diabolical Syndicate. You said the Banque was a very minor shareholder – what does that mean, for God's sake?"

"It has contributed only a very small amount of money."

"To the Syndicate?"

"Yes – now please hear me out, Jules ... When I was approached it seemed a good idea to accept their offer because it gave me a pipeline into their system, a pipeline I could use to feed back data to you. And this I have done."

"That's true. It is also true that you would never reveal the source of your information."

"I felt you would not approve."

"In what form was the offer made?"

The banker was beginning to sweat; tiny beads of perspiration were showing on his forehead. The atmosphere

35

inside the luxurious office was electric and to de Graer it seemed it was becoming impossibly overheated. He made a move in the direction of the drinks cabinet, changed his mind, stood irresolutely behind his desk. Beaurain thought, he's on the edge of a breakdown. He kept his tone distant, repeating the question.

"In what form was the offer from the Syndicate made to the Banque?"

"Over my private phone – God knows how they got the number. They have people everywhere."

"Who made the offer?"

"The woman I am supposed to phone about you. Yes, Jules, for God's sake – about you! I'm supposed to relay every word we have exchanged in this room."

"The woman has a name?"

"Originally she just told me to call her Madame."

"Her accent?"

"Flemish is the language she uses."

"And the offer she made?"

"A shareholding in the Syndicate which would yield enormous profits for the sum we invested. Three hundred per cent annually was mentioned."

"How do you conceal this criminal act from the other directors?"

"I paid the money in cash out of my private account."

"*You are lying, de Graer.*"

The accusation was like a blow in the face to the old baron. Beaurain actually saw him flinch, his face drained of blood. He seemed to age before the ex-chief superintendent's eyes. Beaurain felt sorry for his friend, but he refused to allow it to affect his judgement. He had to break through the barrier he sensed was there.

"You dare to speak to me like that, Beaurain ... "

"I know when you are lying. I've spent a lifetime training myself to know things like that. You're lying now – or not telling me everything. What really happened?"

"She threatened Yvette."

"Who?"

"My niece, my sister's daughter. After what happened to my own child. For God's sake, have a little pity, Jules ... "

"I'm going to smash these people into the ground if it takes me the rest of my life. I just have to know where I stand

36

with you – who I can trust."

"Hardly anyone now, I fear. And you are in great danger."

"And the nature of the threat?" Beaurain still kept his voice a distant monotone, hoping to defuse the terror which had penetrated the heart of one of the most powerful banks in Brussels. De Graer did not reply in words. Taking a chain linked to his waistcoat he produced a ring of keys, chose one, inserted it in a desk drawer, opened it and produced an envelope which he handed to Beaurain. Beaurain took out the card inside, which at first sight seemed like a greeting card until he looked at the picture. It was primitive, crude, quite horrible and fiendishly effective. It was a drawing of a child's doll sitting up in bed. Minus a head. Blood dripped from the truncated neck. At the foot of the bed a photograph of a child's head had been pasted onto the card. Beaurain looked up at the banker. "That's her?"

"Yes, that's Yvette." De Graer couldn't keep still. He kept glancing towards the drinks cabinet and then forcing himself to remain behind his desk. "Can you imagine how I felt when that arrived?"

"You have warned your sister?"

"She mustn't know anything about it." The banker was close to panic now. "Her husband is a prominent lawyer, as you know. He would create a great fuss – which might lead back to the Banque. I have complied with their demands – supplied them with funds – so Yvette is safe."

"You hope."

"Damn you, Jules! Don't say things like that! I have done my best, but the Syndicate has agents everywhere. No doubt there is someone inside this building who watches me."

"Have you told this Madame who calls you about Telescope?" Beaurain asked slowly.

"For God's sake, do you think I would betray the organisation I helped to build? What a question." De Graer mopped his forehead with his handkerchief, beyond caring. Then he made a supreme effort and got a grip on himself. "I am relying on Telescope to destroy the Syndicate. The police and security services are helpless – they are not even convinced this new octopus exists. You would have found that out if you had been able to attend the Commissioner's international conference."

"But I am attending it."

"You will be stopped at the door. Someone influential at that meeting has also received a *Zenith* message to exclude you. Do not ask me who it is – I don't know. Don't ask me how I know."

"This is the end of your connection with Telescope then?"

De Graer smiled bleakly for the first time. Producing the ring of keys at the end of the gold chain again he opened a much deeper drawer and brought out a brief-case which he placed on the desk. The key was in the lock. When Beaurain opened it he was staring at stacks of banknotes which filled the case. Swiss francs; a quick glance told him the serial numbers were not consecutive. Laundered money and quite untraceable. He shut and locked the case and looked at the banker.

"Another contribution to Telescope, Jules. The equivalent of half a million pounds in sterling."

"Thank you, Baron. Thank you, very sincerely. Now, the telephone number Madame gave you to contact her?"

"She will know – Yvette, my niece ... "

"She will not know, but we might decide to trace her and put her out of action. Permanently."

De Graer hesitated only a moment before he riffled through a card index on his desk, extracted a card and handed it to Beaurain. The banker had invented the name Pauline for Madame and he watched unhappily while Beaurain noted the number in his book. "This is getting almost like wartime," de Graer commented. "Your use of the word 'permanently'."

"She threatened a little girl's life, didn't she? And you presumably have to report something to Madame about my visit – since you're convinced there is a spy inside the Banque? Agreed, then. You tell her I came to you as an old friend in some agitation because an attempt was made to assassinate me near the *Grand Place*. Tell her the assassin was able to make his escape. Tell her I looked shaken." He picked up the brief-case. "Thank you again for the contribution. Before I go, is there anything else you can tell me about the Syndicate?"

De Graer hesitated, then stiffened himself. "All the members – shareholders ... "

"Contributors to this criminal international organisation ... "

He saw the banker flinch before he continued. "There will be a full meeting in about a fortnight's time. I have been told I shall have to travel to Scandinavia, although where exactly I don't know."

"Let me know when you get more details," Beaurain told him as he walked towards the door. "And from now on use a payphone in the street for calling the Château Wardin."

The guard on the second floor accompanied him down in the lift. Was there an aura of hostility about the man? Beaurain was looking at everything with fresh eyes. And the guard *was* carrying a gun in a shoulder holster, an innovation for the Banque du Nord.

As he left the lift the guard did not look at him, remaining behind as the ground floor man took over – again in silence – and escorted him to the main doors. Beaurain paused before stepping out. A phone call could have been made, men could have been summoned. Louise Hamilton was sitting in the passenger seat and her expression was grim.

"Something wrong?" Beaurain enquired as he got behind the wheel.

"That creep in the blue Renault in front is what's wrong. He's given you a ticket. I told him who you were, but it made no difference."

"I'll have a word with him. Something odd is going on. I'll explain later."

Beaurain noticed that the policeman was in plain clothes. The man, lean-faced and swarthy, wound down the window at his approach. "I was just considering having you towed away."

"You know who I am?"

"Yes, but that ... "

"I don't know who you are – and only uniformed branch concerns itself with traffic offences. Your action is harassment. Show me your warrant card."

"I don't have to show you anything."

"So now I don't think you're in the police and I'm going to drag you out of that car and find some identity on you."

Worried by Beaurain's expression, the man produced his police card. Beaurain nodded, tucked the traffic ticket into the man's top pocket and walked away, angry and puzzled. Since his resignation he had received the same courtesies as when he had been chief of the anti-terrorist squad. Was this development the result of the *Zenith* signal de Graer had received? Behind the wheel of the 280E, he said nothing to Louise but switched on the ignition and drove off.

"We're being followed," she said. "A cream Fiat with two men inside. It was parked behind me. When that man was giving me a ticket I saw him signal the couple behind us."

In the mirror Beaurain saw the car. Three men in plain clothes had been detailed to watch him. The terror had started.

4

Arriving at police headquarters, Beaurain parked by the kerb and took Louise into the waiting room. Normally he would have told her to take the car to his apartment and wait there. Now he thought she would be safer inside.

"Keep an eye on Miss Hamilton for me, Pierre," he told the duty sergeant.

He was late for the conference called by Commissioner Voisin so he ran up the stairs, leaving Louise alone in the cheerless waiting room.

Outside in the street one of the two men who had followed the Mercedes emerged from a payphone and Pierre, the duty sergeant inside the police station, replaced his receiver. He glanced across to where Louise was sitting with her back to the window and left his post. The reception desk was now unmanned and there was no-one else in sight.

The two men from the Fiat walked into the station, glanced across at the reception desk and entered the waiting room. One stayed by the door to keep an eye on the corridor. Louise, reading a paperback she had taken from her shoulder-bag, glanced up and froze.

"You are Louise Hamilton?"

The man addressing her was tall and bony-faced. He wore a light trench coat, a soft-brimmed hat and dark glasses. Louise stood up quickly and looked towards the reception desk which she saw was unoccupied. That struck her as off-key, as did the manner and appearance of the two men. The man outside the waiting-room was shorter and bulkier than his companion, and chewed gum as he kept glancing along the empty corridor.

"May I see your identity card?" she asked.

She was already moving. The bony-faced man was not in her way and she kept edging steadily towards the doorway.

"I don't have to identify myself in here. Hey! Where are

41

you going ... André!"

Louise slipped into the corridor and headed for the main exit.

André was the next barrier to be eluded. He moved back towards the doorway and she didn't think she could get into the street before he caught up with her. She turned as he came forward, raised her steel-tipped heel and ground it deliberately down his shin. André choked off a scream with his hand.

Louise ran, threw open one of the outer doors and fled into the warmth and freedom of the open air. There was no-one about in the early evening, and the Mercedes was still parked by the kerb. She had the key in her hand as she reached it but froze as she heard André shout. "I'm shooting – she resisted arrest."

She thrust the key into the lock, swung the door open and ducked down behind the wheel, slamming the door behind her. Only then did she look back at the police headquarters and while she did so she was slipping the key into the ignition lock and firing the motor.

The short, bulky André, hobbling with pain, was outside the entrance door endeavouring to aim a pistol with a bulging muzzle. The tall man was struggling with him, forcing the gun up into the air.

"No shooting, André. Pietr will stop her."

Pietr? He had to be the man who had given her the parking ticket outside the Banque du Nord – because now he was parked in his Renault a short distance behind her. The Fiat was parked immediately in front of the Mercedes, blocking her in. Except that behind her Pietr had left a gap – to make things look less obvious? – and was now starting up his own engine to drive forward and sandwich her.

She backed the car. Behind her Pietr saw the Mercedes ram towards him and panicked. He backed out of her way at speed and hit a stationary truck. André and his companion were half-way across the sidewalk. She drove out into the street and slammed her foot down on the accelerator. She had to get away before they could start their pursuit. As she came up to the first intersection the lights were in her favour. She turned left into heavy traffic as the lights changed. Neither car could find or catch up with her now. But would Jules' apartment be safe?

"I'm afraid you can't go in, sir."

Beaurain took a tighter grip on the case the Baron de Graer had given him. His smile concealed his dismay at the uniformed policeman's reply. He had not really believed what de Graer had said. *You may well be refused admission to the conference.* He considered shouldering the gendarme aside, but the latter unbuttoned the flap of his holster, exposing the butt of his pistol. Beaurain had known the man for fifteen years, a reliable plodder with neither initiative nor imagination.

"You value your retirement pension, Georges?" he asked casually, and watched the man, whose eyes could no longer meet his, shuffle his feet uncomfortably as though his shoes were too small.

"I have my orders."

"Whose orders were they?"

"Commissioner Voisin himself posted me at these doors." Beaurain snatched the pistol from his holster with his left hand and pushed the guard aside with his right, bursting into the large room beyond and slamming the door closed behind him.

The conference room was furnished with a long, wooden table seating about a dozen people. Commissioner Camille Voisin, large in body with a wide thin mouth and small eyes which moved restlessly like his plump hands, was in the chair. Beaurain glanced round at the others, all of whom he had known for years, high-ranking security officials from western Europe, and Ed Cottel of the CIA.

"My apologies for arriving late," Beaurain began smoothly, noting there was no place for him, "but I got held up."

"You are not included in this meeting, Beaurain."

It was Voisin who had spoken, rising from his chair to show his displeasure and more of his gross figure. He stared at Beaurain and made one of the obvious comments he was notorious for.

"You have a pistol in your hand."

"Brilliant! It belongs to the idiot outside who tried to refuse me admission."

"Exactly as ordered."

"My invitation came direct from the Minister, Voisin. Do you wish to contact him?"

Voisin's pudgy hands fluttered aimlessly, conveying to his

colleagues how impossible life was. There was a phone on the table but he made no attempt to call the Minister.

"Jules, come and sit next to me." His old friend Ed Cottel had collected a seat from by the wall and placed it next to his own. Beaurain opened the door and shoved the pistol back into the holster of the guard standing disconsolately outside. "Do be careful not to lose this again," Beaurain said severely. As he sat down next to the American he exchanged salutations with the others.

René Latour of French counter-espionage, an odd note in a gathering of policemen. Harry Fondberg from Stockholm, chief of Säpo, the Swedish secret police. Peter Hausen, the shrewd chief of Kriminalpolizei from Wiesbaden, sat in another chair. Voisin stared at him, and he decided to go on the offensive.

"I appreciate being asked to attend this meeting, but perhaps I could be briefly informed of its subject?"

"Voisin couldn't be brief if the doubling of his salary depended on it," Cottel commented loudly.

"There are two subjects on the agenda," Voisin snapped. "The first is the location and destruction of Telescope, the private army of terrorists operating inside western Europe and the United States. We have been instructed by my Minister to identify the top man in this subversive organisation, to locate their base and their sources of finance."

"*You* may have been instructed to do this by *your* Minister," Cottel interrupted, "but his instructions hardly apply to Washington or, I should have thought, to any representative of any other country present. Furthermore ..." Cottel rolled on as Voisin opened and closed his mouth, "furthermore I have to challenge your description of Telescope."

"I was not, of course, suggesting that anyone else is bound by my Minister's instructions ..." Voisin began hastily.

"I have to challenge your description," Cottel continued, "because during the past two years the Telescope people, as they call themselves – perhaps because they see further than some of us – have been responsible for knocking out at least forty-five top terrorists, during airport hi-jacks, embassy sieges and kidnap rescues. There are colleagues of mine who unofficially approve of Telescope for what it has achieved."

"You suggest nothing be done about these pirates?" Voisin was angry at the murmurings of approval which had

44

greeted Cottel's opinion. The American ignored the question.

"Commissioner, shouldn't you tell Jules Beaurain the second item on our agenda?"

"It is a co-ordinated discussion on whether another criminal organisation known as the Syndicate exists."

"Of course it exists. We all know it," Cottel said with disgust, "but we don't like admitting it. We do know that millions of dollars have moved to western Europe to help finance it. We suspect that several American multi-national corporations have transferred vast sums to the Syndicate. Furthermore ..." He raised his voice at Voisin again, who closed his mouth. "Furthermore," he repeated, "the sums of money at the Syndicate's disposal are so enormous that whoever controls it wields power almost without precedent. Gentlemen, I suggest the first priority of this meeting is not Telescope – it is to co-operate in tracking down and destroying the Syndicate." He looked at the Commissioner. "I have finished, M. Voisin – for the moment at any rate."

"I agree with Mr Cottel," said Peter Hausen.

"Commissioner Voisin, I agree with my colleague, Peter Hausen, and, therefore, with Mr Cottel," the French counter-espionage representative added crisply.

"Shall we have a show of hands?" enquired Beaurain gently.

"That will not be necessary," Voisin snapped, anxious to avoid any further demonstration of the united front against him. "The first requirement, surely, is to prove the Syndicate exists."

"Assume it exists and go on from there," growled Cottel and lit a cigarette.

"Who is behind it then?" demanded Voisin.

"The Kremlin," replied Cottel.

It was 7.30 p.m. when Louise Hamilton arrived at Beaurain's apartment off the Boulevard Waterloo. Confident she had not been followed, she parked the Mercedes in the ancient garage and let herself inside the first-floor apartment.

The living-room was expensively furnished, the kind of place you would expect a widower to live in – except that it was tidy and organised. After her experience at police headquarters she didn't feel hungry, so she slipped off her shoes and flopped onto a couch. The reaction was setting in. She could hear the voice of the detective in her mind: *I'm shooting – she resisted arrest!*

The entire Brussels police force knew Jules Beaurain. He had always been popular because he treated his men fairly and was incorruptible. Since his resignation many of them – especially at headquarters where he was a frequent visitor – had come to know Louise as "Jules' friend". They knew nothing about her work for Telescope. The phone rang. She lifted the receiver and said, "*Oui?*"

"Louise Hamilton, *n'est-ce pas?* You had better get back to your own country by the first plane."

"Who is this? I love callers without the guts to identify themselves," Louise said coolly.

The voice was a woman's, probably in her early thirties. Her command of English was good but there was an accent Louise couldn't place. Let the little bitch chatter on a while longer, she thought.

"If you hang around we have people expert in breaking legs. Then they go on to the hands. You are left-handed, *n'est-ce pas?*"

"Why not come and deliver the message yourself?" Louise suggested. "I'd love to meet you face to face."

"When your face has been ruined you will not talk in this way, I am sure of that!" The voice ended with a note of venom, and the connection was broken.

Louise replaced the receiver slowly, automatically noting the time the call had ended. Beaurain had an unlisted number – how had the woman managed to obtain it?

The second – more alarming – thought was how the caller had known that she would find Louise in the apartment. It was the first time for over a week she had entered the place. She might have been trailed from police headquarters – but she had taken great pains to see that she was *not* followed. That left only one other – equally unsettling – solution. The apartment was being watched on a round-the-clock basis.

She went over to the window and peered through the net curtain. Below she saw the narrow, deserted road. She stared at the first-floor windows opposite but they were also masked. Were there watchers behind the net curtains?

Louise went into the kitchen to calm herself by preparing

46

dinner. Somewhere in the same city another woman was probably sitting down to her meal after making a phone call.

"Did she sound scared?" enquired Dr Berlin as he scooped a generous helping of melon.

"No!" Sonia Karnell had paused before reluctantly deciding that – as always – it was much safer to tell the truth to Berlin. He always knew when you shaded a meaning. Outright lying she would not have considered. "She sounded like a woman who was expecting just such a warning and had worked out what her reply would be."

"Like you, she is tough, ruthless – and well-trained. A pity she has to be the sacrificial goat."

Sonia Karnell, dark-haired, five feet six tall, and thirty-two years old, was Swedish by birth, a native of Stockholm and fluent in six languages, including English. Despite the heat of the evening, Berlin wore his normal black suit across his ample form. As he spoke he looked frequently at Karnell across the table to gauge her reactions. He was always watching the people around him, especially those closest – and none was closer than Sonia Karnell – like a man whose greatest fear in life is betrayal.

"We flew here today just so I could phone her?" she asked.

"Eat your melon – it helps replace moisture. Yes, we flew here partly to make a phone call. Had Beaurain answered, you would have made the same menacing noises about Hamilton – but this may be more effective. When he hears what happened."

"A sacrificial goat. What does that mean, Otto?"

"Let me eat. The plan is based on the fact that the first complete meeting of the Syndicate takes place near Sweden in two weeks' time. We have a problem because Telescope has as its objective our destruction."

"How does my phone call fit in? I don't understand."

"Patience!" The eyes behind the thick pebble glasses studied her. "I have contacts inside the European police – high-level informers. There is a discreet understanding between Beaurain and certain of his old colleagues who agree with his methods. It was a police contact who informed me Beaurain is Telescope's chief, and determined to wipe out the Stockholm Syndicate. So we must destroy them first – before the meeting, otherwise there could be a catastrophe.

Beaurain is getting too close."

Sonia Karnell, her white face framed by her close-cut hair, started eating her melon to please Berlin. The heat was appalling! "Why threaten Beaurain's tart?"

"To distract him. One thing is needed before our soldiers can attack – we must know the location of Telescope's main base, which we should learn soon from Serge Litov."

"What's going to happen to her?"

"Gunther Baum will deal with her. That will shake Beaurain's nerve."

She stopped eating, unable to swallow. "You are going to use that animal on her?"

"He will produce the necessary effect – fury on the part of Beaurain. This may well cause him to make a mistake. Terrify those you can. Those you can't: upset their balance."

"And are we going back to Bruges?"

"For a short time, yes. Until Litov returns with the location of Telescope's base. After all, I have to attend to my rare book business if we are to make a living!"

"So this woman threatened you?" Beaurain said as he paced round his living-room. It was ten o'clock: as usual, Voisin's meeting had gone on for hours. Beaurain was very disturbed by the fact that the caller had been able to obtain his phone number; by the fact that it was Louise who had been threatened; above all by the bizarre incident at police headquarters.

"She gabbled on about having my legs and hands broken," Louise said calmly, "as well as cutting my face. A regular little madam. I'd like five minutes alone with her. Oh, and none of this would take place if I caught the first plane back to England. She was trying to rattle *you*, Jules."

"I wonder who the hell it was," he said.

"The Syndicate, of course. They're stepping up the pressure."

"They're certainly doing that – to get into the meeting this evening I had to push aside a guard who had been put on the door to keep me out. That can only have come from the Syndicate."

She sat up straight. "Surely you don't think Commissioner Voisin could have been got at?"

"That does seem unlikely – but someone at that meeting

48

must have asked to keep me away. As you can imagine, Voisin would be glad to oblige – he's too lazy to take any initiative himself. I don't know. It should have been impossible for the Syndicate to penetrate Brussels police headquarters – but they managed. Those two men were certainly not detectives. What's getting me is how they ensured the reception desk was unmanned."

"Just before they came in I heard the policeman on duty take a call. When they arrived he had disappeared."

Beaurain crashed his fist into his palm. "That was Pierre Florin behind the counter when I arrived."

"Has he been with the force for some time?"

"Only twenty bloody years. I'll have a few questions to ask him!"

"That woman is succeeding in rattling you."

"What's rattling me," he snapped, "is the penetration this criminal organisation has apparently achieved. We shall have to release Serge Litov immediately – and see where he leads us."

"You were going to keep him longer," she objected, gripping his arms tightly. "Now they are making you react to their timing."

"Don't forget what Henderson noticed the night Litov tried to shoot me – the safety catch still on his Luger. With a professional like that! They took the opportunity I gave them in order to exploit it themselves. We are using Litov to find the source of the Syndicate. They're hoping Litov will escape and tell them where we're based. Litov is in the middle and probably knows it. After today's happenings I'm going to speed up the process and release Litov."

Beaurain broke off as the doorbell rang repeatedly. Louise tensed and let go of his arms. "Who could that be?" she asked quietly.

"It's the special ring I arranged with Ed Cottel. He said he'd call round."

"You hope it's Ed," she said, extracting her pistol from her handbag.

"You're right – from now on we don't make any assumptions. And, by the way, he's here on a double mission – to help track down the Syndicate, which he is convinced exists – and also to wipe out Telescope."

It was indeed Ed Cottel outside and when Beaurain had

49

re-locked the door, the American, who knew Louise Hamilton well, hugged her, nodding his acceptance of a large Scotch.

"This new Syndicate scares the guts out of me," he said. "I've been talking to Washington – someone I can trust – since that for-ever-and-a-day meeting. The fragments we keep picking up frighten me more each time."

"Why did you say at the meeting you thought the Kremlin were behind the Syndicate?"

"Because I can tap a computer."

Ed Cottel was a slim man in his early fifties. His most outstanding characteristics were his hooked nose, his West Coast accent and his restrained manner reflected in the Brooks Brothers suits he invariably wore. He reminded Beaurain more of an Englishman than an American. He was so independent-minded that the Belgian was surprised Washington had chosen him to come to Europe to collaborate with its security services.

"Tap a computer, Ed? What are you driving at?"

"It's just about the biggest computer in the world, and it contains records on every person of prominence in politics and industry, including the top Russians. You've heard of Viktor Rashkin?"

"The Kissinger of the Kremlin – but so much quieter that the international press doesn't know he exists," Beaurain replied.

"At the moment he is First Secretary at the Russian Embassy in Stockholm." Cottel peered at the bottom of his glass. "First Secretary – that's a laugh. Leonid Brezhnev's wonder boy and top trouble-shooter – and trouble-maker – and he's only a First Secretary. It's the usual cover, of course. Moves about a lot, does our Viktor," he said thoughtfully.

"You said you can tap a computer," Beaurain reminded him. "How does this link up with Rashkin?"

"At Voisin's comic meeting I mentioned the money trans-ferred from the States to finance Syndicate operations over here. I got a tip while I was in Washington, and I went to the computer and found out about a recent transfer of five million dollars from an Arizona bank to one here in Brussels. The recipient at this end, I'm pretty sure, was Viktor Rash-kin. Did you know," he enquired casually, "that Rashkin is in Brussels right now? Flew in with some other people aboard his private jet from Stockholm. It's now under observation at Brussels airport."

"And where did he go in Brussels? You seem to know more about my own back yard than I do."

"Only because of the computer. We lost Rashkin the moment he left the airport with his friends."

"Friends?"

"A man and a woman – and before you ask, we don't know who they are and we have no description. So we're not always that smart, Jules." He stared up at the ceiling, carefully not looking at them. "One thing you might find interesting. Voisin kept me back after the meeting had closed. I had said in a written report on Telescope that we might just be able to identify its personnel – or at least the leaders. Want to hear the damnfool mistake I made?"

"Up to you, Ed," Beaurain said, with a show of indifference. Curled up again on the sofa Louise looked tense. "I could do with some more coffee if you have the strength."

"Of course."

She walked to the kitchen, able to hear the conversation through the door. Cottel's reference to identifying the people in Telescope had shaken her. How the hell could he possibly do that?

"Have another drink, Ed." Beaurain sat in Louise's place on the sofa where he could study the American without appearing too interested. He folded his arms. "You stayed behind with Voisin. That must have been entertaining."

"In my report I suggested that the key men and women running Telescope might have suffered personal losses from terrorism. Wives, sisters, husbands, girlfriends. I suggested we made a list of all those who had recently suffered personal loss through criminal and terrorist action. Among that list we may spot likely candidates – because I'm sure that was the motive for starting up Telescope. Disgust with the incompetence of governments. Dammit, Jules, the motive is one of mankind's most powerful – revenge."

"That list would take years to build up."

"Not using that computer I have access to."

"Oh, I see. And you told Voisin?"

"No. Voisin asked me to use the computer to build up the list. If I don't do it, he'll ask someone else. And now I must get going – I'm catching the night flight to the States." Cottel stood up. "I'll be back soon. And don't forget about Viktor Rashkin."

"You think he's a member of the Syndicate, for God's sake?"

"Not a member – but I think he funnels funds through whoever is running that outfit." He scratched his head. "Don't know if it means anything," he remarked casually, "but have you ever heard of the *Kometa*?"

"No, but it sounds Russian."

"It is. One of our satellites has been following its progress down the coast of the Baltic. It's a huge hydrofoil. Normally the Soviets only use them on rivers like the Volga – but this one is now off Poland. Not so far from Sweden. Where is it headed for and why? No-one can work it out – which is what makes it worrying. See you both ..."

After Cottel had left, Beaurain dialled a number. He settled himself into a chair and perched the phone amid the crockery Louise had laid. "Is that you, Jock? Jules here. The mobile cargo we picked up recently is to be put on a train early tomorrow morning at Brussels Midi. Yes, that's right – *Midi*." Midi was one of the three main-line stations in Brussels. "Organise an all-round escort to supervise proper handling of the cargo. Understood? Next, stock up the floating fuel store with supplies and await instructions. Got it? And take care – someone might be starting a fire and there's plenty of tinder about."

He put down the phone, shifted the receiver off the table and looked up, suddenly aware that all sounds from the kitchen had ceased. Louise was standing close to him, holding an empty scoop. He threw up his hands as though in self-defence.

"I know you've laid the table – but I haven't disturbed your beautiful setting."

"I want to know what's going on – and quickly or the food will be ruined."

"You heard the conversation."

"Which was in code. First of all, where is Jock now? It sounds as though things are moving."

"Jock was at our sub-base near the station, although by now I expect he'll be on his way to the Château Wardin."

She glanced at her watch to check the cooking time and perched herself on his lap. "For 'mobile cargo' I read Litov – who's going to be dropped at Brussels Midi and allowed to run. I'm worried we'll lose him."

"Hence my reference to 'an all-round escort', the full-scale dragnet I want Jock to throw round all Litov's possible escape routes – because elude us he will try to do. And, since he will assume we're tracking him, we must trick him into thinking that he's succeeded. Then see where he leads us. Tomorrow will be a big day. Satisfied?"

"Not yet." She caressed the side of his face with her scoop as she continued. "What about your reference to 'the floating fuel store'? Is that the steam yacht, *Firestorm*? It is? And where is she now?"

"Midway between Scotland and the mouth of the Baltic. I've kept her ready there since I first heard the phrase 'Stockholm Syndicate'. Jock will radio her to take on board provisions, check weapons and ammunition, above all equip her with a team of gunners. He's going to have a busy night is Jock. And now I'm hungry."

"You always are. It's chicken – cooked the way you like it. I suppose tomorrow we'll watch them plotting Litov's movements on the map."

"More than that. Later tomorrow we're visiting the Fixer in Bruges. He may be able to tell us who is the real power behind the Stockholm Syndicate."

5

The Fixer. Dr Henri Goldschmidt, dealer in rare coins, was one of Bruges' most eminent citizens. Beaurain estimated his present age at about sixty but could only guess – the doctor guarded his private life jealously and you dared not ask him the wrong question. The penalty was to be instantly crossed off his list of social acquaintances.

"They are excluded from my *milieu*," he once explained. "And, of course, once excluded they can never be re-admitted."

He spoke eight languages fluently, including French, English and German; he also used his finely-shaped hands to aid his flow of conversation, gesturing with controlled deliberation to emphasize a point. He was the confidant of royalty, American millionaires and French industrialists. Less well-known was the fact that he was on good terms with some of Europe's top gangsters. This was the man Beaurain was going to meet.

One hour before dawn the huge Sikorsky helicopter took off from the Château Wardin. Litov – who had endured his last 'interrogation' at the hands of Dr Alex Carder – was lying on a stretcher, as on the 'outward' journey, his damaged arm expertly protected with a splint and bandages and his left wrist and ankle handcuffed to the stretcher. His right ankle was also manacled.

There were two guards in the gunners' normal battle uniform – denim trousers, crêpe-soled shoes, windcheaters and Balaclava helmets which completely masked their appearance. One was Stig Palme. The second was a twenty-nine year old German, Max Kellerman. A year earlier he had been looking forward to a brilliant career as a lawyer. Then his fiancée had been caught in terrorist crossfire when the police had been tipped off about a bank raid in Bonn.

They were still unaware that the tip-off had come from Jules Beaurain. It was something he had also concealed from Kellerman, as he had once explained to Louise.

"If Kellerman knew I started the whole thing off he *might* blame me for the death of his fiancée."

Litov had been blindfolded before he left the large cell he had occupied for over a week. Once again he was relying on sound and his sense of smell to double-check what he had learned about Telescope's main base. The same bonfire smoke had hit his nostrils when they carried him from the building to the ramp at the rear of the chopper. They took him the same way out – he felt and heard the change from carpet to stone; then the stone steps followed by an absence of sound suggesting grass. The bonfire stench didn't seem strange: from his tour of duty in London he recalled that the British kept foul-smelling fires smoking all summer.

"Don't forget to light that bonfire in good time," Beaurain had reminded Stig Palme. "Litov is bright – he must not get a whiff of the Ardennes pines while he's being carried aboard".

It had been 3 a.m. when they had come to collect Litov. Still wearing his wrist-watch, he had managed to check the time before one of the masked guards applied the blindfold. If he was being returned to the same starting-point the flight from England should take about three hours.

When the Sikorsky landed, Litov, still imprisoned on the stretcher in the cargo hold, found himself re-living his earlier experience in reverse. There was a bump as the chopper came to earth, a pause while the rotors stopped spinning, followed by the purr of the hydraulics as the automatic ramp at the rear of the cargo hold was lowered.

His blindfold was removed by a guard with a Balaclava concealing his face. These people didn't miss many tricks, Litov thought smugly – and then he was being lifted down into broad daylight. The strong scent of Ardennes pines entered his nostrils and above he saw the tops of the trees encircling the secret helipad. The two guards carried him to the familiar van with *Boucher* across the rear doors. They dumped him on the same leather couch alongside the left-hand wall, the doors were closed and Kellerman and Palme sat facing their captive with machine-pistols across their laps.

"We are driving you to Brussels Midi station," Kellerman told Litov in English as the van began to move. "Here are your papers, Mr James Lacey or whatever your name is."

Litov could hardly believe it. Kellerman bent over him and returned his wallet to his inside pocket. Was this a trick to throw him off balance, to make him relax before they subjected him to torture or a trial of endurance?

But he half-believed the guard who returned to his seat as the van gathered speed. Why should they let him go at all? The guard gestured towards the wallet he had returned.

"You will find all your money intact. Belgian francs, deutschmarks, Dutch guilders. Telescope does not steal like the Syndicate."

Litov stiffened, tried to keep his face expressionless. What the hell was going on? This was the first admission that these men belonged to Telescope. And why the casual mention of the Syndicate? To test his reaction? Of one thing Litov was now certain – he was being freed in the hope that he would lead them to the Syndicate's headquarters. He had trouble concealing his satisfaction. They were in for a surprise, a very nasty surprise indeed.

Pierre Florin, desk sergeant at Brussels police headquarters, requested a week's leave soon after the two men had accosted Louise in the reception room. It was the sight of Beaurain running up the stairs to attend the meeting and the realisation that the girl knew Beaurain which had scared Florin. Because of his long years of service his request was immediately granted.

He spent most of the seven days in his bachelor's apartment in south Brussels. One of the fake detectives visited him one evening.

"Why have you taken this leave, Florin?" he demanded. "It draws attention to you at just the wrong moment."

"I am worried. Beaurain . . ."

"You are a fool. Beaurain is no longer on the force."

"He carries enormous influence." Florin could not keep still, and kept moving restlessly about, fussily moving cheap mementoes of holidays in Ostend. "I would not like to be grilled by Beaurain," Florin continued, confirming the other man's opinion that he would crack under interrogation. "I want my money." The lean-faced man extracted a sealed

56

envelope and dropped it on the floor, making Florin stoop to retrieve it. Then he left and reported his doubts to Dr Otto Berlin.

It took Dr Berlin several days to locate Gunther Baum, the East German whose speciality was the removal of people. Baum and his companion, a nondescript individual who carried a brief-case, arrived unannounced at Florin's apartment. Wearing dark glasses, Baum was smartly dressed in American clothes. Outside Florin's apartment he took the silenced Luger from the brief-case and held it behind his back as he pressed the bell.

Gunther Baum was medium built and deliberate in his movements. "Never hurry," he often warned his assistant. "It draws attention to you." He was wearing a straw hat which, with his tinted glasses, masked his whole upper face, revealing only a pug nose, a small thin mouth and a fleshy jaw. Cupped in his left hand he carried a photo of Pierre Florin. It was best to proceed in a methodical manner.

Florin opened the door and glanced nervously at the strangers before starting to close it again. "We are the Criminal Division. A message from headquarters. Concerning the incident there about one week ago. We may come in, yes?"

"Of course ..."

Baum spoke in a sing-song French. He spoke in short sentences as though he expected everyone to accept him at face value. It never occurred to Florin to ask for some form of identification. They proceeded into the apartment, first Florin, then Baum and his companion, who carried the empty brief-case and closed the door.

"You are alone?" Baum asked.

"Yes, I seldom ..."

"Keep walking, please. We have been asked to look at your bedroom. Statements have been made that a woman visits you who keeps bad company."

"That's ridiculous."

"This we are sure of. Keep walking. Open that cupboard – I must be sure we are alone."

They were inside the cramped bedroom and Florin reacted like a robot to Baum's instructions. He opened up the cupboard at his visitor's request. Baum pressed the tip of the silencer against the base of Florin's neck. The Belgian stiffened at the pressure of the cold metal. "Step into the cupboard slowly," Baum commanded in the same sing-song French. "You stay there out of the way while we search for evidence." Terrified, Florin stepped inside the cupboard, his face buried among his clothes. Baum pressed the trigger once.

He slammed the door against Florin's toppling body and turned the catch. Without saying a word he handed the Luger to his companion who immediately hid it inside his brief-case as Baum removed his gloves and shoved them inside his pocket. "Time to go," Baum said.

It was his normal routine when working on a close-up job. Baum never kept the gun a second longer than necessary. It was his companion's task to transport the incriminating weapon so that Baum could never be compromised; it was a risk Baum's companion was paid good money to take.

"Now for the bargee Dr Berlin is worried about. We want to keep our employer happy, don't we?"

At 9.30 a.m. a butcher's van pulled into the kerb at Brussels Midi station. Serge Litov had been released from the handcuffs and was sitting facing Max Kellerman who was pointing his machine-pistol at the Russian's belly. Litov could still not fully believe he was about to be freed; the one thing which reassured him was the sound of heavy traffic outside.

"When you get out don't look back," Kellerman warned, "or this van will be the last thing you'll ever see. One quick burst and we'd be away. And there is a whole team of our people outside to make sure you board a train – any train."

Stig Palme, still masked like Kellerman, unbolted the rear doors, opened one a few inches and peered out. He opened it wider, Litov stepped down into the street and the door was closed. Kellerman now moved very fast.

Stripping off the boiler suit he had been wearing, he stepped out of it. Pulling off the Balaclava helmet, he lifted the top of the couch Litov had been seated on, took out a trilby hat and jammed it on his head. He grabbed a suitcase and a fawn raincoat from inside the couch. The suitcase's corners were tipped with steel to serve as an improvised weapon. Sliding back a plate at the front of the van he spoke to the driver.

"Well?"

"He behaved – went straight into the station booking-hall." Kellerman ran to the back of the van and dropped into the street. No-one noticed. Kellerman walked across to one of the swing doors and entered the booking-hall. Litov was standing at the ticket counter by the first-class window with only one man in front of him. While he waited he glanced behind and saw a Belgian woman with a poodle on a lead joining his queue. She was muttering away to herself as she burrowed in her handbag for fare money. Expensively dressed, which fitted her presence in the first-class queue. Litov noticed things like that.

"Stupid old cow," he thought. "Women never have their money ready."

The man in front of him moved away and with a quick glance at the station clock Litov asked for his ticket in a low tone. The ticket clerk asked him to speak up. Litov did so, anxious not to draw attention to himself.

"One seat on the *Ile-de-France* Trans-Europ Express to Amsterdam. One-way and a non-smoker. I shall have time to catch it?"

"Plenty of time." The clerk was writing out the car and seat number. "Arrives here 9.43, reaches Amsterdam 12.28."

Behind Litov the woman with the poodle was still investigating her handbag and muttering away to herself in French. She irked Litov: people like that ought to be locked up. He paid for his ticket and moved towards the platforms, glancing round at the milling crowd, trying to locate the hidden watchers he knew must be there.

Everything seemed normal. The bustle of passengers criss-crossing the large booking-hall, the general air of frustration and anxiety, the constant background voice over the speakers relaying an endless list of train arrivals and departures all over Europe.

At the first-class counter the woman apologised to the clerk. She couldn't find her purse. Would he serve the next passenger while she . . . She glanced across to see Litov walk out of sight onto the platforms. She hurried over the concourse, her poodle trotting briskly by her side, to Max Kellerman who stood reading a newspaper. Stopping abruptly, she let the poodle walk on and contrived to let the leash wrap itself round the German's legs.

59

"So sorry," she burbled in French, her voice low as she untwined the leash, "Colette does like men. The 9.43 T.E.E. to Amsterdam," she went on. "Five stops – Brussels Nord, Antwerp East, Roosendaal, Rotterdam, The Hague, then Amsterdam ..."

"Get the news to Henderson," murmured Kellerman. "Tell him I'm on my way."

Kellerman quickly joined the short queue which had formed at the first-class window. Behind him the fussy lady in her sixties had made her way to a telephone kiosk.

It was not long until the *Ile-de-France* de-luxe express would be arriving en route for Amsterdam. The T.E.E.s stopped for precisely three minutes. Nevertheless Serge Litov, after walking up and down the platform, suddenly returned to the booking-hall.

Left behind on the platform, Max Kellerman, wearing his raincoat and hat and carrying his suitcase, waited where he was in case Litov reappeared at the last moment and boarded the express. Litov might be standing watching the exit doors to see if anyone followed him. Or buying the ticket for Amsterdam might be the first of his tricks to throw off the shadows he knew were watching.

In the booking-hall Litov hurried to a phone box, shut the door and called a Bruges number. He watched to see if anyone appeared to be dogging his movements. What he didn't notice was a woman with a poodle who was perched on a nearby seat ostentatiously eating a sandwich. If Litov had happened to spot her, the sandwich would have explained her presence – having booked her ticket she had a long wait for her train and preferred to spend it in the booking-hall.

"If he leaves the station, you follow him, Alphonse," she said quietly to the man sharing her seat.

"It doesn't look as though he is catching the Amsterdam express."

"He still has time," Monique replied equably.

"I'd like to know what he's saying," muttered Alphonse.

Inside the phone box Litov's Bruges number had connected and he identified himself quickly. "Serge speaking, your friend from the Stampen. They let me out – just like that."

"Berlin here. Keep this call brief, I'm expecting another.

Where are you?"

"Brussels Midi station. I've bought a ticket for Amsterdam. Which route – and can you get me a back-up? They're bound ..."

"It was our friends?" Berlin interjected sharply. "And you know their home town?"

"Yes and yes. I'm short of time. I have to catch that express. Or don't I?"

"Of course. Then continue on by air, if you understand me. Help will meet you at Copenhagen – to deal with any difficulty you may encounter. Goodbye."

In the tiny terraced house at Bruges, Berlin replaced the receiver and looked across the table at Sonia Karnell pouring out coffee. He waited for the cup before satisfying her curiosity.

"Serge Litov is starting his run. He is at Brussels Midi. Telescope has let him go and he says he knows the location of their main base."

"But that's marvellous."

"Is it?" Berlin looked round the drab walls, the gilt-framed pictures you couldn't see in the gloominess caused by the looming houses on the other side of the narrow street. "We shan't know whether he has succeeded until I have questioned him. The thing now is to sever the link between Litov and Telescope's trackers. He will catch the first plane. Find out when it reaches Copenhagen and have someone waiting there – someone capable of eliminating any tracker. Today is going to be dangerous – for everyone. Including the esteemed Dr Henri Goldschmidt – The Fixer."

The lookout in the first-floor window saw the 280E coming, wending its way through the traffic towards the heavy wooden doors at the entrance to the sub-base near Brussels Midi station. He phoned down to the guards and the doors swung smoothly inwards for Beaurain to drive into the yard. Beside him Louise Hamilton looked back and saw the doors closing off the view of the traffic beyond.

"I wonder where Litov is now?" she said.

"Let's go upstairs and find out."

The cobbled yard was small. It was entirely enclosed by old six-storey buildings. The rooms overlooking the courtyard were the property of Telescope, held in a dummy name by the Baron de Graer. The only other vehicle in the yard was the butcher's van, already refuelled from the petrol pump in the corner and turned round so it could leave immediately.

Henderson was sitting in a functional first-floor room. In one corner a wireless operator wearing his earphones sat in front of a high-powered transceiver. The Scot, who stood up as they entered, had been sitting at a table facing a large wall map of northern Europe. On the map he had marked all the possible air, road and rail routes from Brussels Midi with a red felt-tipped pen.

"What are the little blue pins?" Louise asked.

"Each one shows a gunner I can contact by radio or phone inside three minutes."

"There are scores of them!"

"Only wish I had more," the Scot replied laconically. He looked at Beaurain. "The moment of truth has arrived. Litov, code-named Leper, is at Brussels Midi. He has made one two-minute phone call. He bought a T.E.E. ticket for Amsterdam. Train leaves 9.43." He looked at a large wall-clock. "That's about now."

Serge Litov played it cagey from the moment he returned to the platform. Carrying his ticket, he went up to the special T.E.E. board which illustrated the sequence of the carriages. Voiture 3 was immediately behind the engine.

From behind his newspaper Max Kellerman – who was leaving Litov to do the moving about while he remained in one place – watched him carefully study the ticket and then the board. It was a pantomime for the benefit of watchers.

In his mind Kellerman went over the stops the express made before arriving at Amsterdam. Brussels Nord, Antwerp East, Roosendaal, Rotterdam and The Hague. At all these stops Henderson would already have arranged to have a gunner stationed in case he got off. Kellerman's job was to stay on board until Amsterdam. The T.E.E. glided in, five de-luxe coaches preceded by its streamlined locomotive. The express stopped.

Litov climbed aboard Voiture 3 the moment the automatic doors had opened, pushing rudely past a woman waiting to alight. It was the old trick: wait until just before the automatic doors closed and then jump back onto the platform – leaving your shadow on board, carried away by the train. But Litov reappeared, descended the steps and stood on the platform. What the hell was he up to? Kellerman had one eye on Litov, the other on the red second-hand on the platform clock.

Behind him Alphonse strolled into view and took up a position on the opposite platform. Kellerman climbed aboard, joining a woman who was a late arrival, so they looked like a couple. Once inside the coach he sat down in a seat near the entrance to the next coach, Voiture 3.

There is no warning when a T.E.E. express is due to depart; no call from the guard, no whistle blowing. The doors close, the train draws out of the station. Litov, watching the second-hand on the clock, timed it perfectly. He ran up the steps into the coach a second before the doors met.

"Triple bluff," said Kellerman to himself as the train pulled out.

The next stop, Brussels Nord, was only a few minutes away. Would Litov get off after only one station, despite booking all the way to Amsterdam? Because from Brussels Nord he could catch a train or a cab to the airport. Kellerman could have relaxed now. His assignment was to stay on board all the way to Amsterdam. Instead he sat tensely, trying to put himself inside Litov's mind, to predict how he would react at Brussels Nord.

Inside the temporary headquarters for Operation Leper the tension was rising. Louise kept pacing up and down in the small room. Beaurain sat down next to Henderson, the picture of relaxation as he lit a cigarette. They had done all they could. It was up to the men in the field.

"Who have you got aboard the train?" he asked.

"Max Kellerman. He can be a bit insubordinate."

"He's among the best we've got. Uses his brain." He stopped as the phone rang. Henderson picked up the receiver and spoke briefly in French.

"That was Louis. The Leper boarded at Midi. So he has started to run. All we can do now is wait – for the next message."

At 9.53 the T.E.E. slid into Brussels Nord station and the doors hissed open. This was a two-minute stop. Max Kellerman had made up his mind. He was standing at the exit of his coach furthest away from Voiture 3.

Kellerman was not recognisable as the man who had boarded at Midi. He had taken off his hat and light raincoat and put them inside his suitcase. He had donned a pair of glasses. His thick thatch of dark hair, previously hidden beneath the hat, was now visible.

Alighting from the express he glanced to his left, saw no sign of Litov and swung round to give the impression of a passenger about to board the train. In his mouth he had a cigarette and he was deliberately making the gas lighter misfire: it gave a reason for pausing at the foot of the steps.

"He's going to get off at Nord and head for the airport," Kellerman had decided during his few minutes on the train. "After his confinement he'll be impatient, anxious to reach home base. I would be."

He was disobeying his orders. On no account was he to leave the train before Amsterdam. Kellerman was relying on his observation of how Litov had handled his problem at Midi. And if he was continuing to Amsterdam he would surely have pretended to be leaving the express here – by getting off and loitering near the exit doors.

The German found himself watching the platform clock. In ten seconds the doors would close. Nine-eight-seven-six . . . Litov had fooled him. He was staying aboard. At the last moment Litov rushed down the train steps, onto the platform and hurried towards the station exit. No-one could have got out in time to follow him. Kellerman smiled grimly and strode towards the exit.

There he saw Joel Wilde, the ex-SAS gunner Henderson had sent to Nord for just this contingency. Kellerman out-ranked him. "He's mine," he said as he walked past.

He was through the doors in time to see Litov leaving the station on the far side of the booking-hall. He came up behind him as the Russian waited for the next cab. "The airport. Move it," Litov informed the driver and climbed into the back.

He was so confident he had overlooked the obvious precaution of waiting until he was inside the cab to give his destination. It was out of character. Or was it? They had been careful to keep Litov without food for the past twenty-four hours, giving him only fruit juice. He could be light-headed and over-confident. Or that phone call from Brussels Midi could have arranged back-up to any shadow who attached himself to Litov when he left the express. If so, Joel would sort that one out.

Kellerman glanced over his shoulder before climbing inside the next cab which drew up. Joel Wilde was close behind him. You never heard the bastard – until it was too late. Kellerman lowered the window and looked up at him.

"Thanks for everything. I'm going to make the airport in good time."

"You're welcome. Our love to Sharon. A smooth flight."

Joel watched the cab pull away and turned round to face the station exits. No-one else was coming for a cab. No-one was heading for a private car. But during the next few hours the Syndicate would send someone to take out any man they detected following Litov.

"I'll chew his balls off."

At the headquarters of Operation Leper, Henderson put down the phone, caught Louise Hamilton's amused eye and clapped a hand over his mouth.

"That was Joel Wilde from Nord station. The Leper left the express – as you thought he might – and has taken a cab to the airport. More to the point, Max Kellerman is running his own railway again. He got off too – and he's followed the Leper in another cab to the airport."

"Max is a good man, one of our best," Beaurain commented.

"Where is the Leper heading for?"

Henderson stood up and went over to study the air routes marked on his wall-map. He moved a blue pin – Max Kellerman – to a position on the road to the airport. Just ahead of this he placed the red pin representing Serge Litov.

Beaurain joined him and checked his watch against the wall-clock. "You'll hear soon enough. Get someone to look up all the airline flights taking off within the next two hours. I don't think the Leper will linger longer than he need. You mind the shop till we get back, Jock. We're going to take a train to Bruges and have a word with my old friend, Dr Goldschmidt. It's just conceivable he can tell us the name of the man who is running the Syndicate."

6

Gunther Baum sat perfectly still in the passenger seat of the
Renault, which had been driven by the lean-faced man
beside him. On his companion's lap lay the brief-case containing the loaded Luger. Baum had not yet requested the
weapon.

As during his visit to Pierre Florin he was proceeding with
caution. Again he wore a straw hat and tinted glasses. In his
left hand he held a photo of Frans Darras and his wife, Rosa.
It was best to proceed in a methodical manner.

"I trust they are both on board," Baum said. "And at least
we have found the barge where it was supposed to be – you
can see the aerial."

He held out his gloved hand. His companion had not
replied, knowing Baum often thought aloud to make sure
there was nothing he had overlooked before he completed a
job. When it involved two people at once it always required
a little more finesse.

Baum took the gun, made sure the silencer was screwed on
tight and opened the door with his other gloved hand. "You
follow with your tool-kit in three minutes counting from
now." His companion checked his own watch quickly. In
Baum's world seconds counted.

Baum climbed deliberately and slowly. Reaching the tow-
path he held the Luger behind his back and looked around.
The barge was moored and its deck was deserted but he
heard voices from the cabin below. There was no-one on the
tow-path. The one feature Baum missed was a small boy
perched in the branches of an apple tree. Baum stepped
aboard and pocketed the photo.

Frans and Rosa Darras were arguing so loudly they did
not hear Baum descend the steps into the cabin. They would
not have heard him anyway. Coming out of the daylight it
was difficult to see clearly in the cabin and behind his tinted

glasses Baum blinked.

"I have a message and some money for Frans and Rosa Darras," he said.

Startled, the bargee turned quickly. "That's us. Who are you?"

"Both of you will turn and face the wall."

Baum had produced the Luger from behind his back and aimed it at a position between them. "I have come to remove your transceiver," he continued in his sing-song French. "Face the wall until we have completed the work. Behave yourselves in an orderly manner and you can rest assured no harm ..."

They had both turned together to face the wall. Instinctively Frans grasped Rosa's hand to reassure her. Baum was still talking when he pressed the muzzle against the base of Frans Darras' neck and fired once. Darras was falling when the muzzle pressed into the neck of Rosa who, frozen with terror, was unable to move. Baum pressed the trigger a second time.

His companion appeared with his brief-case and tool-kit. Baum handed the Luger to him at once and the weapon was returned to the brief-case. He stood quite still while his companion swiftly removed the transceiver and its power-operated aerial. On the canal bank above them the little boy in the apple tree had remained in its branches. He was sucking an orange as Baum reappeared at the top of the steps, and it slipped from his fingers, hitting the tow-path with a clunk. Baum turned and scanned the area.

Hidden amid the branches no more than twenty feet away, the boy watched the sunlight flashing off the tinted lenses as Baum continued searching while his companion also reappeared on deck, the brief-case in one hand, the transceiver and aerial awkwardly held under his arm. He was sweating with the effort.

"You heard something?" he asked.

"Time to get back to the car," said Baum.

They were driving along the main highway, heading for Brussels, when a train passed in the opposite direction. Inside a first-class compartment Beaurain and Louise sat facing each other, gazing out of the window. They had a glimpse of a canal, of several barges moored close to a lock, barges with clothes-lines hung along the decks, TV masts and radio aerials projecting into the sunlight.

"Those people must lead a life of their own – they even have TV," Louise remarked.

Beaurain was staring out without seeing anything, his mind on Goldschmidt. He nodded automatically, but registered what she had said to him.

"Shot in the back of the neck? Pierre Florin?"

Chief Inspector Flamen of Homicide sighed inwardly. Voisin had a habit of repeating statements you made.

"Chief Superintendent Beaurain had requested to see him as soon as he returned from sick leave," Flamen continued and then waited for the expected reaction.

"*Ex*-Chief Superintendent Beaurain, you mean. Is it not peculiar that the policeman Beaurain wished to see should be murdered before he saw him?" demanded Voisin.

"It could have significance," Flamen agreed.

"Had I better see Beaurain?"

"As you wish, sir – but it might be better if I saw him first. That way you won't find yourself in any embarrassing situation, if I may so phrase it."

"You may indeed, Flamen." Voisin smirked. Clearly Willy Flamen understood the delicacy of his position, the political importance of never having to take a decision that might backfire.

"Found in his apartment," Flamen continued. "No sign of a break-in."

"So he knew his murderer," Voisin jumped in.

"It would seem so," Flamen agreed tactfully, although he knew it didn't necessarily follow. "Shot in the back of the neck," he repeated. "Reminds me of something nasty – but I just can't recall what it is."

"You had better leave for Brussels now, before Bruges is flooded with police," Dr Berlin told Sonia Karnell inside the tiny house in the Hoogste van Brugge.

"Something is going to happen?"

"A couple of loose ends are being tidied up by Gunther Baum – Frans and Rosa Darras aboard the barge. They were getting slack – it was you who warned me when you delivered the *Zenith* signal about Beaurain."

Karnell had stood up to leave. Her brow was crinkled with

apprehension. "What have I been responsible for? I thought you were only going to warn them."

"It is a warning!" Berlin raised his voice and used the fingers of one hand to stroke the curved ends of his moustache. "A warning to the other people running our communications. But that's why there may be police activity round this area soon. Also because I have decided to teach Dr Goldschmidt a lesson for spying on me with that photographer in the house opposite."

"Not Baum again?" she asked quietly.

"You are too soft-hearted."

"You are getting more brutal and I don't really like it."

He relented and decided to tell her. "Dirk is going to deliver one of his toys. He is a gentle soul. Now run along and I'll meet you later at the Brussels apartment before we go to the airport together."

She nodded and left to find a cab for the station. Dirk Mondy ran the Bruges office when Berlin was not there. What toy could he be presenting to Goldschmidt?

As she left the house and headed down the narrow cobbled street she was relieved that it was not Baum who was calling. Even the mention of Baum, whom she had never met, terrified her. *I wouldn't know him if he came up my own stairs in Stockholm*, she thought.

At Bruges station Louise and Beaurain had to wait several minutes until a cab arrived, bringing a passenger to the station. The door opened, a girl wearing a windcheater stepped out, reached into her handbag for her purse and caught sight of Beaurain. For a fraction of a second she froze, then recovered, paid the fare and hurried into the station.

"Holiday Inn," Beaurain told the driver. It was easier than explaining how to get to Dr Goldschmidt's address in a nearby side street. "This is one of the most beautiful towns in Europe," Beaurain remarked as the cab moved off. "There's an area with canals and ancient bridges with willows dripping branches in the water. It is just the sort of place I'd hide up in if I were running some shady outfit."

"You noticed that girl who got out of this cab at the station?" Louise asked in a low voice.

"Vaguely. Quite a looker." Beaurain lit a cigarette.

"She was staring at you as though you scared her stiff.

Have you ever seen her before?"

"Never in my life. Ah, here we are. I'm looking forward to seeing my old friend."

The Holiday Inn was on the corner of an ancient square – the T'Zand. Down the side street where Dr Goldschmidt lived were old houses, steep-roofed and white. The atmosphere was so peaceful Louise felt ridiculous carrying a pistol.

"Here we are."

Beaurain stopped outside one of the houses which carried an engraved plate on the wall by the door. *Avocat*. Lawyer. No name. He pressed the bell and glanced down the street. Forty yards away a Volkswagen was parked. A man sat behind the wheel. Impossible to see his face at that distance. The door opened on a chain.

"Your card, please."

"Here, Henri. It is Jules."

"Cautious, isn't he?" Louise whispered.

A slim-fingered hand took the card, the chain was removed and they stepped into a hallway. The door closed and Dr Goldschmidt regarded them both, a tall, stooped man with a silver mane of hair and a hawk-like nose. He wore a business suit which could only have been cut in Savile Row and peered at them through a pair of gold-rimmed glasses.

He said mildly: "You are both carrying guns. Correct, Miss Hamilton? No, don't look at Jules for your cue. Am I right?"

"Yes – but how . . . ?"

"Because he's a good bluffer," Beaurain put in. "When we entered the doorway we passed through a metal detector let into the door-frame and the bulb down here in the wall lights up faintly when metal is detected on a visitor. The bluff is he had no way of knowing the metal was a gun so he challenged you with an accusation which threw you off balance. He used to be one of Belgium's most eminent lawyers before he took up . . . the collection of rare coins."

"Any more of my secrets you wish to reveal?" Goldschmidt asked with mock waspishness.

"Not at the moment – but please don't play games with my best girl."

"Mamselle, a thousand apologies. And such a beautiful

70

assistant."

He ushered them through a doorway into a small but comfortably furnished room overlooking the street. The walls were lined with bookcases, a blue deep-pile carpet covered the floor. Goldschmidt pulled forward a leather armchair for Louise and fussed about her courteously. She looked straight at his penetrating grey eyes and decided she must establish herself or be dismissed as second-rate.

"You are afraid someone is coming to kill you, Dr Goldschmidt?"

"All the time – in my business." He turned to Beaurain who was staring through the window at the parked Volkswagen. "You said on the phone I could speak to Miss Hamilton as though I were talking to you."

"That's true." Beaurain sat down in a second armchair and Goldschmidt took a high-backed chair behind a large antique desk – which meant he was looking down at them. He used the technique of intimidation with so many people he even continued it with his friends.

"First things first," said Beaurain in a business-like manner, and took out a long, fat envelope containing £20,000 in deutschmarks of high-denomination notes. He dropped it on the desk. "My contribution towards your favourite charity."

Goldschmidt picked up the envelope, locked it in a desk drawer without opening it and inclined his head. "Thank you. How can I help you?"

"I want to know who is running the Syndicate, some idea of the size of its operations, and where its headquarters are."

"Terror." Goldschmidt plunged straight into his subject. "Terror is the weapon this Syndicate is using on a scale never before seen in Europe – or in the States, not that Washington will admit its existence. I have never in all my experience," he continued, "known such a situation." He stared hard at Beaurain. "The Syndicate controls men and women at the summit of power in this country. If you become its target you cannot save yourself."

"I've never heard you talk like this before," Beaurain said grimly. "How have they managed this in such a short time?" He was thinking of the fear on the face of the Baron de Graer.

"They vary their method to suit the victim. Sometimes money is employed – very large sums, some of which originate in the United States. In other cases they employ terroristic blackmail. You remember the killing of the Baron de Graer's wife and daughter during the so-called kidnap attempt at the Château Wardin?"

"*So-called?*"

"Yes. It was planned from the outset that the wife and daughter would be killed. You look very grim, Jules."

"I happen to know the Baron de Graer. Also I was in charge of the anti-terrorist squad at the time. Brussels stopped me using my normal method of going in with heavy fire-power. Brussels insisted on negotiations." There was an undertone of bitterness in the Belgian's voice.

"It would have been too late anyway, Jules, had you done so," Goldschmidt said gently.

"What the hell does that mean?"

"De Graer's wife and daughter were brutally murdered as soon as the kidnap took place. The rest was window-dressing."

"*Window-dressing?*" There was an ominous note in Beaurain's quiet voice.

"I only learned several months later." Their host turned in his chair to look out of the open windows. "The killings at the Château Wardin were a demonstration of the Syndicate's power. A number of prominent citizens – up to Cabinet level – were phoned and told what was going to happen, that the same thing could happen to their own loved ones if they refused to co-operate. You see, the conspiracy started early." He turned and looked at Beaurain's frozen expression. "As I said, it is the uninhibited use of terror, intimidation and bribery. I suspect that soon whole countries will be practically run by this evil organisation. You are powerless to do anything about it, Jules. Or are you? By the way, I wondered whether your visit was to ask me about Telescope?"

"What do you know about it?" Beaurain asked.

"Very little. It is organised like the wartime escape routes for Allied fliers from Brussels to the Spanish border."

"And its leadership?"

Goldschmidt did not reply at once. He took off his gold-rimmed spectacles and studied Beaurain as he polished them with a blue silk handkerchief. He glanced at Louise whose expression was deliberately blank; she hoped not too blank. He replaced his glasses.

"I know nothing of its leadership."

"Getting back to the Syndicate ..."

"It is controlled by three rarely-seen men. One of them is a dealer in rare books who, when he comes to Bruges, has a house in the Hoogste van Brugge – only five minutes' walk from where we are now. I find that a trifle insulting. Let me show you on the street map."

Beaurain and Louise studied the map briefly. The address was, as Goldschmidt had said, surprisingly close. "These three men have names?" Beaurain asked.

"The one in Bruges is a Dr Otto Berlin." Goldschmidt extracted a card from a drawer and wrote on it. "The second is a Dr Benny Horn, a Dane who operates a rare bookshop in the Nyhavn waterfront area in Copenhagen."

"I know the area," Louise said.

"Good, good. Do not go there alone, my dear, I beg of you. The third is a Swede, a Dr Theodor Norling, and he too is in the rare book trade. He has an address in Gamla Stan, the Old City district of Stockholm. You know that, I believe, Jules?"

"Yes." Beaurain took the card and glanced at the address. "I don't follow why they are all in the rare book trade. It's some kind of cover?"

"They can travel about – officially purchasing some rare volume for a valued customer. Rare books! They are cold-blooded killers."

Goldschmidt spoke with abnormal vehemence. "Trust no-one, Jules. There is treachery everywhere. Unless the Stockholm Syndicate is destroyed quickly it will have the whole western world in its grip."

"Surely that's rather an overstatement," Louise suggested gently.

"You think so?" The rare coin dealer gazed hard at the English girl. "It operates like some international protection racket. Clearly you have no idea who they already have."

"Where does the money come from?" asked Beaurain.

"That's the trouble," Goldschmidt said. "We know that billions of dollars have been transferred to Europe by certain American multi-nationals to support the Syndicate. In secrecy, of course, but the funds have been so huge they have moved the value of currencies and that you cannot hide. So, again, it *seems* like the Americans ..."

"But you think not?" Beaurain asked. "Who then?"

"If only I knew which of Berlin, Horn or Norling was the chief executive. The top controller goes under the code-name Hugo. That is a name you whisper. Find Hugo and you have the Syndicate by the throat."

"Why do you call it the Stockholm Syndicate? Why Stockholm?"

Beaurain had deliberately returned to his old role of Chief Superintendent grilling a suspect, hurling question after question with such speed that the recipient answered without thinking.

"Because that is how it is known. My enquiries have traced funds through many channels – and always the end of the line is Stockholm."

"How do the men who run this Syndicate extract billions of dollars from the States? By the same methods – intimidation?"

"Sometimes – many successful men leave skeletons behind as they climb. There is an American who has built up what he calls 'a blackmail bank'. That could be used by the Syndicate. That, plus the lure of huge, invisible – and so non-taxable – profits when the money is invested in European crime – the drug traffic and so on."

"Are the Soviets involved?" Beaurain demanded.

"Viktor Rashkin, the protégé of Brezhnev, is at the Russian Embassy in Stockholm," Goldschmidt observed. Unlocking the drawer which contained the envelope of money Beaurain had handed him, the dealer handed it back. "Keep this. Use the funds for your investigation. As you know, my dear Jules, I am a supplier of information. May I just for once enter the prediction business?"

"Go ahead." Beaurain pocketed the envelope. "And thank you."

"I have heard there is to be a meeting of all key members and 'shareholders' in the Stockholm Syndicate within the next two weeks. The Americans are flying to Europe – the conference will take place somewhere in Scandinavia. I predict that within the next fourteen days there will be a frightful collision between Telescope and the Stockholm Syndicate. Only one organisation will survive."

At that moment the grenade came through the window

74

and landed on Goldschmidt's desk.

Beaurain reacted with great speed. If he lobbed it back into the street he might cause hideous casualties to passers-by. His hand grasped the obscene object, he rushed to the door, hauled it open and hurled the grenade as far as he could down the narrow hallway. Slamming the heavy door shut he waited for the explosion.

"Superb reflexes, my friend – as always," Goldschmidt commented drily. The emergency had drained the tension out of his system.

"I think it's a dud."

Beaurain was looking at the second-hand of his watch. He waited a little longer. Louise, white-faced but controlled, nodded towards the window. "Just before it happened I heard a car start up and approach. There was a Volkswagen parked further up the road when we arrived. It had one man behind the wheel."

"I noticed it. I'm going to check."

"Be careful."

Beaurain returned tossing the grenade in the air like a tennis ball. "It's a fake," he assured them. "No primer. Who wants to scare the living daylights out of Dr Goldschmidt? There's a note on this spill of paper. It says, 'Get out of Belgium by nightfall.'"

"Undoubtedly a message from Dr Otto Berlin. He objects to my compiling a dossier on his activities."

"That address," Beaurain said quickly. "In Hoogste van Brugge. I think we'll go there immediately. What does Berlin look like?"

Goldschmidt was unlocking a drawer in his desk. "My photographer who took these pictures – I was going to get them when the grenade interrupted us – says Berlin is about five feet ten tall, very fat, hair black and greasy, with a moustache curling down the sides of his mouth. Walks with a waddle like a duck. Short-sighted – wears horn-rimmed pebble glasses, sounds repulsive."

"That's a very precise description."

"Sounds most conspicuous for someone who wants to avoid the limelight," added Louise.

"Here are the photos – you can keep them. They're very good, considering they were taken under poor conditions.

Berlin has a girl assistant. Very distinctive hair-style as you'll see – very dark, cut close to the head like a helmet."

Beaurain and Louise looked quickly at the prints but neither of them said anything. Berlin's assistant was the girl whose taxi they had taken. Beaurain shoved the prints in his pocket with the envelope containing the deutschmarks.

"Thank you, Henri. You have been more helpful than you may ever realise. From now on, be very careful."

At the far side of the T'Zand Square they entered the Zuid-zandstraat, a narrow street which was almost deserted. "Prepare for trouble," Beaurain said as they arrived at the entrance to the gloomy Hoogste van Brugge. It was empty, little more than a cobbled alley hemmed in between two walls of old terrace houses. Beaurain paused, checking house numbers on both sides of the corridor of stone. At the far end was parked a Volkswagen taking up most of the width of the alley.

"I reckon No. 285 is by that car," Beaurain said.

"Which could be the car from which the dummy grenade came?"

"Just might be. Again, be ready for trouble."

They started walking down the alley side by side, their rubber-soled shoes making no sound on the ancient cobbles. The walls of the lifeless houses seemed to be closing in on them. Although only a minute's walk from the bustling T'Zand Square they were in a different world.

They were half-way to the Volkswagen when Beaurain made a swift gesture. He pressed himself in the recess of a doorway on the left and Louise chose a doorway in the right-hand wall. Beaurain's acute hearing had caught the sound of a door being unbolted. They waited.

A man came out of a house on the right-hand side, glanced down the alley, then turned away and hurried to the Volkswagen. A tall, thin man with a springy step, he bore no resemblance to the description of Otto Berlin. They waited until he got inside the car and drove round the corner. Beaurain nodded and they started up the street again.

Another man, carrying a suitcase, emerged from the same house. A fat man with greasy black hair and a moustache whose ends curved down round the corners of his mouth. A man who waddled like a duck. He saw them, stopped, took something from his pocket, made a quick pulling movement and hoisted his right hand like a bowler throwing a cricket ball.

"My God! That's Otto Berlin!" Louise called out.

"*Drop flat!*"

Louise reacted instantly, sprawling on the cobbles. Beaurain fell on top of her, protecting her body. The missile Berlin had hurled fell on the cobbles about forty feet from where they lay. The silence lasted four seconds. It was followed by an ear-splitting blast as the grenade exploded. Chips of stone flew all over the place. As Beaurain and Louise remained prone the shock wave passed over their heads. Beaurain felt a stone sliver whipping through his hair, but Berlin had miscalculated the distance and dropped the grenade too far away to hurt them. Provided they had luck on their side. They had.

"Are you all right?"

Beaurain was on his feet, tugging the Smith & Wesson from its holster. He was too late. Otto Berlin had sprinted round the corner. Beaurain turned to Louise who was brushing dirt off her clothes. Her voice was shaky.

"I'm OK."

"The station ..."

Beaurain shoved the revolver out of sight. Not a soul had appeared so far. The Hoogste van Brugge seemed accustomed to grenades. Or perhaps the unseen inhabitants had found it paid to mind their own business.

"Why the station?" Louise asked as Beaurain grabbed her arm and hustled her back the way they had come.

"Because I think he could be heading there – to get the hell out of Bruges. And I saw a cab rank in the T'Zand Square."

"Why didn't the Volkswagen driver take him?"

"How the devil do I know? Maybe Berlin wanted him out of town fast in case the car had been recognised." They entered the T'Zand Square. "We'll take this cab," Beaurain said.

He only relaxed when the cab was moving. "If only we could get hold of one of the three men Goldschmidt gave us we could crack this thing. Otto Berlin would be perfect. You're sure you're all right?"

"I seem to be in one piece." She said nothing more until they arrived at the station. Beaurain was taking money out of his wallet when she grabbed his sleeve. "Look! There's Berlin – just going into the station. He's still carrying his case."

Running from the cab, they were able to pass straight through the barrier with their return tickets. An express to Brussels was just about to depart. Among the last-minute passengers scrambling aboard they saw the fat figure of Otto Berlin entering a compartment near the front of the train. They just managed to get aboard as the express started moving. Beaurain peered out of the window to make sure Berlin had not jumped off again. The platform was empty. He looked at Louise as they stood in the deserted corridor.

"This is an express. One stop before Brussels – Ghent, which is half an hour away. We've got him – he can't leave a train moving at seventy miles an hour."

7

"We search the whole express – but I want to find Berlin
without him seeing us. So we can track him. We start at the
front of the train and work our way back. You go first, I'll
trail behind you. That way he's less likely to spot us."

The express was about half full. They walked rapidly to
the front of the train but neither of them saw Berlin. They
began working their way back towards the rear of the express
checking every passenger.

"I'll check each lavatory as we go through," Beaurain told
her. "If one is occupied we wait at a discreet distance and see
who comes out."

They had over fifteen minutes to go when they reached the
end of the train. No Berlin. Standing in the corridor
Beaurain lit them both cigarettes and they looked at each
other. Outside the windows the sunlit countryside flashed
past – and again they saw a canal and barges with T.V.
masts and washing-lines.

"I can't understand it," Louise said. "You checked every
lavatory. We've both seen every passenger aboard – so what
the devil has happened to him? He can't have just vanished
into thin air."

"Except that he appears to have done just that."

The stop at Ghent gave no help in solving the mystery.
People got off. More passengers boarded the express. No-one
even remotely resembling Dr Otto Berlin appeared. As the
train left Ghent they made their way to the front, found an
empty compartment in the coach behind the engine, sat
down and stared at each other.

"Do we search all over again?" Louise suggested. "We
must have missed something."

"We stay here until the train reaches Brussels," Beaurain
said firmly. "At Nord we get out pretty sharp, wait by the
barrier and check everyone off. No-one can board a train and

disappear in a puff of smoke."

At Nord the express emptied itself. Standing a short distance away from Beaurain, Louise watched the passengers trailing past, many of them with luggage and obviously travellers from Ostend and the ferry from England. A squabbling family already tired from their journey and the heat; a crowd of locals wearing berets and chattering away in French; the inevitable priest with his suitcase.

They watched the last person off the express and then joined each other and walked towards the exit. Beaurain spoke as they came outside the station into brilliant sunshine. "We'll take a cab to Henderson's sub-base and see how the tracking of Litov is proceeding. Better than our efforts I hope."

He arranged for the cab to drop them a few minutes from the sub-base and they continued on foot. When they arrived in the first-floor room with the wall-map Beaurain only had to take one look at Henderson's face to know a disaster had occurred.

"Pierre Florin, the sergeant you wanted to interview, has been found murdered at his apartment," Henderson informed them. "Commissioner Voisin is anxious to see you as soon as possible." '

"How do you know about Florin?" Beaurain enquired.

"I phoned your apartment to see if you had arrived back – and Chief Inspector Willy Flamen of Homicide answered the phone."

"And what the hell was he doing inside my apartment?"

"I wondered that too," said Henderson, "until he told me the place had been broken into. He called there to give you Voisin's message. And Flamen wants to see you – but he'll be waiting at his own apartment. I told him I was a friend and got off the line."

Beaurain had hoped for so much from his interview with Florin: above all, who had paid him to be absent from the reception desk at the vital moment. Or should the question be who had frightened him so much that he had risked his whole career? *Terror*, Goldschmidt had said vehemently, terror was one of the Syndicate's main weapons.

"How are you getting on with Litov?" he asked the Scot.

"He's boarded a flight for Scandinavia – he bought a

ticket to Helsinki. Max was right behind him and is now aboard the same flight – a Scandinavian Airlines plane flying to Stockholm via Copenhagen." Henderson nodded towards the wall-map. "It's marked there with the red line."

"So his final destination could be Copenhagen, Stockholm or Helsinki," Beaurain suggested.

"That's the way I see it," the Scot agreed. "Unless he's being clever and gets off at Kastrup or Arlanda and switches to another destination. If he does that, I have gunners at both airports to track him. And we always have Max Kellerman travelling in the same first-class cabin as him."

"Where are they now?"

Henderson checked the clock. "En route to Kastrup Airport, Copenhagen. Within half an hour of landing."

"We'd better get over and see Willy Flamen." Beaurain stood up, uneasy about something. How the devil had they let Otto Berlin slip off the Ostend Express? Henderson swung round in his chair.

"Maybe I didn't make myself clear, sir. It is Commissioner Voisin who is anxious to see you. Asked particularly would you give him some idea of your arrival time."

"You made yourself quite clear. We're still going to call on Willy Flamen first. I'll contact you later to find out what's happening to Litov. Come on, Louise." Beaurain had reached the door when he turned and gave a final order. "One more thing, put all our people inside Brussels on a red alert immediately."

Louise waited until they were sitting in the Mercedes before she asked the question. The Belgian had a brooding look and had not yet signalled to the guard to open the gate.

"Jules, what was that about a red alert? That means everyone has to expect an emergency at any moment, doesn't it?"

"The request from Commissioner Voisin to go and see him immediately . . ." Beaurain signalled the guard, gunned the motor and drove out of the archway into heavy traffic. Louise noticed his eyes were everywhere: checking the mirror; glancing at both sidewalks; checking the mirror again. "Plus the fact that Voisin wants me to warn him in advance when I'm going to arrive. It fits in with that *Zenith* signal."

"But he's a Commissioner of Police! Jules, you aren't serious. You don't think Voisin is one of the Syndicate's men?" Her tone of voice expressed her incredulity. "You may not like the fat creep but you're letting your prejudices cloud your judgement. Hey, where are we going? You've missed the turning to Flamen's place."

"We're going to take a look at police headquarters. Flamen we visit later." He eased into the kerb and parked. "And I'd like us to switch places – you drive and I'll be the passenger. Be prepared to drive like hell."

Louise walked round the car and got in behind the wheel. Beaurain had no qualms about giving her the order to drive this way: Louise Hamilton had been a crack racing driver at Brands Hatch in England. Without a word he extracted his .38 Smith & Wesson from his shoulder holster and rested the weapon in his lap.

There wouldn't be much traffic at this hour around the police headquarters, which meant the 280E would be conspicuous to watchers. And Beaurain had no doubt that the Stockholm Syndicate would know the model and the number of his car. It was a crazy idea about Voisin: he hardly believed it possible himself. But he kept hearing Goldschmidt's voice. *Trust no-one, Jules. There is treachery everywhere.*

"If you're so suspicious," Louise said with a hint of sarcasm, "you should have sent a team of gunners to check out police headquarters."

"You're probably right. But to tell you the truth, that didn't occur to me until we'd left Jock."

"Well, here we are. We'll soon know now."

Oh my God! Louise's exceptional self-control prevented her swerving. For a moment she couldn't speak to warn Jules – then she saw he had grasped his revolver with one hand and with the other had lowered his window.

"Jules – on both sides – two cars . . ."

"The one with a single man inside too?"

"Yes – they called him Pietr. He was the policeman in the blue Renault. He tried to block me in when I was getting away."

"Proceed as slowly as you're going now, as though we haven't seen anything. Be ready to accelerate like a rocket when I say 'go'."

"They'll have us in a crossfire if they see us."

"They've already seen us. Hold down the speed. They're

waiting for the moment when they have us sandwiched."

"That couple in the car on the right – the short bulky man's called André and he's a killer."

She continued cruising forward, her eyes whipping from side to side. Both cars were parked facing the oncoming Mercedes. Both could drive out and create a barrier she'd never pass. Was Jules really more tired than she had realised? The Fiat stationed on the right began to move from where it was parked outside the entrance to police headquarters.

As Louise had warned, they were going to be trapped in a crossfire. The cars had been waiting for them, had known that sooner or later Beaurain would arrive to keep his appointment with Commissioner Voisin!

"*Go!*"

Beaurain shouted the command and her reaction was a reflex, her foot ramming down hard on the accelerator which responded with instant action and power. The Fiat containing the two men was heading on a course which would take it across her bows, forcing her to stop, while they poured a hail of gunfire into it.

On his side Beaurain had already seen the thin man beside the driver lifting a sub-machine gun. Out of the corner of his eye he saw what he had foreseen – that the Renault was still parked at the kerb. No man can drive and aim a weapon accurately at the same time, and Pietr was aiming his silenced weapon through the open window.

Beaurain fired four times at the oncoming Fiat. The 280E was surging forward like a torpedo under Louise's expert control. Three of Beaurain's bullets hit the man with the sub-machine gun. Blood splashed the shattered glass of the Fiat's windscreen. The car began to swerve wildly as Beaurain fired again and hit the driver.

"Don't move your head!"

Beaurain turned to his left, laid his arm along the back of Louise's seat and fired two more shots. One hit the target. Blood spurted from Pietr's head and he slumped over his wheel. Beaurain saw it all in a blur as the 280E screamed past police headquarters where no-one had appeared despite the cannonade and the screech of tyres.

Louise's skilful manoeuvring took them past the moving Fiat and then they had left behind the carnage and Beaurain, looking back, saw no sign of pursuit. It was as though police headquarters had been stripped of patrol cars and personnel while the Syndicate killers tried to complete their job.

"You certainly handled that," Louise commented as she changed direction again in case of pursuit. "I wouldn't have known which car to tackle first."

"The Fiat – because it carried a sub-machine gun and it was moving. Now, head for Willy Flamen's apartment."

"Get out of Brussels, Jules: better still, out of Belgium. Both of you. Preferably tonight. The cold-blooded killing of Pierre Florin should be enough warning."

Willy Flamen stared over the rim of his cup at Beaurain and Louise as they drank the coffee and ate the sandwiches provided by his wife. The policeman was a man who spoke his mind and possessed great courage. Which made his advice all the more disturbing.

"You're telling us to run? That's not like you, Willy. Anyway it was agreed at Voisin's meeting that I should investigate the Syndicate." He smiled wrily. "The brief was to confirm its existence, for God's sake."

"Well recent events should have convinced you of that," Flamen commented, pausing to light his pipe. Beaurain recalled that he used it at moments of crisis. "And there is worse to come – if you can believe that's possible."

"Do cheer us up," Louise joked.

He pointed his pipe-stem at her. "Enjoy this, then. Jules let it be known he wanted to interview Florin, the sergeant who was on desk duty just before he took sick leave. As you know, Florin was found murdered at his apartment. When I made a search there, I found a notebook belonging to you, Jules – it had your name in the front. A small black notebook – easily dropped when someone is in a hurry." He sat back in his chair and went on puffing his pipe. Louise stared at him, the muscles of her jaw tight.

"And I believe my own apartment has been broken into and ransacked," Beaurain said quietly.

"That is so," Flamen agreed. "Ransacked to cover the stealing of the notebook later left in Florin's apartment. Voisin wants me to hold you for questioning," he added casually.

"In what connection?" Beaurain asked tightly.

"In connection with the investigation of the murder of Pierre Florin – because you were going to question Florin and also on the evidence of your notebook being found there." Flamen produced a small black notebook from his pocket and pushed it across the table. "That is yours, I take it, Jules?"

"You know it is."

"By the way, Florin was shot in the back of the neck. One shot."

"The old Nazi method of execution."

"Of course!" He snapped his fingers. "That's what it reminded me of. It could be the signature of the executioner – a German trained by the Nazis. By the way, have either of you visited Bruges recently?" Flamen enquired placidly. His pipe was smoking furiously and he was staring out of the window.

"Yes," Beaurain answered shortly. "Today."

He kept his answers as brief as possible and avoided mentioning that Louise had accompanied him. Willy Flamen could be clever and devious. "Why?"

"Because this morning a bargee called Frans Darras and his wife, Rosa, were brutally murdered aboard their barge. The same technique was used – both were shot in the back of the neck. One bullet apiece. Voisin has dived in head first, linked the three killings together because of the *modus operandi* – and linked them all with you because of Florin. The fact that you were in Bruges today won't help when he hears."

Flamen broke off to answer the telephone. He listened and then asked a number of questions rapidly. The topic of the phone call was obvious. Flamen broke the connection, excused himself, and used the phone to despatch a team of investigators and forensic experts. Replacing the receiver, he gave a grunt and then looked at both of them with a grim smile.

"Where have you parked your Mercedes, Jules?"

"In a side street out of sight."

"Good." He stared at the ceiling. "There was a bloodbath outside police headquarters not fifteen minutes ago. Voisin is going mad – as if that were news. Three men attacked a vehicle passing headquarters. All three are dead, and one was armed with a sub-machine gun. Some fool of a woman peering out after it was nearly over says that four men who were attacked were travelling in a Mercedes. She didn't specify a 280E." He waited for comment.

"So?" asked Beaurain.

"I'm glad to see you both looking so well." His manner became very serious as he leaned forward over the table. "More than ever I think you should leave Belgium tonight. Surely you can continue your investigation from a safer country."

"Name one," said Beaurain. "But thanks, Willy." He left it at that. "One thing which puzzles me is how the Syndicate operates its communications – because you can bet your pension it will have a system and a good one. Is anyone working on that?"

Flamen stood up and brought a map of Belgium from a side-cabinet which he spread out over his desk. "There has been an unusual amount of illegal radio traffic during the past six months."

"In these ringed areas?" Beaurain asked, studying the map.

"Yes. A colleague of mine compiled this and I borrowed it – I thought it might interest you. I can't make head or tail of the thing."

"But you think it has some significance?" Louise enquired.

"That's what I'm not sure about," Flamen admitted. "We have a fleet of radio-detector vans scattered throughout Belgium. Some are under the control of counter-espionage."

"And these ringed areas show the areas of the most intense activity during the past six months?" Louise asked. While she and Flamen were talking Beaurain was staring at the map with a scowl of concentration.

"That's right," Flamen agreed. "The trouble is the Syndicate's transmitters keep moving while transmitting. That increases the difficulty of location enormously. They must have the transmitters inside tradesmen's vans – something innocent-looking which wouldn't look out of place travelling along a highway."

"How do you know these are Syndicate transmissions? Has someone broken the code?" Beaurain asked.

Flamen hesitated. "That's top secret information from another department. Frankly, until today I wasn't sure myself, and no-one else is, so this is between the three of us.

86

One of our men did crack one code. Two days later he was killed. Shot in the back of the neck. One bullet."

"Order Captain Buckminster to take *Firestorm* into the Kattegat and then proceed full steam ahead until he's anchored off Elsinore."

Immediately after their meeting with Chief Inspector Willy Flamen, Beaurain and Louise had driven back to Henderson's control headquarters. On arriving Beaurain had begun to issue a stream of instructions to Henderson. Within minutes the atmosphere inside the room – which had been tense before they returned – became electric. At one stage Henderson swung briefly in his swivel chair to ask a question.

"All this means, sir, that Telescope is temporarily evacuating Belgium – including the Château Wardin? Is it really essential to go that far?"

"If we are to fool the Stockholm Syndicate we have to put into action what you have rehearsed time and again, Jock. We withdraw so swiftly we're gone before they suspect what's happening."

"May I know the reason?"

"I'm just coming to it. I'm gambling everything on two people being right – Goldschmidt in Bruges and Ed Cottel of the CIA. They both state that a full meeting of the Stockholm Syndicate is taking place somewhere in Scandinavia in less than two weeks' time. Telescope must be there in force to confront them."

"Why should Goldschmidt and Cottel be right?" Louise objected.

"They don't have to be," Beaurain said, "but we have to take a decision and it's bound to be a gamble. The point is they have entirely different sources – literally in different continents. But they both say the same thing. About two weeks away – a meeting. Locale – Scandinavia."

"Hence you're moving *Firestorm* towards the Baltic?"

"It's so packed with men and equipment it has become a mobile version of Telescope. We now have a force at sea we can land almost anywhere in the Scandinavian zone. My huge gamble," Beaurain admitted, "is that this will be the scene of Goldschmidt's predicted collision between Telescope and the Stockholm Syndicate. Our next move," he told Louise, "is to pay a brief visit to Ed Cottel who is now back at the Hilton."

"If you can reach it alive," commented Henderson.

"It's the Baltic – just as I suspected," said Captain 'Bucky' Buckminster, Captain of the steam yacht *Firestorm*, to his First Mate as he read the decoded signal. "At the moment we sail through the Kattegat and wait at the entrance to the Øresund . . ." His wiry hand traced the course on the chart spread out on the chart-table. "On arrival we anchor off Elsinore – unless we're ordered to proceed at full speed into the Baltic, which wouldn't surprise me."

Buckminster was a tall, restless man of fifty who had commanded a destroyer in the Royal Navy before retiring at his own request.

"We do realise the murder of your daughter in Beirut must have come as a great shock, Bucky," one of his superiors had told him. "But why don't you give your decision more time? You'll lose your pension, you love the sea, and who's going to give you another command like the one you're resigning?"

"No-one, sir," Buckminster had lied, meeting the Admiral's eyes without flinching. It would not have done to reveal that he would be taking over command of a vessel which carried at least as heavy a punch as the destroyer whose command he was relinquishing, even if it was concealed under the guise of a powerful steam-ship built and operated for the Baron de Graer.

Seen from the air, the impression of idle luxury was confirmed by the blue swimming pool. It would have taken a very keen pilot's eye to notice the size of the helipad aft, capable of landing the largest type of Sikorsky in the world, the chopper which the Americans in Vietnam had called a gunship.

The same keen pilot's eye might also have wondered about why so formidable a winch was needed aboard a Belgian millionaire's floating plaything. And had he happened to be flying over when the giant hatch had been open, something else might well have caused him to lift his eyebrows – the size of the hold and the fact that it contained a small floatplane, a very large launch complete with wheelhouse and several power-boats.

Before agreeing to join Telescope, Buckminster had gone secretly to Brussels to discuss what had been presented to him as 'an interesting proposition in view of the brutal and tragic murder of your daughter'. On his arrival in Brussels he had learned to his dismay that he was meeting a Belgian. Impossible for him to imagine himself taking orders from someone who wasn't British. He received a further shock when he was introduced to Jules Beaurain, who, dressed casually in a polo-necked sweater and slacks, became the image of an Englishman when he opened his mouth. Buckminster agreed to take command of *Firestorm* even before he had seen the vessel.

Now he stuffed the signal from Henderson in his pocket. The powerful rotors of the giant helicopter could be heard in the sky.

"Dead on time, sir, as always," First Mate Adams observed, checking his watch.

"Has she brought everything we need?" demanded Buckminster.

"The earlier signal – didn't feel it was necessary to report that to you – confirmed that Anderson airlifted from the Scottish coast two bazookas, extra sub-machine guns, extra ammunition, a supply of hand-grenades and various small-arms. No alcohol was included in the consignment," Adams said with a grin.

Buckminster shaded his eyes as he watched the incoming chopper whose sheer size never ceased to surprise him. His reprimand was the more devastating for being delivered as he stared upwards.

"Adams, I decide what is and is not necessary. In future you will show me all – repeat all – signals reaching this vessel."

"Of course, sir. Fully understood, sir."

"Another point. I run a dry ship, therefore your presumably humorous reference to alcohol is not appreciated."

"Really am very sorry indeed, sir."

In his best quarterdeck manner Buckminster lowered his hand and glared at his First Mate.

"Just so long as it doesn't happen again. Now, I leave you to see to it that Anderson and that bloody great chopper of his land safely on the helipad."

Turning his back on Adams, he studied the chart again

and taking a pencil from his pocket drew his projected course. The Sikorsky lowered its great bulk onto the helipad. The sea was calm, a sheet of rippling blue which sparkled and glittered in the reflection from the sun shining out of a clear sky. All this was lost on Buckminster as he studied the chart. Nor was he dwelling on the fact that below deck he was carrying some of the most deadly killers in the world – a large nucleus of ex-Special Air Service men, and men from various nations who all had their own reasons for hating terrorism.

"Who and where is our opponent?" was the question he was asking as *Firestorm* increased speed and headed for Elsinore.

At precisely the same hour – and also in the glare of a blazing sun – the 2,000-ton Soviet hydrofoil MV *Kometa* was proceeding at twenty knots off the Polish coast near Gdansk. Captain Andrei Livanov turned as Sobieski came onto the bridge and concealed his dislike of the newcomer with an effort. Livanov was a Muscovite and proud of it. Having to consort with such people as Poles did not suit his temperament.

"Is there some problem, Sobieski?" he asked.

"None whatsoever, Comrade."

"Then you had better return to your control headquarters to make sure no problem does arise."

Peter Sobieski, a well-built man of forty with a cheerful and extrovert personality, glanced at his temporary – and nominal – captain and then lit a cigarette.

"If a problem arises you will not be able to eat. If an emergency occurs you will have a nervous breakdown," thought Sobieski, who disliked Russians as much as Livanov disliked Poles. He did not say the words out loud. Instead he blew smoke across the bridge, an action which touched off Livanov's edgy nerves. "You will not smoke on my bridge!"

Sobieski added insult to injury by grinding the cigarette under his heel. At that moment a radio signal received from the shore station was handed to Livanov. It did not improve his temper. The signal asked why *Kometa* was cruising like an ordinary vessel and not using her surface-piercing foils.

Captain Livanov concealed his anger. First the man in charge of the sonar room had been replaced by Sobieski. The Pole undoubtedly knew his job; Livanov had to admit that he was at least as good as the regular man. But Sobieski was Viktor Rashkin's creature. And Viktor Rashkin, the wonder boy of the Soviet political world, was Leonid Brezhnev's creature.

It was Rashkin, the second most powerful man in the Soviet Union, who had ordered *Kometa* to proceed along the Baltic shore on its way to Germany. And it was the brilliant Rashkin who had come aboard briefly before *Kometa* departed from Leningrad, bringing with him Peter Sobieski.

"He will take control of the sonar during this voyage of your remarkable ship," he had informed Livanov.

Livanov was on the verge of asking *Is he qualified?* before he realised the danger of the question. He hoped he was. He dared not cast doubt on Rashkin's judgement.

"He is my assistant," Rashkin had said. "He is also a Pole. Do not look surprised, Comrade Livanov. We and our European allies are one big happy family – so why should we not co-operate?"

Had there been a note of cynical irony in Rashkin's remark? The captain of *Kometa* had glanced quickly at him and a pair of shrewd eyes had met his own. Livanov did not understand this man whose expression changed with alarming suddenness. They said he had been an actor before he served his apprenticeship with the KGB.

Livanov was thinking of this conversation as he cruised off Gdansk and read the signal from shore control. Very well, he would show them. Sending Sobieski back to his sonar room, Livanov issued his instructions and the huge vessel began to pick up speed. He himself operated the lever which transformed *Kometa* from a normal vessel with her hull deep in the water to a streak of power elevated above the sea on massive steel blades like giant skis.

Onshore several pairs of eyes watched the spectacle through field-glasses. Some of the watchers had never seen a hydrofoil. There were expressions of sheer astonishment as *Kometa* flew across the vast bay. Fresh signals were despatched to the captain – this time of congratulation. Livanov chose to ignore them. He was thinking now of the passengers he would be taking on board at his next port of call. A detachment of MfS – members of the dreaded state security from East Germany.

8

Beaurain and Louise found Ed Cottel finishing a meal in an elegant café on the Hilton's ground floor. Overlooking a glassed-in verandah with a dense wall of trees and shrubberies, the Café d'Egmont had the atmosphere of somewhere in the country. It was safe to talk – Cottel was almost the only diner.

"Can I get you something?" he asked without ceremony.

"Just coffee, thank you," Louise said. Beaurain also asked for coffee and declined anything to eat. They were short of time; the Belgian was anxious to return to Henderson's headquarters to check on the progress of Serge Litov.

"I hear, Jules, they're thinking of charging you with multiple murder, rape and God knows what other mayhem. I must say you've been busy while I was away."

"Who told you these interesting titbits? Voisin?"

"Who else? He spent the whole time I was with him telling me what an outrage it was that you should control the investigation into the Syndicate. I think what particularly infuriated him is my insistence that he report this fact to all West European police chiefs and heads of counter-espionage. Now, he's trying to unseat you."

"Was he . . . nervous?" Beaurain enquired casually.

Cottel crinkled his brow and rubbed his crooked nose, which Louise always found attractive. "Now that you mention it," the American decided, "I guess the answer is 'yes'. Like a man who felt threatened." He sipped at his coffee. "Sounds pretty goddam ridiculous."

"Maybe. Have you dug up any more information about the Syndicate, Ed?"

He waited until their coffee had been served and then started talking.

"First thing is that our latest satellite pictures taken over the Baltic show that big hydrofoil – the Soviet job, *Kometa* –

creeping along the coast of Poland and heading for East Germany. It looks as though its ultimate destination could be the port of Sassnitz. And from there it's only a short distance to Trelleborg, a small port in Sweden. There also happens to be a ferry service between Sassnitz and Trelleborg."

"What about that list of people for Voisin – the list you thought might lead to the personnel of Telescope?"

"Dammit! Never did get round to that – you've no idea how these transatlantic trips disappear – you get back and wonder what the hell you accomplished." Cottel drank more coffee. "I told Voisin that as soon as I hit his office – got in first before he asked."

"You always were a good tactician, Ed," murmured Beaurain. "Do you now have Washington's backing to track down the Stockholm Syndicate?"

"In a word, no." The American looked grim and wiped his mouth with his napkin. "Queer atmosphere back home – especially close to the President. No-one wants to know. They all say wait till after the election – concentrate on exposing Telescope. One reason is they're upstaged by Telescope. But more important is the election. The man in the Oval Office isn't exactly the president of the century and there are people who would like to dump him before the Convention. If news of the Stockholm Syndicate ever leaked to the press – the fact that a huge piece of its finance is coming from American conglomerates looking for huge tax-free profits ..." Cottel made a gesture with his napkin and then crushed it. "Out of the window would go any chance of the President being re-elected. You can trace a line from the Stockholm Syndicate almost up to the Oval Office."

"You mean that?" Beaurain asked sharply. "You're not guessing?"

"Do I ever guess?" asked Cottel. "I have more news."

"Less unnerving than what you've told us so far, I hope," said Louise.

"Viktor Rashkin fits into this thing somewhere," Cottel said, keeping his voice low. "We keep a close eye on Viktor, who is not a nice person. I can tell you he has just left Brussels Airport this evening aboard his Lear jet."

"Alone?" Beaurain queried.

"No, not alone. He was accompanied by a fat man very

muffled so you couldn't see his features – and also a girl, likewise with her features concealed." He finished his coffee. "I wondered whether anyone was interested in the flight plan Rashkin's pilot filed. His destination."

"You're going to tell us anyway," Louise said.

"Copenhagen – and then Stockholm. Which is why I'm catching the first plane out of here for Stockholm in the morning," Cottel informed them. "When you need me, you can find me at the Grand Hotel."

"We're going to need your help?" Louise asked innocently.

"We're all going to need each other's help before this develops much further," the American predicted.

The jet taxied to a halt at Copenhagen's Kastrup Airport. Inside the passenger cabin Viktor Rashkin lit a cigarette and gazed at his companion.

"What is your next move, Viktor?" she enquired. "Isn't the opposition beginning to show some teeth?"

"The opposition – Beaurain in particular – is reacting just as I expected." His dark eyes examined the tip of his cigarette. "The important thing is to keep him away from Denmark for the next few days. The big consignment is on its way and nothing can – must – stop it."

"How much is it worth?"

"On the streets something in the region of forty million Swedish kronor. I think we should leave the plane, my dear."

"To go where?" Sonia Karnell asked.

"To pay a discreet call on our friend, Dr Benny Horn."

"Max here, Jock. Speaking from Kastrup Airport. The subject left the flight here instead of proceeding on to Stockholm."

"How can you be sure?" Henderson interjected tersely.

"Because you wait on the plane if you're going on – and the flight is now airborne for Stockholm. Because at this moment I'm watching Serge Litov..."

The large and heavily-built man – he was over six feet tall but like other men conscious of their excessive stature he stooped – had entered the booking-hall and now stood holding a short telescopic umbrella. His gross form was topped by a large head and a tan-coloured hat which partially concealed his strong-boned face. English was the language he used when he conversed with Serge Litov. He appeared unconnected with the Russian.

"Where is the man requiring my attention, sir?"

His jowls were heavy and fleshy; he was about sixty years old and the personification of a successful stockbroker. Litov could hardly believe this was the intermediary sent to cut out any intervention he might have spotted.

"Do I know you?" Litov asked sharply, covering his mouth with his hand as he lit a cigarette. The fool had not used the code. Had he himself walked into a trap? But in that case why had the Telescope people released him in the first place?

"I am, of course, sir, George Land. Coming from London you must know and appreciate as I do the beauties of St. James's Park at this time of the year."

His mouth hardly moved – and yet Litov had heard every word quite clearly. *St. James's Park* – that was Land's identification.

"The lake is what I like in St. James's Park," Litov responded, and the word 'lake' completed the code check. "How did you know someone was following me?" George Land gave him the creeps, though he was not easily disturbed. Like a perfect English butler – and he was just about to despatch a fellow human being permanently.

"I knew someone was following you because I watched from outside the entrance doors. I observed your furtive glances in a certain direction. Also, I see now there is perspiration on your brow, if I may make mention of the fact, sir."

The constant use of 'sir' did not help. Land was so cool and collected; his restrained courtesy was beginning to get on Litov's nerves. "You see that man in the payphone?"

"I can see the gentleman quite clearly."

"Get rid of him – permanently. As soon as I've got out of this place."

"It would be helpful if you would remain where you are until I have reached the phone box. In that way he will notice no change in what interests him – yourself."

Land briefly grasped the dangling umbrella with his left

hand. And then Serge Litov understood as though he had been trained to use the weapon all his life. The umbrella was a camouflaged dagger, spring-loaded and designed so the blade projected from the tip at the touch of a button.

"I'll wait here," he said reluctantly.

"It has been a most profitable conversation, sir," said Land discreetly and proceeded across the almost deserted booking-hall as though bent on making a phone call.

"I said I was watching Litov," repeated Kellerman to Jock Henderson from inside the payphone. "He appears to be waiting for someone to collect him."

"Or he could be playing a game," the Scot pointed out. "He'll still have that ticket to Stockholm."

A large English-looking man was wandering across the hall towards the payphones. He was close enough for Kellerman to see his fleshy cheeks. As he walked with a slow deliberate tread he swung a telescopic umbrella back and forth from his right wrist. Otherwise, the booking-hall was empty. The other passengers had departed for Copenhagen via the airport bus or taxis and no other flight was due to land or take off.

"He's waiting here," Kellerman repeated, "and . . ."

"You keep repeating yourself, Max," Henderson said sharply. "Is anything wrong?"

"No. From Litov's behaviour I'm sure he's going into Copenhagen – maybe just for the night. I anticipate an attempt to evade surveillance while he's here – then he moves on to his next destination, which may not be Stockholm."

"You think he's spotted you, then?"

"I didn't say that . . ." Kellerman's brow was wrinkled as he tried to talk to Henderson and think at the same time. "But with a man of Litov's experience I'm assuming he'll *expect* surveillance."

Kellerman suddenly grasped what had been worrying him outside the payphone. It was the huge English-looking man advancing on the bank of payphones. *He hadn't once looked at the booth occupied by Kellerman.* Which simply wasn't natural behaviour. In fact he was deliberately *not* looking at Kellerman's payphone even as he continued his steady, doomsday-like tread towards it. Beaurain came on the line, crisp, decisive.

"Beaurain. Trouble at your end?"

"Yes ..."

"Louise books into the Royal Hotel later this evening. Goodbye."

Kellerman carefully did nothing untoward. The large man was close to the door of his box, staring fixedly at an empty booth as his outsize feet continued their purposeful advance. By now Kellerman had noticed the telescopic umbrella swinging back and forth. The man wasn't a poof, he was certain.

He maintained his stance until the last moment: phone held to ear, head half-turned away, suitcase propped against side of payphone with one leg. George Land, jowls shaking, took one final glance round the booking-hall, a sweeping gaze which told him it was empty and that Litov was leaving without looking back. He pressed the button and the spring-loaded stiletto blade shot out of his umbrella which he held like a fencer about to make a savage lunge.

His thick lips slightly parted, he turned back to use his left hand to pull open the door of the booth occupied by Max Kellerman. The door was open.

Kellerman was inside the box, stooping to pick up the suitcase. Land stared at the side of the German's neck. He moved in closer, and took a strong grip on the umbrella ready for the lunge.

Everything moved rapidly out of focus for Land as Kellerman straightened up and slammed the steel-tipped edge of his suitcase into the giant's right kneecap. Land gulped with pain but did not cry out. His large face convulsed in fury. Like a handcuff Kellerman's right hand closed over the wrist which held the umbrella. The handcuff twisted and jerked upward in one violent arc of ninety degrees. The vertical stiletto-like blade entered Land's throat and his eyes bulged.

Kellerman had already transferred his grip to the two lapels of the Englishman's jacket and he spun him round before he could fall and heaved him inside the payphone. The receiver was still swinging from its cord as the Englishman's body began to slide down the rear wall, its feet projecting into the booking-hall over the umbrella on the floor.

Kellerman pulled a soft cap from his pocket and rammed it on his head as he moved swiftly across the still deserted booking-hall with only one idea in mind. To catch up with Serge Litov. The cab carrying Litov was just leaving the kerb as he came into the open air. Kellerman climbed into the next cab and closed the door before giving his instructions.

"Please follow that cab. Do not lose it – the passenger inside is responsible for an incident in the airport hall."

The driver was quick-witted. While he checked on the identity of his passenger he was driving away from the airport, making sure he did not lose the vehicle ahead. He could take his passenger back to the airport if the replies were unsatisfactory. His passenger over-rode his questions by volunteering information.

"You will read about the airport incident in the morning papers. I am *Kriminalpolizei* working in liaison with the Belgians and your own people. Here is my card." Kellerman flashed an identity paper which the driver hardly saw. To build up confidence and dispel all doubts, keep talking fluently, confidently ...

"Do not crowd that cab, please. It is vital the passenger does not know he is being followed. There will, of course, be a large tip for your co-operation. Please, also, be careful when the cab approaches its destination. I must not be just behind when it stops. I appreciate it will not be easy."

"I will manage it. No problem," the Dane replied. Kellerman sank back into his seat and kept quiet. It had worked. Near the end of the conversation give them a problem to occupy their minds, then shut up!

"Serge Litov should be here by now. I cannot imagine what is detaining him. One thing I insist on is punctuality."

The Danish antiquarian book dealer, known by the few Danes who met him as Dr Benny Horn, sat in the darkened room polishing his rimless spectacles and fidgeting as he checked the illuminated hands of his watch. His companion, a girl, smiled in the dark and listened to the gentle lapping of the water which came through the open window from the basin of the Nyhavn harbour outside.

"There could have been trouble at the airport," he fussed. "Let us suppose Litov was followed – it is to be expected ..."

"Then George Land will have dealt with the follower. And that might explain the delay."

"Unless Litov involved himself in the fracas."

"He has his instructions which he won't disobey." The girl was amused by his exhibition of an irritable and pedantic dealer in rare books. Outside the open window headlights appeared, an engine stopped. Sonia Karnell saw a cab had arrived. "Make sure he has not been followed," Horn called to her.

"We are very close to Nyhavn," Kellerman's driver said.

They had driven through a maze of streets and squares lined with ancient buildings and the German would have been hard put to it to trace the route on a map. He was fairly sure they were moving in a northerly direction. What the hell was Nyhavn? He waited, hoping the driver would elaborate, and the Dane obliged.

"Nyhavn is the old port area – seamen's bars to the left of the water and tourist trap shops to the right. That's our friend's likely destination."

The cab ahead was the only vehicle in sight now. If they kept on driving much further it was only a matter of time before Litov spotted that he had a tail. The cab in front turned sharp right and the German guessed they had reached Nyhavn.

The middle of the street was occupied by a long, straight basin of water with its level well below that of the street, like a canal in Amsterdam. A forest of masts projected into the night sky. On either side of the brightly-lit street overlooking the waterway was a wall of seventeenth-century houses.

Kellerman's driver earned his tip. Instead of turning right alongside the basin he drove straight on past the end of the water, round a corner, and stopped. The brilliant lighting vanished. There were shadows everywhere.

"He would have seen us. I'm sure he's stopping somewhere down Nyhavn and it's a short distance before you're on the waterfront."

"Thank you." Kellerman gave him money. "Would you wait? I shan't be long."

The problem was that he would be conspicuous walking along Nyhavn carrying a suitcase. It also restricted his movements if he were attacked – and he had not forgotten the assault with the umbrella. That weapon was reminiscent of Bulgarian techniques.

Free of his suitcase, he strolled round the corner back into the lights. Litov was climbing a short flight of steps to a house at the far end. "Tourist trap shops on the right . . ." his driver had said. The Russian was entering one of the houses on the right – easy to pinpoint even from a distance because each house was painted a different colour. A most helpful arrangement.

It was also helpful that there were people about. Kellerman strolled a short distance down the left-hand side and saw the flights of steps leading down to the basement bars. Returning the way he had come, he walked round the end of the harbour basin and continued down the tourist-trap side until he drew level with the house Litov had disappeared into. At the top of a short flight of steps in the blaze of street lights Kellerman could make out a name engraved in large letters on a plate. *Dr Benny Horn.* He had located the base of another of the three-man directorate running the Stockholm Syndicate.

It was time to meet Louise at the Royal Hotel.

When Serge Litov climbed the steps at the Nyhavn address he was relieved to see the name engraved on a plate to the right of the heavy door. *Dr Benny Horn.* Litov pressed the bell.

"Come in quickly."

The door closed behind him and he stood in darkness. There was the sound of a lock being turned, of bolts being shot home. Then a blaze of light illuminated the narrow hallway, so strong it made Litov blink. He looked quickly behind him. A slim, dark-haired girl, her hair cut close like a helmet, stood aiming a Walther pistol. It was Sonia Karnell.

Litov had expected to meet Dr Otto Berlin, the man who had issued him with his instructions to penetrate Telescope's headquarters. Instead, facing him in the hallway, stood a man wearing a skullcap, a bow-tie and a neat suit which was in considerable contrast to Berlin's careless dress. He was also clean-shaven and stood with his hands clasped across his slim stomach while he contemplated Litov in a manner which irritated the Russian.

"Who the hell are you?" he demanded brusquely. "I've come a long way and I'm damned tired."

He stopped as he felt the muzzle of Sonia's Walther press against the back of his neck.

100

"You are also damned impolite," the man facing him remarked in a cold distant voice. "I am Benny Horn, the man Dr Berlin ordered you to report to when you had completed your mission, as I believe the phrase goes in your circles."

Litov flinched at the sneer in Horn's voice; he flinched also as he felt the gun barrel jabbing into his neck.

"Come into this room and report at once what you have discovered," Horn ordered and led the way into a room overlooking Nyhavn. Litov sat down in an armchair indicated by Horn, who himself occupied a stiff-backed chair behind an antique desk. Unlike Berlin, who slouched all over the place, Horn sat erect and again clasped his hands as he stared at the new arrival.

"Coffee, Litov?"

Sonia did not wait for a reply as she poured a cup of black coffee from a percolator and added a generous spoonful of sugar. She knew his tastes, Litov observed. The Walther pistol had disappeared. Unlike the hallway, where he had been so dazzled by the glare he had hardly been able to focus on Horn, here in the book-lined room the lighting was dim, but Horn sat in one of the shaded areas. He waited until Litov had drunk half the cup of coffee and then began to fire a barrage of questions at him.

"You located Telescope's base?"

"It is in southern England – near Guildford in the county of Surrey."

"How do you know that?"

Litov explained how he had seen the red bus with the destination *Guildford* on the front. Horn seemed more interested in the pillar box where letters had been collected. What time of day had the postman collected? Had he seen anyone *post* a letter in the box? The barrage of questions went on and on – almost as though Horn were hoping to catch him out in a lie. Litov couldn't understand the ferocity of the cross-examination.

"How were you able to time the flight of the helicopter in both directions?" Horn demanded at one stage.

"Fortunately they let me keep my watch."

"They *let* you keep your watch? You had it with you all the time? The watch you are wearing at this moment?"

Litov barely concealed his irritation, but remembered the

cold, detached look in Horn's eyes and the cold pressure of the pistol against the back of his neck. "Yes," he said. "While I was at the house near Guildford the interrogator, Carder, even mentioned the watch once. He said it would stop me becoming completely disorientated if I knew the time."

Horn went on asking Litov again and again to repeat the story of his experiences since his capture in Brussels. Then it ended abruptly. Horn stood up and came round to the front of his desk, staring down at Litov as he polished his rimless spectacles.

"Wait here," he said suddenly. "On no account attempt to leave this room."

Horn hurried out into the hall followed by the girl who shut the sound-proof door. They went into a room at the back and sat facing each other across a table. "What do you think?" Horn asked, removing his skull-cap.

"The bus convinces me."

"We must send a heavy detachment of specialised troops by air to locate and destroy that base." He stopped speaking as the front door-bell rang. Sonia Karnell slipped into the hall and returned shortly. "It is Danny."

Waiting in the hall was the cab-driver who had transported Kellerman from Kastrup to Nyhavn when they followed Serge Litov.

Max Kellerman had settled himself into Room 1014 at the Royal Hotel – but he was ready for an emergency departure. He chose the quick-service restaurant – where the service lived up to its name and the food was on a par with the service – for several reasons. It was part of the shopping and reception hall complex, which meant that as he ate he was able to observe the reception counter from a discreet distance. This could pay life-saving dividends – as Kellerman had discovered in the past. It enabled you to observe who booked in at the hotel after your own arrival. A method of assassination employed all over the world was for the hired killer to take a room in the same hostelry as his victim.

If – as Kellerman had done – you left your room key with reception while you ate and watched – you could sometimes spot a caller making an enquiry about you. The receptionist would swivel his head to see whether your key was on the hook. It was impossible to be sure the receptionist had checked your key – but if you were already suspicious it was added confirmation.

Kellerman lingered over his meal, savouring the Scandinavian food. He was already beginning to enjoy the relaxed atmosphere he sensed in the Danes who inhabited Copenhagen, which was refreshingly free of the normal multitude of high-rise blocks. The multi-storey Royal Hotel, oddly enough, was an exception. Jules Beaurain and Louise Hamilton arrived at the reception desk at precisely 10.30 p.m.

"Louise, I've been to the scene of the murder aboard the barge near Bruges – there was *a witness*, a boy who spends half his time in a tree-house he's built."

"Hold on a minute, Willy, here is Jules."

The call came through at the Royal Hotel in response to an earlier call from Beaurain to Willy Flamen at his home address. Flamen had been on his way home and his wife had promised that he would call back the moment he arrived. Beaurain emerged steamily from the bathroom where he had just taken a shower.

"It's Willy Flamen," Louise told him. "About that bargee and his wife. He says he's found a witness."

"I'll take it. You go downstairs and keep Max from feeling lonely. He's still drinking coffee in that restaurant, watching reception."

"Time you gave up," she said to the German when she had joined him and had ordered coffee. Only one man on duty now and a general atmosphere of boredom and closing-down for the night.

"It comes when you least expect it," he replied.

"What does?"

"The breakthrough. The incident which means nothing at the time and everything later on. Waiting is the key to success. Any policeman will tell you that."

"And when you were a lawyer in Munich did you meet a lot of police?"

A flicker of pain crossed his face. He responded in a slightly grating voice behind which she detected a hint of menace – not for herself, but for some unknown killer. She really had blown it. "I'm sorry, Max. It was in the Munich shoot-out that your wife was killed. What was she like?"

"Irreplaceable."

"Sorry again. I'll keep my big mouth shut."

"You don't have to," he assured her. "And I'm sitting here for a reason – I don't understand why the Syndicate mob didn't have more back-up at Kastrup Airport when I arrived with Serge Litov."

"Where is Louise?" asked Beaurain, slipping into the chair alongside Kellerman in the ground floor restaurant.

"She took off after someone."

"What the hell are you talking about?" asked Beaurain, his face devoid of expression.

"It's strange," the German commented. "I was just saying – it comes when you least expect it. A breakthrough. I was just coming up to your room to tell you. We were sitting here when a girl went up to the reception counter and we saw the clerk turn round and look towards where my key was hanging. She rolled his pen onto the floor behind the counter to keep him busy while she checked the register of guests. She could have been anything European. She had a distinctive hairdo – very black hair cut short and close to her head – like a helmet. What's wrong, Jules?"

Beaurain's eyes were hard. "I'm waiting for you to get to the point," he said with an unnerving quietness.

"After she had gone outside, Louise followed her and waited at the door for my signal."

"Why not the other way round? Why didn't *you* take the tail job?"

"For a reason I'll give you in a minute." The German met Beaurain's gaze levelly. "I went up to the receptionist and spun him a story about thinking I'd recognised the girl as a friend of my wife's. He opened up immediately – strange coincidence and all that. The girl was looking for a man who had dropped a wallet her husband had picked up. She described me perfectly and said her husband thought I'd come into this hotel. He – the fictitious huband – had been rushing to a business appointment and would come back in the morning."

"So she got your name?"

"She got that – and my room number."

"And Louise?" asked Beaurain.

"I gave her the go-ahead. The 'black helmet' girl got into a car and Louise followed her in the car you hired. I couldn't – just in case I was recognised from the incident at Kastrup."

"I've just heard someone else call the girl Black Helmet, and since it was an intelligent child's description it is likely to be accurate. She was visiting a couple on a barge near Bruges just before they were murdered."

9

Kellerman was shaken by Beaurain's news. He sat staring at the reception counter where the girl they had christened Black Helmet had played her tricks on the receptionist.

"Who is this intelligent child?" he asked in a toneless voice.

"I was talking on the phone to Willy Flamen when Louise came down to join you. A boy he interviewed had built a makeshift cabin in the branches of a tree overlooking the Darras' barge."

"How does this tie up with Black Helmet?"

"If you'll keep quiet until I've finished, I'll explain," Beaurain told Kellerman coldly. "This boy lives nearby and he sounds a loner. He makes a habit of creeping out of his bedroom after dark and spending half the night in his hidey-hole. The Darras' barge has been moored to the same place on the towpath for quite some time."

"Perhaps their role was to act as a link for the Stockholm Syndicate."

"That was my thought too. Now, this boy – who impressed Willy, I gather – was hiding in his cabin, probably snooping on what the Darras' were up to, when a car arrives long after dark. He saw a girl visit the Darras', someone shone a lamp full on her face. The description fits Black Helmet perfectly."

"It's a long way from Bruges to Copenhagen."

"Well, Louise and I made the trip. Why not Black Helmet? The kid was also there when Darras and his wife were murdered – although he didn't realise what happened at the time. He probably saw the killer and his companion arrive at the barge: an odd-sounding couple from his description."

"This precocious child is a veritable mine of information," Kellerman said cynically, not fully convinced of the danger to Louise.

106

"The killer," Beaurain continued, ignoring the interruption, "was dressed like an American according to the kid. Also he wears a straw hat and dark glasses and is of average height and build. His companion is thin – that was all Flamen could get on him. They operate in a strange way. The kid actually saw the thin man take from a brief-case what he called 'a big gun with a bulging nozzle' and hand it to the 'American' as they stepped onto the barge. My own theory – and Flamen is inclined to agree – is that Black Helmet called on them a few days earlier, gave them some final instructions, and they then became a liability to Dr Otto Berlin who ordered the two killers in to deal with them."

Kellerman pushed away his cup which a Filipino waitress had refilled with coffee. "It's all speculation, though. You still haven't conclusively linked them – or the girl – with the Syndicate."

"Black Helmet's description fits perfectly the pictures Dr Henri Goldschmidt showed us of the two people leaving a house in Bruges. One was Dr Berlin. With him was a girl. Black Helmet."

"Forty million Swedish kronor worth of heroin," said Benny Horn. "Intriguing how much money you can carry in one suitcase."

He was facing Sonia Karnell in the narrow hallway and carried the case in his right hand. On her return she had locked the door behind her and was eager to make her announcement. Horn had been waiting for over an hour, however, and his impatience overrode her sense of the dramatic.

"I have news."

"Tell me quickly. The van for Elsinore is waiting outside. This consignment is so huge I won't be happy till it's outside Copenhagen."

"Armed with Danny's description of the man who followed Litov here from Kastrup, I checked the King Frederik Hotel where Danny left him. His passenger played it clever – obviously a professional. He didn't book in at the King Frederik. I had to start hunting, hoping to God he'd chosen a large place and not some fleapit."

"I have understood you so far," Horn said quietly.

"I tried the Palace. Told my story and gave them Danny's

107

description of the man. All I had going for me was that few people book in as late as this. No luck at the Palace. But I struck gold at the Royal Hotel."

"Yes?"

The excitement in her manner made Horn contain his impatience. She must have uncovered something important. Which was a blasted nuisance when he wanted to leave Copenhagen fast. The consignment of heroin had arrived by a small boat, which had briefly docked at the end of Nyhavn while Sonia was out searching for the mysterious shadow.

"He's staying at the Royal," Karnell continued. "Description fits Danny's. But I got a chance to read the register upside down and two more people arrived even later. One is Jules Beaurain, the other Louise Hamilton." Dr Benny Horn slowly put the suitcase down on the carpet and stared at the girl.

"You have interesting company in town with you tonight, Jules," Ed Cottel of the CIA told him over the phone. "Viktor Rashkin landed at Copenhagen in his Lear jet after flying from Brussels."

Beaurain sat on the edge of the bed in his room at the Royal Hotel, listening closely to his American friend. He had phoned the Grand Hotel in Stockholm on the off-chance that Ed might have arrived. It occurred to him that Cottel didn't seem to worry much about the security of an open telephone line.

Max Kellerman, perched on the edge of a wooden chair, looked stiff and serious, and Beaurain knew he was worried sick about what was happening to Louise. There had been no word from her since she had followed Black Helmet out into the night.

"Ed," Beaurain replied into the mouthpiece, "was there anyone with Rashkin when he left the Lear jet at Kastrup?"

"Yes, a girl. Difficult to see at a distance – just as it was with the big R. apparently. She had dark hair, cut short. End of description."

"So where did they go when they left the plane? And is it still at Kastrup, waiting to take him on somewhere tomorrow maybe?"

"My man lost them again when they left the airport. They had two cars waiting – one for passengers, one to set up interference if anyone tried to tail them. The girl left with the big R. And the man I hoped to contact here isn't at home in his apartment in Gamla Stan – that's Swedish for the Old City. He's a book dealer. Rare editions."

"Has he a name?"

"Dr Theodor Norling. Keep in touch. Bye, Jules."

It was 10.30 p.m. when Beaurain broke his phone connection with Ed Cottel in Stockholm. In Washington, D.C., it was only 4.30 p.m. and the atmosphere in the Oval Office at the White House was tense. The President, who faced an election in less than six months' time, had long become accustomed to seeing the world entirely through electoral glasses. His every action was judged by one criterion: would it gain or lose him votes in November?

The fact that he was already being called 'one of the worst presidents in the history of the United States' had only bolstered his determination to see that his country – and the world – was subjected to four more years of the mixture as before. Seated behind his desk, his legs raised, his ankles crossed and resting on it, he looked at the only two other people with him.

His wife, Bess, sat upright in an easy chair, leaning slightly forward in a characteristic manner which an unkind columnist once described as 'Bess rampant and ready for blood'. The second person, equally unpopular with the press, was his chief aide, Joel Cody from Texas. The subject of the conversation, which – like so many White House conversations – had been initiated by the President's wife, was Ed Cottel.

"You're sure this Ed Cottel was checked out before he was sent to Europe, Joel?" the President demanded.

"Right down to his underpants. He's West Coast – not Ivy League, thank God – and he has a leaning towards this private organisation, Telescope, and its objectives, although he tries to conceal it. He also believes the real menace is the Stockholm Syndicate and that we should concentrate all our fire on that."

"For Christ's sake, Joel!" Tieless, his shirt front open, the most powerful man in the western world sat up straight, whipping his feet off the desk together with a sheaf of papers which fluttered to the floor. "Until we've won the election we don't want to know about that Stockholm Syndicate. There are rumours that some of the top contributors to our campaign chest may have dabbled their fingers in that thing."

"So when the crunch comes we want Telescope to be the target, not the Syndicate?" Cody suggested. "And this way that's what we get."

"You wouldn't care to explain that, Joel, would you?"

"I think you'll find Joel knows what he's doing," Bess reassured her husband and then subsided, for the moment.

"Cottel is sympathetic to these Telescope people, whoever they may be," Cody explained. "We do know further that he is a personal friend of this Belgian, Beaurain – rumoured to be one of the chiefs of this Telescope outfit. So, while officially Cottel is locating the key personnel of Telescope – ready for the western security services to swoop when the time comes – he will really be trying to help the Telescope organisation all he can. We're having him watched – that way he leads us to the whole outfit pretty soon now."

"Why don't we send this Harvey Sholto you keep recommending – you said Sholto hates the guts of Telescope."

"Which is well known," Cody assured the President smoothly, "so Sholto wouldn't get anywhere near them. Ed Cottel only took this assignment so he could secretly keep the heat off Telescope – and he'll end up leading us to the capture and exposure of the whole goddam underground organisation."

"I like it, Joel, I like it." The well-known smile suddenly left his face. "Haven't you overlooked something? Supposing Cottel digs up information we'd just as soon he didn't – such as names of some of the big companies whose chairmen have contributed money to the Syndicate?"

"That's all taken care of," Joel assured him confidently. "If Cottel gets out of line we send over Sholto to take care of him. I may even send him in any case."

"Don't give me those sort of details," the President said hastily. "In fact, I don't know anything about this Harvey Sholto. And I don't really understand what you've just said, so let's change the subject."

Louise Hamilton felt sure she would lose the dark-haired girl. The same girl she and Beaurain had seen outside Bruges station when they took her vacated taxi. Leaving Kellerman with hardly a word, she walked out the back way and got behind the wheel of the hired Citroën.

"I want hired cars waiting for me at Copenhagen, Stockholm, Helsinki and Oslo," Beaurain had instructed Henderson. Thankful for his foresight, Louise drove round near the main entrance and stopped. Seconds later the dark-haired girl came out, summoned a passing cab and got inside. As Louise followed the cab, keeping a rough check on its route with the aid of the Copenhagen street map open on the seat beside her, she soon began to suspect the girl's destination. The house on Nyhavn Kellerman had described.

Within minutes she knew she had guessed correctly. The cab ahead turned right, the basin of water was there in the middle of the street, the forest of masts above fishing boats tied up to the quays. Louise took a quick decision. Tooting her horn, she speeded up and overtook the cab with inches to spare. It was not the act of someone who wished the cab's passenger to be unaware of her presence – and inside the cab Sonia Karnell hadn't even noticed the Citroën as she felt inside her handbag for the front door key. Coming close to the main waterfront, where the wall of houses ended, Louise pulled in at the kerb and watched the cab coming up behind her in the rear-view mirror.

"If you have guessed wrong, my girl," she told herself, "you've had it." The cab stopped a dozen yards behind where she was parked. She watched while the short-haired girl paid off the cab, went up the steps, inserted a key and went inside, closing the door behind her. The cab drove past her and was turning right along the waterfront on its way back into the centre of Copenhagen.

Louise didn't hesitate. The moment to check on a place is when someone has just arrived. Nobody expects a shadow to have the audacity to approach so close when the person they have followed has just entered a building.

She was walking along the pavement within less than twenty seconds of the door closing. She reached the bottom of the short flight of steps, the smell of brine in her nostrils, saw the engraved plate to the right of the heavy door and tiptoed swiftly up the steps.

Dr Benny Horn. The same name Max Kellerman had mentioned. This was the house which had swallowed up Serge Litov after his dash from Brussels. Was this journey's end for the Russian? She doubted it very much. Glancing down she saw a squalid-looking basement area, the glass of the windows murky with grime, the steps streaked with dirt. It was in great contrast to the freshly-painted front door and surrounding walls of the house.

She returned to the Citroën at once, climbed behind the wheel, locked all the doors from the inside, took out a peaked cloth cap and rammed it loosely over her head. With her strong jaw-line the cap gave her a masculine appearance; in the bad light – she was midway between two street lamps – she could easily be mistaken for a man. She slumped down behind the wheel as though asleep and waited, her eyes fixed on the rear-view mirror.

Beaurain felt one satisfaction which offset the considerable anxiety he felt about Louise. He sat on his bed and drank more coffee, watching Max Kellerman pace back and forth with the restlessness caused by enforced inaction. Beaurain voiced his satisfaction to try and cheer up the German.

"At least I guessed right when I sent *Firestorm* into the Kattegat. Serge Litov headed for Copenhagen as soon as he thought he'd shaken himself loose."

"Where will *Firestorm* be at this moment?"

Beaurain checked his watch. "Just after midnight. She'll be just about off Elsinore. It's the narrowest passage between Denmark and Sweden."

"And Henderson?"

"He and his men from Brussels should by now be aboard her. They caught the flight before us as soon as I heard Litov had alighted from the Stockholm flight here."

"And how did they get from here to *Firestorm*?"

"By courtesy of Danish State Railways. They came from Kastrup straight into Copenhagen. From the main station – just across the way from this hotel – they caught an express to Elsinore, which is less than an hour's journey due north of the city and straight up the coast. I'd told Buckminster by radio what to expect and when. At a remote point on the coast just north of Elsinore, Henderson's party onshore exchanged signals by lamp with *Firestorm*, which promptly sent a small fleet of inflatable dinghies powered with outboards o pick them up."

"How do you manage it?" Kellerman had stopped pacing

and was sitting in a chair as he poured them both more coffee.

"I'm lucky," Beaurain smiled grimly. "It helps if you have the pieces on the board in the right squares at the right time. In this case particularly *Firestorm*. Goldschmidt in Bruges was emphatic that a meeting of the Stockholm Syndicate is due to take place in Scandinavia. There was mention of it at Voisin's meeting, the one I had to fight my way into." He frowned. "That was the first time they tried to grab Louise. What the hell can have happened to that girl?"

"I'm sorry." Max spread his hands.

"Shut up! I've already told you it's not your fault. And you both took the right decision."

They were waiting for the van. Dr Benny Horn, wearing a dark-coloured raincoat and a soft, wide-brimmed hat, stood once again in the hallway holding the suitcase which contained heroin to the value of forty million Swedish kronor. He had just completed making several phone calls.

"Have you fixed up anything for Beaurain and Co.?" asked Sonia Karnell, who had changed into a different trouser suit.

"Gunther Baum is now in Copenhagen. He will pay them a visit at the appropriate moment."

She shuddered as always at the mention of Baum. "I thought he was in Brussels."

"He was. Guessing that Beaurain would follow Litov to Copenhagen, I instructed him to make himself available here. I have just talked with Baum on the phone. The great thing is to have one's servants available at the right time," Horn remarked.

"Is it sensible to have our destination – Helsingør – painted in large letters across the side of the van?"

"Yes, it merges into the background at Helsingør which," Horn continued in a contemptuous tone, "is a provincial town, always feeling that cosmopolitan Copenhagen looks down on it."

He stopped speaking as the doorbell rang in a particular way, a succession of rings. Karnell had extracted the automatic from her handbag, switched off the hall light and opened the door. The van had arrived – she could see the bloody great name she objected to: *Helsingør*.

The driver, a short bulky man wearing a blue boiler suit and a beret, handed her the ignition keys and went inside. Out of the corner of her eye Karnell saw Dr Horn make a brief gesture with his head in the direction of the shuttered room where Litov was still waiting for fresh instructions.

Helsingør. Shakespeare's Elsinore where Kronborg Castle was linked with Hamlet's name. No historical foundation for the myth, but it was very good for Elsinore's tourist industry. Louise saw the van out of the corner of her eye as it passed down Nyhavn, heading for the waterfront where it would turn right or left.

Back into the centre of Copenhagen? In her rear-view mirror Louise had seen the couple, the man with the suitcase and the dark-haired girl, come out of the house and climb into the front of the van delivered by the man in the boiler suit.

She had observed that the girl climbed in behind the wheel, that the man clutched the suitcase, casting a quick glance up and down the street and a final look over his shoulder before climbing into the cab as passenger. The final look over his shoulder had been in the direction of the nearest fishing vessel moored to the quay. On the deck stood a seaman looping a cable for no very obvious reason.

Was he a guard who watched the house for the occupants? Who would look twice at a seaman? Louise felt sure there *had* been a signal exchanged between the girl's companion and the sailor. To her relief the seaman immediately went below deck as the van was leaving. He would not be there to see her own departure.

She set off as soon as the van had disappeared round the corner. The word *Helsingør* was obviously a blind: wherever she tracked the van to it would not be Elsinore. There was very little traffic about at this late hour so she was able to follow the red lights of the van at a distance. Was the passenger who had clutched the case so possessively Dr Benny Horn? She shrugged; Jules had taught her the futility of wasting energy speculating to no purpose.

After driving through a district of wealthy suburbs they came out onto the coast road. On her right the dark waters of the Øresund rippled placidly by the light of the moon. There were the coloured navigation lights of an occasional vessel passing up or down the Sound.

The van and the shadowing Citroën were travelling north. Louise knew that with the sea on her right there was only one route they could be taking – and that route took them to Elsinore! Could the name on the van be a piece of double bluff? Or was Dr Benny Horn running an apparently legitimate business which had offices in Copenhagen and Elsinore? Jules had repeatedly said idle speculation was a waste of time.

My God! Jules – he would be doing his nut back at the Royal Hotel! She hadn't managed to inform him where she was or what she was doing. It couldn't be helped; the van ahead was almost the only link Telescope had left with the Stockholm Syndicate.

"Have it out with Jules later," she told herself. "And just hope to God following this van turns out to be worthwhile. Then he can't say one damned thing."

It was one o'clock in the morning when the phone rang in Beaurain's bedroom. Kellerman had fallen asleep in a chair instead of returning to his own room. Beaurain had just checked the empty coffee pot with an expression of disgust. He grabbed for the receiver, almost knocking the instrument on the floor in his haste. It was Louise.

"I'm going to talk fast, Jules." He understood her meaning: at night, hotel operators, bored and idle, had been known to listen in on calls. "I'm in Elsinore – you've got that?"

"Yes," he said tersely.

"The girl at the reception counter took me to the place where Max was a few hours ago. On Nyhavn."

"Understood."

"She drove a man in a van with the word *Helsingør* on the side – nothing else, just the name – to Elsinore. He's hugging a suitcase like a gold-brick. Just south of the town they have stopped at a house which backs onto the rail track. There are shunting yards and loaded freight cars. Two have a large consignment of what looks like compressed paper – packing materials."

"Got you."

She was gabbling on, throwing all sorts of details at him irrespective of whether they seemed significant to her. He understood what she was doing exactly; they had used the same technique before.

"My position is a bit exposed. I'm actually inside Elsinore and no-one's about at this hour. The only hotel I've seen is closed."

Position exposed. She was signalling danger to him. Beaurain recalled the chairman of the Banque du Nord who had warned him about the *Zenith* signal. He told her to hold the line for a second. Checking a map of Denmark, he picked up the receiver.

"Still there? Can you drive north out of the place a few miles?"

"Yes, I'd drive back to Copenhagen but I'm short of petrol."

He gave her the name of a tiny place on the coast, instructed her how to get there by road. "You drive down to the beach, Louise, and wait there with your headlights pointed out to sea. At fifteen minute intervals precisely – commencing on the hour – you flash your lights six times at five second intervals. Henderson will be coming to collect you himself."

"From the sea?"

"From *Firestorm* in a small motor-boat. Now, have you got it?"

"I'm leaving at once."

She broke the connection. No prolonged conversation, no asking of a dozen questions which flooded into her tired mind. Just obey orders. And something in Jules' tone had said, *get the hell out of there fast.* Inside his bedroom, high up in the Royal Hotel, Beaurain replaced the receiver and looked at Kellerman who still sat upright in his chair.

"She's followed two people to Elsinore – one is the girl, Black Helmet, the other could be Benny Horn – who, incidentally, was carrying a suitcase. I'm guessing because there was no time to ask her for descriptions. I think she's in danger. I just hope Henderson reaches her in time."

He put in another call to the address near Brussels Midi station from where, earlier, Henderson had directed the watching operation on Serge Litov. As he had anticipated, it was Monique who answered the phone. She had taken over control of the command centre in Brussels. In as few words as possible he told her the signal to be sent to Jock Henderson aboard *Firestorm*, now somewhere just north of Elsinore. He replaced the receiver again and yawned loudly.

"Time you caught up on your sleep," Kellerman suggested. "You take my room and I'll wait here for Monique to
phone back."

"Thanks, but I can't sleep until I know Louise is safe
aboard *Firestorm*. You go get some sleep."

"You think I'll sleep until *I* know she's safe?" the German
demanded.

Beaurain grunted tiredly and grinned. Then he sighed.

"It's just that I'm not sure how far the tentacles of this
octopus, the Stockholm Syndicate, spread. De Graer shook
me: they've threatened his niece now so how far can we really
trust him? How far can we trust anyone? That's why our first
call in the morning will be on an old friend of mine, Superintendent Bodel Marker of Danish police Intelligence. He runs
his outfit from police headquarters. That's only ten minutes
away. He's dependable."

"Of course, they do know we're here – I'm sure that girl
spotted your name in the hotel register."

"So, we look out for two men – one dressed like an
American, the other carrying a brief-case, the brief-case containing the killer's gun."

Inside the house on the outskirts of Elsinore, Dr Benny Horn
sat polishing his glasses as he watched Sonia Karnell making
up her face. The room was smartly furnished with modern
pieces, the walls freshly painted in white; the heavy drapes
masking the windows were pulled closed.

"Do you have to keep fiddling with those glasses?" Karnell asked irritably. "What about that girl in the Citroën?"

"I'm thinking about her," Horn replied mildly. "Carl is
watching her, and since he hasn't returned yet she must still
be inside that phone booth."

"But isn't it madness?" Karnell became more vehement
the more she saw how calm Horn was. "She is phoning the
Telescope people to tell them where we are."

"I sincerely hope so. My whole plan for destroying them
is based on the knowledge that they followed Serge Litov to
Copenhagen. You located our primary target, Beaurain,
who will be destroyed when he leaves the Royal Hotel. Litov
discovered the main Telescope base in England near Guildford – and we have people already searching the area. Now
the girl may lead us to the remainder of Telescope's force on

the European mainland."

He broke off as a lean-faced man dressed inconspicuously in dark blue came silently into the room. "Developments, Carl?"

"The girl finished phoning. She's on her way back to the car."

Horn turned to Sonia Karnell. "So now you follow her. And use the Porsche parked at the back – she will not recognise it. Carl has placed the explosive device in a box in the boot."

"Why not kill her here?" Karnell snuggled coaxingly against his velvet jacket.

"Because we don't want blood all over the place here. It is our respectable house. I've been known here for many years."

"That's a laugh," she said quickly in French, the language they invariably used together, although it was neither's mother tongue. He pushed her away roughly. The eyes behind the rimless lens had lost their placidity, were cold and darkly intense. Eyes which had frightened countless men in their time.

"You will not joke about such things. You will not argue when I give you an order." She struggled into her duffel jacket, shaken by his reaction. "You will follow her because she may well lead you to another Telescope base in Denmark. Find out all you can, then use the device. Return here as soon as you can. There is much to do tomorrow. Understood?"

"Of course."

"Good luck. Be quick – you must not lose her."

Unlocking the car, Louise Hamilton glanced round in the darkness, listened for five minutes, which is too long for anyone to keep perfectly quiet. Her next precaution was to take her small torch from her shoulder-bag and shine it on the hood. The barely visible match was where she had left it; no-one had raised the bonnet in her absence.

As she started the engine and drove slowly out of Elsinore she had the route map of Denmark open on the seat beside her. It took her two minutes to realise she was being followed. She was not surprised. Never underestimate the enemy – one of Jock Henderson's favourite maxims. Louise

118

Hamilton had assumed only a short time after leaving Copenhagen that the couple *must* suspect that her car was a tail.

To escape any risk of detection she could have hung well back and almost certainly lost the van. The other option was to subordinate every other consideration – including personal safety – to making sure she did not lose the van. She had chosen the second option, and must have been spotted within ten minutes of leaving Copenhagen.

Now the roles were reversed. Heading north from Elsinore towards the remote rendezvous on the shoreline with Henderson, Louise was aware of the Porsche following at a discreet distance – but not so discreet that there was any danger of the sports car losing her.

Karnell concentrated on the red lights ahead, flicking her eyes away from them at intervals to maintain night vision. The Citroën puzzled her – because of the direction it was taking. The girl behind the wheel then disconcerted her more severely because of a sudden change in her way of driving. The car accelerated and disappeared round a bend in the road. Karnell pressed her foot down, tore round the corner and then jammed on her brakes.

"You stupid little cunning tart."

The contradictions of her insult didn't bother the Swedish girl. Coming round the bend she had found the red lights immediately ahead, the Citroën cruising very slowly like someone looking for a turning.

It wasn't that at all, and Karnell knew it. The girl had speeded up and then braked as soon as she was out of sight beyond the bend. Just far enough from the bend to ensure that the Porsche wouldn't ram her – although it might have skidded off the road.

"Bitch! Bitch! Bitch!" Karnell snarled.

The Citroën was picking up speed again. Karnell glanced at the device on the seat beside her, a device which was protected with foam-rubber inside a cardboard box bearing the name of a well-known Copenhagen florist. Much as she disliked handling explosive, Karnell was beginning to look forward to attaching some extra equipment to the car ahead.

She kept the speed of the Porsche down as the Citroën vanished round another bend at speed. Sure enough, round-ing the bend herself she saw the car was only a short distance ahead. Once again the driver had jammed on the brakes as soon as the Citroën was out of sight.

"You caught me once. Twice never, you whore," Karnell said triumphantly.

It happened about two kilometres after these two incidents. It happened without warning. Karnell saw the red lights suddenly leap away and vanish round a fresh bend in the road. It was again impossible for Karnell to see beyond the bend, which was lined with trees and undergrowth. She reduced speed and approached with great caution. Crawling round the bend she gazed stupefied ahead and in her state of shock pulled into the side of the road.

The road ahead was deserted. No red lights. No traffic at all. The Citroën had vanished into thin air.

10

Henderson himself was in command of the dinghy crossing the calm sea under the moonlight to the remote beach where *Firestorm* had seen the flash of Louise Hamilton's headlights from the Citroën. Two other men were aboard and all three were armed with sub-machine guns and hand grenades.

Louise's manoeuvre for losing the Porsche seemed to have worked – for a time. That depended on the determination and ingenuity of the other driver. Everything had hinged on conditioning the Porsche's driver to approaching bends with great caution and *at low speed*. On the third occasion Louise had accelerated as she came up to the bend, swung round the curve, saw the road immediately ahead clear to the next bend and had rammed her foot through the floor. As she roared through the dark she counted the right-hand turnings which were little more than tracks.

Approaching the third, she checked again in her mirror, saw no sign of headlights coming up behind her, slowed and veered sharply off the highway down a tree-lined track which crunched under her wheels. She kept up the maximum possible speed until she had turned a sharp bend in the track, out of sight of the highway. Now she only hoped to God she had chosen the track which led to the remote beach and the sea where *Firestorm* was waiting for her. Five minutes later, standing by the Citroën and watching the incoming outboard, she knew she had chosen well.

Stealthy footsteps in the night – behind her and coming down the track. Above the mutter of the outboard Louise was sure she had heard the hard crunch of slow-moving footsteps, the steps of someone who is careful where they place their feet – but is forced by the thick undergrowth on both sides of the track to make their way along the gravel.

She looked out to sea again and saw the outboard already

cutting its motor. Henderson climbed out over the side. Another man disembarked, took hold of the side of the craft and held it in the shallows ready for swift departure. Louise moved along the water's edge towards the Scot who ran to meet her, crouched low and grasping a sub-machine gun in both hands.

"Anything wrong?" were his first words. As he spoke his eyes were scanning the woods and the entrance to the track.

"I thought I heard footsteps – I must be jittery."

"Anyone follow you from Elsinore?"

"One person – in a Porsche."

"Get into the outboard. Tell Adams to start it up."

Stealthy footsteps. Henderson distinctly heard them before the outboard flared into power. The crunch of footsteps on gravel as someone came closer to the parked Citroën. He ran back, keeping a low profile, giving the order as he scrambled aboard in his half-length rubber boots.

"Masks on. Assume we're observed."

Louise looked back briefly to the hired Citroën which looked sad and abandoned on the lonely beach. But she would be returning soon: to pick up that car and drive back to Elsinore.

Sonia Karnell was irked by the crunching sound of the gravel as she moved forward with her gun held out before her. She could normally move as silently as a cat – but confined to the gravel track she made a noise.

But the fact that the track had been made up of pebbles had been of enormous help. When she had lost the girl in the Citroën, Sonia Karnell's stupefaction had been quickly over-taken by the realisation she had been tricked.

There was a series of turnings off to the right – towards the nearby sea. The problem had been to locate which track the bitch had used. Karnell was convinced she had not driven much further along the highway – since she could see too far for the Citroën to have vanished to the north. No, it had been swallowed up by one of the tracks cut through the woods to the sea. The only question: which track?

Crawling along, losing valuable time, but knowing she had to proceed in a systematic manner, the Swedish girl stopped at the entrance to each track, got out of the car and examined it with her torch. At the third track she found skidmarks where a car had turned sharply off the highway. She followed her torchbeam only a few yards checking the very clear indentations of a car's tyres. When she returned to the Porsche she even saw stones and dirt scattered over the highway.

She drove the Porsche down the track far enough to conceal it from the highway. The last thing she needed at this stage was a Danish patrol-car – and the discovery of the bomb, which would be rather difficult to explain. Then she crunched her way cautiously down towards the beach, her Walther at the ready.

"Oh, I should have bloody known!"

Through the gap in the trees at the end of the track she saw what was responsible for the sudden burst of engine sound – an outboard rapidly growing smaller as it headed for the tip of a headland to the north. Whipping a pair of night glasses from her shoulder-bag, she focused them with expert fingers.

"You clever Telescope bastards! Bastards!"

In the twin lenses the four people crouched in the dinghy came up clearly, but they were all wearing Balaclava helmets which concealed their features. Even with the field glasses, only the eyes showed through slits in the woollen helmets.

There was no vessel in sight they could be making for. What she did not know was that immediately after the outboard had been winched over the side in response to the flash of Louise's headlights, Captain Buckminster – on Henderson's orders – had withdrawn *Firestorm* out of sight behind the tip of the headland.

"Just in case Louise has been followed," Henderson had observed to the ex-naval captain, "I suggest you pull north behind the headland when we head for the shore."

"Then you lack my support," Buckminster had objected.

"At this stage I think it may be more important to conceal from the Syndicate our main and most deadly weapon – *Firestorm*."

And so Sonia Karnell was left swearing on the foreshore as the dinghy disappeared. She vented her fury by taking great care over her actions during the next few minutes.

She would have taken great care in any case: you do not fool about with bombs. The extra care she took was to plant the device underneath the Citroën without leaving any clue to its existence. Once the job was complete, she wriggled herself from under the car and shoved the torch back inside her pocket. She had activated all the systems and she walked round the vehicle before leaving it, to make sure there were no tell-tale traces.

The bomb was controlled by a trembler. If the Citroën were driven at reasonable speed and had to pull up sharply for any reason: *Bang!* If the Citroën were taken up or down an incline at an angle exceeding twenty degrees, no matter how slowly: *Bang!* Before leaving the booby-trapped car she took one last look out to sea where Louise Hamilton had vanished on the outboard.

"Don't forget to come back for your car, darling. I just wish I could be here."

On the sidewalk outside the Royal Hotel two men stood studying a street map of Copenhagen. It was 8.30, a glorious morning on the following day, the sun shining brilliantly out of a clear blue sky with a salty breeze in the air.

Rush hour had begun, streets were crowded with traffic, sidewalks crowded with pedestrians, and the two men merged with the background. They were patient men and they had stood in different positions for over an hour – but each position always gave them a clear view of the main exit from the Royal Hotel.

An observer could have concluded that they were used to working together: they rarely exchanged a word. One man was dressed like an American. His companion carried a brief-case.

On the same morning Dr Henri Goldschmidt of Bruges arrived in Copenhagen aboard a flight from Brussels. A car was waiting for him and the chauffeur transported him to the Hotel d'Angleterre.

He always stayed at the Angleterre when he visited the Danish capital and the manager was waiting to greet his distinguished guest and accompany him to his suite. After seeing that he was satisfied, the manager informed the reception desk that the normal instructions applied: in case of enquiry from the outside world Dr Goldschmidt was not staying at the hotel.

Up in his suite, the coin dealer was well aware that Jules Beaurain and Louise Hamilton were in the same city. Immediately the couple had left his house in Bruges he had summoned Fritz Dewulf, the Fleming who had operated the camera in the house facing No. 285 Hoogste van Brugge.

"Fritz," he had said, "I want you to proceed immediately to Brussels Airport and take up residence, so to speak."

"Who am I waiting for?"

"Jules Beaurain and, possibly, Louise Hamilton. You can obtain their photos from our files."

Among the most important tools of his trade, The Fixer counted his very considerable collection of photographs, many of people who believed no photographs of them existed. Armed with the prints, Dewulf departed for Brussels Airport.

He had to wait for many hours, snatching bites at the buffet, and by evening his eyes were prickling from the strain of checking people's faces. Then he saw both of them – Beaurain and Louise boarding a flight for Copenhagen.

"Copenhagen?" Goldschmidt repeated when Dewulf phoned him. "It really is a beautiful city. I think it is time I visited it again."

Jules Beaurain ordered a large breakfast for two and then called Max Kellerman to his bedroom. The sun shone in through the wide picture windows high above the city as they wolfed down the food and consumed cup after cup of steaming coffee. The Tivoli Gardens seemed to be almost below them, although several streets away.

"I've talked to Monique," Beaurain had informed Kellerman when he arrived, "and she confirmed that Henderson radioed her from *Firestorm*. Louise was picked up and taken aboard. They are landing her again later this morning after I have contacted them again. First, we see Superintendent Bodel Marker at police H.Q."

"I don't see the connection," Kellerman said through a mouthful of bacon and eggs.

"I can't decide whether Louise should wait for us in Elsinore or drive all the way to Copenhagen and link up with us here. Elsinore could be a diversion, something to distract us from the real action elsewhere."

"I don't see it," said Kellerman. "Louise said when she

called us last night that she had followed the girl we saw at the reception counter downstairs. She also mentioned a passenger who could well be Dr Benny Horn, the Dane your friend Goldschmidt named as one of the three men controlling the Syndicate. They're enough to go after, surely."

Beaurain wiped his mouth with a napkin, dropped it on the trolley and went over to stare out across the city. "The van, Max. The van which prominently carries the legend *Helsingør* – and nothing else on the outside. It's too obvious – like a finger pointing us. In the wrong direction."

"Louise did follow it to Elsinore, though."

"Yes, I suppose so. Now, time for us to keep our appointment with my old friend Bodel Marker at police headquarters."

"I thought he was in Intelligence," said Kellerman as he swallowed the rest of his coffee.

"Deliberate camouflage. There he has plenty of protection. No-one is going to notice him coming and going. And he has his own set-up, including his own system of communications."

The phone rang just before they left. It was the American CIA man, who had arrived in Stockholm. His conversation with Beaurain was short.

"Jules, I still can't track down Norling. I'm convinced he's not in Stockholm, but he's expected. I don't think Viktor Rashkin is here either. I gather from certain sources I've screwed the hell out of, that both are expected soon."

"Something wrong, Ed?"

"A funny atmosphere in this city. Noticed it as soon as I began looking up old contacts. Don't think I've gone over the top, but the atmosphere smells of naked and total fear as soon as the Stockholm Syndicate is mentioned. And I've had a weird warning from a Swede I've known for years and whose life I once saved. Oh, I don't know."

"Go on, Ed," Beaurain said quietly, gripping the receiver tightly.

"I was told a signal had been sent naming me. The word *Zenith* was mentioned. Does it mean anything?"

"It means you're on the Syndicate's list. It means you'll be spied upon and your every move reported. It means you're in grave danger. Ed, you need to be armed. There's a place in Stockholm where you can buy ... "

126

"Teach your grandmother to suck eggs," Cottel said quickly. "What the hell is this *Zenith* thing? People make it sound like I have the plague."

"That's how you'll be treated unless you use every ounce of clout when you want something from the authorities. I'm about to find out whether there's a *Zenith* signal out for me in Copenhagen. So, from now on, trust no-one. And the higher you go the more dangerous it could get."

"Great. Just great. Anything else before you tell me to have a nice day?" enquired Cottel.

"Yes. Any idea where the *Zenith* signal originated?"

"Washington, D.C."

There was a glazed look in Beaurain's eyes as he replaced the receiver. A thought occurred to him. Kellerman was gazing out of the window down the street where crowds of cyclists had joined the cars, and the pedestrians were hurrying along the sidewalks. In Denmark people seemed anxious to get to work. Beaurain picked up the receiver again and was put through to Monique in Brussels almost immediately.

"Monique. Check something for me, please. Contact Goldschmidt in Bruges and ask him whether he knows if Dr Otto Berlin has been seen there – or in Brussels, for that matter – since Louise and I were last there. Call you back later."

He put on his jacket and turned to Kellerman. "We'll leave the second car I hired in the parking lot and walk out the main entrance. It's only a few minutes on foot and I could do with the exercise."

The front entrance to the Royal Hotel debouches onto a side street. Leaving by this entrance, Beaurain and Kellerman turned right and began walking towards the main street leading to the nearby Radhuspladsen, the main square in the centre of Copenhagen. On the opposite side of the street from the Royal Hotel which rises into the sky on a corner site, is the main railway station. The station building stands back a short distance from the street and in front is a large well about thirty feet deep through which the rail tracks pass.

It was this curious local layout Kellerman had been studying as he looked out of the bedroom window while the Belgian had been phoning. Reaching the street, they paused at a pedestrian crossing.

"We cross over here," Beaurain explained. "Go down that street over there and the police headquarters complex is ten minutes walk, if that. What's wong, Max?"

The lights were still against them. Other pedestrians were waiting for the lights to change. Kellerman had his hand in his jacket pocket and now his face was tense. Beaurain followed his gaze and saw only the crowd waiting on the other side of the crossing.

"Two men," Kellerman said. "One with a brief-case which contains the weapon. Wasn't that how a little boy described the men who murdered the bargee, Frans Darras, and his wife Rosa?"

Gunther Baum had come to the conclusion that both the Belgian, Beaurain, and the German, Kellerman, were professionals. Their maximum alertness would be when they were in deserted alleys, lonely country lanes – conversely their minimum alertness would be in a crowded street at rush hour first thing in the morning after a good breakfast with the sun shining down and the promise of another glorious day opening out before them ...

Baum was an exceptional psychologist – but he had not grasped that in confronting Telescope he was dealing with exceptional men. He would have been appalled to know that his fellow-countryman had already observed a false note in the manner of the two men constantly studying the large street plan of Copenhagen. The oddity in their stance he had seen from the tenth floor bedroom of the Royal Hotel. At the time, waiting for Beaurain to complete his phone call, Kellerman merely noted the position of the couple.

One with a brief-case which contains the weapon ...

The lights had changed, the pedestrians were swarming over the crossing. Beaurain and Kellerman were caught up in the swirl. Beaurain grasped who Kellerman meant at once and scanned the oncoming crowd. *Zenith!* Desperately Beaurain went on scanning faces, with Kellerman a step or two ahead as though he had some urgent purpose. Beaurain did not distract the German in any way. He had learned to give his trained gunners their heads in an emergency situation. He had almost reached the sidewalk, the crowd had thinned out, when he saw ...

One man of medium height and build dressed in a suit of American cut, wearing a straw hat – apt in this weather – and dark, shell-shaped glasses. He already had his hand inside the brief-case his companion held towards him. They had emerged from behind the map, which was mounted on two high wooden posts with an open gap below. It was through this gap that Kellerman had first noticed the two pairs of legs, had remembered the odd couple he had seen from the tenth floor. The German had watched and seen them come into view seconds before he began to move over the crossing. He'd just had time to make his remark to Beaurain.

As always, Baum had timed his move perfectly; he had been known to plan executions with a stop-watch. Appear from behind the street plan just as the lights changed. Be ready for the targets as they stepped onto the sidewalk. Two shots with the silenced Luger in the confusion of the morning traffic and minutes could pass before people realised what had happened.

Beaurain was not armed. He knew Kellerman was not carrying a gun. He saw Baum, who wore thin brown gloves, withdraw his right hand from the brief-case gripping the butt of a silenced Luger. Baum and his companion were about thirty feet away from their twin targets.

Kellerman was still several paces ahead, striding forward now the crowd had cleared out of his way. His long legs covered the ground at astonishing speed, although he did not appear to be hurrying. And he was striding straight towards Baum, who was taking aim with his left arm extended at right angles to act as a perch for the weapon. Max was going to be shot down in cold blood and there was nothing Beaurain could do to save him.

Suddenly Kellerman's right hand whipped out of his pocket holding the knife he had been nursing. In a blur of movement Beaurain saw Kellerman hoist his arm backwards then the knife was sailing through the air with the thrust of all the German's considerable strength behind it. The missile struck Baum's right shoulder, jerked his elbow and arm upwards and caused him involuntarily to press the trigger. *Phut!*

A bull's-eye! The silenced bullet hit a street light suspended high over the crossing. Sprays of shattered glass fell on pedestrians and there were shouts of surprise and annoyance. Baum still held on to the Luger and snapped off one more shot. His bullet missed Kellerman by a mile and shattered the windscreen of a passing Volvo. The car swerved across the line of oncoming traffic and ended up inside the window of a jewellery shop. Then the screaming began in earnest.

Pulling the knife from his shoulder, Baum dropped the Luger inside the brief-case which his companion still held open and they turned and ran. Kellerman sprinted forward to stop them, crashed into a French tourist who appeared from nowhere and both men fell sprawling. Kellerman dispensed with apologies and was on his feet again as Beaurain reached him.

"Where have they gone?"

"Towards the railway station," Beaurain replied and they both ran – in time to see Baum and his companion, who still carried the brief-case, vanish inside the main entrance to the old station building. Behind them they left traffic blocked in both directions, several cars which had crashed together when the Volvo swerved across their lane, and a growing crowd of tourists and locals forming a mob of sightseers, none of whom had the slightest idea of what had happened.

"We can't miss that American bastard in that garb. Bloody great checks."

"So noticeable you never think he could be anything but normal. Now, watch it – you haven't got your knife now."

They walked casually into a large reception area with places to eat, bookstalls, banks of phone booths, rows of ticket counters. After a swift glance round, Beaurain headed straight for some steps which led down onto the platforms. The flight of steps was crowded with people.

"There they are, Max!"

"Let's get to hell after the bastards!"

"Too late."

The couple had just boarded a red train which started to move into the well-like area they had looked down on from the Royal Hotel. Kellerman was in a rage of frustration increased by the Belgian's outward coolness and resignation.

"Your friend, Bodel Marker, we're going to see. Call him, for God's sake, and get police to check that train."

"Let's see if that's practical, Max."

"How can we see?"

"By checking the timetable here."

Beaurain led the German to a series of wall timetables. He ran his eyes down one timetable after checking his watch and shook his head, pointing with his finger.

"They'll be getting off any second now. That's the train they boarded and it's a local. You can see for yourself where the next stop is – just the other side of the Royal Hotel. We'd never get there in time and I don't think we wish to talk to the local police after what happened back there in the street."

"And I think I can hear police sirens."

"So we walk quietly towards the exit," Beaurain suggested, "trying to look as though we've just arrived in Copenhagen. Someone may have seen us run in here."

And as they calmly walked out, the jackets they had removed during the short walk folded over their arms, two patrol cars screamed to a halt by the kerb and uniformed men went briskly inside.

Police headquarters in Copenhagen is known as Politigarden. A grim, triangular building constructed of grey cement, it faces a square called Polititorvet. Beaurain and Kellerman surveyed it from a distance before they went inside.

"Looks like a prison," Kellerman commented. "Most inviting."

"They're not in the holiday camp business," replied Beaurain.

"And I see they have a wireless mast on the roof."

"It's that wireless mast I'm counting on – on that and Superintendent Marker of the Intelligence Department. He sounded friendly enough on the phone – but he didn't know then what I was going to ask him."

They approached the five arched entrances beneath the flat-topped roof. A patrol car pulled in at the kerb as they were crossing the square and a uniformed policeman carrying a small package dashed inside, leaving his companion behind the wheel.

Beaurain led the way to a side-door which carried the legend *Kriminal Politiet*. He pushed open the door and entered an austere office where a policeman in shirt-sleeves

131

sat behind a desk.

"My identity ... Jules Beaurain ... Superintendent Bodel Marker ... "

He kept his voice low because there was another man in shirt-sleeves who had slipped into the room just ahead of them. The policeman behind the desk seemed to grasp the need for discretion.

"And the person with you?" he mouthed silently.

"My assistant – in charge of an undercover section. Marker will particularly wish to hear from him personally certain events he has witnessed. Name Foxbel."

There followed a brief conversation on the policeman's internal phone. Beaurain could not understand a word he said because he was speaking in Danish. The German nudged him in the back as the policeman stared at his desk. When Beaurain glanced round, Kellerman's eyes pinpointed the man who had entered the room before them: he was studying a notice on the wall. The policeman behind the desk finished his conversation, replaced the receiver and proceeded to fill in a form.

"He is waiting to see you," he informed Beaurain. The man who had been looking at the notice moved towards the door. Kellerman timed it perfectly. One foot projected at the last moment, the man tripped and fell, half-saving himself by grabbing the edge of the policeman's desk.

"I will come back later. I have an urgent call of nature – something I ate this morning."

A small, weasel-faced man with a leathery complexion and the agility of a monkey. Before anyone could react he had left the office. Kellerman heaved open the door and ran into Polititorvet. He was in time to see the patrol-car which had just arrived driving away, but there was no sign of the weasel. The man had vanished. Kellerman glanced up the curving flight of steps which led to the various departments in the building. He met Beaurain coming out, holding the form.

"Disappeared into thin air, Jules. He couldn't have escaped over the square – I was out too quick. He must have gone up there."

Kellerman pointed up a spiral staircase of stone steps which disappeared round a bend. From previous visits to Politigarden Beaurain knew the staircase led to all the main police departments. He also knew that before you could enter any of the departments, there was a police checkpoint you had to pass. The only conclusion left was that the weasel-faced man was a member of one of the many departments. Beaurain explained this briefly.

"Then he must have an official position here. Has the Syndicate penetrated here too?" Kellerman speculated.

"Why do we have to suspect him?" asked Beaurain.

"Because I deliberately tripped him up, he never protested and his reaction was to get to hell out of that room as fast as his legs could carry him."

"You're quite right. Let's get up and see Marker."

Mounting the spiral, they reached the first floor. There *was* a barrier and a uniformed policeman behind the desk. The form was essential: it was checked carefully and then they were told to continue up to the second floor and turn right along the inner corridor until they reached Room 78.

"What is worrying you?" Kellerman asked quietly as they went on up the second spiral which, like the first, was entirely enclosed by a curving stone wall.

"The Syndicate knew we were coming," Beaurain said grimly. "Their organisation and thoroughness is incredible – we've never been up against anything like this before. In some ways the extent of their reach is frightening. The only answer is to go over onto the offensive and hurl them off balance."

Beaurain's reaction was characteristic. Kellerman was intrigued about the reasons for his comment.

"Why is the organisation and thoroughness incredible? Have I missed something?"

"First, as I've just said, they had a man waiting for us here. But we were never supposed to get here, Max. We were supposed to be dead – gunned down near the station by that couple with the brief-case. And that means the man downstairs was simply back-up – warned to keep a look-out purely on the off-chance that the assassination set-up misfired. Next point, how did they know we were on our way to see Marker? Only two possible answers – they have someone on the switchboard at the Royal Hotel or – worse still – they have someone on the central switchboard here at Politigarden. This bloody *Zenith* thing is encircling us with a stranglehold."

They had arrived at the second floor. Beaurain pushed open another heavy door and they found themselves out in the open air on a terrace-like corridor with a railing on the inner side. Kellerman thought it a curious arrangement: on the outside the building had been triangular in shape; now the centre was hollowed out into a huge circular courtyard entirely cut off from the outside world and open to the sky.

The courtyard, resembling the interior of an amphi-theatre, was eerily deserted. They turned to the right and along their right-hand side the wall of the building continued in a circular sweep with more heavy doors at intervals.

"Weird building," Kellerman remarked.

"Unique in my experience," Beaurain agreed.

"I'll be glad when we get off this bloody platform. Anyone could use us for target practice and we're both unarmed."

"Room 78. Relax, Max. You'll like Marker." Beaurain turned the door handle and walked into the large room beyond. Kellerman was behind him when they both glanced into the room next door through an open doorway at the single object on a large desk. *A knife*.

"Forty million Swedish kronor worth of heroin."

The man who had spoken the words and then paused was in his mid-fifties, a man of medium height and rounded stomach whose hair and eyebrows were grey and bushy. His pink complexion and his chubby cheeks, with the brilliant sparkle in his very blue eyes, suggested the keen walker or cyclist. Amiability radiated from him. This was Superinten-dent Bodel Marker, Chief of Intelligence and the man res-ponsible for some of the Copenhagen police force's greatest coups.

His guests, Beaurain and Kellerman, who had been introduced as 'Foxbel', were seated in comfortable chairs, smoking excellent cigars and drinking delicious coffee. Kellerman was forcing himself not to stare at the knife which still occupied the central position on Marker's desk, an ob-ject to which no-one had so far made any reference. The door to the outer office was closed and only the three men occupied the room.

"One of the largest consignments of heroin ever moved in this part of the world," Marker continued in his excellent English. "It is on the move now – at this very moment –

following the same route as always, I am informed."

"Would forty million Swedish kronors' worth of heroin fit inside a suitcase measuring roughly something like this?" Kellerman's nimble hands described in air roughly the dimensions of the case Louise had described the man who had travelled by van from Nyhavn to Elsinore as carrying. Marker looked at Beaurain before replying.

"He is my close associate and friend and I would trust him with my life, Bodel," Beaurain replied quietly.

"Just as you did this morning!"

"Bodel?" Beaurain managed to inject just the right note of enquiry into his voice.

"Yours, I believe, Mr Foxbel."

Marker lifted the knife, threw it across the desk so it fell over the edge and Kellerman was compelled to pick it up. He looked at the knife with a blank expression, gazed at the Dane, and then at Beaurain. Marker's amiability disappeared and his voice was thunderous.

"Less than one hour ago! Before you two arrive we enjoy peace and quiet and ... " He paused, his fist crashed on his desk. " ... I hear that within less than twenty-four hours of your landing we have a murder at Kastrup Airport!"

"Who was killed, Bodel?" asked Beaurain, quite unperturbed.

"George Land. Professional assassin according to Interpol. A big man. Carrying a British passport. He was found lying half-inside a telephone booth killed by his own favourite weapon – an umbrella with a built-in trigger mechanism which operated a knife." Marker leaned forward over his desk and stared hard at each of his visitors in turn, "Mr Foxbel ... that's right, isn't it? Did you see anything odd when you flew in?"

"No," Kellerman replied shortly.

"It's upset you – happening on your own doorstep," Beaurain said to the Dane sympathetically.

"There's more," Marker told him grimly. "Less than one hour ago – while you were on your way here from the Royal Hotel – two men were almost killed by a couple of professional assassins in the very centre of our beautiful Copenhagen, by God! How did the intended victims save themselves? One of them hurls this knife with great accuracy and destroys the gunman's aim."

"And the descriptions of the two potential victims fit us with remarkable closeness?" Beaurain suggested.

"We have your descriptions," Marker admitted. "And so far no-one can give us a clear description of the would-be murderers." He smiled broadly. "I'm glad you survived the attack." He picked up the knife Kellerman had put back on the desk and held it out. "This, I believe, is your property, Mr Foxbel."

"Take it," Beaurain said quickly. "I came here to ask what you know about a certain Dr Benny Horn who has a house on Nyhavn."

"Highly respected dealer in rare books," Marker said promptly. "The house on Nyhavn is both his shop and his home. He travels the world searching out rare volumes, so we are told. I think, Jules, you should be careful – if you are investigating the Stockholm Syndicate."

11

The conversation which followed was so horrifying that Beaurain could in later years repeat it word for word from memory.

"Why bring up the Stockholm Syndicate?" Beaurain asked.

"Because you mentioned Dr Benny Horn. Nothing can be proved, but I am convinced he is a member of the directorate which controls this evil organisation. So far they have tried to kill me twice," he added casually.

"What about your family?" Beaurain asked slowly, watching Marker for any flicker of expression.

"They threatened to gouge out the eyes of my wife and cut off the legs of my ten-year-old boy below the knees. I have sent them both out of the country to a destination I will not reveal even to you."

Beaurain was shaken. He had known Marker since he had become a superintendent and he knew the man had courage, but this was appalling. He stood up, lit a cigarette and fetched himself an ash-tray to give himself time to think.

"Who are 'they'?" he asked eventually.

"Voices on the phone – often a girl, for Christ's sake. She was the one who spelt out the details of what would happen to my family."

Beaurain looked towards the closed inter-communicating door. "It is safe to speak, I assume?"

"There has been an armed guard on the far side of that door ever since you both entered this room. At this moment I am wearing a bullet-proof vest which I put on before I leave my flat every morning. The new system employed by the Syndicate relies on secret intimidation of the most ferocious kind – take my own example."

"The threat must have been combined with some request?"

137

"Of course!" Marker looked savage. "Give me one of your cigarettes, for God's sake. Thank you." He paused a moment, studying the Belgian as though taking a major decision. Then he spoke with great vehemence. "I do not expect you to comment on my statement – but it is vital that Telescope smashes the Syndicate. No government agency I know of can or will – they are like tethered goats waiting for the tiger to strike."

Beaurain looked bemused. Marker sat on the edge of his desk close to the two men as though he needed the reassurance of their proximity. "No government agency at all?" Beaurain asked.

"This man fell ten storeys from a balcony one night." Marker took a small notebook from his pocket, scribbled a name on it, tore the sheet from the pad and gave it to Beaurain, concealing it from Kellerman. "For your eyes only," he said with a mirthless smile, "as the best spies are supposed to say. But this is for real, my friend."

Beaurain glanced at the name, refolded the piece of paper and handed it to Marker who thrust it inside his pocket. It was the name of one of the most well-known political leaders in Europe, who had dominated the Common Market before his 'accident'.

"How do you know that was the Syndicate?"

"Because when they threatened me they said he was going to die within seven days. Most people would have laughed, found it ludicrous. I took them seriously. I phoned my opposite number in the capital concerned. He thought I was mad. At least that's what he said."

"What does that mean?" Beaurain put in.

"I'll tell you in a minute." Marker continued vehemently: "I forced my way through on the phone to the man himself. I warned him to seek immediate protection. He thought I was mad. Forty-eight hours later they pushed him off the balcony and sent him ten storeys down to smash to a pulp on the concrete below. The bastards!" Marker's face was flushed and Beaurain had never known him display such emotion.

"The man he is referring to left behind a wife and several children," Beaurain informed Kellerman.

"Only an invisible organisation like Telescope can smash the Stockholm Syndicate," Marker said. It was the second time he had openly referred to Telescope.

"They rely on the threat alone?" Beaurain asked.

"The swine offered me a bloody fortune in cash if I co-operated. All the big drug runs from the Far East for Stockholm come through here. I would turn my back on that – just for one example."

"What is 'the same route as always', which I believe is the phrase you used earlier," Kellerman enquired, "in connection with the big consignment?"

"Amsterdam through to Copenhagen," Marker said promptly. "On from Copenhagen by train, across the ferry at Elsinore over the Øresund to Sweden. Then the last lap by the same train until it reaches its final destination – Stockholm. The train ferries at Elsinore are a damned nuisance. If they had to take it by scheduled air flight – or by car or truck – sooner or later we would get lucky in our searches. But you can't search a whole train – and whole trains cross from Elsinore on the giant ferries."

"Thank you," said Kellerman, and withdrew from the conversation.

"You said your opposite number you phoned about the danger to a statesman's life thought you were mad. *At least he said that*, you added. What did you mean?"

"I am perfectly sure he had already sold out to the Stockholm Syndicate." Marker stood up and paced slowly round his desk. "It is so easy, is it not? You take the large bribe, salt it away in a numbered bank account, and remove whatever horrible threat has been made against your wife, family, mistress or whoever. They offer you heaven or hell. Is it so surprising that many in countless different countries accepted the former and became part of the Stockholm Syndicate system – if only as informants? Cabinet ministers have made deals. Oh, yes, Mr Foxbel, do not disbelieve me – I have seen it in their eyes when certain subjects are raised."

"It's a kind of leprosy," Beaurain murmured. "It will have to be burned out with red-hot pokers."

"Do not underestimate them," Marker warned.

"Do something for me, please." Beaurain's manner had changed suddenly as he recovered from the shock of sensing that Marker had been close to despair. "Check back on Dr Benny Horn's background – where he came from, how he set up in that house on Nyhavn."

"I can tell you now. He was born in Elsinore – or just outside the port. He built up his business as a dealer in rare editions and two years ago moved to Copenhagen."

"I want more than that, Marker!" Beaurain was brusque. "I want men – a whole team – sent to Elsinore to inverview every person who ever knew him."

"He was something of a recluse – and travelling a lot in his profession."

"I want him *pinned down*! Like a butterfly in a collection! Do you have a photograph?"

"One – he is a difficult man to catch in the camera lens. The picture is not good – taken at a distance with a telephoto lens." Marker unlocked a steel filing cabinet, took out an envelope from which he extracted a photo. Beaurain glanced at it and then showed it to Kellerman who handed it back without comment.

"Show that picture to everyone who ever knew Horn in Elsinore. Find out whether – since he arrived in Copenhagen two years ago – he has ever spoken to or been seen by anyone who knew him when he lived in Elsinore. I just have a funny feeling about Benny Horn. I can call you here?" Beaurain queried.

"Better to call my apartment after eight in the evening. Here is the number. When you call say you are Krantz and give me the number of the phone you are using. Always use a payphone. Then wait for me to call from the payphone in my street."

Beaurain paused. *Zenith*. The terror was appalling and spread across a whole continent, the scale of the terror even greater than he had realised. How many men were there of the calibre of Bodel Marker? Men who would live alone in their own private fortress with their families sent maybe thousands of miles away for safety.

Power was being exploited quietly to enslave and manipulate whole nations. And the most horrible aspect of all – on the surface everyday life proceeded as though nothing abnormal were happening.

"Contact Henderson priority, Monique. Tell him Elsinore is the present objective. Within two hours I want the place flooded with his people searching for a man and a girl. Here are the descriptions."

Speaking from a street payphone near the Royal Hotel, Beaurain reproduced in a few words the vague impression of Dr Benny Horn obtained from the photograph Marker had shown him. The other description was more precise and was based on Kellerman's word picture of Black Helmet. The instruction to Jock Henderson was to find the couple quickly, mount a round-the-clock surveillance on them, but above all not to let them know they were being watched.

"Next request, Monique, please call Dr Henri Gold-schmidt of Bruges and ask him to provide urgently everything possible on the origins and background of Dr Otto Berlin. Then, on my behalf, using the code word Leuven, call Chief Inspector Willy Flamen of Homicide with the same request – everything he can dig up on where Otto Berlin came from, his whole history back to his childhood. OK? I'll call you back when I can. We're on the move so forget the Royal Hotel."

Leaving the phone booth, he joined Kellerman who had been strolling up and down outside as though waiting to make his own call. He relayed the gist of his conversation to the German as they hurried back to the hotel.

"She'll get through to Henderson immediately by radio aboard *Firestorm*."

"Which is still just north of Elsinore? It sounds as though you're launching an invasion of one of Denmark's key ports."

"Almost comes to that," Beaurain agreed briskly. All his previous irritation and frustration had vanished now that he was able to set the wheels of action in motion.

Two outboard-powered dinghies had reached the shore north of Elsinore where Louise had left the Citroën the previous night. In the lead boat were Louise, Henderson and two guards armed with sub-machine guns. In the second boat four men, equipped with the same weapons and various other devices, watched the car which stood parked in the same position Louise had left it, the headlamps pointing out to sea.

It was eleven o'clock on a beautiful morning, the sun shining out of a clear blue sky. It was already very warm and the reflection off the wavelets was a powerful glitter. Louise walked towards the Citroën, shoulder-bag over her arm, ignition key in her hand. Henderson followed close behind while two of the guards fanned out beyond towards the forest and the track with their weapons at the ready.

"You're driving straight into Elsinore to look for those two from Nyhavn?" Henderson asked as she reached the car door.

"Yes, Jock." She turned and he was very close to her. "But only after we have gone over the car with a fine-tooth comb for explosive devices."

"Why?"

"Because I was followed by a Porsche from Elsinore. Because I think sooner or later after checking several tracks the person in that Porsche would find this Citroën. Because since then they have had plenty of time to turn it into a death-trap."

"Top marks!" Jock turned to the men from the second boat who were grinning as they stood waiting and holding small toolkit bags. "Go ahead," he told them. "And for Christ's sake be careful."

Louise let Henderson lead her away by the arm a safe distance from the Citroën as the bomb squad started work, assembling its equipment rapidly, including a circular mirror on a long handle for looking under the car. Louise glanced at the Scot with an amused expression.

"You really thought I was going to get inside and start the engine! If not, why were you practically hugging me when we got there?"

"You damned near fooled me, that's why! The confident way you walked up with the key held in your hand. I admit it – I was ready to haul you back fast if you'd tried to use the key."

"Why not check with me earlier?"

"I never stop testing people's alertness – particularly on a major operation. I think the balloon is about to go up, and the process will start in Elsinore."

"You managed to avoid the railway police? You are sure that no-one saw you hide the consignment?" Dr Benny Horn asked as he polished his rimless glasses and hooked them on again over his ears.

He was talking to Sonia Karnell who had just returned to his room in his new Elsinore headquarters, the Hotel Skandia. Black Helmet was dressed like a man, and wore a white nautical cap. From a paper carrier bag she took out a railway-man's cap and threw it on the bed. She was dressed entirely in black.

"That damned thing gave me a headache – it's too tight. Do you think I'd be here if I hadn't evaded the railway police, for God's sake? As for the consignment, all the heroin is now packed inside the wagon containing packing material."

"No need to get upset, my dear," Horn replied mildly. "I was only ..."

"You were only sitting in this hotel room drinking coffee and generally relaxing while I risked a prison sentence of Christ knows how many years carting that suitcase round the railyard and secreting it aboard the right wagon. Here's the number."

She unzipped her breast pocket, took out a folded piece of paper and threw it at Horn. As she turned away he grasped her by the elbow, spun her round and threw her backwards onto the bed. Then Horn was on top of her, his eyes remote and devoid of all expression as he stared down at her like a specimen from his collection of rare editions which he suspected was a fake.

"You will never speak to me in that way again or I will arrange for a certain Gunther Baum to break your neck."

"Drive like hell to Elsinore. The main station. Use the siren to shove other traffic into the ditch!"

The uniformed policeman who drove Bodel Marker, Chief of Intelligence, dived behind the wheel of the car he had brought to the front of Politigarden. Marker had already settled himself in the back and his chubby face was still flushed with fury. Glancing in the rear-view mirror, the driver caught the expression in Marker's eyes, a look of sheer blue murder. He concentrated on getting out of Copenhagen and onto the motorway where he could make speed to Elsinore.

It had happened as soon as Marker had returned to his office. To his intense annoyance he found his superior had let himself into his private sanctum with the master key. Marker had walked round his desk, sat in his own chair and stared at the man waiting in the visitor's seat. Marker said not a word, forcing the other to take the initiative.

"Sorry to break in here, so to speak, Marker."

"Well, now you're here ..." A deliberate absence of *sir*.

"This huge consignment of heroin which it is rumoured is passing through here on its way to Sweden. You know what I'm talking about, Marker?"

"I will in a minute, I expect," retorted the normally amiable Intelligence chief.

"Forget you ever heard about it, Marker."

"I need that in writing. At once. I'll call my secretary."

"Hold on a moment." The thin man with the curled lips and supercilious manner held out a restraining hand. Marker's own hand was half-way towards the intercom which would summon his secretary. "This isn't something we want on record, if you understand me."

"I don't understand you. Where does this instruction emanate from? I want the original source."

"That is hardly your business, Marker." Sharply, an attempt to wrest the initiative back from his subordinate.

"Come to think of it, my secretary isn't necessary." Marker leaned back in his chair and smiled for the first time since he had entered his office, the soul of amiability. "You see when I sat down I automatically pressed the button which set in motion my cassette recorder."

"You!" Uncontrollable rage – or a shattering reaction of terror? Marker, despite the closeness with which he had watched his superior's reaction, could not decide which emotion was uppermost. Of one thing he was sure; it was a whole minute before his visitor could bring himself to speak. He pulled out a silk handkerchief from his breast pocket and openly mopped his forehead which was beaded with sweat.

"I cannot persuade you ..."

"To erase the tapes, to use a well-known phrase?" Marker completed for him. "On the contrary, my first action will be to hand the cassette to a certain person with instructions that – in the event of a third attempt on my life being successful – it will be handed immediately to a journalist working for the German publication, *Der Spiegel*. I doubt whether the Stockholm Syndicate yet controls that particular magazine," Marker added.

"I don't understand you, Marker. I must go now. As far as I am concerned this conversation never took place," he ended stiffly and left the office.

Within seven minutes Marker had also left the office and was on his way to the car he had summoned. No tape existed; no machine had been activated. But Marker would never forget the look on his superior's face when he had bluffed him that such was the case.

Arriving by train, all passengers alight at Elsinore unless aboard an international express bound for Sweden – because there the rail line ends. Its only extension is to the water's edge – across a road and up an elevated ramp inside the bowels of one of the giant train ferries which constantly ply back and forth across the Øresund.

In June the channel neck of the Øresund – at this narrowest point no more than four miles across to the Swedish port of Hälsingborg – is alive with the monster train and car ferries which have several different landing points round Elsinore harbour. On the morning Beaurain and Kellerman arrived in the Mercedes, the channel was enlivened further by yachts nimbly sailing and turning to keep out of the passage of the lumbering ferries.

Beaurain's 280E, without which he always felt lost, had been driven from Brussels to Copenhagen by the English driver, Albert, who always arrived at his destination in the nick of time. He reached the Royal Hotel fifteen minutes before Beaurain was due to depart for Elsinore. "Why Elsinore?" Albert had asked as he drank his third cup of tea supplied by room service in Beaurain's room. "Isn't that Hamlet's castle?"

"Because," Beaurain explained as he completed his packing, "one of the key Danish police chiefs we have just seen has confirmed a huge Syndicate consignment of heroin is passing along the usual route on its way to Stockholm. The route? Amsterdam to Copenhagen to Elsinore – where it crosses the water to Sweden."

"A vulnerable link in the chain," Albert observed between gulps of the dark tea, "that bit where it crosses water. Means it has to go on a boat, and where do they put the consignment aboard the train?"

"Albert has put his finger on the key factor as usual," Beaurain observed. He told the Englishman briefly about the suitcase Louise Hamilton had seen driven through the night to a house in Elsinore which backed onto the railway line.

Albert Brown, a small, wiry man of forty-two with a face permanently screwed up in an expression of concentration, was an ex-racing driver, a Londoner, and a man who never took anything at face value. He had joined Telescope when his wife had been killed brutally by a murderer released from Broadmoor lunatic asylum.

"So," he concluded after listening to Beaurain, "the Syndicate may still have to put this whopping great consignment aboard one of the international expresses crossing these straits to Sweden?"

"If the heroin really is in that suitcase," Beaurain pointed out.

"And if it is and we can locate it, we deal the Syndicate a good jab in the jugular."

"We do more than that," Beaurain said as he prepared to leave the room. "We create such havoc we'll provoke a major reaction against Telescope by the Syndicate – which is what I want. A head-on collision, as Goldschmidt phrased it. The aim is to wipe out this evil thing."

"We may be the only ones who can do it," Albert said soberly, so soberly that Beaurain stopped picking up his case and stared at him because he had never known Albert, normally chirpy, adopt such a grim tone. "I had a word with Monique before I started my mad dash here," Albert continued. "She gave me a message she said she'd sooner not trust to a telephone conversation. The chap who she spoke to was a Dr Goldschmidt from Bruges. Chap who controls the Syndicate answers to name of Hugo."

"Goldschmidt told me about Hugo – he's one of the three-man directorate running the Syndicate."

"That seems to be the point. I gathered Goldschmidt has only just come up with this piece of information – Monique said he seemed to be working like a beaver trying to dig up data for you. This Hugo – nobody has a clue as to who he is – may, according to Goldschmidt's latest information, not be one of the three-man directorate at all. He thinks there could be *a fourth man*."

With Beaurain behind the wheel, Kellerman by his side and Albert sleeping in the back, they overtook the police car

146

containing Bodel Marker on the motorway to Elsinore.

Marker had heard about Beaurain's 280E and the way he drove it in an emergency; half the police chiefs of Europe had heard about it. Nervous about a third attempt on his life, he looked back at Beaurain who waved to him through the windscreen. Astounded, the Danish Chief of Intelligence relaxed back in his seat.

"What's Marker doing on the same road as us?" Kellerman asked.

"Something must have occurred to him later after he went back to his office – or something happened. This way we get to Elsinore much earlier. Just sit back and relax."

It was the last attitude Kellerman felt like adopting. The police car containing Marker surged ahead, its siren screaming non-stop. Beaurain pressed his foot down and followed in the wake of Marker's vehicle, using it as a trail-blazer.

They passed traffic which had pulled into the slow lane on hearing the approaching siren. Marker's car sailed along the cleared highway, far exceeding the speed limit, and behind him sailed Beaurain's Mercedes, forming a convoy of two vehicles, and when Marker kept glancing back through his rear window Beaurain met the glances with an expression of imperturbable confidence.

Both vehicles arrived at the open space in front of the entrance to Elsinore's railway station with a screech of tyres as their drivers jammed on the brakes. Beaurain had just switched off his engine when Marker jumped out of the rear of his car and strode back to the Mercedes with a grim expression. The Belgian pressed the button which automatically lowered his window and smiled up at Marker.

"What the hell do you think you're doing?" Marker demanded. "I could have you booked for dangerous driving."

"Along with your own driver?"

"Dammit! This is an emergency."

"If it's the heroin, we may be able to help. Don't look behind you, Bodel. Not obviously, anyway. Standing at the entrance to the station is a dark-haired girl called Louise staring watching the ferry coming into the harbour. She's wearing blue and carrying a shoulder-bag. She might just know the present whereabouts of the heroin. Incidentally, while we're asking questions, what made you suddenly decide to take a lively interest in the beautiful old port of Elsinore?"

"Heroin," Marker replied tersely, his lips scarcely moving. He leant both elbows on the edge of the Mercedes window and glanced casually at Louise Hamilton who stood watching the bucket chain of giant ferries plying back and forth across the Øresund with brightly-coloured yachts like toys sailing between the giants. Sweden was a distant stretch of flat coast, a row of miniature oil storage tanks and a plume of smoke.

"Why Elsinore?" Beaurain asked as he lit a cigarette. Marker took the cigarette off him before he could put it in his own mouth. "Thought you'd given up," the Belgian continued, taking out a fresh cigarette.

The Dane's chubby face was thin-lipped with tension, his eyes icy and hard. He smoked the cigarette while he watched Louise Hamilton and scanned the dock area. A Volvo estate wagon pulled into the kerb a dozen yards behind the Mercedes and Beaurain watched it in his mirror. Marker seemed to be gazing in the opposite direction when he spoke:

"Man behind the wheel of that Volvo is Dr Benny Horn, rare book dealer with a shop on Nyhavn in Copenhagen. And, as I told you, he's possibly one of the three most powerful men today in the whole of western Europe. Why has he stopped behind you, I wonder? Sight of my police car or your Mercedes."

"Black Helmet!"

Kellerman said the words almost involuntarily. He had started watching in the wing mirror on his side and she was framed perfectly, the girl he had first seen talking to the receptionist at the Royal Hotel while he watched from the quick-service restaurant.

Black Helmet. Now the description fitted her beautifully and it occurred to Kellerman she looked as sexy as hell – her helmet of black hair cut close to the head without any covering, and wearing a pair of black slacks and a black windcheater. The same outfit as Louise Hamilton's; she even carried a shoulder-bag and only the colour of the outfits was different.

"What was that, Foxbel?" Marker asked quickly. "Black What? You know the lady?"

"We think she may be closely linked with Benny Horn,"

he told Marker. "We haven't seen them together but one of our people gave us descriptions of two people who drove north last night to Elsinore with a suitcase."

"Suitcase the size you described in my office?" Marker interjected.

"The very same. The descriptions of the two people fit Benny Horn and the girl passing the Volvo behind us."

"Horn signalled her to keep moving, not to stop by the Volvo," the Dane observed. Not once since the Volvo had pulled in behind them had Marker turned in that direction. He seemed to have eyes in the back of his head. And he was right, Kellerman thought: Black Helmet had been about to get into the Volvo when Horn had given her a warning signal – a brief movement of the hand – to keep moving.

Black Helmet had speeded up her pace, passing the parked Mercedes without a glance. Reaching the corner she was able to see the exit from the station, and noticed Louise Hamilton standing there. So, the girl she had followed in the early hours had returned to Elsinore. The obvious assumption was that she had used the booby-trapped Citroën. Louise Hamilton should have been dead. Black Helmet reacted instinctively, and walked rapidly across the front of the station as though on her way into the booking-hall. She swerved, changing direction suddenly, coming up silently behind the English girl.

Her right hand was now held motionless by her side, the hand stiff, the edge hard. Her intention was to brush against the English girl, move past her a few feet, swing round and scream, "Thief! You took my purse!" In the ensuing struggle one swift blow to the side of the neck would render her target unconscious.

What the hell is happening?" exclaimed Marker. He had seen the Volvo move away, gliding off so unexpectedly there was no time to stop it. Seconds later Black Helmet had swivelled towards the station and then changed direction to come up behind Beaurain's girl. Marker was thrown off-balance.

Everyone involved assumed Louise Hamilton was so intent on watching the arriving train ferry that she had not noticed Karnell, who moved with the speed of a cobra. They were wrong. At the very moment Karnell brushed against her side and turned to shout the word "Thief!", Louise

Hamilton spun on her heel. "I want you, you bitch!" she hissed. Her right leg snapped forward like a piston, the point of her shoe aimed at Karnell's kneecap. Had the blow fully connected the Swedish girl would never have been able to move once she collapsed on the ground. But Karnell saw the thrust of the shoe and started to spin her own body. The shoe tip cut the side of her leg but she was only hurt, not eliminated.

Staggering back towards the kerb, her right hand scrabbled inside her shoulder-bag for her gun. There was a burst of sound as a motor-bike revved its powerful engine. The machine had been parked close to the ferry point by the kerb, the man sitting on it dressed in helmet, goggles and leather jacket, apparently watching the frenetic activity in the Øresund. Now he sped across the road, over the rail tracks, and towards Karnell.

Louise tried to reach them, to topple the machine over sideways, but Karnell was seconds too fast. Despite her injury she made it to the edge of the sidewalk, swung one leg over the pillion seat of the waiting machine, and grabbed the rider round the waist as he surged off with a roar of power in the direction the Volvo had taken.

Beaurain did not even reach to turn on the ignition: he was watching Louise's reaction. She was staring in a fresh direction – towards the rail line where international expresses waited to move along the lines over the road, up the ramp and inside a ferry which would take them to Sweden.

"Bodel, I think they tried a diversion – at least that girl who got away on the motor-bike did. Her reaction was based on alarm – alarm at seeing a colleague of mine, whom she recognised, watching the ferry terminal. We don't go chasing after high-powered motor-bikes – that may well be just what they would like."

"Why?" Marker demanded irritably.

"Because," Beaurain said grimly, spacing out his words with great deliberation, "the attempt at a diversion suggests to me that what you're after is under your nose." He got out of the Mercedes and closed the door with a hard clunk.

"They would have guards, watchers," Marker protested.

"They had," Beaurain pointed out. "The big man himself was in the Volvo. His girl was about to patrol round the station. There was a third Syndicate member – the man on

150

the motor-bike. There will be more."

"I get the sensation that I'm already being watched," said Marker, his hands plunged deep inside his jacket pockets.

"You are – I have at least a dozen men within shooting distance of where we're walking now."

"I said earlier that Telescope was the only organisation capable of destroying the Stockholm Syndicate," Marker murmured in an undertone. They stopped as they reached Louise.

"Can I talk?" she asked, covering her mouth with a cupped hand as she lit one of her rare cigarettes. She wasn't even looking at them. Curious, Marker glanced quickly along the axis of her observation. All he could see were two large open-sided goods wagons. Behind them an engine was moving along the line to link up with them. A railwayman with a flag guided the engine-driver. It all seemed perfectly normal to Marker.

"This is it," said Louise, once Beaurain had confirmed that she could speak in front of Marker, who was still mystified. He glanced around more carefully, suddenly aware that the previously almost deserted area in front of the station had become populated. Several passengers had drifted out of the reception hall into the open. Tourists with knapsacks on their backs, two men holding fishing rods. At least Marker *thought* they were fishing rods.

Other men were now wandering across the road towards the ferry terminal. One of them, tall and sandy-haired, carrying a long sports bag, walked with a distinctly military carriage.

Crossing the road, he walked a short distance further on beyond the ferry terminal. Marker's eyes narrowed as he watched him put the bag down on the floor and raise a small compact object like a camera to his eyes while he scanned the harbour with the eagerness of a photographic buff always on the lookout for new subjects. It occurred to Marker that the camera could easily be a camouflaged walkie-talkie. Beaurain's face was expressionless as he also watched Jock Henderson take up the best strategic position for viewing the ferry terminal, its approaches, the railway station and the two wagons waiting to be put aboard the next ferry, which was entering the harbour and turning slightly to head for the landing. Everything so normal. The sun beating down,

151

radiating warmth out of a perfectly clear sky. The steady thump of the wheels of the engine approaching the two wagons it would push across the road and up inside the bowels of the ferry once the vessel had berthed and was ready for its new cargo.

"You said 'this is it'. I see nothing out of the ordinary," said Marker.

"You're not supposed to."

"The man with the flag guiding the engine," said Louise. "He's been waiting there for fifteen minutes. He kept looking towards that man on the motor-bike who picked up the girl."

Thunk! The slow-moving engine hit the rear of the two wagons and the railwayman dropped his flag to indicate contact. A shade late, Beaurain noted. The railwayman rolled up his flag. Behind them they could hear a massive gushing as the incoming train ferry displaced quantities of harbour water, the vessel's propellers already in reverse to slow her down and ensure a gentle contact with Danish soil. Customs officials and Immigration men holding brief-cases were moving restlessly in the vicinity of the landing point. All perfectly normal.

"Have you any men with you?" Beaurain asked suddenly.

"No," Marker admitted reluctantly. "I'm not supposed to be here, remember?" He glanced at Louise but she was staring in the direction of the shunting yards and apparently not listening. "I couldn't bring a team – that would have alerted my chief. So, if the Syndicate is here in strength . . ."

"We'll deal with them – and you'll vanish," Beaurain told him crisply. "Officially you were never here."

"I bloody well was – and am! You may need some official backing if it comes to a shoot-out. Where is the dope?"

"The first wagon full of packing materials," said Louise quietly. "Great sheets of it perched on end. That rail guard who flagged down the engine – before it arrived he was patrolling up and down beside the first wagon. During the night those two wagons were further down the track – behind the house I followed Horn to. Work it out for yourself."

"Packing materials?" Marker repeated.

"Ideal for cutting out a secret compartment to take the suitcase with the heroin. And I saw Horn carry just such a suitcase out of his house on Nyhavn only last night – if that was Horn behind the wheel of the Volvo."

"That was Horn," Marker agreed. "This suitcase ..."

"It was driven to Elsinore by that black-haired girl who tried to chop me."

They were running short of time. Already the train ferry from Sweden had stopped its engines, its ramp was being lowered to connect with the rail lines on the quay.

"She tried to chop me," Louise continued tersely, "because I was in the exact position to observe the heroin – for her to risk what she did I had to be in a most sensitive area." She lost patience as Marker looked unconvinced. "Dammit, do I have to draw you a picture? What the hell was Horn showing himself in this area for? Because it's his responsibility to see the consignment gets through. The money and effort they have invested in this load must be enormous. If we can take it away from them we'll have dealt them a savage blow."

"And possibly just before the first full meeting of the entire Syndicate is held," Beaurain murmured. Aloud he said, "So what do we do as the first step, Louise?"

"Scare the guts out of that railwayman with the flag," Louise replied instantly. "I'm convinced he knows where the heroin is hidden, that he's been guarding it until it's safely on its way to Sweden. And we may have only minutes to do it. Any suggestions, Max?" She looked at the German, who nodded and began to move.

Beaurain walked a few paces away and beckoned Louise over. They stopped and stared out at the regatta-like scene in the glittering Øresund.

"We are here in Elsinore for another reason – to meet our chief man in Stockholm, Peter Lindahl. For over a year his whole task has been to locate the head man behind the Stockholm Syndicate. Last night he phoned me at the Royal Hotel from somewhere between Stockholm and Hälsingborg. He has discovered the identity of Hugo."

"Why didn't he tell you on the phone?"

"You must be tired," Beaurain chided. "You think that Lindahl is going to trust a hotel switchboard? Our conversation was well wrapped up, but that's what he meant. He's driving now to Hälsingborg and he'll soon be coming over. He told me he has a car space reserved on *Delfin II* for its midday crossing."

"So within an hour we'll know the monster who is responsible for so much terror and cold-blooded killing."

12

"Bodel," Beaurain began genially, putting an arm round the Dane's shoulder, "you said that only Telescope had any chance of defeating the Stockholm Syndicate. I don't want you out of the way in some bar, just maybe standing over here by the kerb so you can help out if the local police arrive."

"I'll stay." Marker's chubby face was grim and hard as he remembered his superior invading his office back at Politigarden in Copenhagen, recalled how he had been told to drop this case, remembered what the Syndicate had threatened to do to his wife and son. "And I'm armed," he said.

"So are a lot of people round here," Beaurain assured him.

Startled, Marker looked round the whole area. Before wandering round the back of the station to where the wagons were waiting, Kellerman had made a brief hand signal to Henderson. *Give me back-up.* The Scot had again raised the camera-like walkie-talkie and had given the order.

"Cover Max, surround entire action area immediately."

Fascinated, Marker watched as some of the 'hikers' with packs on their backs drifted back inside the station. He guessed that there would be exits from inside the station into the shunting zone where Foxbel had disappeared. Other 'tourists' closed in round the front of the station between the ferry terminal and the shunting zone. Henderson himself picked up his sports bag and unzipped it. Now he could have his machine-gun in action in seconds. Henderson's main fear was that Syndicate men now concealed might appear in strength at any moment. Everything depended on Kellerman.

The Danish railwayman who had guided the engine with his flag was pacing up and down alongside the first wagon when

155

Kellerman appeared. The German realised immediately that the main problem was the engine-driver waiting in his cab to shunt the two wagons aboard the ferry. He was relieved to see two of Henderson's back-up men dressed like hikers appear from the main station beyond the engine. With a swift gesture to them he indicated the engine-driver and continued walking towards the man with the flag, who shouted something in Danish.

"Don't understand the language!" Kellerman called back in English. He was still walking towards him, smiling broadly. It was amazing how a smile threw people off balance, even if only for a few vital seconds. The rail guard spoke again, this time in English.

"You are on private property and must leave at once. Go back! Go back the way you came or I will call the security police!"

"Good idea. You call them. Now! Before these wagons move!"

The back-up team had moved with their accustomed speed. Already one had engaged the engine-driver in conversation while the second man disappeared behind the locomotive, then silently reappeared climbing up into the engine cab behind the driver whose attention was distracted. A hand holding a choloroform-soaked cloth was clasped over the driver's mouth; in less than thirty seconds he was unconscious on the floor of his cab.

"You will get out of this area now!" The thin-faced rail guard slipped his hand inside his jacket and Kellerman leapt forward two paces. His right hand closed over the Dane's wrist, dragging the hand out, a hand which held a pistol. "Danish State Railways issue?" the German enquired. As he spoke he twisted the wrist, broke it and the pistol fell to the ground. The guard's mouth opened to scream and the scream was stifled by Kellerman's other hand. The German was bending the Dane backwards and suddenly he kicked the man's feet from under him. The guard fell backwards and only Kellerman's grip saved him splitting his skull open on the rail. The German lowered him gently until his neck was resting on the rail. He tried to lift his head and something sharp pricked his throat, the tip of Kellerman's knife.

"Try shouting and I'll slit your throat," Kellerman hissed.

156

"The wagon . . ."

"Will move any moment now," Kellerman assured him. "It will neatly slice off your head like a guillotine. Straight across the neck, leaving your head between the tracks, the rest of your body on this side," he elaborated brutally.

"You wouldn't!"

"I would – and will. And if you lift your head to get it off the rail I'll stick you. Comes to the same thing, really, doesn't it? Where's the heroin?"

"What heroin?"

The words were cut off by the prick of Kellerman's knife against his throat. He lay sprawled with the pressure of the iron rail against the back of his neck, and when he looked to the left – the direction from which death would come – he saw the wheel's rim which was now assuming enormous dimensions in his mind.

"The heroin stashed for Sweden," Kellerman said wearily, "I really believe you're stupid enough not to tell me – in which case any second now: crunch!"

"They'll kill me if I speak."

"The Stockholm Syndicate?"

"For Jesus Christ's sake have mercy!"

"And let all that heroin flood the streets? I'd sooner behead you."

Despite the freezing of his emotions after the murder of his wife, Kellerman was impressed by the man's terror – terror of the Stockholm Syndicate even caught in this dreadful position. His gaunt face had almost aged since Kellerman had threatened him; there was the stench of the man's own sweat in the air, the sweat of fear which coursed down his face in rivulets and streamed over his neck, already dirty with rust from the rail. Still he didn't speak and the German was not sure what to do next. A bell began ringing, a steady ding-dong in slow time somewhere in the direction of the ferry terminal.

"The heroin . . . just above you . . . inside the second wadge . . . let me up, the train is moving!"

He jerked his head up violently, staring at the rim of the wheel to his left in gibbering terror. Kellerman withdrew the knife a second before the Dane could impale himself on its point. " . . . *the train is moving!*" Kellerman's reflex action was to grab the man's tie, swing his head to the side away from

157

the wheel and clear of the line. Then, streaming with his own sweat, he realised what had happened.

The steady tolling of the bell continued, warning approaching traffic that a train was on the way. But this train wouldn't be moving because the engine-driver had been knocked out with chloroform, a fact which for a terrible split second Kellerman had forgotten when the bell started its racket. It was no surprise that the Dane had fainted and was lying inert by the track. He heard a rush of feet and hoped they were the feet of friends.

"Did he talk?"

Henderson's voice. Kellerman, his face showing strain, looked up. To his right the two 'hikers' who had dealt with the engine-driver were quietly slipping away to the main station. Gunners disguised as tourists blocked off the approach from the ferry terminal.

"Stop the bell – the train isn't going," he said.

"The heroin?"

Marker's voice. A mixture of eagerness and anxiety. Kellerman used his sleeve to mop the sweat dripping off his forehead. He'd been shaken and he didn't mind admitting it. For a few seconds he'd had a vision of the head rolling free between the rails.

"We've got it," he told them, "if he told me the truth – and I think he did. I would have. In this wagon just above me – the second slat back – 'wadge' I think he called it."

He stood up and stiffened his legs to stop himself swaying. Only Louise saw him surreptitiously wipe the damp palms of his hands on his trousers. He winked at her and she smiled sympathetically. It was at the most unexpected moments that the terrible strain of their work hit them like a sledgehammer, often when they were least prepared for it.

It was being handled with typical Telescope efficiency. Henderson had gone quickly back up the track directing the gunners to form a defensive cordon. Beaurain had climbed up into the wagon with Marker and called down for the loan of Kellerman's knife which was handed up.

"The guard is in it up to his neck." He paused as the potentially unfortunate phrasing occurred to him, then continued, looking at Louise. "The engine-driver may be in it or he could be completely innocent. At the moment he's ..."

He made a gesture placing his hand over his mouth indicating he was out of action. Then, in the near distance, growing louder every second they heard the one sound Beaurain did not wish to hear, the sound of a patrol-car's siren screaming.

It was a potentially dangerous situation. Jumping down from the wagon, leaving Beaurain to wrestle with the compressed paper, Marker advanced to meet three uniformed policemen running down by the side of the wagon, waving his identification card in their faces and gesturing for them to get back. The chubby-faced Dane was magnificent in the emergency, talking non-stop in Danish, ushering the three men back towards the ferry terminal like a shepherd driving sheep.

"Get back out of this area! I have the whole place infiltrated with undercover men! Coming in here with your bloody siren wailing – you may have ruined an international operation planned for months! What the hell brought you here in the first place?"

"We received a message that there was terrorist activity in the region of this ferry terminal."

"And the caller gave you his name and address, of course?" Marker demanded with bitter sarcasm.

"Well ... no, sir," the driver of the car admitted as he continued backing away with his two companions. They had almost reached the road now. "It was the inspector on duty – said we had to get here as fast as we could – we were on patrol when he radioed us."

"*The inspector on duty!*" Sometimes a stray shot hit the bull's eye, Marker thought with a tingle of excitement. No such order would normally be transmitted by the station inspector. The Stockholm Syndicate was here in Elsinore, its corrupt fingers reaching into the local police station. Because of one thing Marker was certain: the patrol car had been sent to disperse and interfere with Telescope's search for the huge heroin haul.

"Have you ever received a direct order personally from the inspector before – over the radio?" he asked, sure that he was right in his incredible long shot.

"First time it's ever happened in my experience," the man told him, "and I've been driving a patrol car for five years. I said to my mate it was odd."

159

"I'm now going to tell you exactly what to do," Marker told the driver, his expression grim. "You will carry out my order to the letter or forget about any further career with the police. Wait in your vehicle. If you receive any further orders or questions from this inspector, tell him your car has broken down, that you have found nothing happening at the ferry terminal after a thorough search. And then, in a few minutes, you will drive me to your station." He looked back to where Beaurain was still inside the rail wagon and saw nothing. God he was taking a gamble!

"What is the name of this inspector?" he asked.

The man gave him a name and then the trio of policemen returned to their car. It now all depended on Beaurain finding the heroin. He made his way back to the wagon where the man he knew as Foxbel stood on guard with the girl. At the foot of the wagon he stared up at the Belgian whose head was just visible above a huge sheet of packing material.

"Get up here fast, Bodel," Beaurain called down.

"You haven't ... not already?" Marker began.

"I said get up here, for Christ's sake. The timing is everything."

It was so simple Marker was overwhelmed with a mixture of disbelief and relief. In the darkened confines of the rail wagon he stared at what Beaurain's torchbeam showed him. Then he was filled with sheer fury when he remembered that less than three hours earlier he had been ordered not to carry his investigations any further by one of the most powerful figures in the Danish police service.

Beaurain had used a nail file borrowed from Louise to pick the locks of the suitcase. Inside the case, which lay in a narrow defile between walls of the packing material, was a collection of transparent bags containing powder. The case was full, the haul enormous.

"Inside there? As simple as that?"

"As simple as that. I was careful not to break the seals."

The hole had been carefully hollowed out of the second wadge of packing material – just where the rail guard had told Kellerman he would find it. Propped against the wadge was the thick panel of the same material which slotted into grooves and was then held firmly in place with transparent sealing material.

"Simple but effective," Beaurain continued. "The sealing

material coincides with the labels designating its alleged destination. We have to take a very quick decision, Bodel, my friend. Only you and I and the two people standing guard outside this wagon yet know we *have* discovered the consignment."

"Which is on its way to Stockholm apparently. If we let it go through, can your people really watch it closely enough?"

"We'll need help from Harry Fondberg, head of Säpo in Stockholm."

Säpo was the Swedish secret police, a department which operated quite apart from the normal law-enforcement agencies. It was becoming stifling inside the wagon and there was a growing stench of something unpleasant like powerful glue. Beaurain assumed it was resin inside the material.

"Who contacts Fondberg – you or me?" Marker asked simply.

It took Beaurain a moment to grasp the significance of what Marker had said. Then he was carefully closing the suitcase, re-locking it and calling for Louise to come up inside the wagon so he could instruct her.

"I'd better not hear you for the next few minutes," Bodel said. "Then if anything goes wrong you'll know I didn't betray you – it has become a way of life you know – betrayal."

"You're actually leaving this enormous haul?" Louise asked when the Intelligence chief had gone. Having closed the case, the Belgian was easing it back inside its secret compartment, prior to replacing the panel and the self-adhering sealer he had taken so much trouble to preserve. "How do you know you can trust Marker?" she whispered.

"I don't – we have to gamble."

"He kept those policemen from the patrol-car away – perhaps it was to protect the consignment."

"So we don't tell him everything we plan. Now, relay all these instructions to Henderson as soon as you can." As he spoke he was continuing the delicate task of replacing the suitcase in its original hiding-place so there would be no signs it had been tampered with.

"Henderson must radio a signal to *Firestorm*. I want Anderson to use his Sikorsky to shadow the express hauling these two wagons all the way to Stockholm. He's to have two men on board he can land if necessary. Anderson is to be warned that the suitcase is likely to be dropped somewhere en route between here and Stockholm."

"And how's Anderson going to see all that in the dark?"

"Because it's likely to be some place out in the wilds, which means they'll need some kind of signal exchanged between the man inside the wagon and those waiting close to the track – a flare, the flashing lights of a parked car, something Anderson will be able to spot from the air."

"Anything else?"

"Plenty. Anderson must have a method of communication with Fondberg of Säpo. I'll phone Fondberg myself as soon as we get clear of this damned wagon. He has a radio outfit and we can send a second message to Anderson letting him know how to radio signals to Stockholm. There, I really don't think anyone could tell we had tampered with their secret compartment. What is it, Max?"

"A suggestion. I travel inside this wagon." Kellerman, who had been standing just below them and listening to the conversation, had shinned up to join them. "Plenty of places to hide," he said, looking round the gloomy interior, "and that way the consignment is under close Telescope observation. Henderson gave me this water bottle."

"One man alone? It could be dangerous," Beaurain commented dubiously.

"I never thought I'd joined a kindergarten," the German said drily.

"You're right," Beaurain murmured. "And this is something we don't let Marker know about," he said firmly.

"Weapon, Max?" Louise offered the pistol she had collected while on board *Firestorm*. Kellerman shook his head, pulled up his right trouser leg and showed them a knife sheathed inside his sock. "If I need something it has to be quiet, I suspect. What's the priority?" he asked Beaurain. "Risking letting the consignment go or trying to track the Syndicate at all cost?"

"The priority, Max," Beaurain said quietly, "is preserving your own life. You'll be working without back-up."

"Any more instructions for Henderson?" Louise asked.

"Find out the exact route of this train from the map inside the station – I think it's Hassleholm, Nassjö, Mjolby, Norr-

162

köping and then Stockholm. Transmit to Anderson not only route but also the timetable. And now we have one or two loose ends to tie up."

"But not Max."

Beaurain had turned to wish the German good luck but already he had vanished into the cavernous depths of the wagon without a trace. How he was going to stick the stench of resin Beaurain couldn't imagine. He leapt down to the ground beside the track. Marker was returning from the patrol-car which was still parked in the distance close to the ferry terminal.

"Everything is organised?" the Dane enquired.

"Your heroin is still aboard."

The ding-dong of the bell warning traffic to steer clear of the road crossing was continuing and the turn-round of the train ferries was very swift. He was asking a very great deal of Marker. Not twenty feet from where they stood was the biggest haul of heroin ever to pass through Denmark. If Marker confiscated it his stock in Copenhagen would rocket; it would solve any problems he might have in fighting his superior; it would quite likely end with his taking over from that same superior.

"We could lose it en route," Marker suggested tentatively, studying the Belgian's reaction closely.

"I have taken certain precautions."

"Which I don't want to know about."

"Which I have no intention of telling you about," Beaurain assured him.

"You think you have a good chance of getting away with it?"

"Providing you personally arrest and hold incommunicado for three days this rail guard and the driver. Can you hold them somewhere in Copenhagen – not here in Elsinore? And you'll need another driver."

"Certainly," Marker agreed with enthusiasm. "Those men in the patrol-car can help. They will handcuff both men and transport them to the police station. From there they will simply disappear for the required three days. You will let me know the ultimate destination of the heroin? I need as soon as possible an official report from Säpo chief Fondberg in Stockholm."

Beaurain and Louise were waiting in the Mercedes, watching the rail wagon being attached to the Stockholm Express. In a matter of minutes it would be aboard the ferry, en route for Hälsingborg – where the express would move on to Swedish soil and begin its journey towards distant Stockholm.

"Do you think Max is going to be all right?" Louise asked as she accepted a few puffs from Beaurain's cigarette. "That wagon looks very tightly sealed to me."

"It is a huge gamble," the Belgian admitted, "but it is our only definite link with the Stockholm Syndicate. Max has to follow whoever collects the heroin and see where it leads him. It may well even lead to Hugo himself – if Max is lucky."

"Is there no way to protect Max?"

"We are doing everything we can," Beaurain replied with a note of irritation. "I admit I'm worried that he is sealed up on his own in that wagon. And there is a chance that it will be handled by Horn in an uncharacteristic way. It was at Elsinore."

"I don't get your reasoning," she said, "because there was Syndicate surveillance at Elsinore, so what different way are you referring to?"

"Horn did not have a platoon of men to back up and watch over the transshipment. If he uses the same method – and it *is* the more effective method – he will use the minimum number of people to take the consignment off the express when the time comes. Maybe only one man. What he loses in strength of numbers he gains by reducing almost to zero the danger that anything will be seen. And it is the normal technique for handling large dope consignments. Few men, much organisation."

"What back-up does Max really have? I heard you talking to Jock Henderson before he drove back with his team."

Beaurain's face, unusually lined with fatigue, became grim as he checked his watch. "Every hour that passes, while Max is inside that wagon alone and nothing happens, increases his chances. Henderson is bringing men down by car from Stockholm to board the express at every stop. Anderson's Sikorsky will be watching the train from the air as far as he can. The point is both Harry Fondberg and I expect the consignment to be off-loaded from the express somewhere before it reaches Stockholm."

"But isn't Stockholm the objective? Won't the centre of the spider's web of the distribution system be there?"

"Yes. But international expresses arriving in the Swedish capital – especially those passing through Denmark – are carefully watched and checked by the Customs and Drug Squad people. Much easier to take off that suitcase at an intermediary stop and transport it the rest of the way by air or road."

Signal from Harry Fondberg, SÄPO, to all units in Southern Zone. Sikorsky helicopter hence designated as DRAGONFLY proceeding very roughly on axis Hälsingborg-Stockholm to be allowed free access and under no circumstances repeat no circumstances intercepted. Regular reports of progress of DRAGONFLY to be sent to this office for personal attention Fondberg and in grade one security code. Any attempt by outside agencies to interfere with progress of DRAGON-FLY to be reported personally and instantly to Fondberg. In case of emergency all SÄPO units will use all resources at their command to protect and preserve DRAGONFLY. Fondberg. SÄPO H.Q. Stockholm. 1640 hours.

The signal caused a sensation when received by local Säpo commanders in southern Sweden – which was roughly bisected by the rail route followed by the express carrying the consignment of heroin. Later, when shown a copy of the signal alerting the Säpo apparatus in the designated area, Beaurain considered it a typical Harry Fondberg ploy – clever, ingenious and misleading. It was what was omitted from the signal rather than what was included which was significant.

Chief Inspector Harry Fondberg of Säpo was one of the best friends Jules Beaurain had made during his years in the Brussels police force – and he personally knew every key police and security chief in western Europe, to say nothing of the counter-espionage people and his contacts inside the United States.

Fondberg was exactly forty years old. Undoubtedly he would have won the prize for the Most Unpopular Man of the Year had a poll been taken of leading Swedish politicians. In a country which prided itself on its tradition of neutrality in all things, Fondberg was the

165

least neutral of men.

"I am not dealing with gentlemen," he once said. "So my methods have to be adapted to my customers."

"Tell me no more," his Minister of Justice had replied. Before he left the Säpo chief's office he added, "But get results."

Now, at the very moment when Beaurain and Louise were expecting the imminent arrival from Stockholm of Peter Lindahl, Fondberg was starting his long wait inside his office. He was prepared to stay up all night until something developed. A methodical man, he faced a wall-map of southern Sweden which showed with a system of pins and string the exact course the train would follow – and, consequently, roughly the route the Sikorsky, *Dragonfly*, would take. The phone rang. It was Erik Lebert, his assistant.

"The American entered Gamla Stan again. Same address. Still no-one there. He watched for a while and then returned to his hotel. I'm speaking from the lobby. Will I continue surveillance?"

"Yes. You will be relieved later."

Fondberg replaced the receiver and squeezed his chin with his hand as he gazed into the distance, a typical gesture when concentrating. The carefully-worded message told him that Ed Cottel, the American CIA man had once more surveyed an apartment near St. Gertrud Church in Gamla Stan, the Old City on an island joined to the main part of Stockholm by a bridge near the Grand Hotel.

Cottel was trying to locate Dr Theodor Norling, antique book dealer and a member of the three-man directorate which controlled the ever-expanding criminal organisation, the Stockholm Syndicate.

"Washington on the line, sir," the operator informed Fondberg.

He was about to ask her to find out exactly who was calling, when it occurred to him that someone might have got round to informing him of Ed Cottel's arrival. He told the girl he would take the call and announced his identity when the connection was made.

"Joel Cody calling, Mr Fondberg. You know who I am?"

His caller was the President of the United States' closest aide! There was a trailing off at the end of the question. Was he supposed to stand to attention while he took the call, showing by his tone how flattered he was that such a man would use a few minutes of his precious time calling someone so far beneath him?

"What do you want, Cody?" Fondberg asked in a blank voice, using his other hand to switch on the recorder.

There was a brief pause, no doubt while Cody patted his dignity back into shape. He recovered quickly, keeping his tone of voice amiable and hail-fellow as though they had known each other for years. It was, in fact, the first time they had spoken to each other.

"First, I want to thank you sincerely for your truly whole-hearted co-operation with D.C., which is greatly appreci-ated. I may say that appreciation is also felt by the most eminent personages in the United States, if you follow me."

The stupid bastard meant the President. He used twenty words where five would do. There was an irritating trailing off at the end of every sentence, presumably to give Fondberg time to register due humility.

"Mr Cody, what is the precise purpose of your call?" asked Fondberg bluntly.

"We always like to maintain normal diplomatic cour-tesies, and in spite of what the press of certain countries says about our playing it close to the chest and not informing our Allies of what we are doing on their territory ..."

"Yes, Mr Cody?"

Fondberg could stand it no longer. With his free hand he opened the bottom drawer, took out a pack of cigarettes, fiddled one into his mouth and used the lighter also secreted in the drawer to get it going.

"We feel you ought to know in advance ..." The voice in Washington went hard. " ... and not after the event, that one of our people will shortly be visiting your country."

Fondberg knew something was wrong. He gave the con-versation his full attention, listening to every nuance in the words being spoken by the President's sidekick.

"The person to whom I'm referring is highly regarded by us, and we sure would appreciate it if you could extend to him all your normal facilities and co-operation. His name is Harvey Sholto and his sphere of activity is security."

"Which department?"

"Now, Mr Fondberg, I'm sure you have found that unfortunately the telephone is not, in the world we live in, the safe instrument we all wish that it might be. May I suggest that Harvey calls you up on arrival and arranges a mutually advantageous meeting, say at the American Embassy in Stockholm?"

"He can phone and make an appointment to see me here. Please let me have the flight number and E.T.A. of this Mr Sholto."

"All I can say is that he will be landing in Stockholm during the course of the next three days and I will pass on to him your message to call you as soon as he has settled in. Now, if you'll excuse me, Mr Fondberg, a certain light is flashing on my desk and I'm sure you'll understand when I say it's the one light I cannot ignore."

Fondberg thought for several minutes before he asked for an urgent call to be put through to the man he knew best at Interpol. While waiting for the call he alerted security at Arlanda Airport to be on the lookout for a passenger travelling on an American passport in the name of Harvey Sholto. When asked how quickly to activate the surveillance Fondberg replied, "At once." It was just like the Codys of this world to play it clever, to inform him only an hour or so before Sholto landed.

When the Interpol call came through he gave his contact the name Sholto, Harvey, and was promised any data before the day ended. Fondberg stared at the wall-map showing the progress of the express carrying the heroin consignment. He suddenly wondered if there could be a link between the train and the unsettling news about Harvey Sholto.

Harry Fondberg's Interpol contact phoned back from Paris at ten that night. The Swedish chief of Säpo was still waiting in his office, convinced that something was bound to happen, that it would happen soon and, pray to God, it would give him the lever he had been desperately searching for to break into the Stockholm Syndicate.

"Harvey Sholto," the Frenchman informed the Swede laconically, "is a highly-trained killer. The Americans give him an X-1 rating. It means I personally would not like to be in the sights of his high-powered rifle."

"If you have a description ... just a moment, I will take this down." Fondberg deliberately had not activated the

168

recording machine because it was understood that each would ask the other before any mechanical record was made. In this case Fondberg did not want any record existing which someone else might get hold of and play back. He scribbled down Sholto's description in a scrawl legible only to himself.

"There is more about this Sholto," the Frenchman continued. "Washington has used him for assassination in Vietnam, Africa and Central America, but we have not been able to discover that he is assigned to any particular agency. He carries very great influence in high places in Washington – which has helped him carry out his assassinations."

"Thank you," said Fondberg. He exchanged the normal pleasantries automatically, then replaced the receiver and cuddled his chin in his hand, gazing into the distance with a grim expression. It was always the same problem: too much was happening at once. But what worried Fondberg most of all was a question which kept hammering away at his brain.

Who was Harvey Sholto's new target?

13

"Send an immediate *Nadir* signal on the police inspector and the railway guard."

Nadir. Even more than *Zenith*, this signal caused sweating palms among the men who transmitted the message. They could not get out of their minds the thought that one day the Syndicate might send out a *Nadir* signal which included their own personal details. And once the word went out there was nowhere to flee to, nowhere safe from the octopus-like reach of Stockholm.

The order had been given by Benny Horn to Sonia Karnell as they sat side by side in a BMW saloon. They had changed cars within minutes of driving away from Elsinore station in the Volvo. It was a policy of Horn's never to stay inside the same vehicle for more than two hours. The BMW was parked by the waterfront in an area quite remote from the ferry terminal and the railway station. She walked across the plank linking the quay to a large fishing boat. For a vessel which could hardly be described as modern it carried some surprisingly up-to-date equipment.

The latest radar device was poised on the bridge, and concealed inside the cabin to which she was descending by a flight of wooden steps was a powerful transceiver. The manner of concealment behind a panel was very similar to the one which Frans Darras had used aboard his barge outside Bruges.

"You want something, lady? This is private property."

Arnold Barfred, the Danish owner of the vessel, deliberately spoke in a loud voice, using the English language, in case a passer-by was listening.

His eyes went blank as Sonia passed on the signal to him in a low voice and told him to hurry. "It is a *Nadir* signal. None of us wastes a minute transmitting a *Nadir*. We just wish to get rid of it – and forget it."

She didn't reply and hurried ashore. Behind her she heard the hatch cover close, sealing off entry into the cabin, the bolt snap home. Barfred was doing exactly what he said he would.

And in another way he had obeyed orders precisely. He had waited below deck for the car to arrive – so that just as the Darras' on their barge had never seen Dr Otto Berlin in Bruges, so Barfred had no idea of the appearance of Dr Benny Horn.

Sonia Karnell settled into the BMW and switched on the ignition, anxious to get away as soon as possible. Beside her Horn looked back at the fishing vessel, doubtless to make sure Barfred did not appear until after they had gone.

"We will just make sure that Beaurain's man from Stockholm is dealt with and then you can drive me back to Nyhavn. We will pick up a few things and fly straight to Stockholm."

"Lindahl? He is coming here?"

"Yes, my dear, he is coming to Elsinore and hopes to arrive here shortly. He is fleeing Sweden by fast car as though all the hounds of hell were behind him. What he doesn't know is that they are *in front* of him."

The huge motor ferry hardly moved in the gentle swell of the Øresund as it lay moored to the Swedish shore at Hälsingborg. A steady stream of cars bound for Elsinore drove up the ramp and vanished inside *Delfin II*'s open maw.

Aboard, the passengers were already taking up position on the upper deck which gave them a good view of Denmark only a short distance miles across the sea channel. Through a pair of high-powered glasses a Swedish tourist gazed at Kronborg Castle which rose up on the far shore, and children clung to the ship's rails.

It was difficult to imagine a more peaceful scene, an atmosphere more removed from violence. Dancing across the sparkling crests of the blue, sunlit waves were innumerable yachts, their coloured sails twinkling triangles flapping in the mid-channel breeze.

A grey Volvo disappeared inside the vast loading deck, and Beaurain's agent guided his vehicle to the position indicated by the ferry loader. Switching off the ignition, Lindahl sank back in his seat and automatically reached for a cigarette until he saw the *No Smoking* notice staring straight at him.

He didn't really mind. For the first time in days he could relax. Within minutes he would have left Sweden. In less than an hour he would be talking to Jules Beaurain in Elsinore.

Lindahl climbed out of his car, locked it carefully, made sure all the windows were closed, and then began to climb the staircases leading to the higher decks. Yes, thank God, it would soon all be over – once the deadly information he carried inside his memory was transmitted to Beaurain. He would be safe again.

Underneath the keel of the motor-ferry *Delfin II* Karl Woltz and his team of three frogmen worked swiftly and skilfully. They had left the large steam-launch, rocking at anchor a few hundred yards away from the ferry, ten minutes earlier. As Woltz had impressed on his three subordinates, "Timing is vital, the crossing is short and the action must occur shortly before landfall."

"Why then?" one man had asked.

"I don't know and I don't care!" Woltz had snarled impatiently. "All I know is we are being paid a small fortune."

Prior to slipping over the side of the steam-launch they had, as instructed, waited while *Delfin II* arrived from Elsinore, disgorged its human and wheeled cargo from Denmark, and started to take on board the cars and passengers waiting at Hälsingborg. Woltz himself had watched through field glasses, seeing only the driver of the blue Mercedes who, in his turn, was watching the cavalcade of vehicles crawling up the ramp inside *Delfin II*.

Woltz had no idea who this man was or what he was looking for. Nor would he recognise him again. The man standing by the Mercedes wore a light trench coat with the collar turned up and a soft hat pulled well down over his face. Then he gave the signal. Using a tightly-rolled newspaper like a baton, he rapped the bonnet of the car five times in an absent-minded manner. Woltz counted the rises and falls of the newspaper, then dropped his glasses, turning to the others waiting in the launch.

"We go! For God's sake handle the equipment carefully."

Woltz had no way of knowing – nor would he have been

interested – that the driver of the Mercedes had only given the go-ahead signal once he had seen Peter Lindahl drive his grey Volvo up the ramp and inside *Delfin II*.

"We want the entire ferry to sink within five minutes. There must be no survivors."

This chilling instruction had been given to Woltz inside an empty two-storey house outside the Swedish town of Malmö. The organisation of whoever he was dealing with had stimulated Woltz's sneaking admiration. They had even gone to the trouble of fixing up a field telephone inside the house. As previously instructed, he had answered the instrument in a downstairs room, knowing that the man speaking was above him on the first floor. And nothing in the world would have tempted Woltz to creep up the staircase.

"Why not sink her in the middle of the Øresund? Why wait until she is close to the Danish shore?" Woltz had objected.

"That is not your problem. Just do as we tell you. You will be watched, of course. If you wish to get the balance of the money instead of a bullet in the back of the neck, start doing things our way."

It had been eerie – the voice, the atmosphere inside the abandoned house. Woltz had been relieved to get out of the place. Now, hidden under the ferry's keel, watching his team through the perspex window of his face-mask, Woltz had no occasion to feel anything but professional satisfaction at a job well done.

Six explosive limpet mines were attached to various parts of *Delfin's* hull. "Do not forget that three of the mines must be attached under the car deck," the voice in the house near Malmö had told him. Underneath the blurry silhouette of *Delfin's* hull, Woltz was trying to concentrate on what he was doing rather than on the consequences of his act which would be swift and horrendous.

The limpet mines had magnetic clamps – so attaching them to the hull was a simple job. You held the mine in the correct position, pressed the switch and the magnetic feet sprang up and affixed themselves like suckers. The last thing was to wait until all six mines were attached like obscene metallic boils and then Woltz himself swam along beneath the hull, pausing at each mine to press another switch which activated the radio mechanism.

As soon as the last man was safely back aboard the steam launch Woltz ordered a crewman to send the signal – the signal confirming that the mines were in position, that the radio mechanisms had been activated, that it now only needed whoever was holding the control device to press a button and detonate all six mines.

The signal was a dipping of the Danish flag at the stern. Borrowing a pair of field glasses, Woltz focused them on the blue Saab which had appeared and was parked where the Mercedes had stationed itself earlier. To his disappointment, the driver behind the wheel wore a helmet and goggles.

Woltz had no way of knowing that he was looking in the wrong direction – that the Saab was simply being used to divert his attention from a very powerful white motor-cruiser behind him. This vessel was proceeding south – away from the car ferry – drifting with the tide at such a slow speed it was barely moving. On the bridge a bearded man wearing a nautical cap lowered the field glasses he had trained on Woltz's launch.

"That is the signal," he said.

"Now we know Lindahl is aboard – and that the *Delfin* is a floating bomb," replied Dr Benny Horn, who stood beside the captain.

Delfin II was two-thirds of the way across the Øresund. Three more ferries were on the move; two crossing to Sweden, the third approaching the ferry terminal outside the railway station at Elsinore.

Deep inside the bowels of the ferry Peter Lindahl was now sitting behind the wheel of his Volvo impatient to disembark. Lindahl, despite his relief at getting clear of Sweden, studied the other drivers carefully. No-one seemed to be taking any undue interest in him.

At the car ferry terminal Beaurain was watching a sleek white motor-cruiser drifting well south of the harbour. It was the drift which had first attracted his attention; you didn't normally just let a vessel like that float about. He handed the field glasses to Louise.

"Take a look at that white boat. There are two men on the

174

bridge. Look at them, too."

She adjusted the focus slightly and stared hard. Then she moved the glasses a fraction and Beaurain heard her intake of breath.

"What is it?"

"The second man – the one with the cap – looks like the man I saw climb into the van carrying the suitcase from the house on Nyhavn. He looks like Dr Benny Horn."

On the bridge of the motor-cruiser Horn was staring fixedly at the progress of the ferry carrying Peter Lindahl to Denmark. He was gauging its distance from the Danish shore.

"*Now!*"

The bearded captain holding the radio-control device pressed one button and at the same second opened up the throttle. Pocketing the device, he opened up the throttle more. The prow of the cruiser lifted like the snout of a shark and the vessel leapt across the waves. "You bloody fool, you'll draw attention to us," cursed Horn, but his words were blotted out by the roar of explosions.

As the bearded captain pressed the button the radio impulse it released travelled in a fraction of a second to the receivers built into each of the six limpet mines attached to the hull of *Delfin II*. Along with the multitude of other victims, Peter Lindahl heard nothing. Sitting on top of one of the mines, it had been instant oblivion.

"Oh, God, Jules!"

Louise grabbed his arm and put a hand over her mouth. The giant ferry had been blown to pieces. A battering shock wave carried the sea in a minor tidal wave into the harbour, sinking countless small moored vessels during its passage before it smashed against the harbour wall.

Louise was frozen with horror. She had the awful impression she could see pieces of cars – wheels and chassis – spinning among the vast cloud of black smoke spreading rapidly into the sky. She looked behind her and saw everyone else frozen like statues. The only movement was the approach of Bodel Marker's car. In the distance sirens were starting to scream, boats were starting to put out to sea.

"What in hell has happened out there?"

Beaurain was facing Marker, watching his expression

closely when he replied, his voice hard and clipped and, Louise noticed, very public school.

"The Syndicate has just blown up a car ferry. The number of casualties will be appalling. I doubt whether any man, woman or child aboard has survived. It will probably become known as 'The Elsinore Massacre' and it will hit the headlines of every newspaper in the world tomorrow. And all to eliminate one, just *one* man."

Louise knew that underneath the clipped, neutral manner was concealed a terrible, raging fury. Beaurain's eyes, always compelling, had an almost hypnotic quality as they watched Marker. The reaction of the Dane took her completely aback.

"And I thought I had bad news. The Syndicate has simply used the necessity for liquidating one of your own people – and for that person I express my sincere condolences – to stage another demonstration."

And now a breeze was wafting in from the sea – and the scene of the 'Massacre' – the faint whiff of petrol and something extremely unpleasant. Instinctively the trio walked a short distance away from the waterfront. Marker continued: "A demonstration of the immense power and *ruthlessness* of the Stockholm Syndicate. A demonstration which will yield them at least as much as the murder of the Chief Commissioner of the Common Market."

"If you're just saying that to ease the situation ... "

"No, old friend," Marker interjected firmly. "I am not trying to ease the pain that you feel for what you erroneously believe is your fault. I did not tell you earlier because I was still not sure of you – that is how insidious and undermining of trust the actions of the Syndicate make all those who are touched by it. But only this morning I received a phone call."

"From a girl?" Louise asked quietly.

"Yes, my dear, as before, from a girl. Again she warned me that sooner or later they would track down where I was hiding my wife and child, that they were already very close. That last bit was, of course, in the hope of scaring me into communicating with them in some way which would be detected by the Syndicate. She closed by saying a fresh demonstration of her organisation's power was imminent – that I would know what she was talking about when I read

176

about the disaster in the world's press tomorrow."

Beaurain thrust both hands into the pockets of his jacket, one of his characteristic stances when he was undergoing deep emotion. "And I presume other people in high places were also phoned the same message?"

"I know they were. Before Miss Hamilton and yourself arrived at my office I had just completed making a number of discreet calls."

"A white cabin-cruiser," Beaurain began in a blank monotone, "flying the Danish flag when last seen, moving at speed on a southerly course about a mile off the Danish shore in the direction of Copenhagen. We believe we saw Benny Horn aboard. It took off like a bat out of hell almost at the moment of the explosion."

"So," Marker replied, "by now he will have been put ashore at any of a dozen landing-stages along the coast where a waiting car will have picked him up – unless he has crossed the Sound to Sweden once out of sight of Elsinore. Still, I will put out an alert. Excuse me a moment."

Marker went over to his car parked nearby, took the microphone from inside and leant against the car while he radioed his report. The driver was staring at the crowds of people who had appeared from nowhere and were growing denser as they gazed seaward where futile rescue activity was going on.

"You think it was definitely Benny Horn?" Louise asked after a silence lasting several minutes.

"I think he was probably the instrument. Whether he was the prime mover is another question," he told her abruptly and turned to Marker who had now returned. "Bodel, when you arrived here you said you thought you had bad news – as though you were going to tell us something else before the ferry was blown up."

"It seemed horrific ... before this." Marker waved a resigned hand towards the debris out at sea as Beaurain watched him closely. "I told you I was going to have a word with the inspector who radioed that patrol car to go to the ferry terminal by the railway station. I found I was just too late. There had been an accident."

"What kind of accident?"

"He received a call purporting to come from his wife. After taking it he left the police station alone by car. They have just dragged the car out of the sea – the inspector was inside it. He was murdered. I know he was murdered because something has also happened to the two Danish railwaymen you asked me to keep out of circulation for three days. They never reached the police station."

"What happened?" asked Louise. She felt her hair standing on end. Beaurain continued to study his old associate as the Dane went on with his story.

"They were in the patrol-car with the policemen. On their way to the station they were flagged down by a man in front of a garage. A woman happened to be watching from about five hundred metres away – fortunately for her. The man who flagged down the car went inside the garage to fetch someone and then there was an almighty explosion. The car just disintegrated – rather like that . . . " Again the resigned hand made a gesture towards the sea.

In a deceptively detached tone, Beaurain said, "They are killing everyone who has knowledge of the heroin. First the inspector they bought – or intimidated. Then the two railwaymen, both of whom must have known the approximate location of the suitcase. That is the Syndicate's method of protecting its investment. Effective, you must admit."

"It's overkill."

"Face it, Marker – the Syndicate runs one of the most efficient killing machines known in history – and each death is exploited to terrorise the maximum number of people who can be of service to the Syndicate in the future. Someone has thought up a foolproof system. Louise and I must go now," he ended coldly.

"I will give you a lift to the railway station."

During the journey Beaurain only spoke once, seated in the back of the car with Louise. She was looking out to sea when he asked for a cigarette: bits of bodies were beginning to float through the harbour entrance and he didn't want her subjected to any more harrowing experiences. During the ride to the railway station Marker relapsed into a sombre silence, staring through the windscreen without seeing anything. Beaurain was relieved when the Dane told his driver to drop them a distance from the station and wait for him. The three of them walked slowly towards where it had all started – the exit from Elsinore railway station.

"It's such an attractive town," Louise said. "All the

houses old but freshly painted ... "

She ended in mid-sentence and Beaurain gave her elbow a reassuring hug. She had been going to add something like, "for such a ghastly horror to be perpetrated here." Beaurain noticed that both his companions studiously avoided looking to their left over the harbour to the sea beyond. There was also an unnaturally quiet atmosphere among the people walking about who *were* staring seaward. Probably a number of them were in the habit of crossing over to Sweden from time to time. Using the car-ferries.

"While at the police station I asked about the enquiries I made about Dr Benny Horn," Marker said in a dull voice. "About his background and history, what he was like when he lived here in Elsinore. I must say they had responded to my request quickly. And they had showed around the photo I had taken of Horn in Copenhagen – I sent that out by despatch rider before I left the city."

"And what did you find?"

"A few people who knew him when he lived here recognised the photo, others didn't."

"What proportion?" There was an eager alertness in Beaurain's voice and manner.

"Fifty-fifty. The normal proportion," Marker replied in the same dull tone. He was, Louise realised, still in a state of semi-shock, overwhelmed by the power and ruthlessness of the Stockholm Syndicate. "Horn lived the same sort of hermit-like existence in Elsinore that he does in Copenhagen," Marker continued. "He was unmarried, had no relatives and spent a lot of time away from the place travelling – presumably to sell and buy rare editions."

"How long had he lived in Elsinore?" Beaurain persisted.

"About twenty years. And he had his place a short distance outside the town in a very quiet area. That's all I could find out." He stopped suddenly on the sidewalk and turned to Beaurain, his brow crinkled in perplexity and frustration. "It doesn't make sense at all, does it?" he burst out.

"No, it doesn't."

"What doesn't? Am I being dim?" Louise enquired.

"No," Beaurain replied, "but I think Bodel means this. For at least twenty years we have a man leading an apparently respectable and sober existence. All right, he keeps himself to himself, a bit like Silas Marner. Then this same

179

man moves to Copenhagen – when would you say, Bodel?"

"About two years ago."

"He moves to Copenhagen two years ago," Beaurain went on, "and what happens – almost overnight? He becomes one of the three men we think control the Stockholm Syndicate."

"I see what you mean," Louise said slowly. "No, it doesn't make any sense."

They had reached the concourse in front of the station where they had left the 280E parked, and Marker forced himself to speak with false exuberance. "Well, what are you going to do now, Jules? Is there any way in which I can help you?"

"Drive back to Copenhagen after we've had lunch and think things over a bit. Thanks for your help and I know where to find you. I suppose you'll be staying on here for a while."

Beaurain nodded in the direction of where a fleet of rescue and police craft were beyond the harbour poking around among the rapidly dispersing wreckage. Marker said yes, he would be staying on in Elsinore, shook them both solemnly by the hand and walked away slowly back to where his car was waiting.

"What are we actually going to do?" Louise asked. "I know you didn't tell Marker the truth. And where are Henderson and his team of gunners?"

"Back on board *Firestorm* by now. I told him to leave once we had seen the ferry carrying the heroin depart. And Captain Buckminster has fresh instructions – to sail through the Øresund and wait at anchorage off Copenhagen. As for us, you are right, of course. I wasn't at all frank with Marker – and not because I don't trust him. But suppose the Syndicate did locate where he has hidden his family. How long do you think he would resist their pressure for information?"

"How long could you expect him to?" Louise shuddered and compelled herself to look out to sea where the flock of boats was milling round aimlessly. One large launch was trawling over the side what looked to Louise like a shallow net. "What is that thing, Jules? The boat with a loud-hailer keeping other craft away?"

"That will be Forensic. They will be gathering specimens of the debris for later analysis in the laboratory. That way they hope to discover what explosive was used."

"Let's get back to Copenhagen – and then?"

"Stockholm."

Beaurain paused as he took one last look at the confused armada beyond the harbour as if he wanted to imprint the scene on his memory. There was a set look to his expression; in some odd way he seemed to have grown younger rather than older, a youthfulness tinged with a merciless ferocity.

Beaurain made one more phone call before he left the Royal Hotel while Louise obtained flight reservations from the S.A.S. airline counter in the hall adjoining the ground floor of the hotel. The call was to Chief Inspector Willy Flamen of Homicide in Brussels.

As he expected, Flamen was ready with the information he needed; in a very short time he had thoroughly investigated the early history and background of Dr Otto Berlin, dealer in rare books.

Berlin came from Liège, one of Belgium's largest cities, where he had built up a small but apparently lucrative business as a dealer in rare stamps. Part of his success lay in the fact that, unlike some of his European competitors, he was willing to travel any distance to conclude a worthwhile deal.

"You did say *stamp* dealer, Willy," Beaurain queried. "He's in rare books now surely?"

"Quite correct. He switched from stamps to books immediately on his arrival in Bruges about two years ago."

Goldschmidt's photograph of Otto Berlin had been shown to the few people who had known Berlin in Liège. Flamen explained that Berlin was a bachelor, apparently totally absorbed in developing his business and with no close friends. Shown the photograph, the few people who had known him by sight had roughly divided into two sections – those who firmly said the picture was of Otto Berlin and those who said they didn't recognise it.

Flamen went on to explain that Otto Berlin had lived for about fifteen years in Liège before moving to Bruges. That was all Flamen had been able to come up with so far. There was an apologetic note in his voice but also, behind that, Beaurain thought he detected some other unspoken doubt. He tackled Flamen directly on the point.

The only other fact was something Flamen had obtained by phoning an acquaintance of Otto Berlin. Apparently Berlin had been excited just before he moved to Bruges, and he had conveyed this excitement over the phone without explaining the reason for it. And no, the man he had phoned had never seen Berlin again from that day to this.

Beaurain thanked Flamen, who then expressed the horror which was being felt all over the western world at 'The Elsinore Massacre'. The fact that there had been not a single survivor increased the dramatic impact, which TV stations and the radio everywhere were exploiting to the full. Louise returned, holding the folder with their air tickets, just as he replaced the receiver. He told her in a few words what Flamen had found.

"Nothing, then," Louise decided after listening to Beaurain's account of the call.

"You don't notice a pattern?" the Belgian queried.

"It's almost a replica of Benny Horn's early days in Elsinore. No close friends. No family. Not at home very often because they spent so much time travelling on business. Jules, it's almost as though these people never actually existed!"

"Exactly!" Beaurain paused. "But they did – do – exist. We have the evidence of two of the shrewdest police investigators in Europe – Marker here, Willy Flamen back in Brussels. In Liège one of these men, Otto Berlin, lived for fifteen years. In Elsinore there are people who confirm without a doubt that Dr Horn lived there for twenty years. Then they both suddenly change their addresses and pop up in Copenhagen and Bruges."

"And almost at the same time," Louise pointed out. "Both men apparently appeared in their new lives only two years ago. Is it significant that there's a break in the pattern? Willy Flamen said Berlin was a stamp dealer in Liège and then switched to rare books as soon as he appeared in Bruges."

"Possibly."

"Who do you think is behind this monster?" Louise asked as she perched on the bed to fix her nylons. "You have the feeling there is no-one you can confide in any more – in case he or she may be a member of the Syndicate, willingly or because they're under pressure."

"Which I suspect is also part of their technique. The terror spreads ever wider, sucking more and more key figures

182

in the West into its web. As to who is behind the monster, the answer appears to be Hugo, whoever he may be." He looked up and handed back the airline folder. "I'm convinced there's only one way to find out – to do what we're going to do. Fly to Stockholm and track down the location of the coming conference of the entire Syndicate. And we have Harry Fondberg of Säpo on our side, who may make all the difference."

"Can we trust him?" she asked.

He was careful to keep control of his expression: not to let her see that she had just asked what he considered could be a leading question with a sinister answer.

14

The express had been stationary for over an hour. Kellerman had no doubt that the wagon was standing in a siding at Stockholm Central: there had been shunting after the express had stopped and he'd heard the distant sound of passengers' feet clumping along a stone platform. So far no-one had come for the heroin.

Kellerman was cramped in every muscle, parched with thirst. Taking the cap off his water-bottle he swallowed a modest portion of the water still remaining, recapped the bottle and then froze. There was a strange hissing sound which he couldn't immediately identify. Then he smelt a faint aroma and saw a whitish cloud drifting from the crack between the doors. The bastards were filling the wagon with some kind of gas.

Hauling his handkerchief out of his pocket he uncapped the water-bottle again and soaked the handkerchief. He was already feeling dizzy when he clamped the damp cloth over his nostrils to minimise the effect of the gas. They couldn't *know* someone was inside: it was another example of the Syndicate's meticulous attention to detail, a precaution *in case* someone was inside waiting for them.

Everything began to blur. Wedged against sheets of compressed paper at the end of the wagon he was out of sight when they opened the doors and two men climbed inside wearing gas-masks. He could just make out the silhouette of the masks through a blurred haze and they looked hideous. Kellerman leaned against the wagon wall, incapable of any action except struggling to keep quiet.

There was a ripping sound and he guessed they were using a knife to open up the compartment secreting the suitcase of heroin. And not a damned thing he could do to stop them. At any second he knew that he might lose consciousness. If he did that he would fall down, make a noise. They would see to it that he never woke up again.

One of the men appeared briefly holding the suitcase, stood in the opening and tore off his gas-mask. Kellerman saw it all as though in a dream. The man with the heroin jumped out of the wagon, there was a brief lack of sound except for the muffled murmur of nearby traffic, then the vrooming roar of a powerful motor-bike's engine, which cut off suddenly, as though the machine had turned a corner. Kellerman eased the handkerchief away from his nostrils and found he could breathe. The gas had drifted out through the open doors. He began to feel better, able to cope, then he froze again as he realised something was not right. *The second man was still inside the wagon.*

Kellerman stuffed his handkerchief back in his pocket and began to ease his way forward down the narrow passageway between the walls of compressed sheet paper. The air was bearable, but the German was horribly aware he was making noises as he moved forward. His sleeve scraped against the sides of the paper – only a slight sound, but more than enough to alert the man still in the wagon, who would be a professional. Why the hell was he still waiting?

Kellerman found him crumpled in a heap at the edge of the open doors, a short, heavily-built man still wearing the gas-mask and with a reddish stain spreading ever more widely over the uniform jacket across his chest. What the uniform might be Kellerman was not sure – it looked like a policeman's – but he jerked off the gas-mask and looked into a plump face with the eyes open. A familiar face, for God's sake, the face of Serge Litov. And someone had used a gun with a silencer to shoot him, although he was still just alive.

"Heroin ... Norling ... traitor," were his dying words.

Passenger who landed Arlanda Airport Flight SK 407 from Copenhagen as per attached photo identified as Gunther Baum. Originates from East Germany. Poses as business executive but is independent professional assassin charging extortionate fees due to reputation for always completing assignment. Present whereabouts unknown.

Chief Inspector Harry Fondberg of Säpo studied the signal which had just arrived from Interpol. He was fuming about the incident at Stockholm Central – where someone disguised as a police despatch rider had seized the haul of heroin from under his nose and murdered his own accom-

185

plice as a bonus. Then the phone rang and he heard Jules Beaurain had arrived.

The Belgian was ushered into his office and shown to a chair. The Swede was studied by Beaurain as they shook hands: no outward sign of nerves here in Stockholm. And his host's appearance was exactly as the Belgian remembered him from their previous meeting.

Thinning hair was brushed over a well-shaped skull. He had the blue eyes of the Scandinavian which, in Fondberg's case, held a hypnotic quality. His nose was strong, his mouth firm and he had a jaw of character. The Chief of Säpo, who worked under a Director solely responsible to the Minister of Justice, showed his guest the signal from Interpol. Attached was a glossy print.

"That's a copy of the picture we radioed to them," Fondberg explained.

There were several people the photographer had caught in his lens and it was obvious they were completely unaware that their arrival was being recorded. Beaurain passed the photograph back to Fondberg.

"He tried to kill me in Copenhagen – in broad daylight close to the Tivoli Gardens. His accomplice is with him."

"Accomplice!" Fondberg grabbed the picture off the desk, glaring at it. "Those damned fools at Interpol never said anything – and we radioed the complete picture. It was taken at Arlanda. The accomplice is ... ?"

"The ordinary-looking man behind Gunther Baum's right shoulder. You can just see he is carrying a brief-case. That is where the gun would normally be – he is Baum's gun-carrier and, I suspect, only hands him the weapon at the last moment. Baum is extremely well-organised. When did he come in here?"

"On the first flight this morning from Copenhagen – what we call the businessman's flight. The distance is so short, many spend the day in Stockholm, conclude their business, and are back in Copenhagen for the night."

"Stockholm has more attractions than that, Harry."

Fondberg smiled. "Yes, indeed. But you see, the business-men's wives also know that. So, if they are not back in their cosy little Danish houses before midnight, chop!"

"How did you happen to take that picture?" Beaurain indicated the radio-transmitted photo of Baum and

186

his companion.

"As you know, we have men watching Arlanda all the time for known criminals. If the watcher on duty is keen, sometimes he takes a picture of a passenger who strikes him as not quite right. Baum's was taken for that reason, I sent it to Interpol, and you see their reply."

"You have his address?"

The Swede winced and lit a cigar before replying. "The shot was random, as I have explained. Since the signal came in I have had people checking at all the hotels, but it is too early for anything yet."

"You won't get anything anyway. He'll register with false papers wherever he stays. As you know, he is a top professional. So that is the man who has travelled here for the express purpose of killing me – or so you suspect?"

"I don't know," Fondberg replied blandly. "There are other potential candidates for the job. This man, for example."·

It was like the old days when they had co-operated together – with or without the agreement of their respective superiors. Beaurain stared at the glossy photo pushed across the desk at him. Again taken at an airport, doubtless Arlanda. An excellent print, this one, taken with a first-rate camera operated by a top-class photographer. The man was obviously totally unaware that his arrival had been recorded.

A big man, probably six feet one, broad-shouldered and with a large round head and cold eyes. Like Fondberg, the few streaks of thin hair were carefully brushed over the polished skull – but unlike Fondberg he was almost bald. Even caught unawares his demeanour was aggressive; the total lack of feeling in the blank eyes was reflected in the thin-lipped, tight mouth. The way he held himself told Beaurain that this man, in his early fifties, was in the peak of physical condition. He probably played an hour's squash before breakfast every morning – and his mood would be mean for the rest of the day if he didn't win.

"Who is the candidate and when did he get in and from where?" Beaurain enquired, his eyes still imprinting the man's features and general stance on his memory.

"American, of course. The dress tells you that. He is known as Harvey Sholto. He got in at Arlanda on the overnight flight from Washington. I was informed by no less a person than Joel Cody of his imminent arrival – person-to-person call. And the bastard tried to trick me."

"Cody? The President's aide? The man who thinks that *finesse* is a French pastry? And how did he *try* to trick you?"

"By officially informing me that Sholto would be coming here within the next few days, when he had already arrived in Stockholm. He didn't allow for the closeness with which we watch all incoming passengers at Arlanda. Sholto's appearance rang a bell in the mind of one of the watchers with a camera so he took his picture. The people who are checking hotel registers for Gunther Baum are also checking for Harvey Sholto, the second killer to arrive just ahead of you."

Fondberg added the final remark casually and puffed at his cigar while he gazed at the ceiling. It was the same game they had so often played in the past and was one of the many reasons Jules Beaurain liked Fondberg as much as any of the host of international colleagues he had come to know over the years.

"You're sure this is Harvey Sholto?" Beaurain queried, tapping the glossy print. "So he's a killer too."

"One of the deadliest. Our agent in Bangkok could have vouched for that. Except that he's dead now. He was very experienced and very good." Some of the toughness briefly evaporated from Fondberg's exterior. "He left a nice Swedish wife and three children. They found him floating in one of the *klongs* – canals. His throat had been cut from ear to ear. The Stockholm Syndicate never does a second-rate job, my friend."

It was the first time Harry Fondberg had linked the Syndicate with the Swedish capital. Smoking his cigar, teeth clenched, he stared hard at his visitor. "Are you going to do something about it?" he asked softly.

"Yes. Kill it."

"You haven't the knowledge, resources or power. Above all you haven't the knowledge. How do they run their communications system? Tell me that. An organisation which has wrapped up a good part of Scandinavia and the Low Countries and is now rapidly penetrating Germany has to have a first-rate communications system."

"Water."

"I beg your pardon."

"Water," Beaurain repeated. "It came to me finally when I was on the terrace of the Grand Hotel looking out over the Strommen. Harry, has there been an increase in illegal radio activity in recent months?"

"Here in Stockholm? Yes." Fondberg's eyes were watchful. "I also know we have been unable to track down a single one of the transmitters – which we suspect are very high-powered."

"Over how long a period?"

"I'm told it started about two years ago."

"Foundation date of the setting up of the Stockholm Syndicate," Beaurain said grimly. "Has anyone kept a record of the general areas of these illegal transmissions?"

"Yes, although I don't see how that will help." Fondberg broke off to speak in Swedish into his intercom, then switched off. "Our radio-detector vans have never been able to get a fix on a transmission. We think whoever is sending the signals uses a van and keeps on the move during the period of transmission."

The Swede stopped speaking as a girl came into the room with a rolled sheet, placed it on the Säpo chief's desk, and left them. Beaurain got up and stood behind Fondberg as the latter unrolled a large-scale map of Stockholm inscribed with red circles. He snorted his disgust.

"Doesn't tell you a bloody thing!"

"Doesn't tell *you* a bloody thing," Beaurain corrected him. "But for me it's the final confirmation that I'm right. Look at all the circles."

"In so many different districts? No pattern."

"You're losing your grip. The pattern is screaming at you. All the roads and districts circled include waterways." Beaurain's tone became emphatic. "Willy Flamen in Brussels showed me a similar record of heavy illegal radio traffic – and he couldn't see a pattern. Neither could I at the time – but all his marked districts throughout Belgium were close to canals. Same thing in Copenhagen when Marker of Intelligence showed me his records. The activity is always close to the Øresund."

"You mean ... "

"The bastards have their transmitters *afloat*. Aboard barges in Belgium which will move down the canal while they transmit. This is why they've never been caught. In

189

Denmark they're on board fishing vessels or power-cruisers, again on the move just offshore while sending a signal. Here they're on the Strommen, on the . . . " Beaurain's hand hammered the city map as Fondberg studied it afresh.

"I believe you could be right," Fondberg said slowly. "If we can crack their communications system we sever the jugular of the Syndicate."

"Let's get the timing right," Beaurain suggested. "I want one smashing Europe-wide hammerblow delivered at the same hour when the transmissions are going full-blast. Everywhere taken out at once including the barges in Belgium, where, incidentally, two Syndicate operators, a man and his wife, were recently executed. Each took a bullet in the back of the neck."

"What?" Fondberg sat very upright and his intelligent eyes gleamed. "That's an old Nazi technique. It raises a hideous new possibility – that the men behind this foul organisation are the Neo-Nazis! God, have we been blind!"

Harry Norsten sat behind the controls of his Cessna, ready to land in the centre of Stockholm. He had just received clearance and in the two passenger seats the man and the girl stirred as travellers do when approaching their destination. Norsten was not coming in at Arlanda, the great international airport many miles outside the city. The Swedish pilot was dropping his tiny aircraft into Bromma Airport, a short drive from the Grand Hotel.

The male passenger glanced out of the window, hardly interested in the familiar view. Of medium height, his hair blond with side-burns and a thick mane extending down his neck, the passenger wore large horn-rimmed spectacles. Dr Theodor Norling squeezed the hand of his companion, speaking to her in French. "You are glad to be back home? You have had a busy time."

A busy time. The girl whose jet-black hair was cropped close to her skull shuddered at the words. She was recalling what she had read in the morning paper about what was rapidly becoming known across the world as 'The Elsinore Massacre'. Then she was frightened because she realised her shudder had communicated itself to Norling who was still gripping her hand.

The blond head turned slowly. Staring straight ahead at

Stockholm coming up to meet them, Sonia Karnell fought to regain her composure. Whatever she did, however she reacted, she must never show alarm, fear or repulsion. *He* disapproved of such emotions, regarded them as irrelevant in the task they were engaged on.

"Do I wait for you at Bromma or go home?" Norsten asked as he skilfully manipulated the controls for a perfect descent. He also spoke in French. The silent Dr Theodor Norling had once told him he liked to practise the language.

"You go home and wait for my call. I may need you again at very short notice."

That was all. A typical Norling command. Clear to the point of abruptness and not a wasted word. Who the hell was he anyway? After acting as his pilot for over a year Norsten knew as little about him as the first day he had been hired – except that Norling expected him to be available at all hours for a sudden trip and paid incredibly generous fees for the service – and his silence. The fact was that Dr Norling scared Norsten ice-cold.

"And one more thing, Mr Norsten," the Swede had told him when they first met at Bromma and concluded their arrangement. "It would be most ill-advised of you to broadcast my activities – or even to mention my existence as a client of yours."

He had paused, his blond head motionless, the eyes behind the tinted glasses equally motionless as they gazed with concentrated intent at the pilot.

"You must realise that success in my business, Mr Norsten, often depends on my competitors being unaware of my movements – unaware even of when I am present in Stockholm. Indeed, it is a cut-throat trade I ply."

Cut-throat . . . Norling had been staring at the pilot's throat when he used the phrase and Norsten was aware of an unpleasant prickling sensation in that region. Ridiculous! But that had been his reaction when he first agreed to do business with the book dealer. *Fear.*

They were a couple of bloody commuters, he reflected as he continued his descent – the sun glittering on the maze of waterways. Commuters between Stockholm and Copenhagen! And often at odd hours – flying through the night and landing before dawn.

He was pretty confident that at times they flew from

Copenhagen to the United States. Once Norling had dropped an airline folder on the floor of the Cessna as they were descending to Kastrup. Norsten had caught a glimpse of the tickets which fell out before the girl grabbed for them. Destination: New York. So why not fly direct from Stockholm by ordinary scheduled flight instead of using the Cessna to cover the first lap to Copenhagen?

It didn't make sense. But Norsten, a prudent man, had long since decided not to question any of the book dealer's actions, or to probe into his background in any way.

As he landed he saw the beige-coloured estate car was waiting for them, empty. As usual. A most methodical man, Dr Theodor Norling. Who brought the Volvo to the airfield Norsten had no idea, but whoever it was always took good care to be well away from the scene before he landed his passengers. It was almost as though no-one was permitted to see what Dr Theodor Norling looked like unless it was essential. The fact that he possessed that knowledge sometimes woke up Norsten during the night in a cold sweat.

"The pilot, Harry Norsten, is developing a dangerous sense of curiosity about my identity and my life-style."

Dr Theodor Norling made the remark to Sonia Karnell as she drove away from Bromma Airport behind the wheel of the Volvo and headed into the city. Removing his tinted glasses, he replaced them with a pair of gold-rimmed spectacles. From his suitcase he extracted a dark trilby hat and settled it on his head despite the blazing sun which was causing Karnell to drive with narrowed eyes. It gave him a professional air, this slight change in his appearance. Taking a pipe from his pocket he gripped it between his teeth, completing the transformation.

"Do we have to take any action?" Karnell asked.

"I have already made all the necessary arrangements to take him out at the appropriate time."

The watchers stationed at Bromma Airport followed the Volvo with great skill, employing the leapfrog technique. Norling, an expert in surveillance, constantly checked in his wing mirror but was unable to detect any signs that they were being followed.

Ironically enough, it was Harry Norsten the Swede was

checking for. Although well aware of the leapfrog technique, Norling noticed nothing. It was, in fact, ideal for the watchers in their vehicles – in heavy city traffic it was most unlikely they could ever be spotted since they were using as many as three cars and one delivery van.

There was a second factor which made it impossible for the ever-suspicious Norling to detect what was happening – the distance involved from Bromma to their destination was comparatively short. Even in heavy traffic, over a greater run Norling might well have eventually spotted what was happening as the four shadow vehicles continued their 'musical chairs' act.

"I drop you this side of the apartment?" Karnell queried.

"Of course. The usual precaution."

They had entered Rådmansgatan, a good-class residential street consisting of old four or five-storey buildings, all of which had been converted into flats. The street was also quiet and deserted as Sonia Karnell pulled in at the kerb, a good two minutes' walking distance to her apartment at Rådmansgatan 490. Norling slipped out of the car holding his case and within seconds she was driving away to park it. A Saab drove sedately by.

Without moving his head Norling registered every detail. Registration number; the two men sitting in the front, one of whom was yawning while the other stared straight ahead, concentrating on his driving. Both were dressed in casual Swedish clothes and Norling could see nothing odd about the car which vanished round a corner.

"Sonia will be able to confirm whether they followed her to the garage," he murmured to himself, then crossed the street and walked at strolling pace towards the entrance.

"I'll drop you off here, Louise," Stig Palme said. "God we got lucky at Bromma."

Louise Hamilton was most uncomfortably doubled up on the back seat and out of sight of anyone studying the passing car from the street. She sat up and eased the ache out of her legs as Palme pulled in at the kerb.

"Not lucky, Stig," she remarked, checking her hair quickly in a hand mirror. "Jules is just a superb organiser. And I can recognise Black Helmet – I should be able to spot the bitch by now."

"Take care," Palme warned.

Then she was gone, walking back down Rådmansgatan, carrying a shopping-bag with *NK*, the name of a leading Stockholm department store, printed on the side. She also carried, looped over her shoulder, the bag which contained the automatic supplied to her after her arrival by air at Arlanda. God, what a rush to reach Bromma! She turned a corner which hid the rest of the street – and the blond man with gold-rimmed spectacles who had left the Volvo was facing her.

This was the risk they had foreseen – that she *would* come face-to-face with him. Which was why Louise had done her best to change her appearance. She had discarded her trousers and windcheater and was wearing a bright yellow summer dress. Her hair was concealed under a silk scarf. Half her face was masked with enormous goggle-like sunglasses. Norling was only feet away from her, standing in front of the entrance to an apartment building. In his free hand he held a bunch of keys, one of them ready to insert into the lock. From behind gold-rimmed glasses distant eyes stared straight at her.

On her side of the apartment entrance there was a shop door. Praying it was open for business, she grasped the handle, turned it and walked inside, closing the door without a glance back.

Norling opened the front door leading into the apartment block and then glanced swiftly into the shop. The girl with the absurdly huge glasses was standing with her back to him ordering something from the woman behind the counter. He frowned, moved out of sight quickly, went into the apartment block and closed the front door. Inside, a flight of stone steps led upwards. It was very quiet and apparently deserted. Norling paused, one foot on the lowest step, his blond head cocked to one side. He was listening for the slightest sound.

Satisfied, he ran lightly up the steps, making scarcely a sound. Arriving on the silent first floor he paused again, this time to look out through a pair of double windows giving onto a curious enclosed roof-like area. There existed, he knew, access to that roof from another staircase.

Again satisfied, he unlocked the door, which involved two

separate keys for two separate locks. Norling walked into a pleasant, roomy apartment and closed the door behind him.

The living-room – which overlooked Rådmansgatan – had a polished wood-block floor covered with colourful rugs. A curious Oriental lantern hung from the ceiling for night-time illumination. Norling sat in a chair, picked up the phone and dialled a Stockholm number.

He had just replaced the receiver when Sonia Karnell's keys rattled in the locks. Norling made no assumptions: when she pushed the door open he was facing her directly, both hands raised and clasping the Luger pistol. "What's wrong?" she asked.

"Arlanda has reported the arrival of Jules Beaurain and his mistress in Stockholm."

In the *patisserie* Louise Hamilton had slipped inside to avoid recognition by the blond man, she was now ordering slowly a range of cakes and pastries. It was a quality shop and the woman behind the counter clearly expected her customers to choose carefully. Louise wanted to give the blond man plenty of time to get off the street before she emerged.

Then it happened. Sonia Karnell appeared on the pavement outside the window and stopped to search in her handbag for her door keys. As she had seen the blond man peer in earlier, Louise now had an excellent view of the dark-haired girl – in the mirror lining the wall behind the counter.

But the girl outside had only to glance into the shop and she might recognise the single shopper: Louise instinctively knew she would be recognised. She stopped herself moving in time. The slightest movement would be caught out of the corner of the dark-haired girl's eye. Was all this frenetic search inside the handbag a cover for the fact that she had already recognised Louise? The English girl became aware that the woman behind the counter was staring at her strangely. She hadn't spoken for half a minute.

"I'll have some of the chocolate gâteau, the one with cherries. About a quarter of the cake – I see it's cut ... "

A clear and direct look at the mirror image of Black Helmet would have told Louise exactly what the situation was – and that was the one thing she knew she must not do. Her head was bent over the counter, examining the display while the woman packed what she had ordered into a carrier.

195

Black Helmet disappeared, moved past the window to the apartment block entrance. Louise pretended to have trouble with the currency, to give the girl time to get well inside the building, then left the shop.

Before she left she was careful to pick up the carrier full of the food she had purchased with her left hand. Her right hand hovered over the unbuttoned flap of her shoulder bag – over the compartment holding the 9-mm. gun. She stepped into the street.

It was empty. Quite empty.

She hurried to the door to the apartment block. Swiftly she ran her eye down the small metal plates with the occupants' names. Only one woman. *Apartment 2. Sonia Karnell.* She walked back up the street to where the Saab was parked with Stig Palme behind the wheel.

"Get me back to the Grand Hotel," she told him as she climbed stiff-legged into the back and slammed the door shut. Stiff-legged with tension, God damn it.

Without being told, Palme chose a different route, one which would not take them past the apartment block – so anyone watching from a window overlooking the street would not see the Saab pass the building a second time. In the mirror Louise caught Palme's eyes and the Swede winked. He had detected the tension she was struggling to control. She began speaking to Palme and his companion as though delivering a report.

"If anything happens to me the address is Rådmansgatan 490. I'm pretty sure the hideaway is Apartment Two – occupied by a Sonia Karnell. Only woman shown as occupying an apartment. Not conclusive – it could be in a man's name."

"She parked the Volvo," Stig pointed out. "Again, not conclusive, but I think you're right. We're moving in on them."

"Or they're moving in on us." Bloody hell, she was still talking through clenched teeth. That episode in the *patisserie* had been murder. She went on giving her 'report' for Beaurain in the same clipped tone. "Male passenger, fair-haired, sideburns, hair thick on neck, wears gold-rimmed spectacles. A little taller than Dr Benny Horn or Otto Berlin. He could just be Theodor Norling, but I'm guessing. That apartment wants a round-the-clock stake-out."

196

While Louise Hamilton and her two companions were following the Volvo from Bromma Airport, Beaurain was still at police headquarters with the Säpo chief, Harry Fondberg. The Belgian had just called London and was talking to Detective Chief Inspector Swift of Special Branch.

Swift had known Beaurain for years and, like many of his international colleagues, still treated the Belgian as though he were in charge of the Brussels anti-terrorist squad. His news was a tonic to Beaurain – at whose suggestion Swift had sent a special team to the Woking-Guildford area of Surrey. Their task seemed strange – they had travelled backwards and forwards on single-decker buses in the hope of detecting suspicious foreign visitors.

"The score so far, Jules, is fifteen – all with false passports and all carrying concealed weapons. Some very tough characters."

The trick played on Litov had been two-edged. Primarily planned to lead Beaurain to the Syndicate's base, it had also been hoped it would syphon off to England a number of the Syndicate's top soldiers – who would not be available if and when the main clash took place. Special Branch had scooped the pool.

"It's all the wrong way round!" Fondberg poured more coffee as he shook his head. "I get this oily bastard of a presidential aide, Joel Cody, on the phone like he's admitting me to some exclusive club. He says Harvey Sholto is *on his way* to Stockholm when he has already arrived – I told you, my people at Arlanda saw him."

"What is really worrying you, Harry?"

"Normally we have good relations with the CIA. But Ed Cottel arrives without a word from Washington. I repeat it's the wrong way round. They tell me about Sholto, a very dangerous and suspect character. Why focus attention on Sholto and hide Cottel?"

"You're assuming they know Cottel is here," Beaurain commented.

"You mean ... ?"

"I'm not sure what I mean, Harry. Do you have a photo of Sholto? An earlier one from his Far East days I mean."

Fondberg reached into a drawer, took out a folder and produced two photographs. One of them was the picture of Sholto taken arriving at Arlanda. The big, broad-shouldered man with the large, round, almost bald skull and the cold eyes.

It was the second photo which interested Beaurain, a photo with crinkled edges and creases which showed a man taken against a background of a hut in a jungle. The build was the same, as was the shape of the head, but it was difficult to believe it was the same man. For one thing he had a thatch of thick hair and a moustache.

"How long ago was this taken and who took it, Harry?"

"Two years ago. A clandestine shot taken by our man in Bangkok. He could have been one of the top European contact men in the drug-smuggling circuit originating in the Golden Triangle. Drugs which eventually end up on the streets of Stockholm, Malmö, Gothenburg and so on."

"This Far Eastern shot is definitely Sholto?"

"That's the name our man in Bangkok attached to it. And there's something else which makes me worry about having Harvey Sholto free on the streets. I told you that our man in Bangkok was found floating in one of the *klongs*?"

"Yes."

"Well, I phoned someone else in Bangkok who hears all the rumours. Remember," Fondberg warned, "I used the word *rumours*. The word out there is that the man who killed our agent flew in from Manila. He used to be one of Harvey Sholto's contacts when he was out there."

"You're not suggesting the Americans ... "

"I'm not sure. But the one who is blanketing this city with eyes is Ed Cottel."

"May I take these photos of Sholto? You have copies? Good." Beaurain took the envelope the Swede had slipped the prints inside and pocketed it before Fondberg could have second thoughts. Only now did he raise the subject which he knew would embarrass the Säpo chief enormously. "Thank you for releasing my man so quickly at Stockholm Central. The drug consignment from Elsinore was ... "

"Boy, did we balls that one up!" Fondberg slapped the top of his desk to emphasize his chagrin. "I surround the whole area with police. I play it clever and tell them to keep well back from the wagon containing the drug haul. The Syndicate sends in two men wearing Swedish police uniforms. Jules, I let it slip through my fingers – forty million kronor.

And what is there to show for it?"

"A great deal, Harry," Beaurain said soothingly. "A direct link between Norling and the drugs – and therefore with the Stockholm Syndicate. Remember Serge Litov's last cryptic words – *Heroin … Norling … traitor*. At long last Norling is tied in with the whole infamous business."

"Except that's not evidence," Fondberg pointed out with unusual bitterness. "The last words of a now-dead Russian. Why a Russian? And on top of that the drug haul is gone."

"Harry, have you *any* information on Norling?"

"Yes. He poses as a dealer in rare editions."

"Poses?"

"May well, indeed, be a genuine book dealer to cover his real activities. It would explain his long absences away from Stockholm, since an international dealer travels a lot. He has an apartment in Gamla Stan – the Old City. Very close to the Church of St Gertrud." The Swede took a street plan of Stockholm from another drawer. "Here, I'll show you." He drew a cross on the plan. "I have also heard that the real power behind this organisation is a shadowy figure called Hugo."

"Hugo?"

"Yes, identity completely unknown. The word is he terrifies even the members of the Syndicate."

The phone rang. Fondberg, normally slow-moving and deliberate, grabbed for the instrument. He listened, spoke several times in Swedish, then slammed it down as he stood up behind his desk.

"Norling has been seen in Stockholm. He's in a Renault heading for what we call Embassy Row – where all the foreign embassies are. Not far away is a large marina with a whole fleet of boats. A car is waiting for us."

In the living-room of Sonia Karnell's first-floor apartment in Rådmansgatan the blond man was checking the mechanism of a Walther .765 automatic. The girl watched him: ironically, the weapon was a police issue pistol. For the third time he rammed home the magazine into the gun and then slipped it inside his shoulder holster.

"As I told you, my dear, Beaurain and Hamilton are in Stockholm – just as the first of our distinguished visitors from the States are beginning to fly in for the conference."

"What are you going to do about it?"

"Ensure that within a few hours no matter where they go they will be paid a visit."

"So much blood."

"Your favourite play is *Macbeth?*" Norling asked genially. He lifted a hand as he saw her preparing to leave with him. "This time I go alone. We must not be seen together any more than can be helped while we are in Stockholm. San Francisco will be a different matter, but I am a little nervous while I have this in my possession." He hoisted the suitcase which had been waiting for him at the apartment. "After all, my dear, forty million kronors' worth is not to be treated lightly."

"And you are going where?"

"First to collect the Renault. It *is* in the garage with the Volvo? Good. The time has come – and this I will handle personally – to send out a *Nadir* signal on Louise Hamilton and Jules Beaurain. They are to be executed on sight."

Sonia Karnell folded her arms quickly and forced herself to relax, to show no sign of the mounting tension she felt. Tension to Norling meant a person's nerve could be cracking – as he had suggested might be the case with the pilot, Harry Norsten. And to safeguard the Syndicate's security he would not hesitate to send out a *Nadir*. The person named could then never survive – often his worst move would be to seek police protection.

"The Renault has a full petrol tank," she assured him as his left hand rested on the door latch. "You still haven't told me where you're going."

"To the marina, of course. The one near Embassy Row."

15

At the moment when the sighting of Dr Theodor Norling behind the wheel of a Renault was reported to Harry Fondberg, activity in Stockholm was building up a steadily increasing momentum in many districts.

Unmarked cars carrying Beaurain, Fondberg and other officers left police headquarters and sped through the city, weaving in and out of the traffic and causing drivers to jam on brakes and curse. The cars were heading for the Royal Motorboat Club, the marina in the Djurgardsbron district. In the front car, which he was personally driving, Fondberg explained to Beaurain: "We have a written description of Norling and one photo taken with a telephoto lens. Both have wide distribution among officers I hope I can trust."

"You can't trust everyone inside the police?" asked Beaurain quietly.

"What do you think?" replied Fondberg. "My department, of course, comes under the ultimate control of the Minister of Justice. I had to go over the head of my superior to get some freedom of action. Can you guess what the Minister asked me to do if he agreed to let me quietly probe into the Stockholm Syndicate?"

"I'd rather not."

"Mount a twenty-four hour guard on his home with Säpo men. And these days he travels everywhere in a bullet-proof limousine with Säpo outriders on motor-bikes. That was the price for keeping me in business."

"It is happening in other countries."

Fondberg's normally controlled voice rose to a pitch of fury. "I don't care. It's time it was stopped!"

"That's why I'm here. Be ready to look the other way. Aren't we close to the Grand Hotel? Good. Can we stop there for a couple of minutes? There may be someone I want to pick up if they've returned to the hotel."

Behind the wheel of his Renault, Dr Theodor Norling was making slower progress than he had hoped, but he was driving more carefully than Fondberg's cavalcade surging through the city. He had no desire to be stopped by a *Polis* car for a traffic offence – bearing in mind the contents of the suitcase by his side.

Even so, he was close to Diplomatstaden, the foreign embassy area which was very close to his ultimate destination – the boat marina where a whole cluster of vessels would be bobbing at anchorage. He checked his watch. He should be there in about ten minutes with a little luck.

Sitting in the rear of the Saab which Stig Palme was driving back to the Grand Hotel, Louise eyed the cloth-covered weapon at her feet. It was Stig Palme's favourite gun and in standard use in the Swedish Army. A model 45 9-mm. machine-pistol, it was equipped with a movable shoulder-grip, could be used for single shots with a gentle pressure on the trigger – or fire a lethal continuous burst of thirty-six bullets in six seconds.

Telescope had gradually built up secret caches of arms and ammunition all over Europe. It was too dangerous to move across borders with weapons – although the steam yacht, *Firestorm*, purchased from a Greek millionaire, had been cunningly re-designed to provide so many hiding-places it was a floating armoury. In Sweden, Stig Palme's weapons cache was in the cellar of a house out in the country – just off the E3 highway leading to Strängnäs.

"Here we are," Palme called out cheerfully. "The Grand Hotel."

"Stop here!"

The Swede reacted instantly and smoothly, pulling in at the kerb before he reached the main entrance. To the right there was the usual row of Mercedes and Citroëns parked, their well-waxed surfaces gleaming. To the left the window-boxes of geraniums gave a splash of brilliant red, and a gardener was trimming them ruthlessly.

"Beaurain is waiting for us," said Louise.

She had just spoken when the Belgian opened the rear door, pushed his head inside and spoke quickly. "The hotel said you were out – I had a feeling you might be back any minute. We're on an emergency – Theodor Norling has been spotted by himself in a Renault."

"He came in to Bromma Airport in a Cessna – with Black Helmet! She seems to turn up everywhere. Her name could be Sonia Karnell. Address of apartment is Rådmansgatan 490. Norling was carrying a suitcase, *hugging* it."

"Christ! Has he fooled us? Was it about the same size as … "

"The one which was hidden aboard the express for Stockholm? Yes, it was."

"You see that Saab over there, with the man behind the wheel carefully not taking any notice of us? That's Harry Fondberg. Don't lose him, Stig. We think Norling's destination could be the boat marina near Embassy Row."

"I know it."

Beaurain forced himself to stroll casually the short distance back to Fondberg's car although his legs were screaming at him to run. He got inside, closed the door and lit a cigarette. "Norling has a suitcase which sounds exactly like the one snatched from the wagon you surrounded at Stockholm Central station. He flew into Bromma from somewhere."

"God Almighty!" Fondberg had started up his car which was the signal for the other two cars parked further back to prepare to move. "You mean he could be carrying the big consignment, the one for which my man in Bangkok died? Hold on to your seat-belt!"

The American behind the wheel of the hired Citroën wore a Swedish-style nautical cap. In his mirrors he had observed everything – Beaurain waiting inconspicuously on the sidewalk after a brief dash into the hotel; the arrival of the Saab which contained Louise Hamilton in the back and two unknown men in the front. He had noted the urgent conversation between Beaurain and Louise; the Belgian's careful stroll back to another Saab, with Harry Fondberg waiting behind the wheel. He waited until the convoy departed – with the second Saab carrying Louise bringing up the rear – then he drove out from the row and followed. Ed Cottel of the CIA knew a crisis when he saw one.

From the moment they left police headquarters they preserved radio silence. Fondberg had taken the precaution of sending a message to the man who had spotted Norling that only if the target was *not* heading for the marina was he to send a brief message over the radio.

There had been no signal by the time the 'convoy' left the Grand Hotel, a convoy consisting of two unmarked police cars, followed by Stig Palme and Louise Hamilton who, in their turn, were closely followed by Ed Cottel's Citroën – equipped with a radio that had been skilfully attached after the hiring of the vehicle. It kept Cottel in touch with what Fondberg had called his 'eyes'. Remaining one vehicle behind Stig Palme's Saab he was using his radio link.

"Carmel calling. You read me? Good. Any sign of Ozark?"

"Monterey here, Carmel. No, repeat, no sign of Ozark. Am continuing surveillance pending further instructions."

"OK, you do that."

With an expression of resignation the hooked-nosed American replaced the microphone and concentrated on not losing the Saab. It had been going on for days and the only thing to do was to persist; sooner or later something had to break.

Ozark was the code-name for Viktor Rashkin, First Secretary at the Soviet Embassy in Stockholm. The odd thing was he seemed to have vanished off the face of the earth.

"Pass me the gun – lay it on the seat beside me."

Stig Palme made the request to Louise as they continued in the wake of two unmarked police cars. Palme knew that they were close to Embassy Row, which meant they were close to the marina. Without asking why, Louise lifted the weapon wrapped in oil-cloth and gently laid it on the empty seat in front.

"I may need Christine," he remarked. It was typical that Palme should confer a girl's name on his favourite weapon. When using her in action he was accustomed to use some pretty racy language. "We're being followed. *Don't* look round. He's driving a cream-coloured Citroën."

"Any idea since when?"

"He was parked with his back to us outside the Grand Hotel. And he's been using the usual technique of keeping one vehicle between us all the way. The Syndicate obviously has a team watching the Grand Hotel."

"Just one man, you said?"

"With a highly-trained killer they only need one man. Better for getting away after he's done the job. Beaurain could be the target," he said, and relapsed into silence.

Fascinated she watched while Palme drove with one hand and used the other to unwrap the oil-cloth and expose Christine. The machine-pistol was already fully-loaded. "We're on top of the possible target area," Palme warned and then stopped the car.

Dr Theodor Norling pulled in at the kerb by the landing stage. The marina was vast. There was a breeze coming off the water which freshened the air and countered the blaze of the high sun glaring down out of a cloudless sky. For a few seconds he paused after locking the car, standing quite still with the suitcase in his hand.

Arne, reliable as usual, was walking towards him. Norling was trying to sense anything unusual in the scene before committing himself to water. A whole fleet of craft of varying sizes and types bobbed at anchor, a galaxy of vibrating colour in the intensity of the sun. Already Norling could feel its heat on the back of his neck. There were expensive cruisers equipped with all the latest electronic devices, small power-boats, larger launches, a whole diversity of yachts, some with coloured sails.

"The power-boat is ready to take you out to the *Ramsö*," Arne informed his employer.

"I'm in a hurry," Norling replied curtly.

Behind him, beyond a screen of shrubs and trees and across the unseen road rose the buildings of the American Embassy with a flight of steps leading up to them. From a flagpole the Stars and Stripes fluttered in the breeze. Before getting into the power-boat Arne held waiting for him, Norling turned and gave the flag a brief salute. An onlooker would have found it impossible to decide whether the gesture was ironic or serious.

"God, that's him – and he's getting away!"

Three cars had arrived alongside the marina. It was Louise, jumping from the third car and running up to where Beaurain and Fondberg stood, who confirmed the worst.

205

Before leaving Stig Palme, who had pulled up a cautious distance from the police vehicles, she had snatched a pair of field glasses from the glove compartment, nearly dislocating herself leaning over the seat. Focused on the receding power-boat, the lenses brought up the two figures on board only too clearly.

She had not recognised the man steering the craft towards the powerful cruiser riding at anchor. The second man, nursing a suitcase, was only too horribly familiar. The encounter outside the shop on Rådmansgatan when he had stared at her through his gold-rimmed glasses. In the lenses the sun – for a brief second – flashed a hint of gold off those same glasses.

"It's him," she told Palme, and ran to Beaurain to repeat the warning.

"Are you quite sure?" asked Beaurain, glancing uncertainly towards Palme.

"Bloody hell, do you think I'm blind!" she screamed at him. "I was as close to him as I am to you!"

"Harry, can you have that cruiser intercepted – if that's what he's headed for?"

Fondberg shook his head dubiously and there was a grim look on his face. "Point One, I have no authority or reason to intervene. I could always argue I didn't know it was Norling, but . . . Point Two, that vessel can really move – and the river police are never where you want them."

"Then this, Harry, is where you look the other way."

The power-boat carrying Dr Norling had now arrived alongside the cruiser. Through her binoculars Louise watched the Swede move nimbly aboard, holding the suitcase in his left hand. Crewmen had appeared on the bridge of the vessel which was clearly about to depart.

"Forty million kronors' worth of heroin in that suitcase," the Belgian hammered home. "Soon it will be flooding the streets of Stockholm, creating more untold misery."

"*For Christ's sake!*" protested the exasperated Swede. "Don't you think I feel helpless enough?"

Louise studied the so-called dealer in rare books through her field glasses. Beaurain was standing next to her and behind Fondberg's back. She lowered the glasses and saw him make a brief gesture describing the outline of a suitcase. Suddenly she looked behind her and over to the right where

Stig Palme had parked the Saab.

Palme was leaning against the car to steady himself. He was holding at shoulder level the machine-pistol. The muzzle was aimed out across the water towards the cruiser which was still motionless. Then the silence of the peaceful morning was splintered.

It lasted six seconds – the time it took for Stig to empty thirty-six 9-mm. bullets. And Palme was a crack shot. Louise had the lenses of her field glasses screwed into her eyes. Norling was still clutching the suitcase when the hail of bullets ripped into it, shredding the casing and the contents. The suitcase was literally blasted over the side of the cruiser and into the water, scattered in a multitude of fragments which littered the surface of the water and began drifting away. And so accurate was the Swede's fire that – so far as Louise could see – not one bullet had touched Norling.

"What the hell ... !"

Fondberg was sliding his hand inside his jacket and under his shoulder when he felt Beaurain's hand grip his arm: "I said, Harry, this is where you look the other way, God damn it!"

"Sorry. Instinctive reaction. I hope your man moves fast."

He called out a brief command to his men, who froze, and then turned back to watch the white cruiser. Palme was already behind the wheel of his car. The weapon had vanished. Without haste he backed the Saab and drove quietly away. A flock of birds, disturbed by the fusillade, had risen with a beating of wings and headed out over the water. In the sudden silence the noise of their ascent could be heard clearly. Then it was drowned by a distant, muted rumble as the white cruiser began to move.

"He must be mad as hell, wouldn't you say?" Beaurain observed.

Aboard the *Ramsö* Norling had given the order to *move*! Again he looked at the hand which had been holding the suitcase, still unable to believe he was completely unscathed. When the bullets started coming he had felt a hard tug, the case had been wrenched from his grasp as though by supernatural forces, then came the cascade of fragments, a cloud of precious powder. All gone! As the cruiser started moving he could actually *see* a white scum on the water. He hastily went below decks into his cabin and sank into a chair. He was shaking with uncontrollable rage. Alone in his luxuriously-furnished cabin he sat with both hands gripping the arms of his chair.

"Beaurain! First in Brussels, then Copenhagen and Elsinore – now here in Stockholm itself!"

He was talking to himself, a habit of which he was fully aware and of which he occasionally made use as a safety valve. It had started long ago with another life, so far away from Sweden. Behind the lenses of his gold-rimmed spectacles his eyes were remote and cruel. He looked up as a man descended the steps and came into the cabin, Olof Konvall, the wireless operator.

"I'm sorry, sir." Konvall, a small, highly-strung man with a grizzled face, took a step back when he met Norling's gaze. The venom in the stare was scaring. "I didn't intend to intrude – but normally when you come on board you have a signal you wish to send."

"Stay where you are, for God's sake!" Norling's show of rage was most unusual; his normal manner was an icy calm. "Tell the captain I wish to switch to another vessel at the earliest possible moment."

"I will tell him at once."

"Don't go! I haven't finished yet." Norling paused, forced himself to loosen his clenched grip on the wooden arms of the chair, to let his fury dissipate itself. Now he had himself under perfect control. His voice became remote, detached, like a chess-player who has decided on the next move.

"You are to send out immediate *Nadir* signals on Jules Beaurain. The other recipient is his mistress, Louise Hamilton. Let the word go forth. And first Hamilton alone is to be subjected to a demonstration at grade three level. Now you may go."

"*Oh my God, how horrible!*"

Louise froze with shock and revulsion, the key to her bedroom door still in her hand. Like most people in a hotel she had walked in and closed the door behind her under the odd delusion that this was – temporarily at least – a safe refuge.

"*Christ! I think I'm going to be sick!*"

She leant back against the door and forced herself to recover. Her stomach obeyed her and then she caught sight of herself in the mirror and was shocked by her appearance: her lips were drawn back over her teeth in an expression of murderous fury – and she knew in that second that if the person responsible for the outrage had still been in the room she would have killed them. Someone rapped on the self-locking door.

She stood to one side and turned the door handle. Palme walked into the room and stared at the gun aimed point-blank, then his gaze swivelled. He closed the door.

"Isn't it sickening," she said as lightly as she could, but she didn't fool the Swede as she slipped the gun back inside her shoulder-bag. He said the one thing which could have lightened the atmosphere.

"I think the management will agree to changing your room."

There was a second knocking on the door. Stig Palme motioned her to slip into the bathroom, which was a mistake because it was even more hideous there than in the bedroom. She gritted her teeth, then thankfully heard Beaurain's voice, a sharp tone. "Where's Louise? Has she seen ... ?"

"She's in the bathroom. I sent her in there when ... "

He found her sitting on the bathroom stool with her legs crossed, one arm supporting the other as she gazed directly at him and calmly smoked the cigarette she had just lit, her only concession to the experience she had just undergone.

"Only a sick mind ... " she began.

It *was* – if possible – even worse in the bathroom. An aerosol paint spray had been the weapon used – used with such diabolical skill that Beaurain suspected the perpetrator must be a trained artist. Sprayed over every surface in the bathroom were obscene pictures involving a woman indulging in every type of perversion imaginable. And in every instance the face depicted was a caricature – but immediately recognisable – of Louise Hamilton.

The bedroom walls and every other available surface had been similarly treated. Beaurain watched her smoking her cigarette and then reacted in just the right way.

"We must at once reserve another bedroom on a different floor and with an entirely different layout. In actual fact, as long as we stay at this place I suggest you spend each night in my room. God knows the bed is big enough."

"Thank you," she said gratefully.

"Can I have a word with you in a minute?" Palme asked Beaurain.

"After we've got the room business sorted out."

"What are you going to tell the manager?" Louise enquired.

Beaurain knew instantly what was worrying her – that the manager was bound to wonder what sort of people she knew who could act in this way. She felt besmirched by such vile obscenity. Again he knew exactly the right reply. "That my ex-wife is insanely jealous and has already in another country been charged with the same type of offence. Also," he paused to smile, "that she will by now have left Sweden to escape the attention of the police."

Fifteen minutes later they had ensconced Louise in an entirely different room, this time on the second floor. It overlooked the street up which marched the mounted horse troops after the changing of the guard at the Royal Palace, explained an assistant manager who was obviously going out of his way to make her forget her recent experience. At the door he paused before leaving.

"May I take it that Madame had not propped her door open for a short time while she left the room?"

Louise smiled, her face still bloodless: "No, I certainly had not propped the door open in any way."

"Of course! Madame does not, I trust, mind my asking? Thank you. Ah, here is a bottle of champagne. Please accept it as a small present from the management."

Stig Palme was conferring with Beaurain as they sat in the Swede's Saab parked outside the hotel. The choice of locale for their conversation had been Palme's.

"This way we know we are not being recorded. You have seen how the bedroom doors lock, how from the outside you must turn the key before you can enter the room? I think," Palme continued, "it is possible the Stockholm Syndicate have committed their first major blunder – opening up a trail I can follow which just might blast their organisation wide open."

"It's going to be a race against time," Beaurain warned. "I have the strongest feeling Hugo is going to launch an all-out offensive to wipe *us* out."

"Because we've just lost him his major heroin delivery?"

"Partly – but maybe even more because of this." Beaurain nodded towards a large Mercedes which had just glided to a halt outside the Grand Hotel. Out of the rear door a short stout man holding a brief-case had emerged while two other men, who had left the car seconds earlier, took up positions near the foot of the steps and were staring in all directions.

"Who is the little fat man who needs armed guards?" Stig asked.

"That is Leo Gehn, president of the International Telecommunications and Electronics Corporation of America. One of the richest and most powerful industrialists inside the States – they say he contributed a million dollars to the President's electoral campaign. Maybe he contributes even larger sums to the Stockholm Syndicate."

"I don't follow, Jules."

"After leaving the marina we returned to police headquarters – to see if Fondberg's Säpo people had any further information. They had. A whole list of European and American power élite are arriving aboard a stream of aircraft – some aboard scheduled flights, some in their private jets – putting down at Arlanda. They seem to be staying at two hotels – the Saltsjöbaden Hotel and here at the Grand. So far, apart from Leo Gehn, the presidents or chairmen of five of America's biggest corporations have flown in – to say nothing of men like Eugène Pascal from Paris and a score of others. Fondberg suspects they are here for the secret meeting of the Stockholm Syndicate – that they're all men who have either voluntarily contributed money in return for the vast profits they'll gain from international crime – or they have been subjected to the most hideous intimidation. I need just one I can crack, Stig – just one."

Taking the cigarette out of his mouth, he stared through the windscreen at the person alighting from another chauffeur-driven limousine at the entrance to the Grand Hotel. Out of the rear door stepped one of the most elegant and striking women Palme had ever seen, her jet-black hair piled up on top of her head.

"I said I needed just *one!* That, Stig, is the Countess d'Arlezzo."

"But surely her husband is the man who will run their affairs?"

"Her husband, Luigi, was bought by Erika for his aristocratic connections. She personally runs the banking empire she inherited from her father. Wait here."

The Countess lingered on the sidewalk at the foot of the flight of steps, dismissing all attempts to hurry her inside with a casual wave of her slim hand while she drank in the view of the Royal Palace and the Houses of Parliament. Beaurain grinned to himself as he saw the gesture; how like Erika. He was within a few feet of her when a heavily-built man in a dark suit stood in his way.

"Stay back an' 'old da position," he ordered.

"Out of my way or I'll break your arm," Beaurain said politely and smiled.

"Jules!" The woman, in her early forties, had swung round at the sound of his voice and stepped forward. Impetuously she embraced him while the guard stared in confusion.

"You must come up to my suite," she continued, linking her arm in his. "Luigi? I expect he's somewhere with a bottle – didn't you know? These days he's hardly ever sober."

When her cases had been brought up and they were alone she took him by the hand and was about to lead him into the bedroom. He shook his head, turned on the radio loud to counter any possible concealed microphones and faced her as he threw the question in her teeth.

"I take it that your banking consortium has contributed money to the coffers of the Stockholm Syndicate?"

"The equivalent of several million pounds," she replied without the slightest hesitation. "It is supposed to be a loan but I don't regard Hugo as a particularly good risk."

He studied her for a moment. She stood very erect and, while she spoke, inserted a cigarette in a long holder. He lit it for her. Of all the people caught up in the labyrinth of the Syndicate, she was possibly the only one with the nerve to tell him the truth without a second's hesitation. So why had she given in to them in the first place?

"I was one of the people who was told over the phone about the death of the Chief Commissioner to the Common Market – one week before he died in his so-called 'accident'. That was how it began."

"And how did it go on?" he pressed.

"I was told what would happen to me if I refused to transfer funds to Stockholm. The murder of the Chief Commissioner convinced me they meant what they said. I am a coward, so I gave in."

"What did they threaten you with?" the Belgian demanded.

"That I would be found – I can remember the exact phrase – hung and twisting like a side of meat turning in the wind. I didn't fancy that too much, Jules."

"Why are you here?"

"To attend the meeting, of course. The conference of the Syndicate, if you like. I gather Hugo – or his representative – will carve up the loot, allocate territories to different groups, and then the profits from these will be shared among investors in proportion to the funds supplied. That is what he calls us," she remarked, her expression bitter. "Investors – as though we were engaged in a legitimate enterprise."

"And you are engaged in?"

"Prostitution, gambling, drug-trafficking, blackmail, extortion, you name it, we're in it – up to our lousy necks." The bitterness in her manner increased as she stubbed out her cigarette, inserted a fresh one in the holder and again waited while Beaurain lit it for her. They were still standing close together in the beautifully-furnished room and the tension of their discussion seemed to preclude any thought of sitting down.

"Thank you," she said after he had lit her cigarette and continued, her voice low and vehement, which was unlike Erika: in the past he had always admired her sense of detachment. "And one crime is cleverly dovetailed in to aid another."

"How do you mean?" he asked sharply.

"Oh, the high-class prostitutes – and they are among the classiest and most expensive in Europe – are used to compromise leading political figures, who then have to do the Syndicate's bidding or be publicly ruined. You remember there was a man in Milan."

"I know who you mean, Erika. You were rather fond of him."

"Not as much as of you, but yes, I was fond of him, Jules. A week before the scandal broke I was phoned and told that he was about to be ruined. I called him to warn him but there was nothing he could do – the photos had already been taken, the pictures which were then sent to the newspapers and TV. He shot himself – so it appeared."

"And what does that mean?" Beaurain was startled. It had always been his understanding that the Milanese politician concerned had committed suicide.

"He was murdered by the Syndicate and his death faked to look like suicide. In ruling circles in Rome it was clearly understood this was simply another 'demonstration' organised by the Syndicate – like the fatal fall of the Chief Commissioner. Can you imagine the horror of it? Even we who have so much money and once controlled international businesses are now puppets of this foul thing, the Stockholm Syndicate."

"Who do you deal with? Hugo?"

"No. I have no idea who Hugo is. On the rare occasions when I am contacted, it is by the member of the directorate who is in charge of the Mediterranean Sector – a Dr Otto Berlin."

"And, finally, where is this so-called summit meeting to be held?"

"We have not been informed yet – but I have been told to be ready to fly to the south coast of Sweden as soon as the instruction comes." Again the bitter note. "Yes, that is what they give us – instructions. At least I *tried* in Rome."

"You must not reproach yourself. Does Luigi . . . ?"

"Know anything about it? Of course not! Can you imagine what sort of help I'd get from that broken reed? Within a day of being told anything he would probably be blabbing it to the world in a drunken stupor. Jules . . . " She came very close to him, so close he could savour to the full the very faint aroma of the scent she was using. "Jules, can you do anything?"

"Yes, and first I want you under my protection. You will put on a coat and walk straight out of this hotel with me. Leave everything else and come with me this instant. I have people outside and we'll hide you until this is all over."

"I can't, Jules."

"Why the hell not!" The exasperation was genuine. This was not like Erika.

"Because of Luigi. If I disappear they will kill him. He is

214

in Rome."

"One phone call and I can have him scooped up and flown out of Italy."

"No, Jules!" She put her index finger over his mouth, removed it as he relapsed into silence and kissed him full on the lips. He found he could even remember her taste. "I must act normally, go to the meeting – but if you give me a phone number I will call you and tell you where the meeting is being held as soon as I know."

Beaurain didn't like it. He felt uneasy but he couldn't budge her. Eventually he gave her Harry Fondberg's private phone number and the code-word *champagne* which she must use if she found it was impossible to reach Beaurain; then she could leave a message. As he walked out of her room and closed the self-locking door, he passed a man who was slowly pushing a service trolley along the corridor. The trolley's contents were concealed under a large white cloth. It was only later that he remembered the man. Too late.

Stig Palme drove his compact car up the steep road alongside the Royal Palace and turned into Stortoret, the main square where an ancient stone pump stood protected by stone bollards. A few minutes later he parked the Saab close to the entrance to one of the maze of alleyways in this medieval quarter of Stockholm.

The tiny shop he was visiting was situated half-way along the deserted alley, cobbled underfoot and so narrow he could have easily reached out his arms and touched both sides. He entered without ceremony, noted that the place was empty except for the owner and shut the door. He then turned the card hanging against the glass to indicate Closed.

Outside the shop over the door hung a huge key symbol. And the man who supplied master keys in Stockholm was its owner, Tobias Seiger. The price varied according to the status of the hotel and Seiger's estimate of how much he could screw out of the buyer. In return, complete secrecy was guaranteed. It was this wall of secrecy Stig Palme had to break down.

His mission was not helped by the fact that Seiger knew and disliked Palme. A short, bull-headed man, Seiger had a jeweller's glass in his right eye when Palme entered. Observing Palme's action in closing his shop Seiger carefully removed the jeweller's glass and placed it in an open drawer below Palme's eye level. Palme moved. His left hand whipped over the counter, gripped the pistol Seiger had been feeling for and pocketed it. Seiger found himself staring into the barrel of Palme's own gun.

"I have very little money on the premises," he began.

"We're going to talk, Tobias." The locksmith stood in a permanent stoop, brought on by years of cutting keys. His manner was a mixture of aggressiveness and oily persuasion. He had the morals of a brothel-keeper. "The Grand Hotel ... "

"Did you say the Grand?"

The shop was cluttered with cupboards and there was dust and grime everywhere, including a film of dirt on the outside windows – so it was very dark. Even so Palme's sharp eyes caught the brief flicker of expression which vanished off Seiger's slack-lipped face almost before it appeared. *Alarm. Terror?* This was going to be more difficult than he had anticipated.

To overcome Seiger's fear he was going to have to produce an atmosphere of hideous terror to prise open the oily bastard's mouth. Palme pressed the muzzle of his gun into Seiger's left ear.

"I can make you a key – the master key," Seiger babbled.

"Don't get naughty with me, Tobias. You know exactly what I'm after – I saw it in your eyes. The identity of the person who has recently asked you to do just that – supply him with a master key for the Grand Hotel."

When discussing the horrific vandalisation of Louise's room, both Beaurain and Palme had realised only one explanation was possible. The culprit had obtained a copy of the master key and probably from a nearby source. And, Palme thought to himself, where could be nearer than the establishment of Tobias Seiger in Gamla Stan just across the water from the hotel itself?

"I cannot tell you! It would cost me my life. The people involved are ruthless, totally ruthless."

The terror was in Seiger's eyes, in his tone of voice, in the way he physically cringed away from Palme until the wall prevented him retreating any further. Palme's left hand caught hold of Seiger's necktie and tightened it, his knuckle pressed against the locksmith's Adam's apple.

216

Seiger would have screamed with the pain but the pressure of the knuckles made it impossible for him to utter a sound. The gun muzzle was pressed lightly against his right eye and the large Swede loomed over the stoop-shouldered shopkeeper.

"You can always leave Stockholm until the trouble is ended," he said with an engaging smile. "When did you last have a real holiday? Ages, I expect. An honest man like yourself, plying his trade, *deserves* a holiday."

He released his grip on the necktie suddenly and Seiger collapsed in a heap against the wall, his legs spread out at an absurd angle across the stone-paved floor. He used one hand to massage his bruised throat, glaring up at the intruder, then when he saw what Stig Palme was doing his expression changed, he tried to climb to his feet, found he hadn't the strength and held up a hand as though to ward off a blow. What words had not managed a gesture was achieving. Terror!

Stig Palme stood over the collapsed figure, doing what he was doing with great deliberation and without a glance down at the locksmith. He was screwing a silencer onto the muzzle of his Luger.

The atmosphere in the tiny shop was nauseating. On entering the place Palme had been aware of a musty, damp odour – a smell associated with a place which never sees the sun and where the ventilation leaves much to be desired. Added to this now was the stink of sweat streaming down Seiger's body, staining his armpits, moistening his face, the smell Palme had encountered more than once before, the stench of terror.

"These people kill!"

"We are aware it is the Stockholm Syndicate. I need a name, an address," said Palme matter-of-factly.

The latter he had no hope of – the most was a name, the least a description he could circulate in the Stockholm underworld and hope to come up with something.

"The alternative is I blow you away."

And Tobias Seiger, who spent most of his life in this pit of semi-darkness, came up with pure gold.

"A blond-haired man – I can't give you a name. It was strictly a cash transaction, of course ... fair-haired with sideburns ... The hair was thick on the back of his neck ...

and he wore gold-rimmed spectacles. A little shorter than yourself – but not small . . . about five foot eleven. We conversed in French. I have seen him twice before . . . I know where he lives."

Stig Palme was careful to maintain a perfectly blank expression. It increased the pressure, keeping a sense of detachment when he was screwing on the silencer. Christ Almighty, Seiger was actually describing Dr Theodor Norling, one of the three men controlling the directorate of the Stockholm Syndicate. Why had he not sent some minion to get the master key? Then he recalled Beaurain telling him that Norling had an apartment not far away in the posh area near St Gertrud's Church. When Seiger came to *I know where he lives* Palme forced himself to keep silent. In interrogation the art was so often to know when to keep your mouth shut.

". . . it was a strange coincidence," the locksmith babbled on, "I could hardly believe it myself when I saw him on my way to work . . . I often spend the night with my sister who lives in Strängnäs . . . Driving in on the E3 highway I had an urgent call of nature. I stopped by the roadside . . . can I have a drink?"

"No!"

It was such a delicately poised thing: any pause could stop the flow of words if Seiger thought better of what he was doing. And what the hell was all this about the E3 and out in the country? Norling's apartment was in Gamla Stan. Denied a drink, the voice, now cracked, railed on.

"As I was behind a tree I saw this man come out of a house in the distance . . . I always carry a small pair of field glasses in my pocket . . . my hobby is bird-watching. It was him! I waited as he got out his car and drove off in the direction of Stockholm, the way I was going. I followed in my own car until the traffic was heavier and caught him up. He did not see me! The Volvo he was driving carried American diplomatic plates."

It was coming at Palme fast but he kept his head. In a monotone he asked about the location of the house. This involved some detailed explanation even though Palme knew the route to Strängnäs well. He had to pinpoint the location of the house which, apparently, stood back off the highway but in view of it and was quite isolated.

"One of those old-fashioned houses," Seiger ran on.

"Gables and bulging windows like they used to build. It must be at least fifty years old."

"Stay where you are!"

Palme gave the order in a cold voice and Seiger remained on the floor behind the counter. Palme walked slowly towards the door, turned the key quietly and stepped out. As he did so he moved to his left, sliding along the glass of the shop window – the last thing someone waiting for him would expect. And someone was waiting for him. Two of them. Medium height. Heavily-built. Wearing sunglasses. Something wrong with their shoes. Definitely not Swedish.

The man on the left darted forward, his knife extended from his hand. They'd made only two mistakes. They hadn't realised he'd seen the silhouette of one man from inside the shop as he glided slowly past the window. And the other man had gently tried the locked door, making the slightest of sounds.

Their second mistake was in not noticing Palme's right hand down by his side as he emerged from the shop, the hand still holding the Luger with the silencer. As the killer darted towards him he whipped up the Luger and fired. *Phut!* A small hole appeared in the assassin's head between his eyes. The second man had seized his chance to dash inside the shop, confident his companion would eliminate Palme. The Swede followed him inside the open door just in time to see him lean over the counter.

Had Seiger not compelled Palme to relieve the locksmith of his Walther automatic he could have saved himself. Palme had hardly re-entered the shop when the assassin rammed home the knife deep into Seiger's chest. There was a choking cry, a slithering sound as Seiger sank to the floor again out of sight. Palme pressed the muzzle of his silenced Luger into the back of the neck of the killer. It seemed rough justice: these bastards were fond of using the old Nazi method of execution.

The man froze, began to say something *in German*. Palme pressed the trigger once. *Phut!* In the silence of the unsavoury-smelling shop it sounded like no more than the expelling of a breath of air. The assassin sprawled his arms across the counter as though trying to hold himself up. Palme stood back as the man folded up and fell in a heap on the floor. Taking Seiger's automatic out of his pocket he quickly cleaned all fingerprints off it and dropped it inside the drawer which was still open.

He left the shop cautiously, using the handkerchief to wipe the handle. The gloomy alley was still deserted – except for the crumpled form of the first assassin at the foot of the window. Palme concealed his Luger inside his belt and behind his jacket. Moving swiftly back up the alley to the road where he had parked his Saab, he climbed in behind the wheel and drove slowly away.

16

A modern complex of buildings painted in yellow and ochre, the Russian Embassy in Stockholm is cut off from all contact with the outside world by walls and wire fences which are patrolled round the clock by guards supplied, curiously enough, by A.B.A.B., one of the two leading security services in Stockholm. On the inside it is different. All entrances are controlled by the KGB. The walls of the complex are festooned with the lenses of TV cameras which watch all who approach, lenses which project towards the outside world like hostile guns.

Only a privileged élite are allowed ever to leave the confines of the embassy. From outside you may see a Russian woman with her hair in a bun walking behind the wire – one of the wives of the personnel staffing the embassy. She will serve her term there and return to Russia without ever having seen anything of the beautiful Swedish capital. None of these restrictions, of course, applied to Viktor Rashkin.

"Welcome back, Comrade Secretary," greeted his assistant, Gregori Semeonov, as his chief entered his office.

"Anything to report?" Rashkin asked curtly as he sat down in his large leather-backed swivel chair behind his outsize desk. He had not given even a glance to the stunning view through the bullet-proof picture windows behind him. Heavy net curtains masked them, making it impossible for anyone in a block of nearby flats to see into the room. The view looked out across a trim area of well-kept lawn and beyond, the waters of the Riddarfjärden glittered in the noon-day sun. Rashkin was tense. Semeonov sensed it.

"There is a signal requesting your urgent presence in Leningrad. You have arrived back in Stockholm just in time – the First Secretary is visiting the city tomorrow and wishes to confer with you while he is there."

Semeonov handed his chief the decoded signal. He watch-

221

ed while the Russian studied it with half-closed eyes.

Only forty years old, Rashkin was of medium height, average in build and his dark hair was cut very short. Clean-shaven, his eyes were penetrating and had an almost hypnotic quality. As a young man he had spent two years training to be an actor before a senior KGB talent-spotter observed his intensely analytical mind. He was recruited immediately into the élite section of the KGB where he quickly learned the wisdom of suppressing his gift for mimicry.

Despite the fact that his first-class mind swiftly assimilated the flood of information and training directed at him, Viktor Rashkin was not at home inside the KGB. But he had also become fluent in six languages by the time he met Leonid Brezhnev at a Kremlin party. The meeting of the two men was a decisive moment for Viktor Rashkin, a moment which, if mishandled, would never occur again.

Most men would have played it safe, striving to impress the master of Soviet Russia, and being careful to agree with everything he said. Rashkin gambled all on one throw of the dice. He released himself from the mental strait jacket imposed on him by the KGB and for the first time in three years became his natural self. Those nearby who witnessed his conduct were appalled.

Rashkin let his natural gift for mimicry re-assert itself, imitating members of the Politburo who were actually present in the room under the glittering chandeliers. Gradually a hush fell over the great hall in the Kremlin where the party was being held. Only two sounds could be heard – the sound of Rashkin brilliantly imitating world-famous figures on both sides of the Iron Curtain, and the roar of Leonid Brezhnev's laughter as he shook with amusement at such a wonderful contrast to the sombre expressions of the Politburo members.

From that night Viktor Rashkin's future was assured – from being an obscure but promising recruit of the KGB, he became Brezhnev's trusted and secret trouble-shooter. The fact that he was a natural linguist – and that his flair for acting made him a brilliant diplomat – helped to rocket him to the dizzy heights.

The Washington dossier on Viktor Rashkin grew thicker and thicker, but the few privileged to read it complained that

222

despite the quantity of the data, the quality left a great deal to be desired. "It's so damn vague," the U.S. President grumbled. "Now you see him, now you don't"

April ... Believed to have spent three days in Addis Ababa. Purpose of visit: presumed discussion of further military aid to present Ethiopian regime.

May ... Reported to have made lightning visit to Angola. Dates of visit uncertain. Rumoured agreement concluded with Angolan regime.

July ... Presence reported in Havana. No positive confirmation of visit. Previously reliable Cuban woman agent code-named Dora signalled arrival of important personality in Cuban capital. Strong suspicion visitor to Castro was Viktor Rashkin.

December ... Presence of Viktor Rashkin positively confirmed in Stockholm where he holds position First Secretary at Soviet Embassy. This official position believed to mask his real activities. Was observed attending royal reception at Palace in Stockholm. Next day believed he left Sweden for unknown destination.

For the CIA and National Security Agency analysts it was infuriating. As one of them had expressed it after reading the above extracts from agents' reports and a host of other material, "I'm not even sure Viktor Rashkin exists. *Believed to ... presumed ... Reported to have ... Rumoured agreement ... No positive confirmation of visit ... Strong suspicion ...* What kind of dossier is this?"

The man was a will o' the wisp, a shadow flitting in the night. To his assistant, Gregori Semeonov, a senior officer of the KGB, his chief existed but he was almost as elusive as the Washington analyst had suggested. As they conferred in Rashkin's office at the Soviet Embassy in Stockholm the short, burly Ukrainian had no idea where his chief had arrived from.

"I have made your reservation on Flight SK 732 departing from Arlanda for Leningrad at 13.30 tomorrow. Normally this flight is from Gate Six," Semeonov continued pedantically. "The ticket is in your right-hand top drawer."

"A return ticket, I hope?"

Rashkin was studying the contents of a folder from another drawer to which he alone held the keys. As he expected, the stupid, peasant-like Semeonov completely missed the irony of his question.

"What is the exact location of the hydrofoil, *Kometa*?"

"Captain Livanov is waiting at Sassnitz until you give the order for him to proceed to the agreed position off the Swedish port of Trelleborg. I gather he has again complained that we are risking his vessel in asking him to cross the Baltic."

"I have ordered him – not asked him – to proceed to Trelleborg when I give the signal. We must remember to tell him to keep his hull below the horizon so he cannot be seen from the shore. And the Swedish liner, *Silvia*, is in position?"

"Yes, Comrade Secretary." Semeonov paused and Rashkin waited for the next piece of bureaucratic idiocy. He was not disappointed. "I cannot understand why we have hired the *Silvia* and put aboard only a skeleton crew. She is in no position to make a long voyage."

"Just so long as you have carried out my instructions. You may go now."

Rashkin had no intention of revealing his strategy to this man who was, after all, only the creature of Yuri Andropov, head of the KGB and a powerful member of the Soviet Politburo. And he was perfectly aware that it was Semeonov's chief task to report back to Andropov all Viktor Rashkin's activities, a task Rashkin was at great pains to frustrate by never revealing to the Ukrainian anything of the least importance.

Semeonov, his hair cut so short that Rashkin secretly termed him 'Bristle-Brush', was not able even to leave the room without further comment. At the door he turned and spoke in his measured, deliberate manner.

"I will confirm that you may be expected in Leningrad aboard SK 732 from Arlanda tomorrow."

As the door closed Rashkin shut the folder embossed with a small gold star indicating its extreme level of secrecy, pushed back his chair and swore aloud. "Five minutes in this place and I'm screaming to get out again. Bristle-Brush is becoming impossible to live with."

"I can do nothing more, Jules. I have received specific orders that our distinguished guests are not to be interfered with in any way – on the contrary, while visiting this country they are to be granted every courtesy and consideration. The trouble is, Sweden stands to gain a considerable amount of international business while hosting this conference."

"They admit a conference is taking place?"

Harry Fondberg and Beaurain were again in the Swedish security chief's office at police headquarters. But on this second occasion the atmosphere was quite different. To Beaurain's astonishment, Fondberg's manner was formal, as though he were covering up a deep sense of embarrassment.

"There has been a reference to a conference, yes," Fondberg admitted.

Beaurain stood up. "I presume this means I can no longer rely on you for any assistance? That is the situation, is it not?"

The plump-faced, capable Swede paused, clearly reluctant to let his old friend leave. "There was a message for you, by the way," he said. "It was phoned through to me just before you arrived. I was not able to persuade her to leave her real name."

"*Her?*"

"Yes, it was a woman. The message for you was simply, *Offshore from the port of Trelleborg. A hydrofoil. Champagne.*" Fondberg excused himself as the phone rang. He listened, spoke a few words and then replaced the receiver, his expression sombre. "There has been a death at the Grand Hotel. An important lady."

"The Countess d'Arlezzo."

Beaurain made it a statement and Fondberg's sensitive ear did not miss the inflection. He stood up behind his desk, his eyes alert, his mouth hard as he met the Belgian's grim gaze. Beaurain continued, "Earlier today I was talking with Erika – the Countess – in her suite at the Grand. I have known her for a long time. She told me she had been threatened by the Stockholm Syndicate. That phone call tells me roughly where the conference of the Syndicate will take place. We had arranged she should use the code-word *champagne* to identify herself. I believe I passed the person who must have been keeping an eye on her for the Syndicate, a waiter pushing a trolley."

"One of the Grand Hotel's regular staff – a waiter – has been found trussed up and stuffed inside a broom cupboard."

"How did she die?"

Beaurain walked over to the window with hands clasped behind his back while he waited for the reply, and stared out

225

at the sunlight which Erika would never see again. His eyes were quite still.

Fondberg was beginning to feel very uneasy. He cleared his voice before he spoke. "She was found hanging from the shower in the bathroom. She used her bath-robe cord, a common ... "

"*I would be found ... hung and twisting like a side of meat turning in the wind.*" Beaurain repeated for Fondberg's benefit the words Erika had used. The Swede sank into the chair behind his desk and stared dully into the distance, tapping the stubby fingers of his right hand on the desk top, a sure sign that he was deeply disturbed. He listened while Beaurain related the whole of his conversation with the woman who had been one of the most powerful figures in western Europe.

The Belgian's voice grew harsher as he concluded his version of his last meeting with Erika. "So these are the people to whom you are extending every courtesy and consideration – that was the phrase, was it not? And they – all these members of the Stockholm Syndicate – are as guilty of Erika d'Arlezzo's murder as if they personally had tied round her neck the cord of her own bath-robe and strung her up to that shower."

"I said nothing about a murder." Fondberg wriggled uncomfortably behind his desk and, for the first time in their long friendship, he was unable to meet Beaurain's gaze.

"Christ Al-bloody-mighty!" Beaurain's fist smashed down on the desk-top. "You are not going to stoop so low that you will allow them to get away with this faked suicide?"

"*No!*" Fondberg came out of his mental daze and stared straight at Beaurain. "Of course I know it wasn't suicide! Had you understood Swedish you would have known I was speaking to the forensic expert who has already arrived at the Grand. I told him to send his report to me personally at the earliest possible moment. No-one else will be permitted to see it. I shall myself announce its findings to the international press now gathering here hoping for news of the 'business' conference. It will cause a bombshell!"

"The Syndicate will come after you," Beaurain warned his old friend, but, he admitted privately to himself, he was also testing him. Such was the quicksand atmosphere of treachery and fear the unseen organisation had generated. Fondberg's reaction made him feel a little ashamed.

"Wrong, my friend. I am going after the Stockholm Syndicate! In committing this murder they have made a big mistake. They hoped their influence was strong enough to squash any attempt at a legitimate investigation. They overlooked the fact that I might intervene."

Events moved at bewildering speed during the next few days. On receipt of Beaurain's urgent signal sent by Stig Palme from a transceiver hidden in the basement of a house in the town of Strängnäs, Captain "Bucky" Buckminster left his anchorage off Copenhagen and proceeded south and east into the Baltic.

"We have to wait off the coast near Trelleborg," he told Anderson, the chief pilot of the giant Sikorsky which they carried on the helipad. "Just below the horizon so we cannot easily be seen from the Swedish shore."

"Any exercises once we get there?" Anderson enquired.

"Yes. Intensive training with the power-boats and dinghies equipped with outboards – in fact all the fleet of craft in the hold. Another activity Beaurain wants toned up is the training of frogmen in underwater warfare."

"The Countess d'Arlezzo, president of the well-known group of banks, who was discovered hanging from the shower in the bathroom of her suite in the Grand Hotel was, in the opinion of the well-known pathologist, Professor Edwin Jacoby ... "

Harry Fondberg, who was addressing a press conference called at very short notice – other reporters were still arriving, pushing their way into the crowded room – was possessed of a certain dramatic sense which he now used to the full. Beaurain watched him from a position at the back of the room. Heads craned as the pause was stretched out. Most of the western world's leading newspapers, TV stations and magazines were represented.

" ... was MURDERED!"

Pandemonium! The small plump chief of Säpo waited as men and women milled in the room – some already rushing for phones to catch editions about to go to press with the staggering announcement. The Countess d'Arlezzo's beauty had been compared with that of Sophia Loren; her business influence with that of Onassis. As the initial reaction subsided, Fondberg ruthlessly piled on the drama. Now it was too late for anyone to try and hold down the lid on the case. It was his first promised blow at the Stockholm Syndicate.

"In a moment Professor Jacoby will tell you his reasons for stating that in his opinion the alleged suicide was faked, could not have taken place in the way meant to fool the police. Or, shall we say, certain powerful criminal groups with international connections believed their influence was so great that no-one would ever dare reveal the truth?"

Louise whispered to Beaurain. "God! That's really blasted the case wide open. Whoever Hugo is, he's going to go crazy!"

"That's Harry's tactic," Beaurain murmured. "He hopes that by throwing him off balance he'll provoke him into making yet another blunder. And listen to this!"

The questions were now coming like bullets as reporters fought to catch Fondberg's eye. High up on a platform, he selected his questioners for their influence. Someone ran onto the platform with a note – doubtless from some Minister. Fondberg waved the messenger away and stuffed the message unread inside his pocket.

"Are you saying the Countess was mixed up in criminal activities?" asked someone from *Der Spiegel*.

"I am saying she was being blackmailed and intimidated in a way which would only be used by animals. I have the most reliable of witnesses that she was actually threatened with death in the form her murder took."

"Your witness?"

"Would ex-Chief Superintendent Jules Beaurain of the Brussels anti-terrorist squad, previously in charge of Homicide, satisfy you?"

"Thank you. Yes!" said *Der Spiegel*.

"Christ!" Louise whispered. "He's blowing the whole works."

"And the one thing the Syndicate can't stand is publicity," Beaurain whispered back. "It's a dark evil creature which operates in the darkness."

"Would you care to elaborate on the structure of these powerful criminal groups you refer to?" *The Times* – of London.

"Check up on likely personalities at present in Stockholm."

"Names, we need names!" *The New York Times*.

"You are here! Do some of your own investigative work, may I suggest!"

"Leo Gehn has just arrived in the capital, I hear." *The New York Times*.

"I have heard that also," Fondberg replied blandly. "Next question, please."

"Who controls the international criminal groups you referred to in reply to an earlier question?" *Le Monde* of Paris.

There was a prolonged pause. Tension built up in the packed room as Fondberg, one arm supporting another, a hand under his chin, seemed to be considering whether to answer the question. One thing was clear and heightened the tension until the atmosphere became electric: the chief of Säpo *did* know the answer ...

"A directorate of three men." Fondberg spoke slowly and with great deliberation. As he paused again, the door next to Beaurain was pulled open. A man took three paces forward and stopped, holding a Smith & Wesson with both hands, the muzzle raised and aimed point-blank at Harry Fondberg.

Louise had a blurred impression of a short, burly figure wearing a boiler suit. Beaurain grabbed the man's wrist and elbow. There was a single explosion. The bullet fired in the tussle – which would have blown Fondberg off his feet – embedded itself in the ceiling. There was a shocked, incredulous hush which lasted several seconds, during which the only sound was the scuffle of feet as Beaurain overpowered the gunman. Uniformed guards were appearing in the hall beyond the open door. Beaurain hurled the would-be assassin with all his strength backwards into their arms.

"Check him for other weapons!" he snapped. "Or do I have to do the whole damned job for you? He came within an ace of killing your boss."

Chaos broke loose. The room erupted into movement as the mob of reporters stormed towards the doorways. Beaurain hauled Louise back out of the path of the turbulent crowd and pressed her back against the wall. In thirty seconds the room was occupied by only three people: Beaurain, Louise and Harry Fondberg.

The Swede jumped agilely from the platform and ran towards the Belgian, holding out his hand. "For saving my life I can only say thank you."

"We stage-managed that rather well. Maybe we should go into the theatrical business," Beaurain whispered.

"I have the information you asked me to dig up on Dr Theodor Norling's background before he came to Stockholm. It tells us nothing," Fondberg informed his listeners.

Beaurain and Louise were sitting at a round table in the Säpo chief's office, eating hungrily from a selection of dishes which Fondberg had ordered from a nearby restaurant. Beaurain nodded at Fondberg's remark as the Swede studied the report without enthusiasm.

"It is the same with all these provincial police forces – they think we live the high life here and they can't even answer a civil request without grumbling at how busy they are."

"Tell us what there is to know about Norling," Beaurain suggested.

"Born in Gothenburg, his parents moved when he was seven years old to Ystad." He looked at Louise. "That is an old medieval port on the southern coast in the province of Skåne. The people in Skåne are very different."

He might have been talking about the end of the world, as certain New Yorkers refer to the Deep South. Perhaps this was the Deep South of Sweden, Louise reflected. Fondberg continued reading from his folder.

"When I say Ystad I mean a small place close to it. The first thing Theodor Norling's parents did when they arrived from Gothenburg was to separate. His mother ran off with a ship's engineer while the father managed to get himself killed in a traffic accident a few weeks later. Young Norling was taken in by some aunt who had money and he was partly educated abroad. He returned to Skåne when he was twenty, attended the funeral of his aunt who had just died, and promptly used the legacy she had left him to set up in business as a collector."

"Let me guess," interjected Beaurain. "A collector of editions of rare books?"

"Wrong!" Fondberg chuckled delightedly at having scored a point when he saw Beaurain's expression. "As a collector and dealer in old coins."

"And he travelled a lot," Beaurain persisted, "during the course of his business."

"Yes," Fondberg admitted.

"And most of his business was done abroad and locally he was known as a bit of a hermit and he never got married?"

"Yes," Fondberg agreed, almost reluctantly. "It is a waste of time my reading this folder since you seem to know the contents. It is true he was a hermit – and disliked on that account since he gave the impression he felt himself superior to the locals." The Swede chuckled again. "The truth of the matter probably is that he was very superior! Any more predictions?"

"Only one. He arrived suddenly in Stockholm to set up business as a dealer in rare books about two years ago."

"Ten out of ten!" Fondberg did not even bother to refer to the folder.

"So," Beaurain suggested, "to sum up, Theodor Norling has now no known living relatives. Correct? And have your people down there in darkest Skåne found any close friends he left behind who could identify a picture taken of him?"

"Yes – and no. As you suggested I sent the picture we have of Norling, a picture which had to be taken secretly because of a directive from higher up. The Ystad police showed it to the very few people who knew Theodor Norling when he was in business down there. Some immediately identified him from the photo. Others said they didn't think that was the man they had known as Dr Theodor Norling."

"*The man they had known as Dr Theodor Norling.*" Beaurain repeated the words slowly as though relishing every syllable. The chief of Säpo was now looking thoroughly piqued. Louise did nothing to enlighten him.

"It's bloody uncanny," was her unladylike remark.

"What is?" Fondberg pounced.

"How we've heard this story before. Twice to be precise." She looked at Beaurain who nodded giving her permission to go ahead. "What you have told us about the background and origins of Dr Theodor Norling is an almost exact replica – with a few minor variations – of the background histories of the other two members of the so-called directorate controlling the Stockholm Syndicate."

"You mean these men are sleepers who are now activated?"

"No, oddly enough, the other way round." It was Beaurain who spoke.

"You mean someone has invented dummy men?" Fondberg suggested.

"Not even that, Harry. Dr Berlin certainly existed, was quite definitely brought up in Liège in his early days and started his business as a book dealer there. There are still people who remember him. Vaguely."

Fondberg shook his head and lit a cigar. "I am lost. Which, I suspect, is your intention, you bastard." He turned to Louise and bowed formally. "Please excuse my language, but you work with him, so ... "

"I agree with you," Louise assured him.

"Let's try to find you – since you're lost, Harry," Beaurain continued imperturbably. "Dr Theodor Norling's background is vague because his parents vanished from his life early on, because his life-style was that of a hermit, because he travelled a lot on business and was seen very little before he came to live permanently in Stockholm. *Two years ago.*"

"All that is in the goddamn folder," Fondberg pointed out.

"Dr Otto Berlin's background is vague because Liège is a large city, because he had no relatives and few acquaintances, because he also travelled a lot owing to the nature of his business. His character, too, was hermit-like. Perhaps it goes with the trade. So again, as with Norling, old acquaintances shown a photograph say 'Yes, that's him,' or 'No, doesn't look much like him.' Only one photograph is available of Berlin. These men seem to be very camera-shy."

"I am still lost," Fondberg growled.

"The third man was – note the past tense – Dr Benny Horn who now lives in Copenhagen but originally came from Elsinore. And while I remember it, when do you think Dr Otto Berlin moved himself from Liège to Bruges? *About two years ago!*"

"It is getting interesting," Fondberg was compelled to admit. He glanced at Louise. "This dishonest and devious man you choose to work for plays these games with me whenever he gets the opportunity. In England I think they call it dangling you on a string."

"Benny Horn's background antecedents are equally vague when you go into them with a sceptical eye," Beaurain continued. "He was in the book dealer business for fifteen years in Elsinore before he moved suddenly to Copenhagen.

Since then, no-one in Elsinore has seen him – not that there are many who would be interested."

"Another hermit?" Fondberg enquired.

"As I said, it seems to go with the trade. So, although he has a solid background of fifteen years' residence on the outskirts of Elsinore you can't track down many who actually knew him – and then only vaguely. The local police produce his photograph and we get a repeat performance. Some say 'yes' and some say 'no' when asked to identify Horn. It's quite normal, as you know."

"I still don't understand it," complained Fondberg. "They're not sleepers, they're not dummy men."

"Someone went to a lot of trouble in Belgium, in Denmark, and here in Sweden searching out these men, Harry. The whole thing is quite horribly sinister – worked out by a brilliant mind and manipulated in a diabolical manner. What we are actually looking for is the fourth man."

"The fourth man?"

"The one they call Hugo, the man whose very name evokes terror, sheer terror."

17

The temperature was a comparatively pleasant 42°F., an east wind sweeping over the airport chilled the face, the expressions of the airport staff were sombre; a prejudiced observer might even have used the word 'sour'. As far as the eye could see the landscape and buildings were depressing. Scandinavian Airlines Flight SK 732 from Stockholm had just touched down at Leningrad.

Ignoring the stewardesses waiting by the exit, Viktor Rashkin left the plane and walked briskly to the waiting black Zil limousine. The KGB guard saluted, held open the rear door while Rashkin stepped inside, closed it and motioned to the chauffeur who started the machine moving at once. Rashkin was known for his impatience.

The cavalcade – a Volga car full of KGB agents preceded the Zil limousine while another followed in the rear – sped away from the airport and Rashkin glanced outside unenthusiastically. Why the hell did Brezhnev need to have personal reports on progress of Operation Snowbird? Rashkin suspected the old boy, surrounded by old-age pensioners, simply wanted a few hours of his company. He always asked for impersonations and roared his head off while Rashkin mimicked his victims.

Relaxing back against the amply-cushioned seat he gazed out through the amber-coloured curtains masking the windows. In the streets the people were curious – and resentful. Apparatchiki were on their way to some unknown destination and, ahead of the cavalcade, police were stopping all traffic to allow Viktor Rashkin swift passage. The driver of one car forced to halt by the kerb carefully waited until the second car-load of KGB men had passed and then spat out of the window.

"Arrogant sods – living off our backs."

It was a common sentiment Rashkin would have seen in

the eyes of the staring pedestrians – had he looked up. He didn't bother. He knew what he would see. One day the lid would come off. There had to be a limit to the patience of even these stupid serfs.

Earlier at the Europé Hotel situated off the Nevsky Prospekt there had been more dissatisfaction as all visitors had been moved out of their rooms to other hotels at a moment's notice. No explanation had been given as squads of KGB agents moved in to replace the normal staff.

Now the Europe resembled more a fortress than a hotel with special squads of agents checking the identity of everyone who approached the entrance. Guards patrolled all the corridors and armed men displayed their presence aggressively. First Secretary Brezhnev was in town. His announced purpose was to visit Leningrad. His real purpose was to confer with his protégé, Viktor Rashkin.

"So," Leonid Brezhnev continued, "the Stockholm Syndicate can be said to be flourishing?"

"We can say more than that," Rashkin announced confidently, his manner totally lacking in the usual servility shown to the master of the Soviet Union. "We can say that we have now placed puppets under our control in most of the key positions in western Europe – chairmen of huge industrial concerns, heads of transport systems, controllers of some of the great banks and – above all – certain cabinet ministers. By involving them – through one method or another – in the Syndicate, we have compromised them so all they can do is to obey our instructions."

"A takeover without war, a takeover which is invisible and not even seen by the masses to have taken place!" Brezhnev's tone expressed his immense satisfaction with what he obviously regarded as a great victory.

"It is like Hitler's Fifth Column practised on a far vaster scale," Rashkin commented.

"These three men you found who form the directorate – Berlin in Bruges, Horn in Copenhagen and Norling in Stockholm. Why are they needed?"

Rashkin prevented a sigh of exasperation escaping. This was caused by the First Secretary's advancing years – his infuriating habit of changing the subject for no apparent reason. Yet oddly it was combined with a flair for remembering an extraordinary amount of detail over a vast range of projects. You had to watch the old boy – underestimate him and he'd catch you out in the flick of a horse's tail. And that, Rashkin reminded himself grimly, only happened once. He explained crisply, careful not to appear patronising.

"These three men are essential. Each controls a certain geographical sector – Berlin, the Mediterranean up to the mouth of the Rhine, Horn the United States ... "

"Yes, yes, I remember that bit."

"So any member of the Syndicate in that sector co-operates with the sector commander, who is a west European. This camouflages totally the fact that real control is in our hands."

"How do you explain to them why the conference is taking place aboard a Soviet vessel – the hydrofoil, *Kometa*?"

A shrewd point. *But oh God, we have gone all through this before!* Rashkin smiled to relax himself. "They already believe that much of the Syndicate's profits will come from surreptitious dealings in the proceeds from crime inside the Soviet Union, that there are *Soviet* members of the Syndicate!"

"Good, good, Comrade!" Brezhnev smiled slyly, leaned forward and squeezed Rashkin's shoulder. The younger man guessed what was coming next and was not disappointed. "Now, what about a few of your impersonations to cheer up an old Bolshevik who has to sit all day long staring at sour-faces? For a start, why not our esteemed Minister of Defence, Dimitri Ustinov?"

A moment later he began to laugh out loud: in that short space of time Rashkin's acting genius had transformed him into a different human being. He had become Marshal Dimitri Ustinov.

Attempt on Life of Security Chief Fails.

"God damn it, what crazy maniac acted without my orders and committed this supreme idiocy? And if ever there was a time we do not want anything like this it is now! Now! Now! Now! Do you hear me? Well, why don't you say some-thing instead of standing there like a whore on a street cor-ner?" Rashkin demanded. Karnell grabbed a decorative plate from the wall and hurled it at him. It shattered on the side of his head – and when he put his hand up it came away

236

streaked with blood.

Rashkin looked at Sonia Karnell and took a handkerchief from his pocket with the other hand. He wiped the blood from his fingers, his manner suddenly frigidly calm. While talking he had been raving like a madman, shouting at the Swedish girl as though it were all her fault.

"It was a bumpy ride back from Leningrad," he told her. "The turbulence was most unusual."

"The turbulence since you arrived has not only been unusual," she said viciously. "*It has been unbearable. Do you hear me, Viktor Rashkin?*" she suddenly screamed at the top of her voice. "And the plate I broke over your stupid head was your present to me."

"I know."

"I just wanted to make sure you know – because I'm glad. Do you hear me, you pimp? I'm glad."

Her well-defined bosom was heaving with passion and her white face was a mask of rage. His reaction, as always, was unexpected and disarming. He sat down on a sofa, lit two cigarettes and offered her one.

"The newspaper story disturbed me," he remarked mildly. "Coming on the eve of the conference when we want everything peaceful with nothing to disturb our influential guests. Such men and women like to live without any publicity. There is only one solution, Sonia."

Karnell played with the large diamond ring he had given her and waited for his next pronouncement. She had asserted her independence; Viktor despised and mistrusted all those who played up to him. She had by now learned how to handle this brilliant and strange man.

"We quietly wipe out Beaurain's organisation, starting at once," he decided. "We now have plenty of troops in Stockholm, including Gunther Baum."

"But how are you going to find them? We know Beaurain and his tart are at the Grand but the rest?"

"Our people will call discreetly at all major hotels in the city. They will check on any new arrivals during the past week. They should not be difficult to identify – we are looking for Commando-style men, a number of whom we suspect previously belonged to the British terrorist SAS."

"Who, of course," she interjected sarcastically, "are far worse than the KGB execution squads."

"I must leave now. You can alert our people and get the search under way at once. Gunther Baum is to be put in charge of both search and subsequent liquidations – as many of them as possible to look like accidents. I am going to the house to collect all the folders before the conference commences aboard *Kometa*."

One of those old-fashioned houses ... Gables and bulging windows like they used to build ... must be at least fifty years old ...

Stig Palme recalled the description the murdered locksmith had given him of the house in the country where he had seen Dr Theodor Norling.

"At least I assume it was Norling," Palme continued while Beaurain, Harry Fondberg and Louise Hamilton listened to him as they sat eating lunch in the Opera House restaurant. It was a convenient meeting-place because it was close to the Grand Hotel and was quiet. No-one occupied a table anywhere near them.

"It's all right, Stig," Beaurain assured the Swede, "I'm damned sure it was Norling. He was personally attending to organising another of the Syndicate's 'demonstrations'. Don't forget – poor Erika was supposed to have committed suicide – but other members of the Syndicate would have known better. Now, Harry, this raid on the house in the country, which Stig can locate for us. Can it be soon? And a combined operation between my people and Säpo. Unofficially, of course?"

"It can be today!" Fondberg announced and took a deep puff on his cigar to show his satisfaction at the prospect of action.

Six cars were moving along the E3 highway beyond the outskirts of Stockholm and out in open country. Palme had been chosen to lead the assault convoy because he was Swedish, and because he knew the location of the house which the dead locksmith, Tobias Seiger, had described. In the second vehicle Jules Beaurain sat behind the wheel of his Mercedes which Albert had driven to Stockholm.

"You really think this house could be the H.Q. of the Stockholm Syndicate?" Louise asked as she peered eagerly out of the window.

"I'm guessing – but it would fit the basic requirements of

a headquarters from Stig's own recollection of the place. Hugo won't want anywhere in Stockholm. It's OK for Theodor Norling to have his apartment in Gamla Stan – I think Norling just meets people there, just like Otto Berlin meets people in Bruges."

"In mobility they find safety?"

Beaurain paused. "Something like that. But an old house right out in the country, well back off the road so it attracts no attention, and yet close to a highway which gives swift access to Stockholm. As I said, I'm gambling, but it fits the basic requirements."

"Some gamble!"

Louise twisted in her seat and looked back down the curving highway through the rear window. She could see at least two of the four cars following them – and inside each car Henderson had installed a team of four men accustomed to working together as a group. And – the thought occurred to her – had Harry Fondberg known the arms concealed aboard these vehicles he would have had a fit. Sergeant Jock Henderson, riding in the third car, was organised for a small war. And he was in radio contact with all the other vehicles, using a pre-arranged code which would have meant nothing to any outside listeners.

"Of course it could all be for nothing," Louise remarked. "And where is Harry Fondberg? Incidentally, I presume you know there's a traffic helicopter flying along the highway?"

"I had noticed the chopper," Beaurain informed her solemnly. "I happen to know Harry Fondberg is aboard it. And, as you so cheerfully predict, it could all be for nothing."

The Cessna was waiting for Viktor Rashkin – he could see it in the distance. Throwing his peaked cap onto the rear seat, he grabbed the pilot's helmet by his side and confidently climbed out of the car, locked it in the parking zone and strode across the airfield.

In the control tower a man picked up a pair of field glasses, focused them on the figure striding towards the Cessna with a springy step and asked to be excused. Instead of heading towards the lavatories he stepped inside the nearest payphone and dialled Ed Cottel's number. In his room at the Grand the American answered with his room number.

"Westerberg here," his caller identified himself. "Ozark is just leaving. Official destination Kjula, as usual."

"Understood," Cottel replied laconically. "Goodbye. And let's hope we win a bundle."

Kjula was a small military and civil airfield about fifteen kilometres from the town of Strängnäs which you reached by travelling along Highway E3 – the route Beaurain and his gunners were now moving along.

Before leaving the Grand to join the convoy Beaurain had slipped into the CIA man's room to tell him what he planned and the location of the strange old house where the locksmith had seen a blond man with sideburns leaving. The only fact Beaurain had omitted to mention to Ed Cottel was that the locksmith had reported the fair-haired man as leaving the house for Stockholm in a Volvo estate wagon carrying American diplomatic plates.

Two minutes later Cottel was behind the wheel of his hired Renault parked outside the hotel. He was going to have to make speed to catch up with Beaurain's convoy.

They were travelling through the province of Södermanland along the E3 highway and Louise was fascinated by the beauty of the scenery. "I had no idea the countryside just outside Stockholm was so lovely."

"Yes, it's attractive," Beaurain agreed.

Louise sat entranced as the sun blazed down once again out of an immaculate sky and the highway spread ahead, passing through tiny gorges where granite crags closed in on the road, then opened out again to reveal rolling green hills covered with fir trees, fields of yellow rape, the occasional wooden farmhouse painted a strong rust-red standing out in stark contrast to the surrounding green. She glanced in her wing mirror and stiffened.

Taking the field glasses from the glove compartment she swung in her seat and aimed the glasses through the rear window at the Renault roaring up behind them. Behind tinted glasses the face of Ed Cottel came rushing towards her.

"We're being followed," she said tensely. "Ed Cottel's right behind us. Any second he'll drive through our rear window."

"I know."

240

The Renault was too damned close for Louise's comfort. Beaurain waved Cottel to move ahead of the Mercedes. Within minutes, moving round a curve, Beaurain spotted a roadsign, a large white letter "M" on a blue ground. He pointed it out to Louise.

"That indicates a lay-by coming up. We can pull in there and see what Ed is getting so excited about. I told him where we were going."

Beaurain hooted and signalled that he was pulling into the lay-by. When he had stopped he remained seated behind the wheel of his car and waited while Cottel, who had parked further along the lay-by, climbed out of his Renault and began walking back towards them.

"Wouldn't it be nice to get out and greet him?" Louise suggested.

"Not until we find out what he's up to," Beaurain replied.

They were now well out in the country and there was very little traffic on the E3. More rolling green hills capped with dark smudges of fir forest, a landscape which seemed to go on forever. The warmth of the sun beat down on the Mercedes as Cottel approached them on foot.

For his normal sober and well-cut suit he had substituted a pair of old jeans, sneakers and a shabby anorak. The American leaned on the edge of the open window, greeted Louise politely and then said, "My people tell me Viktor Rashkin – piloting his own Cessna – took off from Bromma some time ago with a flight plan giving his destination as Kjula airfield."

"Which leads you to think, Ed?"

"That if you wanted to fool someone you might fly to Kjula and then drive back from the Strängnäs direction as though heading *into* Stockholm. Just a thought. Mind if I continue tagging on behind?"

"Suit yourself, Ed."

While Cottel walked back to his Renault, Beaurain pulled out of the lay-by and sped past the American to catch up with Palme's Saab. In his rear-view mirror he saw the car with Henderson at the wheel approaching. The other three carloads of gunners would not be far behind.

"You were pretty rude to Ed," Louise observed.

"I merely used as few words as possible in the conversation. We are, in case you've forgotten, working to a time-

241

table with Harry Fondberg."

"Now give me the real reason."

"Supposing you wanted to divert someone's attention from a certain direction what would be the most effective way of doing it?"

"Point them in another direction. You can't mean Cottel keeps drawing your attention to Viktor Rashkin's movements to divert your attention from Washington, for God's sake?"

Harvey Sholto, the man from Vietnam, the man whose past and present were clouded in vagueness, and the man about whom presidential aide, Joel Cody, had taken the trouble to phone Harry Fondberg to tell him of his imminent arrival, was staying at the Hotel Reisen.

He had chosen the hotel with care. It was located on the island which contained Gamla Stan. Its front overlooked the Strommen belt of water. With a pair of field glasses used from his bedroom window the tall, heavily-built, bald-headed American could see across the water clearly to the front entrance of the Grand Hotel, the cars parked outside and anyone who entered or left the hotel. He had been sitting astride a chair watching through his field glasses when he saw Beaurain and Louise leave the hotel and climb into the Mercedes.

Hurrying downstairs, he got in behind the wheel of the Volvo he had hired and drove swiftly along the river front and over the bridge to the mainland. He arrived in time to insert his vehicle into the traffic within tracking distance of the Mercedes.

Wearing a straw hat – which completely concealed his bald head – and a large pair of shaped tinted glasses, he had changed his appearance so that only a face-to-face encounter would make him recognisable to someone he knew. Glancing to his left he saw a Renault driving briefly alongside him. The two cars were parallel for only a few seconds, but long enough for Sholto to recognise the hooked-nosed profile of CIA agent Ed Cottel.

Sensing that he was following Beaurain, Sholto changed to shadowing the CIA man. He observed the forming-up of the convoy of cars which followed a Saab being followed by Beaurain's Mercedes as they changed direction and, in a matter of minutes, were moving out in the direction of Strängnäs on Highway E3.

It was Sholto who formed the invisible tail of the convoy, careful to keep the last car in sight while he lit cigarette after cigarette and his button-like eyes gleamed with concentration. As he continued driving, staring through the tinted glasses at the unrolling highway, he felt under his armpit the comforting bulge of the Colt ·45 in its sprung holster. On the seat beside him an Armalite rifle was wrapped in a blanket. It was beginning to look as though his urgent mission decided on in Washington was almost completed.

For long stretches in the open country the E3 has no barrier protecting the flat farmland alongside – the road simply merges with the level grassland. Palme had hidden his Saab by driving straight off the deserted highway over the grass and parking his vehicle behind a copse of trees. When Beaurain appeared he waved to him to follow suit and waited to guide the other vehicles in the convoy off the highway.

"What's Ed doing?" Louise asked as Beaurain skilfully and slowly manoeuvred the ton-and-a-half of metal along the same route and behind the same copse.

"Doing his own thing – as usual," Beaurain observed laconically.

The American continued along the highway and was soon out of sight beyond a curve. Overhead the traffic helicopter had appeared again, the machine carrying Harry Fondberg.

"Lose altitude," Fondberg ordered, sitting in the seat alongside the pilot. He rested his elbows on the arms of his seat to give stability and focused his high-powered binoculars on the Renault which had earlier stopped for a brief consultation with Jules Beaurain.

"Got you." Fondberg made a note of the registration number and then told the pilot to regain height. His next focus of interest was the convoy of vehicles leaving the road, ploughing over the grass and assembling behind a copse of trees to form a *laager*. It seemed to the chief of Säpo that interesting developments were about to take place.

Concerned with the movement of the convoy out of sight behind the trees, Fondberg missed the passage of a beige Volvo driven by a man wearing a straw hat. Having noted where the vehicles had left the road – and also aware of the traffic helicopter overhead – Harvey Sholto proceeded at a sedate pace along E3 until he was out of sight beyond the bend.

One of those old-fashioned houses ... Gables and bulging windows like they used to build ... must be at least fifty years old ...

Concealed with the others behind a second copse of trees, Palme used his left hand to scratch at his crew-cut. The murdered locksmith had been incredibly accurate when he described both place and location. The house was just where he had expected to find it. It looked like the house in *Psycho*.

Even Palme, who was not overly sensitive to atmosphere, felt there was something distinctly wrong with the place.

"I don't like it," he told Beaurain who stood alongside him with Jock Henderson just beyond. The Belgian was scanning the place with his own field glasses. He was inclined to agree. It looked a little too damned quiet. Curtains at all the windows, half-drawn to keep out the strong sunlight the way people do to protect rugs and carpets – or when they are away.

The steps up to the open verandah had a rickety look and the paint was peeling, but the rest of the house looked in good condition. The tarred drive ran straight up to the base of the steps and then curved round the right-hand side of the house. On the same side there was the silhouette, partially masked by the trees, of an ancient outhouse.

"Any sign of occupation?" Louise whispered.

There was something about the atmosphere of the place which encouraged whispering, something about the heavy, hot silence which hung like a cloud over the strange building.

"Can't see a damned thing," Beaurain said as he lowered his glasses, but there was a lack of conviction in his voice. "What do you think?" he asked.

"I don't like it," Palme repeated and again scratched his head with his left hand; his right was holding a loaded machine-pistol.

"I suggest we surround it first, sir," Henderson suggested crisply. "Then move in from all sides at an agreed moment. There's a drainage ditch just behind us with grass grown up all round it – a perfect conduit if we wriggle on our bellies and head for the rear of the house and then circle round."

"There's a lake not far away," Palme observed. "A lot of them in this area. This one's reasonably large." He showed the map to Beaurain, who made a remark he was later to regret.

"Can't be of any significance. I agree, Jock, we approach with extreme caution. Surround the place and then move in from all sides. Jock, get it organised – and *get it moving!*"

The "traffic" helicopter with Harry Fondberg aboard had flown away some distance and when Louise shaded her eyes against the glare of the sun she saw it as little more than a speck. Fondberg was deliberately moving out of the battle area so as not to alert the opposition. Louise stood behind the trees which concealed them from the highway, staring again at the house through her field glasses.

Henderson and his team of twelve armed gunners, equipped with walkie-talkies, had already disappeared along the drainage ditch. Watching the grasses above the ditch Beaurain could not see the slightest sign of movement. He just hoped that from an upper window in the house it was not possible to see down into the ditch. He heard an exclamation from Louise, who had moved a few yards away and was still surveying the general area of the house. He joined her.

"What is it?"

"When Stig was interviewing that locksmith in his shop didn't he say he'd seen a Volvo station wagon with American diplomatic plates?"

"Yes, he tried to follow the car on its way into Stockholm and lost it. Why?" There was a note of impatience in Beaurain's tone.

"Because parked behind the house there is a Volvo station wagon – the only thing is the diplomatic plates are Russian, not American."

"Seiger must have been so terrified he tried to hold back some of the truth. And that car means someone *is* inside that house!"

18

Dr Theodor Norling stared from behind the curtain of the first-floor window. There were gaps in the sea of grass along-side the drainage ditch and there he had seen the approaching men slithering along like snakes on their bellies.

He had just collected what he had come for – a sheaf of red folders which had been concealed beneath a trap-door on the ground floor. Now they were safely inside his brief-case, and he had to get away. The upper part of his body was clad in a loose-fitting hunting jacket with capacious pockets. He was holding the brief-case in his left hand; his right hand dug into one of the pockets and felt the hard metal pineapples – grenades.

Swiftly he left the room and darted down the curving staircase. The place was almost empty, barely furnished, and the heels of his shoes echoed throughout the house as he descended.

The furniture which did exist was of a curious nature. Under each window stood a large box which might have been mistaken for an old-fashioned radiator. They were nothing of the sort. Before leaving the ghostly house Norling was careful to collect a compact device with a red button and a slide. He raised the miniature aerial and moved the slide across into the 'active' position. He now had to be very careful not to depress the red button too early.

Outside he ducked behind the parked Volvo and ran under cover of some trees to cross the ditch where it turned and continued behind the house. As he had hoped the ditch was empty; the first man had not yet reached the corner. Behind him he was leaving a powder keg.

Crouched low, he was now moving directly away from the house and the highway, taking advantage of every piece of natural cover: a patch of undergrowth, a group of trees, an outcrop of granite rearing up out of the earth. When he reached the outcrop he stopped, climbing up a small ravine and peering cautiously over the rim.

Some distance behind him the blue waters of a lake rippled and glittered in the sun like mercury. This was the lake which Beaurain had thought couldn't be of any significance. From the summit of the granite crag Norling could just make out, among the reeds lining the shore, where his float-plane was hidden.

He turned his attention back to the house which he could see clearly from his position – the house, the parked estate car, and the line of men who, having encircled the house, were rising up from the ditch and staring at their objective without advancing. Norling clutched the radio-detonation device firmly in his right hand, his index finger close to the red button. One push would detonate the vast quantity of high-explosive installed inside the house.

Ed Cottel drove only a short distance beyond the drive to the house, which reminded him of the old houses still preserved in faraway San Francisco.

"Probably built about the same period," he speculated aloud – and knew immediately that the fact that he was talking to himself was a sign of tension. Wanting to use his transceiver, he drove the Renault off the highway and pulled up behind a clump of undergrowth.

He lowered the flap, exposing the dials, fiddled with them and then called his man at Kjula, the military and civil airfield fifteen kilometres from Strängnäs. "Sandpiper calling ... Sandpiper calling ... "

"I read you, Sandpiper. I read you. Ozark has landed. Repeat Ozark has landed."

Cottel signed out and glared at the shimmering haze dancing over the fields. For Sweden it was getting pretty goddam hot. So – Viktor Rashkin had made his usual landfall at Kjula. The pattern was repeating itself.

It had been clearly established by the watchers at Bromma and at Kjula that the Russian made regular flights along this route. He left the Cessna – piloted by himself – at Kjula, climbed behind the wheel of a waiting Volvo 245 station wagon, and eventually drove along Highway E3 as though heading back to Stockholm – the place he had just flown from. It hadn't made sense.

The trouble was Cottel had always lost the Volvo long before it reached the turn-off to the old house where Beaurain appeared to be about to start his own private war.

The Cessna left behind at Kjula was always flown back to its home base of Bromma by a hired pilot, presumably waiting for Rashkin's next outward flight.

Cottel caught a flash where there shouldn't be a flash. He flung open the door, ducked his head, rolled out bodily over the rough ground.

The first high-velocity bullet shattered the Renault's windscreen, punching a hole through the glass behind where Cottel's head had been. *The second and third bullets hit their targets, destroying both front tyres.* Under shelter of the Renault Cottel loosed off three shots in rapid succession as near as he could manage to where sunlight had flashed off the lens of a telescopic sight. He waited and heard the sound of a car engine starting up. By the time he reached the highway the vehicle and the would-be assassin had gone.

Harvey Sholto was furious with himself for missing the target – something almost unique in his experience. There was a traffic control chopper floating about somewhere – he'd seen it earlier and the one thing he could do without was interference from the local pigs. Covered in the rear of the Volvo lay the Armalite rifle, its barrel still warm from the three shots he had fired. As soon as he'd realised he'd missed Cottel with the first shot he had switched his aim to the tyres.

Using one hand to drive, he removed the straw hat and mopped sweat off his bald head. This was cleaning-up time – knocking off all the loose ends. It had worked well at Stockholm Central. Wearing Swedish police uniform and equipped with the powerful motor-bike, Sholto had slipped through the cordon with the suitcase of heroin strapped to the pillion and delivered the consignment to the apartment in Rådmansgatan.

It was also Sholto who had used the silenced gun to kill Serge Litov after they had retrieved the heroin. Litov was an important part of the cleaning-up process. He rammed the wide-brimmed hat back on his head and pursed his thick lips. So, Cottel was still on his list. He would get a second chance.

"There's someone on that granite crag, Jules," said Louise

urgently.

"Where?"

"That bloody great rock sticking up behind the house."

Beaurain had to take an instant decision. He had to assume that Louise *had* seen something. Instinctively he sensed there were only seconds left before something happened ... a man or men on the crag overlooking the house ... a clear view of Henderson's men surrounding the house ... a clear field of fire for automatic weapons to mow down everyone ...

"Withdraw! Withdraw! Henderson withdraw for God's sake now!"

To make his voice carry Beaurain had cupped his hands into a man-made megaphone. He was risking blowing the whole operation. He was risking getting half his men killed if he had guessed wrong – if Louise had imagined something. His desperate shout would have given the whole game away, wiped out Henderson's most important weapon – the element of surprise.

Henderson reacted instantly, but used his own judgment. *"Take cover! Take immediate cover! Attack imminent ..."*

Beaurain and Louise saw the horror from their distant vantage point by the copse of trees.

The bay windows burst outwards, disintegrating into a hail of debris which cascaded over a huge area. The steps leading up to the front door took off like a rocket: a huge amount of explosive must have been placed underneath them to catch anyone trying to reach the verandah. The walls of the house were hurtling like shrapnel through the air, shards of wood with jagged ends. The roof rose up as though clawed skyward by a giant hand. And all this was accompanied by an ear-battering roar which temporarily deafened Beaurain.

Harry Fondberg, returning to the house area in the helicopter, stared in sheer stunned horror at the aerial view. The chopper shuddered briefly as the shock wave hit the machine. Fondberg recovered his wits swiftly, and gave the pilot a natural and humanitarian order.

"Put down on the highway at the entrance to the drive," he said into the mike. "And fast!"

And now the fire came. Like so many Swedish dwellings the house was built of wood. A fierce tongue of yellow flame speared its way up through the spreading black smoke, a tongue which danced and grew. The sinister crackle of flames spread fast, devouring the remnants of the house which had stood alone for so many years.

Dr Theodor Norling had not waited at the top of the crag to see the result of pressing his red button. He had scrambled down the side of the crag furthest away from the house and by doing so had saved himself. At the back of the house had stood a large log-pile, ready for the coming winter. The explosion had taken these ready-made missiles and hurled them away from the house with the force of an artillery barrage. Norling heard the thunderous clatter of the logs bombarding the far side of the rock. Then he began moving towards his objective, half-running and half-crouching to escape detection.

The helicopter had been damaged on landing. It had been a chance in a thousand, possibly compounded by the pilot's shock at seeing a whole house fly into pieces – but when he landed at the entrance to the drive the rear of his machine was a shade too close to Beaurain's parked Mercedes. It caught the car only a glancing blow, taking out no more than a sliver from the roof – but it was the small tail rotor whose tip had struck the car. The rotor spun off the chopper and skittered across the highway.

"We can't fly again," Fondberg was informed. "I'm sorry – but without the tail rotor we've lost our rudder."

"Not to worry." The Säpo chief was preparing to leave the helicopter. "Be ready to radio for medical help – but not, repeat not – until I have checked the situation."

He met Beaurain returning down the drive while Louise remained near the wreckage, scanning the countryside with her field glasses. Beaurain was running and his expression was grim. He waved Fondberg back and the Swede stood where he was until Beaurain had reached him.

"Harry, get that chopper into the air and start looking."

"Rotor tail's gone. Pilot chipped your Mercedes when we were on the ground. What's happened up there?"

"Place was one gigantic boobytrap," Beaurain told Fondberg. "Suggest anything to you, Harry?"

"Should it?"

Beaurain was talking fast, filling Fondberg in on the

position as swiftly as possible. "How long ago since the Elsinore Massacre? Another case of a large quantity of explosives detonated by remote control. The same hand pressed the button here to turn this house into a pile of rubble. I wanted your chopper in the air looking for the mass-killer – the maniac – who seems to be getting madder."

"Your men ... " Fondberg spoke quietly and looked up the drive to where there was a scene like the smoke of battle. "How are they? I can call a fleet of ambulances."

"Not necessary, but many thanks. Henderson reacted a split second too early for the killer, radioed everyone to take cover – so they dropped flat. Result – the blast-wave and the shrapnel-effect passed right over them. One or two have cuts and bruises, but nothing they can't fix up themselves. Otherwise you wouldn't see Louise back there doing her bird-watching act."

"I think she may have found an interesting specimen," Fondberg observed. "I'll stay here with the chopper to cover for you if a patrol car arrives. They do creep about on the E3."

Beaurain turned and saw Louise beckoning him. He ran back up the drive and now the stench of charred wood was increasing. Black smoke billowed, the fire inside the smoke-filled nest was a searing, crackling inferno. As he came close to Louise who was standing where she could see behind the house, he saw the familiar figure of Henderson in the distance running towards a granite crag rearing up out of the ground.

"What is it, Louise?" Beaurain demanded.

"Norling."

"Where?"

"I'll tell you if you'll shut up for ten seconds, for Christ's sake!"

"I'm mute," he told her.

"To the right of that large crag Henderson is heading for with some of his men." She handed him her field glasses. "I thought I saw movement in the grass, then I thought I was wrong – then I saw it again. The trouble is his blond hair merges with the landscape. And Stig is puzzled."

Palme was standing a few yards away, his face smoke-blackened, his stubble of hair singed with the heat which had flared out from the house, holding his machine-pistol ready for action. Now Henderson had reached the base of the crag while Beaurain continued scanning the field of yellow rape Louise had indicated. Surely there was nowhere there a man could hide, let alone keep moving. Then Beaurain saw what she was driving at. And at almost the same moment something else happened. Palme began receiving a message on his walkie-talkie.

There was a deep gulley running across the field of rape and along it a fair-haired man was moving at a steady trot – not so fast that he could easily be picked out, but fast enough to be putting plenty of ground between himself and the house he had just annihilated.

"Why is Stig puzzled?" he asked Louise.

"Stig says the fair-haired man – Oh, hell, it must be Norling – is heading straight for a lake which bars his way."

"Message from Sergeant Henderson, sir," Palme put in, proffering his walkie-talkie. "He says he can see a blond man running towards a lake which he will reach in about two minutes. He has a good view of the target from the top of the crag but the range is too great for opening fire. He proposes sending a cordon across country to surround the fugitive – but would like a word with you."

"Beaurain here," the Belgian said into the instrument. "I want that man at all costs – preferably alive, but dead rather than let him escape."

"We're moving now, sir," Henderson's voice confirmed. "And at the base of this crag I found something odd – show you later."

Palme took a firmer grip on his machine-pistol and spoke with great conviction. "We can get him. He has kept to the gulley to make himself invisible, but that gulley winds – it's marked on the map. An old stream-bed. We go straight across country. OK?"

"OK," Beaurain agreed. He had hardly spoken when Palme was moving at a steady trot away from the blackened ruin, his weapon held diagonally across his body ready for immediate use. Behind the sturdy Swede followed Beaurain and Louise.

They soon saw that Palme knew what he was talking about. Because of their starting point and Norling's present position they had a good head start on Henderson and his circling cordon. The trio led by Palme would reach the blond-haired man first. Arriving at the deep gulley, they went down one side, crossed it, climbed the other side, and Louise gasped when she saw the view.

Without her realising it they had been climbing gently since leaving the area of the house and now they were on a low ridge with the ground ahead falling away from them. The boomerang shape of a lake spread out below, unruffled by even a whisper of breeze, the sun blazing down on the startling blue surrounded by the yellow of the rape. Norling was only a few hundred metres ahead. They had got him!

"The plane – the float-plane – concealed in those reeds!"

It was Beaurain who first grasped Norling's plan of escape and – because of the accident to Fondberg's chopper – how close he was to succeeding. Away to their left and behind them Henderson's men were spread out, in correct military fashion, in a fan-shaped cordon. It was Beaurain who detected the terrible danger.

"Get down! Drop flat for God's sake!"

The fair-haired man had turned, seen the trio and his reaction was immediate. Standing quite still he fumbled inside one of his pockets, fiddled briefly with something between both hands, hoisted his right arm up and bowled the missile overarm. His hand returned to his pocket for a second object. The first grenade was sailing though the air heading straight for where Beaurain and his companions had been standing.

They sprawled flat among the rape, hugging the ground. There was an ear-splitting explosion. Debris rained down on their reclining figures. Norling had their range. Beaurain shouted a second warning. "Lie still, don't move, don't show him where we are." He had just finished his warning when the second grenade burst. Again debris was scattered all round them.

Beaurain did not have to shout a third warning. Both Louise and Palme remained perfectly still. Seconds later a third grenade detonated. Then a fourth … a fifth … a sixth …

The grenades were landing further and further away from where they lay. Norling was running to the lake, stopping briefly to hurl another grenade, then running again. Beaurain stood up cautiously. His caution was wasted.

Norling had already reached the float-plane and was inside the cabin, and the engine burst into action. As Louise and Palme climbed to their feet, Beaurain aimed his Smith & Wesson and fired twice. It was quite hopeless. Out of range. "Use the machine-pistol!" he shouted to Palme.

Palme was already cuddling the stock against his shoulder, but as he did so the float-plane streaked out across the lake and he didn't even bother to press the trigger. As Henderson came running up followed by two of his men Beaurain shrugged his shoulders and lit a cigarette. He watched as the float-plane lifted off and continued its flight at a low altitude, vanishing over the fold of a hill.

"Fondberg's chopper," Henderson suggested. "If we get him in the air fast ... "

"Which we can't – because in landing he lost his tail rotor." Smoking his cigarette, Beaurain looked down towards the lake where the float-plane had been half-hidden inside the belt of reeds. "Stig, he took off in one hell of a hurry. Go down to where that float-plane was and see if you can find anything. We'll meet you back at the drive."

When they arrived back on the highway Beaurain told Fondberg the bad news and the Säpo chief put out a call for the float-plane on his radio. "Not that you can expect much," he warned Beaurain. "The trouble is we have plenty of those machines buzzing about in this part of the world – and especially further south where the country is littered with lakes. So what have we discovered?"

"You tell me," Beaurain suggested.

"The Syndicate's explosives dump – probably stock-piled for bank robberies – and their temporary headquarters which is now a pile of smoking rubble. That's it."

"Except look who's coming down the road."

Ed Cottel had walked. Since the unknown gunman had shot out his two front tyres he had been walking back down the highway. And Cottel objected to walking, couldn't see the point of it when there were things called automobiles available. He gave Fondberg and Beaurain a terse account of his experiences while Louise listened; then he absorbed what Beaurain told him about what had happened to them.

"You say there was a Volvo 245 parked behind the house?" he checked when Beaurain had completed his story. "None of this makes much sense. One of my watchers reported Viktor Rashkin had left in a Cessna – piloting himself

– taking off from Bromma with a flight plan for Kjula. Then he gets in a Volvo 245 and drives in this direction. It turns out that there was a Volvo 245 parked out of sight behind this house. Now you tell me the guy who peppered you with grenades before he took off in his float-plane was Dr Theodor Norling. Are you sure?"

"There's nothing wrong with my eyesight," Louise rapped back.

"Ed, I'm more interested," Beaurain interjected, "in who might be the killer who tried to wipe you out when you were sitting in that hired Renault off the highway."

"No idea," Cottel said brusquely.

"And who are all these watchers you keep occupied tracking the movements of Viktor Rashkin?" Beaurain persisted. "You seem to have an obsession with the Russians."

"Just with one Russian – because I'm convinced he fits in with the Stockholm Syndicate somewhere. I'll provide you with my record of those movements and see whether you can spot any pattern. As to my watchers – it's taken me God knows how long to build up a network of people throughout Scandinavia at all the airfields and seaports, people who've no idea who is employing them but like the money they get." A dry smile wrinkled his tanned face. "I guess Harvey Sholto would blow his top if he knew how I was using the funds I get from Washington. You've no idea how adept I've become at what we call creative accountancy."

"What we call fiddling expenses," Louise remarked.

"So now perhaps you understand," the American continued, directing his remark to Beaurain with a hint of sarcasm, "my obsession with the Russians."

"No, frankly I don't. You seem to have forgotten that one of the Syndicate's own people deliberately murdered Serge Litov at Stockholm Central after he had served his purpose. *Touché* – you said the Russians fitted in with the Syndicate somewhere."

"To hell with you," Cottel replied amiably.

"How much power does Harvey Sholto have in Washington?" Beaurain asked out of the blue.

"You don't mention his name – even favourably – if you want to keep your job on the Government payroll. Officially he doesn't even exist."

"I see," the Belgian replied, and Louise wondered what he saw.

Harry Fondberg suggested that the entire Telescope force started back for Stockholm before the patrol-car he had summoned arrived. He was going to be the innocent bystander who had spotted the house exploding from the air while on another mission.

On the return journey Palme waited until they were well clear of Fondberg before producing something from inside his windcheater. "You were right to ask me to check round where Norling took off in his float-plane," he commented to Beaurain. "He must have been climbing into the cockpit when he dropped this and there was no time to go back for it." 'This' was a slim red folder.

"Norling carried a brief-case," Beaurain recalled. "It looks as though at the wrong moment the case came open and in his haste to get away he never noticed. The brief-case looked pretty heavy, probably crammed with these folders."

"Anything interesting?" Louise enquired.

"Give me time – I've only just released the security device. One surprise: the language used is English – or American. The spelling is American – *labor* instead of *labour*."

"It's a good thing Ed Cottel is travelling in one of the other cars," Louise remarked. "I think if he heard that remark he'd blow his top."

"It might be a better thing than even you realise at this stage," Beaurain replied cryptically, his eyebrows furrowed as he rapidly read through the sheets contained inside the folder. "This is a little too damned convenient, isn't it? It could be a plant left behind deliberately. How come if it did drop out of his brief-case when he was climbing into a float-plane on the edge of a lake that the bloody thing isn't even wet?"

"Because," Palme informed him smugly, "I found it resting on the edge of an old bird's nest made of reeds and God knows what else – a big nest. And don't ask me what bird! I don't watch them."

"OK, Stig. We can take it that this is genuine."

"With Stig's discovery my own little contribution isn't going to rate very high in the history of Telescope discoveries," Henderson said apologetically. "I found it at the foot of the far side of the big crag behind the house from where Norling detonated all his explosive."

Henderson handed his discovery to Beaurain who had turned in his seat and was staring fixedly at the object Henderson was holding. As though mesmerised he reached out a hand, took the object and held it in the open palm of his hand.

"What's so exciting about that?" Louise asked.

"Thank you, Jock," Beaurain said slowly, balancing the object as though it were made of gold. "You have just handed me the final key and proof I needed as to what the Stockholm Syndicate is really all about."

"It's the broken-off heel of an elevated shoe," Louise objected. "That's all."

"That's all," Beaurain agreed sardonically.

From his room in the Hotel Reisen overlooking the Strommen and the Grand Hotel across the water Harvey Sholto had put in a call to the home of Joel Cody, the President's aide. It was an arrangement that had been made before he left Washington to fly to Stockholm. Any operator intercepting a call to the White House just had to listen in to *that* kind of call. This way Sholto could be phoning any ordinary individual.

"Appalachian calling," he opened cautiously.

"Rushmore here."

Joel Cody himself had answered, and he was alone, so Sholto could start talking. He kept his voice so low that twice Cody had to ask him to speak up.

"Cottel ... " He said the name quickly and deliberately mispronounced it. " ... is getting close. I persuaded him to keep his distance earlier today but he's breathing down our necks."

"Real close?" enquired Cody. "I mean, you're not panicking over nothing? This is a delicate situation and we wouldn't like it to blow up in our faces."

"I'm telling you Cottel is within spitting distance of what you wouldn't like your best friend to tell you about. To say nothing of the guy you work for. And that's not all! You ever bought a telescope, one of those things you look through to see the girl taking off her bra in the window across the way? Well, they're also breathing down our necks. Correction – they're breathing down *your* neck. And you know something? I thought you had an election coming up."

"OK, OK," Cody replied hastily. "You're the man on the spot, you decide. You have, of course, our complete backing."

"With that I should start running. But Harvey Sholto stays in business while presidents come and go – so shove it. And I'll see what I can do."

Sholto rammed down the receiver onto the cradle before the man in Washington had time to respond. High-powered rifle or revolver, the next time he would be shooting for real. And there were a lot of people to deal with in a short space of time. Just like the old times in Vietnam. He caught sight of his bald-headed reflection in the dressing-table mirror. Still, he had once killed twenty individual men in Saigon in different parts of the city in one day. And that had been to please Washington. Correction: to *save* Washington.

The news which determined Beaurain's final strategy came from an old friend just arrived at the Grand Hotel. The agitation Beaurain had detected when he had visited the Baron de Graer in his office in the Banque du Nord had disappeared. This time the Baron's expression was composed as he sat in an armchair close to the bathroom where Beaurain had turned on all the taps to scramble any possible listening device hidden in the room. But despite his placidity Beaurain saw in his eyes a steely determination.

"We – you – have to destroy the Syndicate, Jules," he remarked as he trimmed off the tip of his cigar and then lit it slowly, puffing with evident pleasure. "You might say I have recovered my nerve."

"Did you ever lose it?"

"The last time I saw you in Brussels I was a trembling wreck – I have had time to think since. The information you need is this. I am, as a minor member of the Syndicate, invited to what they are pleased to call their summit conference. *The scum!*"

"We'll deal with them."

"Meeting place is supposed to be the liner *Silvia*, now lying a few miles off the coast of southern Sweden near the port of Trelleborg. That's a blind. The real conference takes place aboard the Soviet hydrofoil, *Kometa*. All the leading European financiers, industrialists and politicians who have become members will be taken out aboard power-boats and cruisers from Trelleborg – to meet their American counter-parts. They are moving out of Stockholm at this very moment."

"By what route?"

"Mostly by air. Some aboard scheduled flights from Arlanda to Malmö and then on by car. Others will use smaller and private planes to get them to an airstrip close to their destination." He began pacing restlessly round the room. "This Hugo has to be identified and hunted down, Jules. He is the real leader and yet no-one has ever seen his face."

"But we have heard of him," Beaurain said soothingly. "When is this summit due to take place?"

"Hugo – whoever he is – has chosen a curious time. Once on board *Kometa* the visitors will be taken on a short voyage – it will take place between 20.50 hours and 2.43 the following morning, which coincides tomorrow precisely with the few hours of darkness at this time of the year."

"And you have no idea at all – even remotely – who Hugo might be?" Beaurain pressed.

De Graer threw up his hands in a gesture of frustration. "Do you think I have not asked myself that question a thousand times and more?"

"How long have you known these details of the summit conference?" asked Beaurain.

"A message came through on the telephone less than an hour ago. The short notice is obviously deliberate – to give no time to react."

"Who phoned – a man or a woman?"

"I'm pretty sure it was that girl who phoned me when I was in Brussels. The one I called Madame."

"Always it is a woman, a girl, who makes these phone calls," Beaurain said reflectively. He looked at the Baron. "I cannot thank you enough for the information you have provided. Can I take it that under no circumstances will you attend this meeting on board *Kometa*?"

De Graer stopped pacing and grasped Beaurain's arm. "I only came here to see if I could help. I am now catching the first flight back from Arlanda to Brussels – but I am taking the precaution of booking my ticket only when I get to Arlanda. No-one except yourself will then know of my departure."

"Very wise. Take care." Beaurain shook the old warrior

by the hand. "Louise and I will be leaving for Trelleborg shortly. That is all I am going to tell you."

Descending in the hotel's splendid lift with its red leather padding and gilt-framed mirrors – which seemed to go so well with the world of the Baron de Graer – Beaurain pondered on what the banker had said. Who, he wondered, really was Hugo?

19

The short time before Beaurain's departure for Trelleborg was packed with activity. Beaurain was preparing very carefully for the final clash between Telescope and the Stockholm Syndicate.

His temporary headquarters was the interior of a laundry van, a mobile headquarters Palme kept in reserve in a garage in Stockholm. Similar mobile headquarters inside a variety of vehicles were available in every country in western Europe. The interior of the laundry van was fully equipped with a high-powered transceiver, a telescopic aerial, maps of every major province in Sweden, charts of the seas offshore, and long-life rations. The van was parked in a side street close to the Grand Hotel.

As Beaurain, sitting on a flap seat at the rear of the van, read signals which had come in from *Firestorm* at sea, Louise stood by his shoulder. Some time earlier, Palme had driven off in his Saab to Rådmansgatan 490. Beaurain's instructions had been simple and direct.

"If the place is empty, rip it apart. I don't know what we're looking for – something unusual, something you feel doesn't fit in with a normal middle-class Swedish girl's way of life, something Norling keeps in that apartment."

"*Firestorm* is lying off Trelleborg," Louise remarked.

"Bucky Buckminster is doing exactly what I told him to – keeping below the horizon and using his chopper to mount a series of recces."

"Well, they've found both the liner *Silvia* and the Soviet hydrofoil *Kometa*."

"Yes, and the significant thing is that *Kometa* is situated a few miles further out to sea and due south of *Silvia*. So any power-cruiser ferrying VIPs from Trelleborg to *Kometa* can make it appear from shore that it is *Silvia* they are heading for."

"Will it be a savage encounter?" Louise asked quietly.

"I expect a most brutal and bloody clash with no quarter given on either side. This is an organisation with billions behind it, with men of enormous influence involved. They live in a world all their own where the only thing that counts is the maximum profit. Look at the horror of the Elsinore Massacre – and that was just to make sure one man – one man! – didn't reach us with information. I'm not too happy about any of it."

"Why?" asked Louise. She watched him while he lit a cigarette and took only a few puffs before stubbing it out. One of the disadvantages of holding a meeting inside a stationary laundry van.

"I think Hugo may have gone over the edge," Beaurain told her.

"You mean ..."

"Hugo still, I'm convinced, has his first-class brain functioning perfectly. It's just that he no longer takes human life into account at all."

"What's going to happen?"

As if on cue, there was a rapping on one of the rear doors, Palme's signal that he had returned from the apartment on Rådmansgatan. Checking through the one-way glass window in the door, Louise released the latch and the Swede scrambled inside. He was holding a blue cloth bag.

"Something very peculiar," were his first words.

"Which is?" Beaurain prompted him.

"This bag – hidden where women always think no-one will ever look," Palme said laconically. "In a recess on top of a wardrobe well above eye level. Contents are interesting."

Beaurain took the bag and burrowed inside. Two items were neatly stored inside plastic envelopes. They were American passports and when Beaurain showed them to Louise they saw that the photographs and details of the holders were still to be added. "Final proof – and the mystery deepens," was his tantalising observation.

"Very illuminating ..." Louise began.

"We have to make one more visit to Harry Fondberg, another to Ed Cottel, then we all make our way to Trelleborg by different routes and modes of transport. Scheduled air flights, cars – this laundry van must go as our mobile headquarters – and some can go direct to *Firestorm* by boat. Inform Jock to organise the move south *fast*," he told Palme.

From Harry Fondberg's office at police headquarters, Beaurain used the phone to call both Willy Flamen and Bodel Marker. Fondberg and Louise sat listening to his conversations and Fondberg smoked another of his cigars as he listened and nodded his approval. Eventually Beaurain put down the phone after making his last call.

"You'll all have to collaborate very closely and get the timing synchronised right across western Europe," he warned Harry Fondberg. "You heard me arrange with Willy to co-ordinate with Wiesbaden for Germany and with Paris – and Bodel Marker links up with Amsterdam. God knows they have enough water in Holland."

"It will be the biggest mass-arrest Europe has ever seen," Fondberg promised Beaurain. "And it will happen everywhere at the same time, as soon as the next set of signals start transmitting – you predict tomorrow about midnight."

Beaurain stood up. "And now Louise and I must get moving." He hesitated before he continued. "We have an appointment which concerns the American connection."

"The American connection?" Fondberg was puzzled.

"Yes. It's the key to the whole evil system."

The rendezvous with Ed Cottel took place late in the evening at a remote spot off Highway E3 which leads towards Strängnäs. Beaurain had chosen a location on a side road on the way to an old iron mine which had ceased working. The mine was called Skottvångs Gruva, and the meeting point was deep inside a fir forest which closed in on either side of the road like a wall.

The location had been suggested by Palme and marked on a map delivered to Cottel in his room at the Grand so that on receipt he barely had enough time to drive to the rendezvous. The dramatic atmosphere, heightened by the time of the meeting – 10 p.m. – was all part of Beaurain's plan, as he explained to Louise while they were driving along the E3. In the back of the Mercedes Palme sat in silence, his machine-pistol concealed in an oil-cloth sheath.

"I'm playing on Ed's nerves," Beaurain told her, "screwing them up to the maximum pressure point, hoping he'll blow."

"I thought he was your friend," Louise observed.

"And who is in the best position to fool you? Read history – it always turns out to be the one closest to you. Julius Caesar could have told you – Brutus."

"But you've known him for decades."

"Don't forget that house that damned near blew up in our faces – and Ed Cottel kept well clear of it. Another thing, he keeps pointing me at Rashkin and away from Washington. It could even be that Harvey Sholto is in Stockholm to find out who Ed really is. I'm just not sure – I hope to be after this meeting."

On this cryptic note Beaurain fell silent, turning off the main highway onto a forest-lined road which had no traffic at all, a road which Louise found creepy in the gathering dusk.

"Sorry about that mistake I made in the lobby of the Grand Hotel," Palme called out from the rear seat.

Beaurain shook his head dismissively. In a rush when delivering the rendezvous message to Cottel, Palme had used a hotel pad to scribble brief written instructions on the route to reinforce the marked map. On his way back from Cottel's room he had hurried down to the lobby to rescue the pad in case the impression of his writing was imprinted on it. *The pad had disappeared.*

The Mercedes was moving at no more than thirty miles an hour, its headlight beams lancing across the enclosing palisade of tree trunks. Palme leaned over frequently to check the odometer, checking the distance from where they had turned onto the road leading to Skottvångs Gruva. Beaurain was still cruising, watching the dashboard clock which registered 9.50 p.m. "We're ten minutes early – deliberately," he remarked. Louise didn't like the atmosphere: Beaurain had not told her what was going to happen. And now there were only three of them left in Stockholm.

The main movement south towards the port of Trelleborg had started and was well under way. Commanded by Jock Henderson, all the gunners were being withdrawn from the Swedish capital and sent by various routes and differing forms of transport to reinforce the heavy contingent of troops already aboard the fast and heavily-armed steam yacht, *Firestorm*.

"Drop me off here, Jules."

It was Palme who had spoken after leaning forward again and checking the odometer for the last time. Beaurain dipped his lights, cruised a few more yards, hardly moving, then switched off all the lights and stopped the car.

"Don't worry, Jules, I'll be close enough," Palme whispered as he opened the door.

"Happy to rely on you. But watch it, Stig. We can't be sure."

Can't be sure of what? Louise bit her knuckles to stop herself asking questions. Sitting rigidly in the dark with only the illumination from the dashboard she noticed something else. As Palme left the car he did not close the heavy door with his normal *clunk!* He went to considerable trouble to close it as silently as he could.

Then they were moving again, Beaurain switched on all the lights and they were turning a bend and the headlight beams illuminated another stretch of highway hemmed in by dense forest. Here and there tracks led away through the wall of trees, tracks for timber wagons by the look of the deep ruts bored into the ground. They had moved only a very short distance beyond the bend when two headlights came on and glared at them, stayed on for three seconds – Beaurain was checking by his wrist-watch – and went out.

Beaurain stopped the car and Louise sensed the tension although there was no physical contact between them. The twin headlights repeated the process twice – switching on for three seconds and then going out again. So far as Louise could gauge, the car beaming its lights at them was parked at an angle just off the road on one of the tracks. It was ridiculous and yet eerie. In her nervousness she giggled.

"It's like Checkpoint Charlie – you know, an exchange between East and West."

"Except that this time it's an exchange between West and West."

"What does that mean, for Christ's sake?"

"An exchange of views. That should be Ed Cottel in his new car."

"Then it's all right – if it's Ed?"

"If you say so."

Louise felt a tremble of fury. "Why the hell do we have to

meet him in this godforsaken spot?"

"I told you earlier."

"To put pressure on Ed? That's crazy."

"His idea," Beaurain told her. "We're here at his request – a meeting between me and him well outside Stockholm."

"I don't like being out here. I feel something is desperately wrong."

"Something is desperately wrong. We have to try and find out what it is, who Hugo is, who really is running the Stockholm Syndicate before we move down to Trelleborg."

"These signals – car lights flashing on and off."

"Were agreed when we arranged this rendezvous. They're supposed to identify us to each other."

"Supposed to?"

"And now the exchange of signals has taken place we head straight for Cottel's car, then stop. So, we will do just that."

Beaurain, who had kept the engine idling during the exchange of signals, released the brake and drove forward at very slow speed. The Mercedes was hardly moving as he swung off from the road onto the springy grass at the edge of the forest. And as he approached the stationary Renault the vehicle remained dark and without any sign of life.

Beaurain turned the wheel slightly, swinging Louise's side of the Mercedes away from the Renault. He stopped and whispered in her ear before switching off the engine. "Open your door, slip out and back onto the road. Don't close the door – just push it to. If you hear shots take cover and wait for me to call out to you."

She hated obeying the order, leaving Beaurain on his own, but her training at the Château Wardin asserted itself. Without a word she did as she had been told, using the Mercedes to hide her from the Renault as she slipped back through the forest to the road.

Left alone, Beaurain took his Smith & Wesson from its shoulder holster, held it by his side and quietly slid out of the car.

"I have a machine-pistol trained on you! Drop the gun, Hugo."

Hugo!

Two things jolted Beaurain – the use of the name *Hugo* and the fact that the voice was definitely the gravelly tones of Ed Cottel. Also the American had switched on a powerful torch which almost blinded Beaurain – but let him see the barrel of the machine-pistol. Beaurain estimated the muzzle was just about aimed at his gut. At that range and with that weapon the worst shot in the world couldn't miss. And Cottel had taken medals on the firing ranges at Langley. Beaurain dropped his revolver.

"That's better, Hugo. Now let's place our hands on the top of our head, shall we? That's better." The torch light was doused, which again affected Beaurain's vision. But the American didn't need it – not with a blaster of a gun at such close range.

Beaurain's excellent night vision was now reasserting itself. He could make out clearly the American's silhouette – and the silhouette of the machine-pistol which never wavered as it remained aimed point-blank at its target. He asked another question, enunciating his words with great clarity so they echoed among the dusk descending on the forest. There was a strong smell of pine in Beaurain's nostrils.

"Who fooled you, Ed? Who took you for a ride in a big way? I have a feeling you've been manipulated like a puppet."

The gravelly voice sank to a monotone as Ed Cottel began reciting a list of events like a litany, his tone remote and cold. "You were in Bruges at the same time as Dr Otto Berlin, director of the Syndicate's southern sector. Department of Coincidence? You were in Copenhagen when Dr Benny Horn, director of the Syndicate's central sector, was in the city on one of his rare visits. Department of Coincidence? To say nothing of your presence in Elsinore when God knows how many innocent souls were massacred aboard that ferry to shut the mouth of one man."

"Watch it, Ed," Beaurain said very quietly. "Before I smash your teeth in."

"*No! You watch it, you bastard!* I arrive in Stockholm and try to locate the elusive Dr Theodor Norling, director of the Syndicate's Scandinavian sector. He can't be found anywhere. Then he arrives. And hell, who do you think also arrives at the same moment? Ex-Chief Superintendent Jules Beaurain."

"If you say 'Department of Coincidence' again I'll kick your kneecap off," Beaurain told the American. "Who's been feeding you this poison?"

"Very clever, Jules. You pretend to be tracking down this Hugo, so who is the last person in the world anyone is going to suspect just could be Hugo? Yourself. And now I'm going to feed you on a platter to Washington – unless I have to press this trigger."

"Which would be a very convenient conclusion to the whole complex case – from your point of view."

"What do you mean?" Cottel demanded.

Beaurain's voice had hardened when he made his statement and the American detected a subtle change in the Belgian's personality. He noticed there was also a physical change: Beaurain suddenly stopped wriggling his shoulders as though trying to ease the cramp out of his muscles. Cottel was sensitive to personality changes and an interrogator of many years' experience. He was still trying to work it out when a cold hard rim of metal was pressed against the base of his neck.

"You have three seconds to drop the machine-pistol before I blow your head off your shoulders," Palme told him. "My orders are to pull the trigger even if you open fire on Jules Beaurain. I have started counting."

The shock tactic approach had been worked out by Beaurain in advance and was based on his knowledge of the American's psychology. Cottel was a realist and had long ago learned never to buck the odds if there was another option, a chance to live and fight again another day. He didn't hesitate. He dropped the machine-pistol.

"Walk two paces forward," Palme ordered.

The American obeyed and behind him Palme quietly stepped to one side before he scooped up the weapon – in case Cottel had kicked out behind him seeking a vulnerable part of the Swede's anatomy.

"So now, the Swede, at long last, we get to meet Hugo," Beaurain said, "and we have penetrated the American connection."

"What the hell are you talking about?" Cottel blazed.

"Shut your trap, Ed, for ten seconds. Louise," Beaurain called out, "come here and listen to this rubbish." He waited until she had arrived. "Meet Hugo," he invited.

"*Hugo?*"

"To cover his tracks he was going to offer me up to his

chiefs in Washington – on a platter was the phrase, I believe. Who is the big man in Washington, Ed? The one you really report to? I offer Joel Cody as a suggestion."

"I don't report to anyone back in the States any more than I can," Cottel replied quietly. "And when I do send anything it amounts to no more than meaningless words."

"Why?" Beaurain pounced.

"You should know – because I don't know who I can trust. Your Syndicate has penetrated the highest echelons."

"Someone did tell you I was Hugo." Beaurain was suddenly convinced the American was not lying. And yet there had to be an American connection. He had proof. "Who told you?" Beaurain persisted.

"One of my watchers. No, you don't get his name. Tell your thug to pull the trigger now, but you still don't get his name."

"Even though he was bought?" Beaurain asked softly. "Bought to twist the existing facts in a way only Hugo could have done to make everything seem exactly the opposite to what it is? Have you a transceiver in that Renault? You have? Then get through now to the contact who pointed the finger at me."

"Why?" Cottel asked.

"Because you'll find he's not available. By now he will be dead. He's served his purpose and when a man has served Hugo's purpose he's eliminated. Go on, Ed, get back into that car and use the transceiver to call your contact. He should be available?"

"Round the clock." The American sounded doubtful. "Every one of my watchers is now holding himself available round the clock. I'd expected to clean up the whole business within the next twenty-four hours."

"Starting with me? You were fooled, Ed! *Fooled!*"

"Give me a couple of minutes. Get your man to check me for extra weapons." He waited while Palme obliged. "He can hold me in the sights of his machine-pistol."

Cottel didn't wait for a reply. Slipping behind the wheel of the car he fumbled in the dark, attached a head-set and reached for the microphone. It seemed to Beaurain it was a one-way conversation. Only two minutes later the American climbed slowly out of the car and accepted the cigarette Beaurain offered.

"There are things you should know, Jules," he said dully. "And there is an American connection. Stupid Ed Cottel was chosen to come to Europe because Washington thought he was more concerned with tracking down the Telescope organisation. Making enquiries, quote, as to whether the Stockholm Syndicate existed, close quote, was supposed to be a side-line. I think Washington found out I was directing all my resources and firepower on locating the Syndicate after I came over. I've had trouble making contact back home."

"You just tried to call up your contact who said I was Hugo, who *convinced* you I was Hugo. Any reply?"

"None at all. And he was supposed to be waiting for a signal from me, staying up all night if necessary."

"He's probably floating down the Riddarfjärden by now. You see, Ed, he'd served his purpose, so Hugo has disposed of him. You're supposed to have served your purpose now ..."

"Which is?"

"You should have shot me as Hugo. Then sat down and written out your highly confidential report for Washington. End of any rumours about a Stockholm Syndicate, end of any speculation starting in the American press about who was financing it, end of any horrendous scandal which might break and lose the President the coming election."

"I think I got most of it wrong." Ed was deliberately looking at Louise when he made the statement. "I was conned, but good. Jules, you have any information on the financing of the Syndicate?"

"One of the big contributors is Leo Gehn, chairman of the I.T.E. combine, who is also a generous contributor to the President's campaign war chest. Just imagine those two facts hitting the headlines."

"You think this definitely goes all the way up to the White House?" Cottel asked tersely.

"Harvey Sholto arrived in Stockholm direct from Washington a few days ago," Beaurain threw at him. "Joel Cody phoned the Säpo chief to let him know of Sholto's imminent visit – but didn't let him know Sholto was already in the city. Luckily Fondberg's men at Arlanda spotted him coming in, but didn't follow him. Why should they? And Sholto hasn't surfaced. No contact with Fondberg or anyone. He just went to ground."

"Sholto! Jesus Christ!"

"And," Beaurain pressed on, "neither Cody nor anyone else reported you were coming into Stockholm."

"They didn't?" There was sheer incredulity in Cottel's voice. "I kept a low profile to do a better job but I assumed the Säpo people would know I was in town. I don't like this, Jules. Who's next?"

"You are."

Beaurain raised the .38 Smith & Wesson he had picked up from the ground and fired.

Further along the road towards the old iron ore mine at Skottvångs Gruva, a large man wearing a wide-brimmed straw hat and outsize tinted glasses sat behind the wheel of his hired Audi. He had not been able to get any closer for fear of being seen. He heard the sound of three distinct shots being fired.

He waited twenty minutes. Earlier that day he had taken up a position behind a pillar in the lobby of the Grand Hotel. He had seen the Swedish peasant with a head like a melon writing on a notepad. As soon as the man had disappeared inside the elevator he had palmed the pad and walked out. Back at the Hotel Reisen the careful scraping of a pencil had brought up the impression on the next sheet of the pad, showing clearly the words *Skottvångs Gruva*. Now the plan had worked. Cottel's watcher at Bromma had been bought, the information passed to Sholto, who had directed him in turn to pass the misinformation to Cottel, implying that Beaurain was Hugo.

After twenty minutes he drove away towards the mine. In due course he would swing round in a loop which would bring him back onto the E3. A cautious man, Sholto had no desire to encounter any survivors of the forest shooting on his way back to Stockholm – and then on to Trelleborg.

20

The following morning it was a main item on the news. The mystery lay in the identity and – more precisely – the occupation of the two foreigners who had shot each other. Jules Beaurain had fired the first shot with a .38 Smith & Wesson revolver, so the theory went. A Belgian, he had at one time been in the Brussels police and had risen to the rank of Chief Superintendent. This detail alone was enough to give the item major billing in a news editor's eyes.

The American, a visitor to Stockholm identified as Edward Cottel, had fired one shot at Beaurain from a .765 Walther which, oddly enough, was the hand-gun carried by the police. There had been a second bullet from the Smith & Wesson found in Cottel's body and presumably Jules Beaurain had transported him from the scene of the shooting in a hired Renault.

The macabre location of the American's body was the bottom of a deep hole close to the mine. A wire railing which normally protected visitors from any risk of falling into the hole had been flattened, again presumably when Beaurain man-handled the body out of the car and into the pit.

The Belgian's own corpse had been found a short distance away, collapsed as he tried to reach the Renault. End of story. The detective interviewed had been very firm on this last point. "The investigation is proceeding ... no further information available at this stage."

Harvey Sholto used a payphone on his way to Bromma Airport, dialled the Trelleborg number, and identified himself as soon as the familiar voice came on the line. "It worked," he said, hardly able to conceal his satisfaction. "You've seen the news bulletins?"

"Several times. A classic case of the mirror image technique. You show a man what he's waiting to see and he

272

reacts logically."

"Except that the logic isn't there."

"But has it ever been there since we started?" the voice enquired. "I will see you in Trelleborg. The sea is most pleasantly calm."

They watched them flying into the airstrip outside Trelleborg. Using the laundry van which had been Telescope's temporary and mobile headquarters in Stockholm, they sat in a concealed position behind a clump of trees. And they recorded on a notebook the identities of some of the most powerful and wealthy figures in the western world.

"That's Leo Gehn," said Palme, staring through his binoculars from the front passenger seat. "He's chairman of ..."

"International Telecommunications and Electronics – I.T.E. for short," Albert said crisply as he noted the details – name, time of arrival, type of aircraft and whether guards accompanied the newcomers.

"He's brought someone with him as a passenger – Count Luigi d'Arlezzo, the husband of that poor woman who was strung up at the Grand."

"Does he look very upset?" Albert enquired.

"He looks relaxed and relieved, the bastard. I suppose now his wife is conveniently out of the way he's playing at running his own banking empire. Hence Gehn taking an interest in someone he wouldn't normally give the time of day to – bet you anything Gehn is making a play to take over the controlling interest."

"Look at this one who's just arrived aboard a Cessna all by himself," Palme said. "Funny thing is he's landed on a quite different part of the airstrip as though he isn't with the main party. Dr Henri Goldschmidt of Bruges."

A car was waiting for the coin dealer. It was only later that they learned Goldschmidt had been driven straight to a hotel, that he had stayed in Trelleborg after strolling round the harbour area as though interested to see who was attending the conference. He did not even stay at the hotel overnight; very late in the day he proceeded on to Copenhagen.

And on the sea-front at Trelleborg another Telescope team was similarly checking the passengers arriving from the airstrip in a steady flow of limousines. The two-man team, sitting in a Peugeot equipped with a transceiver which kept them in direct touch with Henderson, were compiling their own record as the passengers transferred to waiting power-boats which immediately put to sea.

Henderson, who had returned from his second visit of the day to *Firestorm*, took a cab to within a hundred yards of the Savoy Hotel. There he paid off the vehicle, waited until he was sure he was not being followed, and walked the rest of the way to the hotel.

Room 12 was his destination. He had a brief word with the receptionist who phoned Room 12 and then informed Henderson that M. Chavet would be glad if he would go up immediately. The Scot ignored the lift and ran lightly up the stairs. He paused outside Room 12 and then rapped on the door with an irregular tattoo. The door opened almost at once.

"Come in, Jock," said Beaurain. "Louise and I thought you'd have news for us soon."

"And this is Ed Cottel," Beaurain said to Henderson, introducing the American. "He's officially in Room 14, registered under the name Waldo Kramer. You can talk freely in front of him."

The trio – Beaurain, Louise and Cottel – listened in concentrated silence while Henderson reported on the intense activity at the airstrip and then on the waterfront. He handed Beaurain a list of names of all the people who had arrived for the Syndicate's summit conference. Cottel looked over Beaurain's shoulder, ran his eye down the list and whistled.

"God Almighty, there are men there I'd have sworn were completely above suspicion."

"Which is what makes the Syndicate so dangerous," Beaurain murmured.

There were two lists – the one recorded by Stig and Albert and the check list compiled by the two men sitting on the sea-front watching the VIPs transferring from their limousines to the power-boats.

It was the second list Beaurain was studying with a frown; where the watchers had been unable to identify someone – and there were very few such cases – they had written a brief

274

description of the unknown arrivals. One description read, *Two men. One dressed like an American with a straw hat. His companion carried a brief-case.* With his thumb underlining the comment, he showed the sheet to Henderson.

"That has to be Gunther Baum and his companion, the one who carries the Luger in the brief-case until Baum is ready for it."

"Gunther Baum?" Ed Cottel was interested. "He's reputed to be one of the most professional assassins in the world. From East Germany but nothing to do with the Commie régime according to our information. Not something to be added to the asset side."

"He's in charge of security aboard *Kometa*. I'm convinced of it." Beaurain looked at Henderson. "When you hit the hydrofoil don't underestimate Baum."

"What are we going to do now we know where they're meeting?"

Henderson looked at Beaurain who opened a drawer in the dressing-table, took out a ship's chart and unrolled it on the double bed while Louise held the other end. "This was obtained from a Polish member of *Kometa*'s crew, a man who needs help to get his wife out of East Germany. Remember, Captain Buckminster has stood off Trelleborg for several days. During that time various gunners have been sent ashore in the guise of tourists and made it their business to frequent the waterfront bars. That is how the Pole was found. He is just the man we need secretly working on board that vessel – he controls and watches over the radar defences. I'm not even giving you his name, Ed."

"My question was, what are we going to do?" Cottel repeated.

"Destroy them."

"Just like that?"

"Yes – and with the aid of this chart which clearly shows the course planned for *Kometa* during the four hours of darkness when the actual conference takes place." Cottel was now alongside the Belgian, studying the chart. Beaurain's index finger traced the course of a dotted line drawn on the chart.

They met Harry Fondberg at a pre-arranged rendezvous on the outskirts of Trelleborg. Beaurain was behind the wheel of the Mercedes when he picked up the Säpo chief at a bend in the country road. Fondberg's vehicle was nowhere to be seen and the only other occupant of the car was Louise who sat by herself in the rear. Fondberg settled into the front passenger seat alongside Beaurain, and the Mercedes moved off, heading away from Trelleborg.

"East German MfS – state security men – have been coming in on the ferry from Sassnitz both yesterday and today," the Swede told Beaurain. "It has almost assumed the proportions of an invasion. A handful linger in the town, trying to look like tourists, which is laughable."

"Why?" asked Louise.

"You know what the weather is like. This marvellous heatwave during the day and it's still warm at ten o'clock at night. These cretins from Sassnitz are all walking around in short leather jackets and trilby hats! My men tell me they have to be careful not to burst out laughing when they see them. But the majority have gone out by power-boat to *Kometa*, presumably – to act as security."

"Under the command of Gunther Baum," Beaurain informed him.

"That homicidal maniac? What does it all mean? He's not MfS."

"Intriguing, isn't it? I think Hugo has waved his wand again. And you did a marvellous promotion job on the 'double murder' yesterday night out at the old iron mine of Skottvångs Gruva. Hugo will be bound to be just that little over-confident now he thinks Ed and I are dead."

"Just so long as the media never learn the truth," Fondberg said gloomily. "They'd crucify me. If you're going to launch an all-out assault on *Kometa* from *Firestorm* tonight – and officially I've never even heard of either vessel – why is it so important you appear to be dead? To make Hugo less cautious – I can see that, but . . ."

"To throw him right off-balance when I eventually come face to face with him," Beaurain said grimly. "And that might well not be tonight. I have a funny idea. Hugo could be holding a party and not attending it himself although he's supposed to be the host."

"No, I don't see," Fondberg said. "I don't see at all. And you might like to know that at this moment I'm in Gothenburg – and have witnesses to prove it."

On the June evening of Beaurain's final attack on the Stockholm Syndicate sunset was at precisely 20.50 hours. Over the Baltic darkness fell, concealing the presence of the 2,500-ton motor ship *Firestorm*. Against all international regulations Captain "Bucky" Buckminster, the ship's captain, was showing no navigation lights. If any vessel approached him on a collision course the radar screens would warn him in good time. Beaurain was going over the details of the assault plan for the last time in the main cabin.

"I trust that everyone fully understands the complex nature of the deception operation we shall be practising?"

Twenty gunners clad in underwater gear, oxygen cylinders on their backs and an assortment of arms and explosives in their possession, stared back at Beaurain and said nothing. Beaurain sensed the usual tension which was inevitable before a major operation.

"I can now tell you we have an ally on board *Kometa*." Beaurain turned to the outline drawings showing the composition of the various decks of the Soviet hydrofoil. "It is thanks to this ally that we have this diagram which should make all the difference to the success of our attack."

"Don't we help the poor bugger?" muttered Albert rebelliously. "If he's left aboard he'll ..."

"I was just coming to that." Beaurain placed his wooden pointer on a particular cabin. "That is where you will find him waiting, sitting in front of his apparatus. He is a Pole; he is the sonar controller; his name is Peter Sobieski; he speaks English and the password he will repeat to you to ensure identification is *Waterloo, Waterloo*."

"Pretty bloody appropriate," Albert commented, "considering we're trying to wipe out the whole lousy outfit with one blow."

"Then don't forget that Wellington said afterwards it was a pretty damn close run thing – and I come from Belgium. Now, any questions?"

"Sobieski's sonar is the one thing which could give us away," Palme observed. "He will see us coming."

"So aren't you pleased we have an ally who will be the only person checking the sonar screens. Next question."

It was important to defuse the tension as much as possible – and yet not let any feeling of complacency or overconfidence arise. A difficult combination. Beaurain tackled the over-confidence problem now.

"But even though we have Sobieski watching those screens don't forget the opposition is – what would you call it, Henderson?"

"Formidable!" Jock Henderson stood up quickly on cue, swung round and addressed the assembled men. "Sobieski reckons the conference will be guarded by thirty heavily-armed state security types from a special unit in East Germany. For some reason not one of them speaks a word of English."

"That," Beaurain interjected, "I suspect is so they don't overhear or understand a word said at the conference which obviously will be conducted in English. Leo Gehn, the boss of I.T.E., for example, has no other language than American."

"I had the funny idea," interjected Ed Cottel who was sitting next to Louise at the back, "that both languages were the same."

"We all dwell under our illusions," chirped the irrepressible Albert.

There was a burst of over-loud laughter. At least, Beaurain reflected, that had eased the atmosphere a bit. He nodded to Henderson to continue.

"These MfS people have been well-trained, may have been warned to expect an intrusion, and Sobieski – again – has warned they are armed with percussion grenades for dropping over the side."

There was a general groan, which was only half-facetious, and Beaurain decided any complacency was rapidly disappearing. In the front row Palme shrugged his shoulders without making a sound. He was one of the most formidable fighters in the room.

"They are also armed with automatic weapons," Henderson went on. "We expect them to be patrolling the decks – and yet the object of the exercise is to seize control of the vessel without any undue noise until the last possible moment."

"Knives in the dark and this," Albert said laconically. He held up his hand, the edge stiff and hardened ready for a lethal chop.

"On the plus side," Henderson told them briskly, "we have the complex and confusing deception operation worked

278

out by Jules Beaurain. With a bit of luck the man controlling *Kometa*'s defences won't know what the hell is going on until it's too late."

A crew member slipped into the room, made his way to Beaurain and handed him a message. Beaurain looked at it, handed it to Henderson, who glanced at the few words and stood up again.

"Gentlemen! *Kometa* has started to move on her prescribed easterly course. Our own plan now starts to move – phase by phase as arranged."

21

"Put *Regula* over the side."

This had been Beaurain's first order and was the opening phase. The large launch, flying the Danish flag, had been lowered into the sea and released. Her engines – far more powerful than anyone would expect inside such a vessel – started up and she disappeared into the distance, heading after *Kometa* at a speed and on a course which would soon bring her up on the port side of the Soviet hydrofoil. And it was no coincidence that *Regula*'s size, shape and colour was very similar to that of a Danish coastguard vessel.

"Launch Smithy."

Beaurain had given this command when *Firestorm*'s radar scanner showed that the 'coastguard' vessel *Regula* would shortly overhaul *Kometa*. The float-plane, hauled out of the same cavernous hold which had carried *Regula*, was winched over the side and gently lowered onto the calm black Baltic. From the bridge Beaurain watched with field glasses as Smithy took off on a course which would take him precisely between the stern of *Kometa* and the bow of *Firestorm*. Beaurain had worked out the whole plan on the back of an old envelope. He now gave his third order.

"Launch Anderson."

Captain Buckminster gave his own order, briefly slowing down the speed of *Firestorm* while Anderson, the pilot of the giant Sikorsky, lifted off from the helipad aft of the bridge. Alongside him sat his co-pilot, a Frenchman from Rheims, Pierre Cartier. Thirty-one years old, small, lightly-built with a pencil moustache, Cartier nursed a sub-machine gun in his lap as the chopper climbed vertically and flew on an easterly course. Like Smithy in his float-plane, their course was aimed for the stern of *Kometa*.

"You think I get a chance to use my weapon?" Cartier asked.

"Don't be so bloodthirsty," Anderson replied, his eyes on the controls. "That's just for emergencies."

"Then I must hope for emergencies!"

On the bridge of the motor vessel Captain Buckminster watched his radar screen as Beaurain walked a few paces to the huge bridge window and peered into the night. They had picked up speed as soon as Anderson had taken off and he thought he could just discern the lights of the Soviet hydrofoil.

"You think it's going to work?" Buckminster enquired.

"If I was in command of *Kometa* I would be as confused as hell within the next fifteen minutes. And we need only about ten minutes for Henderson and his underwater team to hit *Kometa*."

"Let's hope to God it doesn't start moving and rear up on its foils. Henderson will never board her if that happens."

"Which is why Phase One concerns a convincing-looking Danish coastguard launch," Beaurain replied.

Captain Andrei Livanov swore silently as Viktor Rashkin appeared. The latter wore a dark blue naval blazer ornamented with gold buttons and pale grey slacks. His step was springy, his manner brisk. He established a sense of his supreme authority with his opening words.

"Our guests are now comfortable in the main dining-room, so our meeting is about to start. Please proceed at full speed round Bornholm as planned. Get this thing up onto its skis or whatever you call them."

"Surface-piercing foils."

Livanov, a thin-faced man of fifty who hated having so many Germans aboard, was staring out to the port side where his First Officer, Glasov, was making notes on a pad. Rashkin glanced in the same direction and then his look riveted on what he saw in the distance. The lights of another vessel, and the flashing of a signal lamp.

"What the hell is that?" he demanded.

"Danish coastguard vessel," Livanov replied, keeping his words to a minimum. It was one safe way he could express his intense dislike.

"Tell it to go away."

"You do not tell coastguard vessels to go away."

"Why Danish?" rasped Rashkin irritably.

"Because the island of Bornholm, which we are approaching, happens to belong to Denmark. What is the signal, Glasov?"

"We are to heave to and identify ourselves."

Without referring to Rashkin, the captain gave the order and the former only realised what was happening when he felt the vessel slowing down, noticed the absence of vibrations beneath his feet and realised *Kometa* was now stationary. Glasov was using a lamp to signal their reply when Viktor Rashkin blew his top.

"Who gave the order to stop the engines? I shall report this act of sabotage to Moscow."

"Report away!" Livanov snapped. "If you want our brief voyage to attract no attention we must adhere to international law, we are already in Danish territorial waters, we must comply with the coastguard's requests."

He broke off and walked rapidly to the window on the port side. Out of nowhere a float-plane had appeared, had *landed* on the calm black sea between the Soviet vessel and the coastguard ship. With its navigation lights on it had the appearance of a firefly and its actions were extraordinary. And now that Glasov had completed his reply to the Danish coastguard, the lamp was flashing again, sending *Kometa* a new signal.

"What's that thing out there?" Rashkin asked.

"A sea-plane. I think the pilot must be drunk. Let's just hope he doesn't head our way."

The tiny plane did indeed appear to be in the control – if that was the word – of someone who had imbibed too generously. The machine, scudding over the dark sheet of water, was now zig-zagging. It was crazy, quite crazy. And so many things were beginning to happen at once.

That was the moment when Anderson lowered his Sikorsky over the bridge of *Kometa*. His arrival was heralded by a steadily increasing roar. Livanov pressed his face against the glass and stared up into the night. What he saw astounded him.

"Look above us, for God's sake!" he shouted at Rashkin.

The belly of the chopper, which seemed enormous in the night, was almost touching the top of the bridge. Livanov couldn't see any sign of how many men might be aboard the machine. Livanov could only see that if the pilot came down

282

a few feet more there was going to be a holocaust on his bridge. To add to his agitation the din churned up by the Sikorsky's rotors was deafening. A hand grasped his arm; his First Officer, Glasov, was pulling him gently towards the rear of the bridge so he could get a better view of the Danish coastguard vessel. A searchlight slowly began to sweep the sea from aboard the coastguard ship. Glasov shouted in his captain's ear.

"That searchlight from the coastguard vessel is searching for a floating mine."

"*Oh, my God!*"

Another voice shouted in his other ear, the voice of Viktor Rashkin, but Livanov detected for the first time a note of uncertainty in the Russian's voice. "Start up the engines! Immediately!"

"You have seen what is happening just ahead of us and directly in our way?"

Rashkin followed the line of Livanov's stabbing finger. For the first time he noticed the fresh tactics of the drunken pilot with his bloody float-plane. The machine was criss-crossing over the course *Kometa* would be taking if the ship did start moving, moving at right-angles to the Soviet hydrofoil.

"*And,*" Livanov took great delight in informing this swine of a party boss, "that searchlight is looking for a floating mine. You wish us to move before they have located it? You look forward to the outcome? *BOOM!*"

Rashkin was suspicious. Too much was happening at once. But he found the appalling din of the chopper's rotors made it hard to think straight. What was happening? He watched the probing finger of light, fighting to detach himself from his present surroundings, from the noise and the activity which was overwhelming his brain. *Never permit the enemy to disorientate you.* During the time when he had trained with the KGB his mentor, a veteran, had drilled the advice into his brain. But where was the enemy?

On the 'coastguard' vessel *Regula* there were very few lights – no more than the orthodox navigation lights. Harry Johnson, who had monitored the arrival of the KGB security squads in Trelleborg aboard the ferries from Sassnitz in East Germany, commanded *Regula*.

A lean, tense man of thirty, his face had a scowl of concentration as he stood close to the helmsman inside the wheelhouse and held his wrist-watch in his right hand. The chronometer on the bridge of *Regula* was accurate, God knew – but it was his wrist-watch he had used to synchronise with all the other timepieces before he had left *Firestorm*.

Alongside him stood Jock Henderson clad in his wet suit, oxygen cylinder on his back, face-mask pulled up on his forehead, his automatic weapon clasped in its waterproof sheath. The explosives were inside a separate container strapped to his lower back.

"You'll be leaving soon, Jock," Johnson said.

"I know." Henderson was watching the sweep hand of his waterproof watch. He glanced up and checked again: the lights of the Sikorsky which appeared to be sitting on *Kometa*'s bridge; the flitting back and forth of Smithy in his float-plane across the path of the Soviet vessel to discourage any movement. Then the searchlight beam shone out from *Regula*'s stern.

"*Go!*" said Johnson.

Henderson led the twenty-man team over the port side of *Regula*. Once in the water, his face-mask in position, he passed under the keel of *Regula* before swimming underwater direct for the hydrofoil. The magnetic compass attached to his left wrist showed him the precise course to follow – and this was very important considering what Johnson was going to activate in the near future. It was also the aspect of the assault that had most worried Johnson when discussing it with Henderson earlier.

"The underwater vibrations will be terrific," he had warned.

"So we make sure we're far enough away, we get the timing right and we don't feel a thing – or very little," Henderson had replied.

"Bloody tricky. I wouldn't like to be coming with you."

"You'd manage."

"Then there are the bubbles from your breathing apparatus – from the apparatus of twenty men. Those damned bubbles could easily be spotted by lookouts aboard that Soviet hydrofoil."

"Which is where Jules Beaurain's scenario comes in – to

284

make them look in the wrong place – or places – at the crucial moment of our approach."

"There's always the unexpected factor," the dour Johnson had replied. "Like the sonar room on the Soviet vessel."

Alone inside the sonar room aboard *Kometa* the Pole, Peter Sobieski, who had agreed to co-operate with Telescope, was studying the screen which clearly showed the approach of Henderson's assault team. On such a calm night it was impossible that they should not show up on one of the screens.

Peter Sobieski, a thin, nervous but intelligent man in his early forties, was worried. He had taken all possible precautions. The door behind him was locked so no-one could walk in and surprise him. As he continued staring at the screen, one thing above all else preyed on his nerves. The presence of Gunther Baum aboard as head of security. Sobieski knew he could turn a dial which would fog the scanner, obliterating all tell-tale trace of what was moving steadily closer to the hydrofoil second by second. But, try as he might, he was unable to stifle his anxiety about Gunther Baum.

Gunther Baum was suspicious. As he patrolled the open deck on the port side he tried to work it out: the combination of that ridiculous float-plane, the Danish coastguard ship and the large helicopter hanging over the bridge like a time-bomb. He had suggested to Viktor Rashkin that six of his men riddled the machine with automatic fire.

"Very clever," Rashkin had commented. "Positively brilliant."

Baum had basked in the glow of apparent approval. He was totally unprepared for Rashkin's next statement. "Suppose the chopper is also Danish coastguard, which seems likely since there is an airfield on Bornholm. We don't want an international incident with the guests we have below! And if I had said, yes, where would the chopper have crashed? Right on top of our bridge! So could you please return to your duties of patrolling the ship and overseeing its defences?"

All this had been taken into account when Beaurain worked out his original plan: if the helicopter hovered low enough no-one aboard would dare open fire for fear of causing a conflagration to break out on *Kometa*. And Baum returned to the open deck fuming, with his companion at his heels, still carrying the brief-case holding the silenced Luger.

Checking that his men were on the alert, he wandered slowly along the port side staring at the inky blackness of the water. Standing by the rail he found First Officer Glasov, a mean-faced man whose every action was based on how it would advance potential promotion.

"Everything does not seem to go according to plan," Baum said.

"If you had been at sea as long as I have that is what you would expect," Glasov replied rudely.

Baum was under the distinct impression that the rudeness was calculated, that Glasov wished to get rid of him. Shrugging his shoulders he moved over to the starboard side to check the position there. Glasov watched him go and then turned back to stare at the sea. In the distance a searchlight aboard the coastguard ship was probing for something, but immediately underneath where he stood Glasov saw the light from a porthole reflecting on the water.

Glasov clenched the rail tight with both hands and stared again to make sure his eyes had not played him a trick. Then he saw it again. *A circle of bubbles . . .*

First Officer Glasov practically threw open the door into the sonar room – at least that was his intention. Unexpectedly the door, locked from the inside, refused to budge and he slammed into what felt like a brick wall. When he had recovered he began hammering his clenched fist against the upper panel. Sobieski took his time about unlocking the door quietly, turning the handle and opening it suddenly. He confronted Glasov, fist raised in mid-air for a fresh on-slaught.

"Have you gone mad?" Sobieski enquired calmly.

Glasov stared at him in sheer disbelief. He out-ranked the controller of the sonar room and Sobieski was a Pole which, in Glasov's view, made him a member of an inferior race.

"You cannot speak to me like that!" Glasov snapped and pushed past the Pole who closed the door and quietly locked it again. Glasov swung round. "Why was the door locked?"

"Security," Sobieski replied with a wooden expression. "On the instructions of Gunther Baum," he lied.

"To hell with Baum. I think skin-divers are at this very moment approaching us and you should have detected them on the sonar by now."

Sobieski had returned to his seat in front of his screens and controls and he folded his arms over a half-closed drawer. He had to play for time.

"These skin-divers," the Pole replied in a flippant tone, "you have seen them riding across the sea blowing trumpets?"

"I have seen the bubbles which rise to the surface from their breathing apparatus," Glasov told him between clenched teeth. "So you also must have seen them on your sonar." He stared for the first time at the screen. "What is wrong with the sonar screen?"

It was the question the Pole had been waiting for and had been dreading. Since he had deliberately fogged the reception with a turn of a switch nothing showed but static. The Russsian walked a few paces further and stood in front of the equipment, the corners of his mouth turned down as he glared at the meaningless image. And Glasov knew enough to work the switches – Sobieski surreptitiously checked the time. This was the very moment when the screen must not be clear. And still the ship vibrated with the roar of the Sikorsky's rotors.

"It is interference," Sobieski explained.

"We are being jammed? Enemy interference!"

"Nothing of the sort." Sobieski sounded weary. "No machine is perfect and they all develop bugs. It is likely that there is a . . ."

But then Glasov turned the switch, the static vanished and a clear image showed of an unknown number of swimmers approaching *Kometa*.

"You bloody traitor! You will be shot! And your family will be . . ."

Sobieski raised his right hand out of the half-open drawer holding a Walther PPK and fired two shots at point-blank range. Glasov staggered, spun round in a semi-circle and crashed to the deck. The Pole dragged Glasov by the ankles across the planks and bundled him into a huddled heap which fitted the inside of the bottom of a cupboard. Fetching Glasov's cap, which had fallen off, he crammed it over his slumped head, closed both doors and locked the cupboard, then ran to the sonar screen and turned the switch again – in case of fresh visitors. The invading force would be aboard within minutes or less – provided they were not spotted by Gunther Baum's security patrols.

In the large dining-room of *Kometa* many small tables had been brought together to create one huge and impressive table around which were seated the guests from so many nations. Even aboard the *Titanic* there was less power and influence than was gathered that night aboard the Soviet hydrofoil in the Baltic.

At the head of the table, as befitted his status, was the American industrialist, Leo Gehn, occasionally drinking mineral water, while the rest of the guests consumed ever larger quantities of champagne, encouraged by Viktor Rashkin who made frequent visits from the bridge to soothe his guests.

"A little local difficulty ... concerning some officious Danish coastguard. Doubtless he knows who we have aboard ... it is his brief hour of glory ... briefly to detain with his minor authority such a distinguished gathering ..."

Then the mine detonated.

From this moment on the terror started – terror for those who had themselves used their money and their power to terrorise so many in different countries to do their bidding.

"Explode the mine!"

Aboard the 'coastguard' vessel *Regula*, its captain, Johnson, was still holding his wrist-watch in his hand when he gave the order. He spoke into the small microphone slung round his neck – so the message reached not only the man who detonated the mine let loose to float with the current but was also transmitted to the members of the crew operating the mobile searchlight and the swivel-mounted machine-gun.

The trio receiving the order knew precisely the sequence of events they must bring about. First, the man with the searchlight swung its beam to light on the mine itself; not too difficult a feat since he was wearing infrared glasses.

The moment that happened the second man – controlling the swivel-mounted machine-gun – swung its muzzle, being careful not to aim his gunsight at the mine but only in its general direction, and opened fire. He was using tracer bullets and the Baltic was suddenly illuminated with a miniature fireworks display.

The man whose job was to set off the detonation by remote radio control waited for the first two events to take place. Only when the mine was visible in the searchlight beam, only when a curve of tracer bullets was streaming through the night did he operate the switch. The result was spectacular.

The mine exploded with a dull resounding boom suggesting enormous power. An eruption of water like the Yellowstone Park geyser was superbly illuminated in the searchlight beam. The machine-gun ceased firing. The searchlight went out. Aboard *Kometa* everyone was temporarily stunned. At that moment – on schedule – Sergeant Jock Henderson passed under the hull of the still-stationary hydrofoil.

Kometa was a 'surface-piercing hydrofoil' – a kind of craft invented in Messina, Sicily, a fact not advertised inside Soviet Russia. A large vessel of 2,000 tons, its top speed was thirty knots, which could only be achieved when it was skimming over the surface of the water so that no 'drag' factor any longer applied. Basically the entire vessel, at the pull of a single lever on the bridge, reared up out of the water on what were really massive steel wings.

By careful checking of his waterproof watch Henderson had timed the boarding of *Kometa* to coincide with Johnson's detonation of his mine – the moment of maximum distraction for those aboard the Soviet vessel. A large number of his underwater team were still in the sea, concealed now beneath *Kometa's* hull, when the mine exploded. They felt a sharp push in the back as the shock wave of the blast reached them. By now Henderson was perched on the starboard surface-piercing foil at the stern.

Half out of the water and just behind him Palme stared upwards at the overhang of the ship's rail, holding a harpoon-gun in his right hand. Using the rope and drag-hook like a lasso, Henderson had swung it round his head until the momentum was strong enough, then hurled it upwards and heard the gentle *thunk* as the rubber-covered hooks took a firm hold on the rail.

It was very bad luck – but in Henderson's view they had

used up their share of luck – that one of Gunther Baum's East German security men happened to be patrolling the stern as the ladder took hold. He was taken aback for a few seconds when the grapple appeared out of nowhere, then he un-looped his automatic weapon from his shoulder and peered over the rail. Henderson was a perfect target, silhouetted in his frogman's suit. The security man raised his weapon and took swift aim.

There was a hiss of compressed air, no other sound at all, as the spear released from Palme's harpoon-gun thudded into the German's chest. He slumped forward over the rail, dropping his weapon into the sea. Henderson climbed the ladder, reached the rail, glanced along the deserted deck. Using one hand, he tumbled the man over the side. Palme had already climbed the ladder and a file of men were ap-pearing, their heads bobbing in the water like sea-monsters. Henderson, now over the rail and standing on the deck with Palme, glanced at his watch.

"Less than two minutes before Johnson signals the Russian captain he can get moving."

"We have just made it."

Before the engines of *Kometa* began throbbing underfoot, all the twenty men were aboard the hydrofoil. Advance scouts had been sent a short distance forward to deal with any fresh patrols. And Henderson had been very explicit in his instructions regarding this stage.

"According to Sobieski, the Polish sonar controller aboard, we'll be out-numbered by the East German security guards – and those johnnies are trained to prime condition. There are thirty of them. So for as long as possible we use the silent kill."

The advance scouts – under Palme's command on the port side, under Max Kellerman's command to starboard – were armed with knives and wire garottes. Their instructions were to use firearms and grenades only as a last resort – and preferably not until one of the two section commanders gave permission.

On the port side a second security guard in a leather jacket took a step forward and then stopped, staring in disbelief. He was still trying to decide whether he had seen the outline of men in frogsuits when one of them stepped out behind him from between two lifeboats and plunged a razor-edged stiletto with a savage upward thrust just below the left shoulder-blade. The East German grunted. He was dead before he hit the deck.

His executioner reported the incident and then cautiously moved again towards the bridge. The head count of guards eliminated was important: it told both Palme and Kellerman how many of the opposition were still alive. As the hydrofoil began to get under way Henderson's task was quite different and exceptionally hazardous.

Several times Jules Beaurain had emphasised the danger of the mission Henderson had suggested for himself. "You could be very exposed," the Belgian had warned, "if they start the vessel up while you're still working on the main foil."

"I have allowed for that," Henderson had assured his chief. "It is a chance I have to take. It is the only way I can attach timer-and-impact explosives to the most vulnerable part of *Kometa*."

Timer-and-impact explosives were a new device which the mild-mannered boffins at Château Wardin had recently invented. The device worked initially like time-bombs. But the refinement covered the possibility that the timing mechanism might not work.

Independent of the timer, the explosive detonated instantaneously on impact with another object, and the force of the impact needed for detonation could be varied by setting a meter which was an essential part of the device.

Henderson's objective was now to reach the bow of *Kometa* in the shortest possible time, attach the special explosives to the giant foils in the shortest possible time, and, assuming he survived what Beaurain had called "a real Russian roulette risk", he would then make himself available for the final assault against the bridge.

The Sikorsky had been lifted high into the night. In his float-plane the pilot, Smithy, had suddenly adopted more sober behaviour and was flying across the Baltic away from the Soviet ship prior to taking off – leaving the sea clear for Captain Livanov to resume his course. On the bridge the Russian had received the signal from the coastguard vessel informing him that the floating mine had been destroyed, that it was safe to proceed.

Both Livanov and Viktor Rashkin now felt confident that all was well – that the extraordinary behaviour of the helicopter pilot was simply the Danes taking every precaution to ensure *Kometa* obeyed instructions until the danger was past.

"After all," Livanov pointed out, "we did see the mine explode! I would not like the bow of this ship to have collided with that."

"You are, of course, right,"Rashkin agreed. "And now I suggest we proceed at top speed round Bornholm – which means demonstrating to our guests the thrill of skimming the wavetops. And I must now return to the dining-room."

Livanov gave the order to increase speed and *Kometa* began to move, a dart of glowing light shooting towards the flashing lamp which was the lighthouse close to The Hammer on the island of Bornholm. '*Skimming the wavetops*' was not the phrase Livanov would have used but it did describe the sensation of travelling aboard the hydrofoil at full power. Reaching out a hand, Livanov personally pulled at the lever which operated the foils. The ship rose up until its whole length of hull was clear of the Baltic – supported only by its immense blades of steel.

As Rashkin left the bridge the two teams of invaders, one led by Palme, the other by Max Kellerman, had silently despatched five of the thirty East Germans guarding the ship. They were also putting into effect the second part of Beaurain's plan – which involved stationing men at the head of all companionways and exits leading to the main deck. Anyone attempting to mount the steps from a lower deck would immediately feel the impact of a harpoon. Both to port and starboard Stig and Max were now in control of the rear half of the ship. Only one man was facing problems: Henderson was in danger of losing his life.

The magnetic clamps Henderson had activated held him by the forearms and legs to the huge steel blade as he fought to complete his task. He was now lifted clear of the Baltic which was flashing past below at incredible speed. And the forward movement of the hydrofoil was creating a powerful wind which blew in his face, half-blinding his face-mask with spume and surf, tearing at his body in its attempt to rip him free from the blade and hurl him down into the water where the stern foils of *Kometa* would pass over him, cutting him to mince.

"*God damn them!*"

He had hoped to finish attaching the explosives and to have hauled himself over the rail and onto the ship's deck before the vessel continued its cruise. Cruise? This was more like a bloody race he thought, and when he wiped his face-mask free of surf smears he could see in the distance a flashing lamp. The lighthouse above The Hammer, the dreaded cliffs at the northern tip of the island of Bornholm which they were approaching fast.

As he positioned the second device underneath the foil – out of sight from anyone looking down from the deck above – the vibrations of the engines pounded his body as though he were operating half-a-dozen road drills. Henderson literally found he was shaking like a jelly. Only by making a supreme effort was he able to position the second device, activate first the magnetic clamps which attached it to the blade, then turn the switch which activated both timer and impact systems.

To negotiate the steep-angled support he had to repeat his earlier performance, switching off the magnetic clamps strapped round his left leg and arm, supported only by the other two holding his right forearm and leg. He then had to haul himself higher with his free left leg and arm. The process then had to be reversed so he could climb higher still up the prop, closer to the hull, this time employing his right leg and arm. His progress was not helped by the wind plucking furiously at him, by the roar of the hydrofoil thundering through the dark, by the engine vibrations which were rapidly weakening his remaining physical reserves.

Don't give up or you're finished!

It was the first time Henderson could remember having felt compelled to consider the possibility, and now he was realising it would be wiser never to look down. In his weakened state he was beginning to suffer from vertigo. The sight of the surf-edged water sheeting past below was dizzy-making. Every movement was a reflex of will-power. He didn't really care whether he made it or not – and the thought galvanised him with self-contempt.

A million years later he hauled himself over the rail and collapsed on the deck, lying still while he waited for his natural resilience to assert itself. That was when the machine-gun fire started, punctuated by the crack of stun and fragment grenades.

"Give me the gun, Oscar."

Gunther Baum reached out a hand without looking and Oscar gave him the Luger immediately. The East German was standing on the port side and had no reason at all to suspect anything out of the ordinary. Ahead of him stretched the open deck. He could see dimly the sway of the lifeboats slung from their davits as *Kometa* showed her honoured guests what she was capable of, moving like a bird. Behind Gunther Baum his companion, Oscar, took a tighter grip on his own automatic weapon now he was no longer concerned with the brief-case.

"Is there something wrong?" Oscar shouted. It was the last sentence he ever uttered. The words were hardly out of his mouth when a missile hurtled towards him. He screamed and staggered back, Palme's harpoon protruding from his chest. Swiftly Baum, who was concealed in the darkness, aimed at a moving shadow and fired. The shadow dropped. Baum shouted in German at the top of his voice.

"Mass on the bridge! Withdraw from the deck!" Then he unscrewed his silencer and fired into the air twice.

Theoretically it was sound strategy, as Palme was the first to recognise. Baum was planning on assembling his men on the ship's equivalent of the high ground – the bridge from where they could pour a hail of gunfire down onto the intruders approaching from the deck below.

Baum reached the bridge because of the swiftness of his movements, running crouched up the steps and pressing himself upright against the rear of the bridge. From here he could see exactly what was happening. He witnessed a massacre – of his own troops.

On the port side Palme projected the beam of a powerful lamp on his staircase; on the starboard side Kellerman employed the same tactic. Caught in the glare of the two lights, the MfS men jammed on the staircases were targets which could not be missed. There was a continuous rattle of automatic fire from the Telescope men and Baum saw his guards collapsing and tumbling over each other as they went back down the staircases. He raised his Luger and aimed it at the glaring lamp. As though anticipating he had pushed his luck far enough, Palme turned off the lamp at that moment and jumped to one side. Two bullets from Baum's Luger thudded harmlessly into the woodwork beside him.

It was Henderson, emerging on the rear of the bridge from the starboard side, who saw the almost invisible Gunther Baum pressed close to the woodwork. A brief glimpse, he pinpointed his position when the German fired his two bullets. Taking a grenade from his pocket, Henderson removed the pin, counted and then *rolled* it along the deck. The grenade stopped rolling a few inches from the feet of Gunther Baum. There was a flash which illuminated the whole of the rear of the bridge, showing Baum as its sole occupant, a thunder-crack as the grenade detonated. Baum fell forward, arms out-stretched, slithered over the rail and hit the deck below.

It was time to storm the interior of the bridge, take complete control of the vessel – and destroy it.

22

"Slow down to five knots," Rashkin ordered as he ran back onto the bridge. He had come up from below via a small stairwell which led to his cabin and the main dining-room.

"Slow down?" Livanov was confused.

"For Christ's sake give the order – we are under attack."

He broke off as he heard a loud explosion beyond the rear of the bridge. He did not know that this had killed Baum but he immediately grasped that the opposition had won – they had reached bridge level. Without issuing further orders he disappeared down the small stairwell, paused cautiously at the bottom, a Walther automatic in his hand, saw that the passageway was deserted and ran to his cabin.

He had already warned all his guests to remain in the dining-room, assuring them that they were in the safest place, that the intruders would be dealt with speedily. Rashkin had sensed that Baum's defences were being overwhelmed, that this would be followed by the destruction of *Kometa* and all aboard her. Someone was taking violent vengeance for the killing of Jules Beaurain. Telescope were in action.

The speed of *Kometa* had been considerably reduced by the time he reached the cabin. A man of great agility, it took him hardly any time to strip off his outer clothes and wriggle himself into the skin-diver's suit he had brought aboard secretly in a hold-all bag. Rashkin had only survived in his present position by always preparing for every contingency – and he never neglected his escape route.

As he unscrewed the porthole cover he was armed with two weapons – a sheath knife and the waterproof watch attached to his wrist. It was most fortunate that his cabin was on the starboard side. As he swung back the cover he could see clearly the warning flashes of the lighthouse above The Hammer on Bornholm. And he calculated the hydrofoil was no more than a couple of miles from the Danish island.

Climbing backwards through the porthole, he lowered himself until his body was hanging against the hull, supported only by his hands. He let go without hesitation or trepidation, knowing that at this position there was no risk of his hitting the submerged foil – the speed *had* dropped to five knots and the vessel was moving like an ordinary ship. There *was* a risk, however, in getting caught in the stern undertow, hurled into the wake and chopped to pieces by the propeller.

He felt his feet catch the slow-moving hull and kicked out with all his strength, lunging himself backwards and away from the hull which was gracefully sliding past him. Then, still lying on his back, he began to swim with strong purposeful strokes. Behind him the hull went on gliding past. Above he saw the lights of the dining-saloon. The ship seemed oddly deserted.

The interior of the bridge resembled a slaughterhouse. A few of Baum's surviving security guards had retreated there to join Livanov just before Henderson ordered the final attack to begin. He used one word.

"*Grenades!*"

Three minutes later, followed by Palme and several of his gunners, he entered the deathtrap. He first checked the steering gear. Someone – doubtless Livanov – had at the last moment turned the vessel onto automatic pilot. Like a robot – or a ghost ship – the huge hydrofoil *Kometa* was cruising slowly across the Baltic. He began organising the evacuation of his own men: three were dead, seventeen had survived due to the element of surprise and the co-operation of Peter Sobieski. Palme had personally found the Pole and brought him to the bridge. Henderson was talking to Max Kellerman who had just arrived on the bridge.

"What is the position with that international scum waiting in the dining saloon? The élite of the Stockholm Syndicate?"

"Trapped inside the saloon. The special section fought its way down, wiped out the guards and then welded up the doors with the equipment they brought. The passengers might get out if they try smashing the windows, but I don't think they will try it in time. The shooting rather discouraged exploration."

297

"Fix the bombs to the doors, then leave – all of you – by the smashed windows," said Henderson. "I stay until I get this damned ship moving."

"You'll have trouble leaving her," Palme interjected. " I mean when she's travelling at top speed. And the rescue boats are coming in."

"I said fix those bombs," Henderson repeated.

It was the green Verey light Henderson had fired into the night sky which had summoned the rescue boats. Coming up fast behind *Kometa*, the British motor vessel with Beaurain and Louise aboard and commanded by Captain Buckminster had paused after the green flare exploded like a firework.

"My God! Jock's done it!"

Louise was so relieved that she hugged Beaurain publicly as they stood on *Firestorm*'s bridge. Already power-boats lowered over the side were plunging through the night towards the slow-moving *Kometa*, their searchlights turned on full power to locate Telescope's gunners who would be diving into the sea.

Behind the wake of *Kometa*, which was still moving at five knots, a series of tiny lights were beginning to appear, all bobbing on the water. Power-boats despatched from *Firestorm* were already slowing down, each heading for a light.

The 'coastguard' vessel *Regula* had returned to its mother ship and was being winched aboard prior to being lowered, dripping with sea water, into the cavernous hold of *Firestorm*. And by now Henderson was alone on the bridge, leaning out of a smashed window as he watched the last gunners leaving. He was enclosed inside the bridge with the bodies of the dead East German security guards and attached to all entrances to the bridge were the special bombs – bombs which exploded outwards on detonation *away* from the interior of the bridge. The objective was to ensure that anyone who might escape from the dining-room could never reach the controls on the bridge alive.

It had been Viktor Rashkin's plan to swim the two miles to Bornholm's shoreline, taking his time, but as he saw a power-boat with one man aboard heading in his direction he took a swift decision. The power-boat was heading on a course which would take it past him by about twenty yards.

He waited for the right moment, hoisted himself briefly out of the water and waved.

The crewman from *Firestorm* saw him and changed course, reducing speed. His orders were to pick up as many men as he could in the shortest possible time. The fact that the man swimming in the sea carried no flashing light did not strike him as strange, nor did he notice that the colour of the frog-man's suit was wrong. He hauled his first rescue aboard.

"How did it go?" he asked before he started up the engine to continue the night's work. He was gazing at the man he had picked up who was removing his face-mask with his left hand while his right hand tugged at some equipment behind his back. Both men were now seated and facing each other.

"It went well. All according to plan," Rashkin replied. "Beaurain will be pleased . . . "

The rescuer broke off in sentence. He had seen Rashkin's face – which briefly expressed alarm at the reference to Beaurain – and knew that this was not one of Henderson's gunners. And then Rashkin's right hand swung round from behind his back and plunged the knife it held up to the hilt in the chest of his rescuer.

The man gurgled, his eyes stared, he slumped forward. Rashkin used both hands to heave him over the side and then gave all his attention to what was happening around him. Switching off the searchlight at the bow of his own power-boat, he turned on the throttle. Then he guided the power-boat towards the west coast of Bornholm. He had earlier taken the trouble to read about the island and he was heading for a quiet stretch of the Danish shore. It always paid to take every contingency into account. He was now trying to recall the flight times of the local aircraft which flew from Rønne airfield to Copenhagen.

Inside the huge dining-room of *Kometa* the members of the Stockholm Syndicate seemed to be gripped by paralytic fear, an emotion which froze all power of decision. At the head of the table Leo Gehn, one of the most powerful men in the western world, sat like a Buddha, apparently working out the potential profits from the region of the north European sector allocated to him earlier in the meeting. When Count d'Arlezzo, a slim Italian who, conversely, could not keep still, peered over the American's shoulder he saw to his horror that Gehn was repeating on his pad the same figures over and over again.

Most of the rest of the thirty people present stayed well away from the doors and pressed their faces against the windows. They were staring at the flashing lamp of the lighthouse above The Hammer of Bornholm. Ironically, the arbiters of blackmail, murder and wholesale intimidation were stricken with indecision.

On the bridge Henderson left the ship following the route the others had taken, but under rather different circumstances. The *Kometa* was now reared up on its giant foils. The vessel was moving at its top speed of thirty knots. The hydrofoil was on a fixed course plotted by the Scot and was working on automatic pilot. He climbed out of one of the smashed windows and made for the rail as the wind hit him. Holding on to an upright, he flexed both legs, waiting for the ship to ride on an even keel if only for a few seconds. *Now!*

He dived outwards and downwards, passing well clear of the foil and plunging vertically into the Baltic – far enough away, he hoped, and deep enough down to clear the lethal clawing suction from the propeller. As he surfaced he was amazed to see how far *Kometa* had travelled, a receding cluster of lights. He pressed down the switch which turned on the red light attached to his head-gear. Recovering from the impact of the deep dive he saw close by the power-boat despatched from *Firestorm* with the sole purpose of rescuing Henderson.

The vertical cliffs of The Hammer are protected by isolated pinnacles of rock which rise up out of the sea like immense rocky daggers. Round the base of these leviathans of nature the sea swirled gently, hardly moving, so still was the Baltic on that night and at that hour. *Kometa* hurtled on like a projectile, reared up on its foils, approaching The Hammer at right angles. The last moments must have been a terrifying experience for the men who had planned to weld all the evil in the West into one huge crime syndicate. Then *Kometa* struck.

The collision between flying metal hull and immovable rocky bastion was shattering and thunderous. But fractions of a second later it was followed by the detonation of the explosives Henderson had attached to the foil – explosives which were timed to go off within fifteen minutes, but which also detonated on any major impact. The meeting between *Kometa* and The Hammer was a major impact. The ship fragmented instantly. The explosion hurled one of the foils high in the air before it crashed back into the sea. The hull actually *telescoped*, squashing like a concertina before the bow sank, so, for a few moments, the stern hung in the air.

A plume of black smoke rose from the base of The Hammer, dispersed by a gentle breeze which was now blowing. Then there was nothing. No trace that *Kometa* had ever existed. And only the sound of the power-boat's engine as it sped back towards *Firestorm*.

Sitting motionless in the stern Beaurain was unusually silent. He pointed out to no-one what he had also seen – the cotton-thin wake of a power-boat proceeding south of them at a measured pace towards the west coast of Bornholm. When he later heard that one power-boat had mysteriously not returned he knew that Viktor Rashkin had escaped.

23

The signals went out from *Firestorm* at midnight. Beaurain sent them in prearranged codes to Fondberg waiting in Stockholm, to Marker waiting at the strangely-shaped police headquarters in Copenhagen, and also to Chief Inspector Willy Flamen in Brussels.

By ten minutes after midnight the biggest dragnet ever launched on the continent was under way as detector vans and fleets of patrol cars waited for a spate of Syndicate transmissions. They started at exactly three in the morning. Fondberg phoned Beaurain over the ship's radio-telephone shortly afterwards.

"What was the significance of your timing?" the Swede asked.

"Because someone must have reached Bornholm about midnight. His first task would be to send a message warning what is left of the Syndicate of the catastrophe."

"What catastrophe?"

"Wait for news from Bornholm tomorrow morning."

"Anyway you were right! It's working!"

Fondberg sounded excited. All over Europe the detector vans were homing in on the sources of the mysterious transmissions – because for the first time they were not looking on the roads. They were concentrating on the *waterways*. And due to the emergency the transmissions were prolonged.

In Belgium, France and Holland, barges were being boarded as the Syndicate's radio operators were caught in the middle of transmitting. In Denmark, ships in the Øresund were being boarded. In Sweden, launches and cruisers on the waterways inside Stockholm were being raided. In Germany the barges were on the Rhine. And by launching synchronised attacks at precisely the same moment there was no opportunity for one section of the Syndicate to warn another. At one sweeping blow the entire

302

communications system – without which the Syndicate could not operate – was wiped out.

"A fair-haired girl left the aparment at Rådmansgatan 490 and took the airline bus to Arlanda. She is expected to arrive in Copenhagen at . . ."

Fondberg called Beaurain again on *Firestorm* as the vessel raced westward away from Bornholm, heading for the Øresund and Copenhagen. As arranged with Beaurain earlier, Fondberg had mounted a round-the-clock surveillance on the Rådmansgatan apartment. Two of his men had followed her and, on arrival at Arlanda, they had watched her check in at the Scandinavian Airlines counter for the next flight to Copenhagen.

" . . . 08.30," Fondberg continued. "And the first Danair flight out of Rønne on Bornholm is Flight SK 262 departing Rønne at 08.10 and arriving Copenhagen at 08.40. Who do you expect to be aboard that aircraft?"

"Better you don't know, Harry," Beaurain had replied. "And thanks for the information on the blonde girl. Be in touch."

He broke the connection on the radio-telephone and looked at Louise who had been listening in. She was frowning with perplexity.

"Blonde?" Louise queried. "Can that be Sonia Karnell?"

"It can be – and it is," Beaurain assured her as he rubbed his bloodshot eyes. When had he last slept? He couldn't be sure. "A blonde wig," he explained.

"Of course. God, I must be losing my grip. But I'm completely shattered. What did you mean by saying we must break the American connection before Harry Fondberg phoned? And who is flying into Copenhagen from Bornholm?"

"Answer both your questions when I'm sure." Beaurain took one of his sudden decisions. "I think we'll get to Kastrup Airport ahead of everyone – we'll get Anderson to fly us there in the Sikorsky. And we'll take some back-up, including Stig."

He checked his watch. Four o'clock in the morning. It had been daylight for over an hour and the sky had all the appearance of yet another glorious, cloudless day of mounting heat. They should be at Kastrup by five o'clock; there would be very little activity at that hour and – with a little luck – no-one to observe their arrival in the Danish capital.

They had passed perfunctorily through Customs and Immigration and were moving into the main reception hall when Louise stopped and gripped Beaurain's arm. Gently she pulled him back behind a pillar, then gestured with her head towards a closed bookstall. Beaurain peered cautiously round the pillar while Palme and the other three men froze behind them. Beaurain studied a man standing in profile by the bookstall, holding a magazine which he appeared to be reading.

"Ed Cottel," he murmured.

"The American connection," Louise said.

They retreated out of the reception hall and deeper inside the airport buildings. Palme conducted his reconnaissance and returned with the news.

"They have troops all round the airport," he reported. "All possible exits are covered and we're heavily outnumbered. Men in cars apparently waiting for passengers. Men in taxis. There are two men out on the highway pretending to deal with a defective street lamp."

"Where did you get the boiler suit from, Stig?" Louise asked.

Palme looked apologetic. "I found a cleaner in the toilets."

"You knocked him out cold and hid him in a closet," Louise told him.

"Yes. But in this I was able to wander everywhere – especially when I was carrying the pail. No-one *ever* notices a man in a boiler suit carrying a pail."

Only Beaurain appeared unperturbed. Palme looked round to make sure they were unobserved, then produced from his jacket underneath the boiler suit three guns – a Colt .45, a Luger and a small 9-mm. pistol which Louise promptly grabbed as Beaurain took the Luger.

"The mechanic who handled the chopper when we landed here," Palme explained, "is a friend of mine and keeps weaponry for me so he can slip it to me after we've passed through what are pompously known as official channels."

"Ed Cottel is going to take us out through his own troops," said Louise. She took a firm grip on the pistol with her right hand and covered the weapon with her folded coat. "Any objection?" she asked Beaurain.

"Go ahead."

She walked briskly back into the main reception hall and Beaurain followed more casually. She made no attempt to conceal her presence and marched straight towards where Ed Cottel was still standing pretending to read his magazine. Not for the first time Beaurain admired her sheer nerve, her audacious tactics. She reached Cottel who looked up and spoke.

"Don't any of you leave the airport, Louise, for God's sake. It is surrounded by extremely professional killers."

"Under this coat I have a gun aimed at you point-blank. Now, as a matter of academic interest, who are these killers?"

"They're the American connection," said Cottel matter-of-factly. "But that's not me. I guess I still have some explaining to do."

Beaurain was behind her. He took Louise's arm and squeezed it.

"I'm going to use that payphone over there for a minute," he said. "While I'm doing it, why don't you two exchange experiences – and maybe it would be safer to walk back further inside the building complex and join Stig and the rest of them."

They sat on a seat by themselves while Cottel explained it to Louise. A short distance away Palme kept watch. It had all started when Washington had asked Ed Cottel to come out of retirement and do one last job for them – track down the Telescope organisation. He had agreed and then at the last minute, when it was too late to substitute anyone else, had informed his superiors he was combining the Telescope mission with a personal investigation into the Stockholm Syndicate.

"When Harvey Sholto said 'What's that?' in front of certain top aides who are next to our President – and they all tried to look as though they didn't know what the hell I was talking about – I knew something was wrong. From that time on I was a marked target on a limited schedule."

"What does that mean?" Louise asked.

"That I would be allowed to proceed to Europe in the hope that I'd expose Telescope." He gave a lop-sided grin.

"Whatever that might be. Once I'd done that, I'd be liquidated – probably by Harvey Sholto himself. Luckily the Säpo chief's men in Sweden spotted the early arrival of Sholto so I took extra precautions to keep underground. Once they realised I was devoting all my energies – using all the network of informants and helpers I built up over twenty years – to crack the Stockholm Syndicate, my limited schedule, as they so nicely phrase it, ran out. They sent out a *Nadir* signal on me. To be terminated with extreme prejudice."

"Why is Washington so worried?"

"Because most of the President's electoral campaign funds come from precisely those American industrial corporations who are members of the Syndicate." Cottel's voice became briefly vehement. "You know how our President avoids issues likely to embarrass him – he looks the other way, pretends they don't exist."

"I still don't understand it fully, Ed. This Harvey Sholto – how much power has he? What is his official position?"

"No official position at all any longer. More power than anyone else in Washington below the rank of president – because of what he knows. Christ, Louise, I've as good as told you – that's the guy who photocopied all Edgar J. Hoover's files! Those files had all the dirt on every influential figure in the country. He's built up dossiers so dangerous, no-one in Washington dare touch him. But what was the use of just scaring people? And then he thought up the idea of the Stockholm Syndicate. He contacted Viktor Rashkin in Stockholm – I suspect they must have met secretly in the Far East earlier."

He broke off as Beaurain reappeared, his former fatigue no longer apparent, and he checked his watch as he came up to the seat. "We'll be out of here in five minutes, maybe less."

"How?" Cottel asked sceptically.

"By courtesy of Superintendent Marker of Danish police Intelligence. At the moment a fleet of police cars full of armed men is racing to Kastrup. I told him where Sholto has placed his troops – it is Sholto, isn't it, Ed? I thought so. Those two pretending to repair a street lamp are in for a shock."

"There'll be shooting?" Cottel queried.

"Not a shot fired would be my guess. Viktor Rashkin is

due here aboard a Danair flight from Rønne and they won't want the place swarming with police. I think I can hear police sirens now."

"You can't touch Rashkin," the American warned. "The bastard can always claim diplomatic immunity."

"So we wait a few hours and I think Rashkin will solve the problem for us. Yes, you can hear the sirens. Sound to be a hell of a lot of them."

There was no shooting. Bodel Marker had sent an overwhelming force to Kastrup and none of the men waiting for Beaurain put up resistance. The fact that they carried firearms was more than sufficient reason for putting them behind bars. Beaurain then explained the final move in detail to Marker, one of the key men responsible for smashing the Syndicate's communications system. He obtained the Dane's full agreement to his plan, not all of which was strictly in accordance with the law. And it was Marker who provided transport in the form of unmarked police cars for Beaurain and his companions to move into the city.

"What was all that about?" Louise asked as they drove away from Kastrup.

Marker had provided them with three cars. In the lead vehicle, a Citroën, Beaurain was driving with Louise beside him while in the rear sat Palme and Anderson, the laconic Sikorsky pilot. The two cars following them, both Audis, contained Max Kellerman and five of Henderson's gunners. Henderson was driving the third car, guarding their rear.

"I will guide you to the arms depot," Palme announced.

"Here in Copenhagen?" queried Louise.

"Over this bridge and turn right," said Palme calmly. "Into the Prinsesse Gade." The three cars pulled into a drab side street and parked. Minutes later Palme had returned with his suitcase and they were on their way again, heading back to the main road.

"Where are we going now Stig has tooled up, as he would say?" Louise enquired.

"To the house on Nyhavn – which is where the whole horrendous series of events is going to end unless I've guessed wrong."

"You wouldn't care to elaborate?" They drove over the Knippels Bro into the heart of Copenhagen.

"The American connection is Harvey Sholto – Ed explained about the Edgar Hoover dossiers. With those and his high-level connections Sholto organised the Syndicate membership in the States. He links up with Rashkin, who organises the European end. I suspect that Rashkin has been running a one-man band."

"With the aid of a three-man directorate?"

"Let's see what happens at the house on Nyhavn," Beaurain said.

Ed Cottel, who had stayed behind at Kastrup, watched through a pair of high-powered glasses the arrival of the DC-9 jet – Danair Flight SK 262 from Rønne. As he watched passengers filing off the plane he began to worry. He couldn't identify Viktor Rashkin. Then he had an idea. He hurried to the main exit where cabs waited for fares.

He was rewarded for his flash of inspiration – or so he thought, when he saw a Mercedes with Soviet diplomatic plates pull in at the kerb. A slim man carrying a Danair flight bag appeared, the rear door was opened by the chauffeur, closed, and the limousine glided away, followed by one of Superintendent Marker's 'plain-clothes' cars when Cottel gave the driver a signal. Sweating with the anxiety he had felt, Cottel waited a little longer, watching the departing passengers before he walked rapidly along the airport building front to a parked car which was Marker's control vehicle and equipped with a transceiver. He slid in beside the man behind the wheel.

"I'd like to report to Jules Beaurain."

"Be my guest," the Dane invited, handing him the microphone. "If you can get through it will be a miracle – on a clear day like this the static is bloody murder – what with the high pressure area over Scandinavia."

"Talking of high pressure . . ." Cottel mopped his damp forehead as he called Beaurain. The Belgian replied at once with great clarity.

"The big R.," Cottel began, referring to Viktor Rashkin, "had a Merc with C.D. plates waiting to pick him up. Our friends have followed. Funny thing, when I watched the passengers disembarking earlier I couldn't spot him through the glasses."

It was just one of those throwaway observations you make,

particularly when you have been keyed up, when you are short on sleep, when you thought you had blown it and then found you hadn't. The Belgian's reaction was tense, almost explosive.

"Listen to this description, Ed. A grey-haired man of medium build. Probably a snappy dresser, could even be wearing a velvet jacket with gold buttons. Rimless glasses. May be wearing a skull-cap like orthodox Jews go in for."

Cottel stared at the microphone open-mouthed, then got a grip on himself. "A guy just like that got into a beat-up Volkswagen as the limousine took off. I didn't take much notice of him – and he wasn't carrying a Danair bag."

"He wouldn't be," Beaurain informed him. "You wouldn't recognise him, but Dr Benny Horn has just arrived in Copenhagen. You're waiting now for the flight bringing in Sonia Karnell from Stockholm? Good. I think we're all going to meet up at the house on Nyhavn. And good luck – no-one has yet located Harvey Sholto."

"You think he's in the city too?" Cottel asked grimly.

"He has to be."

For the first time in weeks the weather changed as they approached Nyhavn. The sky clouded over, a faint hint of mist drifted in from the sea and, as they arrived at the familiar basin of water, the seamen's bars on the left and tourist shops on the right, it began to drizzle. A fine spray of moisture descended on the tangle of ship's masts in the basin. The stones in the street were moist. The convoy of three cars drove a short distance past the end of the basin, out of sight of Nyhavn, and then parked.

"They *may* have watchers observing Horn's house," Beaurain warned, "so our first task is to locate them and take them out"

"*May?*" Louise queried. "The Syndicate always has watchers."

"That was before this morning."

"But they still had Kastrup airport staked out with men," she objected. "You had to get Marker to send out a whole team to pick them up."

"That was because Rashkin was coming in. He would have phoned Copenhagen from Bornholm and asked for protection – heavy protection – to be laid on after what

309

happened to *Kometa*. But the Syndicate in Europe is coming to the end of its resources, its power is broken, the leaders went down with the Soviet hydrofoil."

"Then who are we expecting to see at the house on Nyhavn?"

"Hugo."

Palme opened the suitcase from the arms deposit flat in Prinsesse Gade, and handed out weapons and ammunition. All hand-guns were equipped with silencers. He conferred briefly with Max Kellerman.

"There is a man watching from the flat almost opposite – there. I'll take him. Then there is a man on the deck of a fishing vessel making too much of looping up coils of rope. He's moored outside Horn's place. You take him."

It was very quiet in the drizzle as Palme and Kellerman moved off down different sides of the basin, both of them adopting a sailor's way of walking, merging with the odd man who even at that hour came staggering up the steps from one of the basement bars. Palme went into the building and up to the first floor flat where he had spotted his watcher. He kicked the flimsy door in and let the force of his own momentum carry him straight across the sparsely furnished room. In his right hand he held a Luger with a silencer. A man who had been staring out of the open window, sprawled on a sofa, grabbed for the automatic weapon by his side. Palme shot him twice and peered out of the window.

The seaman tending coils of rope had disappeared from the deck of the fishing vessel. In his place crouched Max Kellerman who was now doing the same job. It put him immediately facing the front door leading into Dr Benny Horn's house.

A few minutes later he signalled to Beaurain and Louise as they stood looking into the window of an antique shop. The area was clean. And, standing on the top step and close to the front door of Horn's house, Palme had found the right skeleton key to open the expensive security lock. He walked in ahead of Beaurain and Louise, Luger extended in front of his body, eyes flickering up the narrow staircase, along the narrow hallway, his acute hearing sensitive to the slightest sound. The place *smelt* empty to Palme; occupied not so long ago but empty for the moment.

The calm waters of the shipping basin were dappled with drops of fine rain – and Max Kellerman laboriously coiled rope on the deck of the fishing vessel. Louise stepped over the threshold of Dr Benny Horn's house and Beaurain closed the door.

"The place is clean."

In an astonishingly short space of time Palme had checked the ground floor, run upstairs, checked the first floor, returned to the hallway, vanished down a flight of steps behind a door leading to the basement and reappeared to make his pronouncement. He was a big man, Louise thought, yet he could move with the grace and speed of a gazelle.

"A kind of library room at the front," Palme explained, pointing to a door. "Bookshelves from floor to ceiling, heavy lace curtains masking the window overlooking the front ... Kitchen and dining-room at the back with rear door on the first floor opening onto a fire escape down into a small yard. There is an exit into a side street from the yard. One of the gunners found it and stationed himself there. No-one gets in here without us knowing."

"Then the front room to await our guests?" Beaurain suggested.

Outside the drizzle continued to fall and Max Kellerman ignored the fact that he was getting wetter and wetter.

Sonia Karnell was the first to arrive at Nyhavn. She arrived in a taxi from Kastrup Airport, paid off the driver and climbed the steps, the drizzle forming a web of moisture on her jet-black hair. In her left hand she had the key ready; in her right she carried a suitcase and from a strap dangled a shoulder-bag.

It was the shoulder-bag Louise Hamilton was studying as she kept well back inside the library room and watched through the heavy lace curtains. Beaurain was also inside the room, standing pressed flat against the wall close to the opening edge of the closed door.

"She's suspicious of something," Louise hissed.

The Swedish girl had looked back at the deck of the fishing vessel moored to the quay. She saw the wrong man coiling rope. *She saw Max Kellerman.*

Kellerman reacted instinctively. From under a fishing net he raised the barrel of his sub-machine gun, one of the weapons Palme had distributed from his arms deposit. No-one else was close enough to see it. Karnell saw it. She turned the key, dived into the hallway, slammed the door shut behind her and leant for a moment against the side wall. Louise walked out of the library room.

"Hello, Sonia. A long way from the Rådmansgatan."

Louise was holding the pistol aimed point-blank, but the Swedish girl was either a suicide case or guessed these people did not want the sound of shooting yet. She leapt at the English girl like a tigress, dropping the suitcase, her hands extended like the claws of an animal. She aimed for the eyes. Louise hit her with the barrel of the pistol across the side of the temple. Karnell felt the side of her face and blood oozed between her fingers, the colour matching the tint of her nail varnish.

"Drop the shoulder-bag, Sonia," Louise ordered. "Slowly – try and grab your weapon and I'll shoot you in the stomach."

She watched while the shoulder-bag dropped on the hallway floor to join the suitcase. She was alone with the girl; Beaurain had remained invisible inside the library room and Palme had not shown himself at the top of the narrow staircase. It would be easier to scare the guts out of Karnell if the girl thought she was alone with Louise. Then Louise got it! Of course! A signal that the coast was clear, that it was safe for Horn to come inside when he arrived. Of course!

"What's the signal?" Louise asked viciously, advancing closer so that Karnell backed against the wall.

"Signal?"

"*You stupid bitch!*" Louise raised her pistol. "And you had good bone structure! This gun should re-arrange it so no man will look at you, let alone ..."

Louise's mouth was slightly open, her teeth clenched tight; her gun arm began to move, the gunsight aimed to rake over the bridge of Karnell's nose, which like the rest of her was perfectly shaped. Karnell screamed, "The front room ... a card in the window ... it means everything OK. Come on in!"

"*What card?*"

"In the drawer ..." In her terror she pushed past Louise, ran into the library and opened a drawer. Louise was close behind her but the only thing Karnell took out of the drawer was a postcard of old Copenhagen. Running to the window, she pulled aside the curtain, perched the card on the window and let the curtain fall into its original position.

Then she saw Beaurain for the first time. "You *know* – don't you?" she said.

"I know," Beaurain agreed, "so now we just wait."

Louise body-searched the Swedish girl but the only weapon she was carrying was a pair of nail-scissors. Presumably she would have found a weapon in the house, given time.

Harvey Sholto came to Nyhavn unseen and took up his position unnoticed. Flying in from Copenhagen on the same flight as Sonia Karnell, he mingled with the other travellers on arrival at Kastrup, selected a cab, gave the driver careful instructions and a generous tip, then settled in the back seat with the tennis bag he had collected from a locker at Kastrup.

His large bald head was concealed beneath a black beret and he was wearing a shabby raincoat he had taken from the suitcase he had left inside the locker. Most people – asked to guess his nationality – would have said Dutch or French.

"I drop you here?" the cab driver checked.

"Yes. And don't forget where you pull up for a short time. I want to surprise my girl friend as I explained."

"Understood."

The cab had stopped a few yards before Nyhavn came into view round the corner and Harvey Sholto stepped out and left the cab parked at the kerb. The drizzle suited him well; it linked up with his shabby raincoat. He paddled past the end of the basin and walked down the *left-hand* street, past numerous seamen's bars. He drooped his shoulders, which made him appear a shorter man.

He walked head down, like a man absorbed in his own thoughts, but his eyes were everywhere. The place had to be crawling with that bastard Beaurain's troops. Yes, he was pretty sure one of them was stationed on the fishing vessel moored to the quay outside Horn's house. The cab arrived just in time before the man looked up and saw him, crawling past Sholto as though unsure of its destination.

Aboard the fishing vessel Max Kellerman slipped one hand under the net concealing the sub-machine gun. There was something wrong about this cab. He watched it crawl past, reach the end of the basin, and then stop. No-one got out. It just stopped while the driver gazed up the basin. *The driver!*

Out of the corner of his eye Kellerman watched while the driver took his time over lighting a cigarette and flicked the match into the water. Kellerman revised his opinion. The man was due to pick up a fare and was early so he was enjoying a quiet puff and a few minutes' peace. The cab drove off out of sight.

It was during this charade that Harvey Sholto slipped into the doorway Palme had gone through himself before killing the watcher on the first floor. The sight of the dead body shook him, but only for a second.

He next dragged the sofa over to the window to act as a back support. From the tennis bag he took the Armalite rifle which was separated into its various components and assembled the weapon. At this range the telescopic sight he screwed on was superfluous, but Harvey Sholto was a careful man.

Checking that everything was arranged to his satisfaction he settled down to wait. They were all coming to the house on Nyhavn. As Cottel mounted the steps he would blow him away with one shot. Then he need only lower the firing angle a few degrees and he could blow away the man on the deck of the fishing vessel before he recovered from the shock. He lit a cigar and willed himself to stay still.

The Volkswagen also crawled alongside the Nyhavn basin, but this vehicle was moving down the tourist-trap side of the street. When Kellerman saw it coming he ducked out of sight. At the wheel Dr Benny Horn drove on past the entrance to his house and then parked at the kerb. Clambering out of his ancient vehicle, he adjusted his skull-cap, screwed up his face at the drizzle and walked back to the house with the plate bearing his name. Like Sonia Karnell he had the key in his hand when he reached the top step. Inserting it, he walked inside and closed the door. Beaurain appeared from the open doorway leading to the library, holding his Luger and aiming it point-blank at the new arrival.

"Welcome at last, Viktor Rashkin."

Ed Cottel, who had followed Sonia Karnell from the airport and then lost her in a traffic jam, was further delayed by a puncture in one of the busiest sections in the city. He was then delayed by traffic police until he persuaded them to use the transceiver in his car to call headquarters. Eventually he found himself a cab.

In the first floor flat on Nyhavn, Harvey Sholto was satisfied he could do the job. He had stood well back in the shadows of the small room and zeroed in the Armalite telescopic sight on the front door of Horn's house. It was like taking candy from a baby. Then he saw the cab approaching on the other side and took a firmer grip on his weapon.

The cab blocked off his view while Cottel was paying off the driver and Sholto took one final puff on his cigar and ground it under his large foot. The cab moved off, Cottel glanced round and then mounted the steps. Sholto zeroed in on the centre of his back and between Cottel's shoulderblades, slightly to the left. His finger took the first pressure. He spoke under his breath without realising he was doing it.

"It's been a long time, bastard, well, here it comes."

It hit Harvey Sholto in the middle of the chest, lifted him clear off his feet and jerked him ceilingwards like a manipulated marionette. In mid-air his large body jackknifed. Gravity brought him back to the floor which he hit with a tremendous thud. He lay still, outstretched, like one of the chalk silhouettes police draw to show where the corpse was found.

It was the cigar smoke which had attracted Kellerman's attention to the open window originally. Little more than a wraith, dispelled by the drizzle as soon as it came into the open air, the movement of the smoke had been sufficient for him. Someone was waiting inside the room supposedly occupied only by a dead man. At the sight of the rifle aimed at Ed Cottel he had sprayed the window with one short burst from his sub-machine gun.

Beaurain pushed the man with the skull-cap against the wall of the passageway and stuck the barrel of his Luger into his prisoner's throat. Cottel slipped into the house, and at the head of the staircase Palme appeared. Louise closed the door and Beaurain ushered Horn into his own library, followed by Ed Cottel.

"Sharpshooter opposite," Palme explained as he came down the stairs. "His target was Mr Cottel. Max took him out."

"*Viktor Rashkin?*"

They had entered the library and it was Louise who repeated the name Beaurain had used with incredulity in her voice. Beaurain used his left hand to remove the skull-cap, to tug free the wig of false grey hair. The rimless spectacles he unhooked and threw on the floor.

"It's not as though he needs them to see. Let me introduce Dr Benny Horn, better known as Viktor Rashkin, First Secretary at the Soviet Embassy in Stockholm. And we mustn't forget other people know him as Dr Otto Berlin of Bruges and Dr Theodor Norling of Stockholm. A trio of eminent and murderous dealers in rare books."

The light in the library was dim. It would always be dim behind the heavy lace curtains, but the drizzly morning made it even more difficult to see. Louise had no trouble seeing what she still found almost incredible – stripped of his guise as Benny Horn, the man she was staring at was a young forty, eyes intensely observant, his prominent cheekbones Slavic, and even with Beaurain's gun at his throat he exuded an air of authority and confidence. He met her gaze boldly. Then Beaurain said something else and Louise thought she saw a flicker of fear for the first time on Rashkin's face.

"This is also Hugo, controller of the Stockholm Syndicate and the man who masterminds bloodbaths like the Elsinore Massacre."

"Are you sure?" Louise began. "Why the elaborate deception?"

"To give him three different 'front' men for dealing with the members he was recruiting for the Stockholm Syndicate. No-one at the outset would be happy dealing with a Soviet Communist. But most important of all to fool the Kremlin – especially Comrade Leonid Brezhnev, his patron."

This time Louise, who was studying Rashkin closely, saw all expression leave his face; it went completely blank. Beaurain was striking very close to home.

"And why would he do that?" Louise asked.

"Because he was going to defect from Russia once the Syndicate was set up!" The accusation came viciously from Sonia Karnell who had remained silent up to this moment.

316

"Billions of dollars you said we would have, and now look where we are!"

"Shut your trap," he told her. It was the calm, detached manner in which he uttered the words which Louise found so frightening. And Rashkin did not look frightened. She noticed Palme had left the room with Ed Cottel after a whispered remark from Beaurain. They were alone with Rashkin and his Swedish mistress, Sonia Karnell. Why did the Russian still seem so confident?

"He was going to defect," Sonia repeated. "He knew he'd never make the Politburo with all those old men standing in his way. He deceived the Politburo – and Brezhnev especially – into believing he had formed a directorate while he remained at a remote distance as Hugo. Once the Syndicate was organised we would leave for America and run it from there. *Yes* – he's Hugo. And *yes*, he secretly worked with Harvey Sholto who used the J. Edgar Hoover files brought up-to-date to persuade key Americans to join the Syndicate. Not that they were reluctant when they realised the enormous non-taxable profits they'd make."

"But he didn't *invent* Berlin, Horn and Norling, did he?" Beaurain queried gently. "They were murdered, weren't they?"

"I had nothing to do with that!" Karnell burst out. "He looked for recluses, men who wouldn't be missed if they suddenly 'moved away' – men he could disguise himself as reasonably well."

"How did you find out, Beaurain?" Rashkin asked, again calm.

"All their backgrounds were similar, too similar. When you vanished off the Brussels express from Bruges I later realised you had disguised yourself. Litov's dying words at Stockholm Central – '*Heroin . . . Norling . . . traitor*' – pointed to a Russian. Otherwise why should he, a Russian, use the final word? As Norling, you blew up the house outside Stockholm and left behind *an elevated heel* – to vary your height from your other two 'creations'. Also your reported movements as Rashkin always coincided with the appearance of one of your three 'inventions'." The Belgian moved as Rashkin aimed a blow at Karnell.

Rashkin gave a gulp and a grimace of pain. Beaurain had tapped his Adam's apple with the Luger. Then he smiled, a smile which was grotesque because it reflected the pain. But the will-power which had enabled him to come so far still showed. With an immense effort he spoke the words.

"You cannot touch me. I am Viktor Rashkin. I am First Secretary at the Soviet Embassy in Stockholm. I have diplomatic immunity."

"He's carrying a French passport in the name of Louis Carnet," Sonia Karnell screamed. "I can testify against him. He's a mass murderer."

"Oh, I agree," Beaurain interrupted. He searched Rashkin carefully for weapons and extracted from an inner pocket a French passport. Karnell had been telling the truth. It was made out in the name of Louis Carnet. He returned it to the Russian's pocket.

"But I agree," he said. "Viktor Rashkin has diplomatic immunity and is, therefore, untouchable." Keeping his Luger aimed at Rashkin he stared again through the window, and Louise saw he was looking across the basin to where Ed Cottel stood in front of the house where Harvey Sholto had positioned himself. Pulling back the curtain, Beaurain showed himself. Cottel gave a thumbs up gesture, which seemed to combine the signal for all's well with a gesture pointing towards the window of the room where Sholto's body lay. Rashkin watched him like a cat but he did not see the American or his gesture.

"You know where the front door is," Beaurain told him.

Rashkin did not hesitate. He gave Sonia Karnell a glance which terrified her, then left the room. They heard him open the front door, close it and run down the steps. Beaurain beckoned Louise to join him at the window. Karnell seized her chance to run out into the hallway and up the stairs. There was a rear exit from the building, a flight of iron steps which was the fire escape leading to the cobbled yard. In the library Beaurain gripped Louise's arm.

"Let her go."

"But she'll get away. She tried to kill me."

"No-one is going anywhere. The whole of Nyhavn is sealed off. And from the front window of the room above this one Stig – with a pair of binoculars – got a good view of the position in the room across the way."

Outside Viktor Rashkin had run down the steps and walked rapidly to his parked Volkswagen. He was confident his reference to diplomatic immunity had checkmated the Belgian. Slipping behind the wheel of his car he switched on the engine, started the wipers to clear drizzle from the windscreen and backed to a bridge crossing over the basin.

At the far end of Nyhavn where he had planned to turn right for the city centre he had seen a cordon of cars blocking the route. He crossed the bridge and turned down the other side of Nyhavn.

He pulled up in front of the building where Harvey Sholto had settled himself in position to take out Ed Cottel. As the Russian left the car he saw again what he had spotted in his rear view mirror on entering his car – another cordon closing off the other end of the basin. What he overlooked was Ed Cottel concealed in a nearby basement area. He was Beaurain's back-up – in case the Belgian's basic plan didn't work out.

Beaurain and Louise continued watching from the library window. "Rashkin saw that both ends of the street are blocked so now he's gone into his safe house to decide his next move," Beaurain commented. He turned as Palme came into the room.

"There has been a tragedy," the Swede said with a wooden face. "The Karnell woman tried to get away via the fire escape. She was in a hurry – somehow she lost her balance on the top step and went all the way down. I am afraid she is dead. Her neck is broken. What is happening to Benny Horn?"

"I don't know." The words were hardly out of Beaurain's mouth before he jerked his head round to stare at the house opposite.

Inside the house, Viktor Rashkin, whose whole success in life had hinged on his supreme self-confidence, his conviction that he was capable of out-manoeuvring any opponent on earth, had run up the stairs with his springy step. He reached the door leading into the room, pushed it wide open and stood framed in the doorway.

Harvey Sholto was not dead, although he had taken terrible punishment from the fusillade of bullets Max Kellerman had fired up at the window. Since then, as more blood seeped onto the sofa onto which he dragged himself, he had been waiting with the Armalite rifle propped in readiness, the muzzle aimed at the door, his finger inside the trigger guard.

The door flew open, a man stood there, a blurred silhouette, the silhouette of the man on the fishing vessel who had emptied half a magazine into him. He pressed the trigger. The bullet struck Viktor Rashkin in the chest. He reeled backwards, broke through the flimsy banister rail and toppled all the way down to the hall below. He was dead before he was half-way down.

Later

The Baron de Graer, president of the Banque du Nord of Brussels, arrived in Copenhagen by plane the same afternoon as the events just described took place in Nyhavn. He met Jules Beaurain, Louise Hamilton and Ed Cottel in a suite at the Royal Hotel. At the request of Beaurain he handed to Cottel photocopies of a whole series of bank statements, many emanating from highly-respected establishments in the Bahamas, Brussels and Luxembourg City. They showed in detail the movements of millions of dollars transferred via complex routes from certain American conglomerates to the Stockholm Syndicate.

"I'll take these at once, if I may," Cottel said, and left for another part of the hotel. The reporter he had earlier contacted from the *Washington Post* had just arrived and wished to fly back to Washington the same night with the photocopies.

"People are impressed with documents, Jules," the Baron said as he drank the black coffee Louise had poured. "Documents can be concocted to say anything you want them to say. But print them in a newspaper and they are taken for gospel."

"It's the end result that counts," Beaurain agreed.

Ed Cottel also returned to Washington the same evening. In addition to the incriminating bank statements, he had handed the reporter photocopies of the contents of the red file Viktor Rashkin had dropped from his brief-case when – disguised as Norling – he had fled in his float-plane from the devastated house outside the Swedish capital. The file named names – the company executives of American and European conglomerates who had approved the contributions to the Stockholm Syndicate. Unfortunately many were financial supporters of the President of the United States.

In Copenhagen Superintendent Marker was spared any hint of an international incident since the dead body of Viktor Rashkin was in due course buried as that of an unknown Frenchman, Louis Carnet, identified by the passport found on him. The same neat solution also was applied to the man armed with the Armalite rifle. Marker did later hint to an exceptionally inquisitive reporter that information from Paris led him to believe the deaths of the two Frenchmen were a gangland killing, something to do with the Union Corse. The reporter filed his story but it never appeared; a plane crash with a high casualty rate took over the space instead.

On 4 November in the United States the incumbent president was defeated in a landslide victory by his opponent. Much of the credit for the victory was laid at the door of the *Post* reporter who had, after a relentless search, come up with evidence suggesting the holier-than-thou occupant of the White House had not lived up to his image.

Fiction

☐	**The Island**	Peter Benchley	£1.25p
☐	**Options**	Freda Bright	£1.50p
☐	**Dupe**	Liza Cody	£1.25p
☐	**Chances**	Jackie Collins	£2.25p
☐	**Brain**	Robin Cook	£1.75p
☐	**The Entity**	Frank De Felitta	£1.75p
☐	**Whip Hand**	Dick Francis	£1.50p
☐	**Secrets**	Unity Hall	£1.50p
☐	**Solo**	Jack Higgins	£1.75p
☐	**The Rich are Different**	Susan Howatch	£2.75p
☐	**The Master Sniper**	Stephen Hunter	£1.50p
☐	**Moviola**	Garson Kanin	£1.50p
☐	**The Master Mariner**		
	Book 1: Running Proud	Nicholas Monsarrat	£1.50p
☐	**Platinum Logic**	Tony Parsons	£1.75p
☐	**Fools Die**	Mario Puzo	£1.50p
☐	**The Boys in the Mailroom**	Iris Rainer	£1.50p
☐	**A Married Man**	Piers Paul Read	£1.50p
☐	**Sunflower**	Marilyn Sharp	95p
☐	**The Throwback**	Tom Sharpe	£1.50p
☐	**Wild Justice**	Wilbur Smith	£1.75p
☐	**That Old Gang of Mine**	Leslie Thomas	£1.25p
☐	**Caldo Largo**	Earl Thompson	£1.50p
☐	**Ben Retallick**	E. V. Thompson	£1.75p

All these books are available at your local bookshop or newsagent, or can be ordered direct from the publisher. Indicate the number of copies required and fill in the form below   5

....

Name_____
(Block letters please)

Address_____

_____

Send to Pan Books (CS Department), Cavaye Place, London SW10 9PG
Please enclose remittance to the value of the cover price plus:
35p for the first book plus 15p per copy for each additional book ordered
to a maximum charge of £1.25 to cover postage and packing
Applicable only in the UK

While every effort is made to keep prices low, it is sometimes
necessary to increase prices at short notice. Pan Books reserve
the right to show on covers and charge new retail prices which
may differ from those advertised in the text or elsewhere